"How are ye now?" Elminster asked.

"Well enough," she said. "I feel weary, a little, but not sick or strange."

"Good," the old mage said gently. "I shall cast more lightning at thee. Gather and hold it as long as ye can. If it starts to hurt thee, or ye feel it trying to burst out and ye cannot stop it, fair enough. Let it flow out at the sky or at the rock you struck earlier. Do not release it until then, so that I may roughly learn thy capacity. We have healing means near at hand. Be not afraid."

Shandril merely nodded and stood waiting, hands at her sides. When the sage's bolt struck her, she flinched but then stood quiet as Elminster hurled bolt after bolt at her. The air about the hill crackled and tingled upon the faces of those who watched. Narm trembled and twisted his hands about in the robe he wore, but could not look away.

More and more energy poured into Narm's lady, and she stood silent and unmoving. At last she bent at the waist with a sob, threw her arms wide as she took a few steps to steady herself, and burst into a pillar of coiling flame.

"Mother Mystra!" Narm prayed hoarsely, in horror. Merith laid hands upon him quickly then, to prevent him running to his beloved—and a fiery death. Narm screamed Shandril's name and wrenched at Merith's grasp. He dragged the silent elf forward until Florin arrived to set his strength against the young spellcaster's. Narm struggled helplessly in their iron grip. On the hilltop above them a pillar of living flame writhed where Shandril had stood.

FORGOTTEN REALMS®

FANTASY ADVENTURE

SPELLFIRE

Ed Greenwood

Cover Art
CLYDE CALDWELL

SPELLFIRE

Distributed to the book trade in the United States by Random House, Inc. and in Canada by Random House of Canada Ltd. Distributed to the hobby, toy, and comic trade in the United States and Canada by regional distributors. Distributed worldwide by Wizards of the Coast, Inc. and regional distributors.

TSR, Inc. is a subsidiary of Wizards of the Coast, Inc.

First Printing: July 1988
Printed in the United States of America
Library of Congress Number: 88-50056

9

ISBN: 0-88038-587-1

U.S., CANADA, ASIA,
PACIFIC, & LATIN AMERICA
Wizards of the Coast, Inc.
P.O. Box 707
Renton, WA 98057-0707

EUROPEAN HEADQUARTERS
Wizards of the Coast, Belgium
P.B. 34
2300 Turnhout
Belgium

Visit our website at http://www.tsrinc.com

This one's for all who have brought the
Realms to life over the years:
To Jenny, Andrew, Victor, John, Ian, Jim,
Anita, Cathy, Dave, Ken, Tim, and Kim.

And to new-found friends who have joined
the ride: Jeff, Mary, and Bruce; well met!
It hasn't always been easy being Elminster,
but it's been worth it.

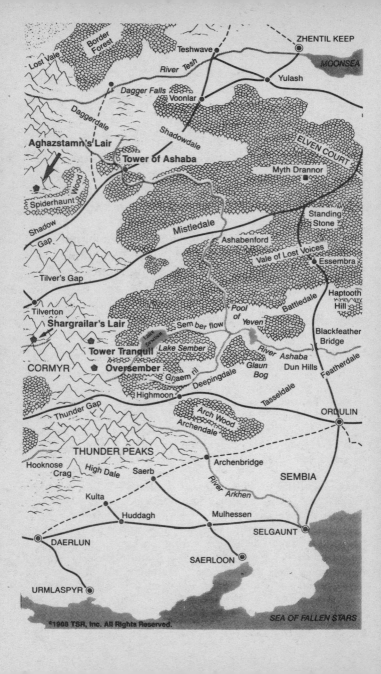

❧ 1 ❧

At the Sign of
The Rising Moon

*Neglect not small things, for all ruling and war
and magecraft are naught but small things, one
built upon another. Begin then with the small,
and look close, and you will see it all.*

Seroun of Calimport
Tales of Far Travels
Year of the Rock

It was a good inn, but sometimes Shandril hated it. She
was crying at the pain in her scalded hands, the tears running down her chin and arms into the suds, as she washed a
small mountain of dishes.

It was a hot Flamerule noon. Sweat stood out all over her
like oil, making her slim arms slippery and glistening. She
wore only her old gray tunic, once Gorstag's. It stuck to her
here and there, but only the cook, Korvan, would see her,
and he would slap and pinch even if she were bundled up in
furs like some northern princess. She blew, sharply, and the
lank blonde hair falling from her forehead parted reluctantly in front of her eyes. Tossing her head to fling her hair
aside, Shandril narrowly surveyed the stack beside her and
concluded with a sigh that there were at least three hours'
worth of dishes left.

Not enough time. Korvan was starting the roasts in the
hearth already. He'd be wanting herbs cut and water
brought soon. He was a good cook, Shandril allowed grudgingly, even if he was fat and he stank and his hands were
always hot and sticky. Some folk came to The Rising Moon
just because of Korvan's cooking.

Shandril had heard the story about how Korvan—younger and slimmer then—had once been a cook in the Royal Palace of Cormyr, in the fair city of Suzail. There had been some trouble (probably over a girl, Shandril thought darkly, perhaps even one of the princesses of Cormyr), and he'd had to leave Cormyr in some haste, banished there-from upon pain of death.

Shandril wondered, as she eyed a soapy platter critically, what would happen if she ever managed to get Korvan drunk senseless or knocked cold with a skillet and some-how could drag him through the Thunder Gap and over the border into Cormyr. Perhaps King Azoun himself would appear out of thin air and say to the Cormyrean border guards, "Here he is!" and without hesitating they'd draw their swords and hack off Korvan's head. She smiled at the thought. Perhaps he'd plead for mercy or cry in fear.

Shandril snorted. Great chance, indeed, of *that* ever hap-pening! He was here, now, and too lazy to ever go anywhere—and too fat for most horses to carry him, if it came to that. No, he was trapped here, and she was trapped with him. She scrubbed a fork fiercely until its two tines gleamed in the sunlight. Yes, trapped.

It had been a long time before she'd realized it. She had no parents, no kin—and no one would even admit to knowing where she'd come from. She had always been here, it seemed, doing the dirty work in the old roadside inn among the trees. It was a good inn, everyone said. Other places must be worse, Shandril reasoned, but she had never seen them. She could not remember ever having been inside any other building, ever. After sixteen summers, all she knew of her town of Highmoon was what she could see from the inn-yard. She'd never more than thought of running away or just slipping off to have a look. She was always too busy, too behind with her work, or too tired.

There was always work to be done. Each spring she even washed the ceilings of all the bedchambers while tied to a ladder so she wouldn't fall off. Sharp-eyed old Tezza did the windows, all those tiny panes of mica and a few panels of blown glass from Selgaunt and Hillsfar, which were far too valuable for Shandril to be trusted to wash.

Shandril didn't mind most of the work, really. She just hated getting extra tired or hurt while the others did little or, like Korvan, bothered her. Besides, if she didn't work, or she fought with the others—all more necessary to the running of The Rising Moon than Shandril Shessair—she'd upset Gorstag. And more than anything (except, maybe, to have a real adventure), Shandril wanted to please Gorstag.

The owner of The Rising Moon was a broad-shouldered, strong man with gray-white hair, gray eyes, and a craggy, weathered face. He'd broken his nose long ago, perhaps in the days when he had been an adventurer. Gorstag had been all over the world, people said, swinging his axe in important wars. He had made quite a lot of gold before settling down in Deepingdale, in the heart of the forest, and rebuilding his father's old inn. Gorstag was kind and quiet and sometimes gruff, but it was he who insisted that Shandril have a good gown for feast-days and when important folk stopped at the inn, even though Korvan said she'd serve them better by staying in the kitchen.

It was also Gorstag who had insisted that she have a last name, when, years ago, the chamber girls had called her "a nameless nobody," and "a cow too runty to keep, so someone threw it away!" The innkeeper had come into the room and spoken in a voice that had frightened Shandril into silence in mid-sob, a voice that made her think of cold steel and executioners and priestly dooms. "Such words—and all others like them—will never be spoken in this house again." Gorstag never hit women or spanked girls, but he had taken off his belt then, as he did when he thrashed the stable boy for cruel pranks. The girls were both white-faced, and one started to cry, but Gorstag never touched them. He closed the door of the room and set a chair against it. Then he walked over to the girls, who were both whimpering and, saying nothing, he swung the belt high and brought it crashing down on the floorboards so hard that the dust curled up and the door rattled. Then he put on his belt, took the shocked Shandril gently by the shoulder, and led her from the room, closing the door again behind him.

He had led her down to the taproom and said thickly, "I call you Shandril Shessair, for it is your truename. Do not forget, for your name is precious." Then Shandril had asked him, voice quavering, "Was I so named by my parents?"

Gorstag shook his head slightly and gave her a sad smile. "In the Realms, little one, you can take any name you can carry. Mind you carry it well."

Yes, Gorstag had been good to her, and The Rising Moon was like him: kind and good, well-worn and bluntly honest, and lots of hard work. Day after day of hard work. It was her cage, Shandril thought fiercely, reaching for another dish while the sweat ran down her back.

With some surprise, she saw that there were no more dishes. In her anger she had washed and scrubbed like a madcap, and now she was done, and it was early yet. Time enough to change to her plain gown and peek into the tap-room before cutting the herbs. Before Korvan could come in and give her extra work to do, Shandril vanished, her bare feet dancing lightly over the narrow loft stairs to her trunk.

She washed her face and hands in the basin of cool water she'd left for Lureene, another young woman who waited on the tables and shared the sleeping-loft with Shandril, except on nights when she had a man and Shandril was banished to the cellar for her own safety. She changed her clothing and crept quickly downstairs again along the passage to the deserted taproom. Gorstag would be seeing to the food, she knew, and he would have started the evening fire already. A party of adventurers had come in from Cormyr earlier, and Gorstag would be busy. The flagstones were cool under her feet.

The taproom was warm and smoky. Light blazed up from the crackling hearth and the several sputtering torches mounted on the walls and hooded with grim black iron. Shadows leaped on the walls and the great beams that ran low overhead the length of the taproom, bearing the sleeping chambers of the inn's upper stories upon their mighty backs. In the shifting play of light, the scenes on faded, flaking paintings seemed to live and move. The high deeds of heroes of the dales were remembered there, and the glories of battles long past. Massive tables of dark oak planks with squat, thick-carved legs crowded the room, and about them were plain, smooth benches and stout chairs covered in worn leather.

Over the bar hung a two-handed broadaxe, old but proud, well-oiled, and kept sharp. Gorstag had borne it in far-off lands in days long gone and adventures he would not speak of. When there was trouble, Shandril remembered, he could still toss it from hand to hand like a dagger and whirl it about as though it weighed nothing. Whenever Shandril asked him about his adventures, the old innkeeper only laughed and shook his head. But often in the mornings, when Shandril crept down the stairs to start the kitchen fires, she would stop and look at the axe and imagine it in Gorstag's hands on sun-drenched battlefields far away, or amid icy rock crags where trolls lurked, or in dark caverns where unseen horrors dwelt. It had been places, that axe.

The bar itself was surrounded by a small, gleaming forest of bottles of all sizes and hues, kept carefully dusted by Gorstag. Some came from lands very far away, and others from Highmoon, not half a mile off. Below these were the casks, gray with age, which the men filled from smaller traveling kegs at the upper bungs, kept sealed with wax and emptied by means of brass taps. Gorstag was very proud of those taps, since they had come all the way from fabled Waterdeep.

Above the bottles, just over the axe, there was a silver crescent moon, tilted to the left just as it was on the creaking signboard outside the front door: The Rising Moon itself. Long ago, a traveling wizard had cast a spell on the silver crescent, and it never tarnished. The house was a good inn, plain but cozy, its host well respected, even generous, and Highmoon was a beautiful place.

But to Shandril, it seemed more and more to be a prison. Every day she walked the same boards and did the same things. Only the people changed. The travelers, with their unusual clothing and differing skins and voices, brought with them the idle chatter, faint smells, and excitement of far places and exciting deeds. Even when they came in, dusty and weary from the road, snappish or sleepy, they had at least been *somewhere* and *seen* things, and Shandril envied them so much that sometimes she thought her heart would burst right out of her chest.

Every night folk came to the taproom to smoke long pipes and drink Gorstag's good ale and listen to the gossip of the Realms from other travelers. Shandril liked best those times when the grizzled old men of the dale who had themselves fought or gone adventuring in their younger days told of their feats, and of the legendary deeds of even older heroes. If only she were a man, strong enough to wear coat-of-plate and swing a blade, to set foes staggering back with the force of her blows! She was quick enough, she knew, and judged herself fairly strong.

But she was not strong like these great oxen of men who lumbered, ruddy-faced, into the inn to growl their wants at Gorstag. Even the long-retired veterans of Highmoon, some nodding and shrunken with age, others scarred or maimed in ancient frays, seemed like old wolves—stiff, perhaps, slower and harder of hearing, certainly, but wolves nonetheless. Shandril suspected that if ever she looked in the house of any of these old men of Highmoon, an old blade or mace would be hanging in a place of honor like Gorstag's axe. If ever she got to see *any* of the other houses in Highmoon, it would be a wondrous thing, she reflected sourly.

She sighed, her scalded hands still smarting. She dared not smear goose-grease on them before getting the herbs, or Korvan would fly into a rage. His aim with kitchen utensils was too good for her health, Shandril knew. Smiling ruefully, she took the basket and knife from behind the kitchen door and went out into the green stillness of the inn garden. She knew by now what to cut, and how much to bring, and what was fit to use and what was not, although Korvan made a great show of disgust at her selections and always sent her back for one more sprig of this, and chided her for bringing far too much of that. But he used all she brought, Shandril noticed, and never bothered to get more himself if she was busy elsewhere.

Korvan was still absent when she returned to the kitchen. Shandril spread the herbs out neatly in fan patterns upon the board and exchanged basket and knife for the wooden yoke and its battered old buckets. I'm used to this, she realized grimly. I could be forty winters old, and still I'd know nothing but lugging water. Hearing Korvan coming down the passage into the kitchen, grumbling loudly about the calm thievery of the butcher, she slipped out the back door. She darted across the turf to the stream, holding the ropes of the pails with practiced ease to keep them from banging against each other.

She felt eyes upon her and looked up quickly. Gorstag had come around the corner of the inn. Trotting head down, she had nearly run into his broad chest. He grinned at her startled apologies and danced around her, making flourishes with his hands as he did when dancing with the grander ladies of the dale. She grinned back after a moment, and then danced to match him. Gorstag roared with laughter, joined by Shandril. Suddenly, the kitchen door banged open and Korvan peered out angrily. Opening his mouth to scold Shandril, he closed it again with an audible snap as the innkeeper leaned over to smile closely at him.

Gorstag turned back to her and said, for Korvan's benefit, "Dishes done?"

"Yes, sir," Shandril replied, giving a slight bow.

"Herbs cut and ready?"

"Yes, sir." Shandril bowed again hastily to hide her growing smile.

"Going straight out for water. I like that . . . I like that indeed. You'll make a good innkeeper yourself someday. Then you could have a cook to do all those things for *you!*" They both heard Korvan's sniff before the kitchen door slammed. Shandril struggled to swallow her giggles.

"Good lass," Gorstag said warmly, giving her shoulder an affectionate squeeze.

Shandril smiled back at him through the hair that had fallen over her face again. Well, at least *someone* appreciated her! She hurried off down the well-worn, winding path of beaten earth and exposed tree-roots to the Glaemril, to draw staggeringly heavy buckets of water for the kitchen. Tonight would be a busy night. If Lureene did not bed with one of the travelers, she'd have much to tell as Shandril hissed questions in the darkness of the loft: who came from where, and where they were bound, and on what business. News, too, and gossip—all the color and excitement of the world outside, the world that Shandril had never seen.

Gratefully she waded out into the cool water, her bare feet avoiding the unseen stones with long practice as she filled the old wooden buckets. Then, grunting with the effort, she heaved them up onto the bank and stood for a moment, hands on hips, looking up and down the cool, green passage of the stream through Deepingdale's woods. She could not stay long, or swim or bathe and get herself wetter than she was, but she could look . . . and dream. Past her feet, the Glaemril—Deeping Stream, some called it—rushed laughingly over rocks to join the great river Ashaba that drained the northern dales and then turned east to slip past rolling lands, full of splendid people and wondrous things, lands that she would see, someday!

"Soon," she said firmly, as she climbed from the stream and took up the worn wooden yoke. A heave, a momentary stagger under the great weight and she began the long climb up through the trees back to the inn. *Soon.*

Adventurers were staying at The Rising Moon this night; a proud, splendid group of men by the name of the Company of the Bright Spear. Lean and dangerous in their armor and ready weaponry, they laughed often and loudly, wore gold rings on their hands and at their ears, and drank much wine. Gorstag had been busy with them all afternoon, for as he told Shandril with a wink as he strode down the cellar stairs in search of old and cobweb-covered bottles of wine, "It pays to keep adventurers happy, and it can be downright dangerous if you do not." They would be in the taproom by now, Lureene already flirting and flouncing saucily as she brought them wine and strong cider and aromatic tobacco. Shandril promised herself she'd watch them from the passage, while Korvan was busy with the pastry.

Shandril kicked the rusted pot by the back door so that the cook would hear and let her into the kitchen. The chain rattled as Korvan threw up the half-bar and snarled, "Get in!" The expected pinching and slap came as she staggered across the uneven floor with the water. "Don't spill any of that, mind! There are dishes waiting, sluggard! *Move* that shapely little behind of yours!" Korvan rumbled, ending with his horrible, barking laugh. Shandril set her teeth grimly under the yoke. *Someday* she'd be free of this!

The evening grew cool, as it often did in the dale after a hot day, mist gathering in the trees. The Rising Moon's taproom filled up quickly. The townsfolk of Highmoon had done business with the Company of the Bright Spear, and the veterans had come to take their measure and perhaps swap some tales. Shandril managed one quick peek at the taproom and saw the company holding court, all boisterous jests and laughter, at the central tables. A scattering of local veterans sat nearer the bar, and at the small tables along the wall were other visitors. Shandril noticed two lady adventurers close to the bar. Noticed, and stared.

They were beautiful. Tall, slim—and free to do as they pleased. Shandril gazed at them in wonder from the shadows. Both of the women wore leather and plate half-armor without color or blazon. Long, plain scabbards at their hips held swords and daggers that looked to have seen heavy use. Their cloaks were also plain, but of the finest cloth and make. Shandril was surprised at the soft beauty of the two and the quiet grace of their movements—no red-faced oxen, these. But what struck her most was their calm self-assurance. They were what she longed to be. Shandril stared at them from the darkness of the passage—until Korvan came out of the kitchen with a roar. He plucked Shandril up by grabbing a fistful of tunic and hauling roughly and carried her down the passage and into the kitchen.

"Do *I* stand and gawk? If I did, what would the guests eat *then?*" was all Korvan said, in a fierce whisper with his stubbled face an inch from hers, and Shandril feared for her life. If there was one thing Korvan cared about, it was his cooking. For a wild moment, as he thrust a bowl of potatoes at her, Shandril considered attacking her tormentor with a kitchen knife, but that wasn't the sort of 'adventure' she wanted.

But as she washed and cleaned out three hares under Korvan's hot glare, Shandril knew that she'd had more than enough of this treatment. She was going to do *something* to get out of here. Tonight.

* * * * *

"A good place, I've heard," said the mage Marimmar in the

last blue light of dusk, as their ponies carried them down through the trees toward the lanterns of Deepingdale. "Mind you say nothing of our business or destination, boy. If asked, you know nothing. You are not even all that interested in Myth Drannor."

Narm Tamaraith nodded in weary silence, and his master turned on him sharply in the gloom. "Do you hear, boy? *Answer!*"

"Aye, Lord. I—nodded, not thinking you would not see. I beg full pardon. I will say nothing of Myth Drannor." Narm's master, Marimmar "the Magnificent" (Narm had heard him called other things occasionally, but never to his face), snorted.

" 'Not thinking'! *That's* the problem, boy, too much of the time. Well, *think!* Deep but sharp, boy, deep but sharp—don't let the world around escape your notice, lest it sticks a blade in your ribs while your wits are off somewhere considering Xult's Seven Sigils! Got it?"

"Aye, Lord," Narm replied, sighing inwardly. It was to be one of *those* evenings. Even if this inn was nice, he'd scarcely have the chance to enjoy it, with Marimmar holding forth on all of Narm's many shortcomings. Narm could see now why the Mage Most Magnificent had so readily agreed to take on an apprentice. Marimmar needed someone around to belabor, and no doubt few stayed long to listen. His master's art was good, though; Narm knew enough of magic to be certain of that. But Marimmar certainly knew how to ruin the delight and enthusiasm of any adventure—or even daily chores, for that matter. Narm turned into the yard of The Rising Moon, pronouncing silent curses upon his master. Maybe there would be pretty girls inside. . . .

* * * * *

After the hares and four pheasants and too many carrots and potatoes to count, Shandril stole away for another look at the inn's guests. The company of adventurers might talk of their deeds, or even show off some treasure. Moreover, she might learn who the two ladies were. Flitting barefoot down the passage in her greasy tunic and apron, Shandril peered out cautiously into the noise and bustle.

Across the smoky taproom sat an imperious man in fine gray robes, a thin pipe between his fat fingers as he spoke to his companion, a much younger man. This one was handsome, even in nondescript gray robes that were too large for him. He was dark-haired and slim, with a very serious face. His eyes were intent on the cup of wine he clasped on the table before him. Shandril was about to turn away when suddenly his gaze met hers.

Oh, his eyes! Belying that stern face, they were dancing. They met hers merrily and did not ridicule her wild-tousled, long blonde hair and greasy garb, but winked at her as an equal—one, moreover, lucky to be in the shadows and not facing a steady barrage of questions.

Shandril flushed and tossed her head—and yet could not go. Snared by his gaze, by being regarded as a—*person* and not a servant, Shandril stood watching, mute, hands clenching in the folds of her apron. Abruptly, the youth's gaze was jerked away, as a hooked fish is pulled from the water regardless of its will to stay, by the impatient snapping of the older man's fingers.

Shandril stood alone in the shadows, as always, trembling with excitement and hope. These folk who traveled about the world outside were no greater than herself. Oh, they were rich enough, and had companions and business of import, and experience—but she could be one of them. Someday. If ever she dared. Shandril could look no longer. Bitterly she turned back to the kitchen, railing inwardly at the fear that always held her there, despite the endless pots and scalding water, despite Korvan.

"Get in!" Korvan rumbled, red-faced, as she came to the kitchen. "There's onions to chop, and I can't do it *all*, you know!" Shandril nodded absently as she walked toward the chopping board at the back of the kitchen. Korvan's bruising, pinching fingers as she passed, and the roar of uneven laughter that followed, were expected now; she hardly noticed. The knife rose and fell in her hands, twinkling. Korvan stared at her. Shandril had never before hummed happily while chopping onions.

* * * * *

🍷 17 🍷

It was hot and close in the low-beamed room. Narm blinked wearily. Marimmar showed signs of neither weariness nor relaxation in the cozy warmth of this place. *I suppose all inns are the same, more or less,* Narm thought, *but to take this*—his gaze strayed again around the noisy camaraderie of the room—*all for granted!*

But before Marimmar snapped at him to mind his studies and not the antics of drunken locals, Narm noticed that the girl who had stared at him from the dark passage across the room was gone. The darkness there didn't seem right without her. She belonged in that spot, somehow. And yet—

"Will you heed?" Marimmar snapped, really angry now. "What has hold of your senses, boy? One drink and this? You'll have a short life indeed, if you gad about like this when you're in the wild! Some creatures would look upon you as a quick meal. And they'll not wait for you to notice them before they feed!"

Obediently, Narm faced his master and dragged his attention back to queries on casting spells: casting in the dark, casting when the proper components were lacking, casting (Marimmar added acidly) when drunk. Again, Narm's head swam with the picture, his forever now, of the girl gazing into his eyes from the shadows. He almost looked to see if she was there, but checked under his master's gaze.

* * * * *

One of the adventurers had chanced to spill a platter of food, so Shandril was there when it happened. The Company of the Bright Spear were six in number, led by an important, square-bearded, young giant of a man who was fast becoming too drunk to keep his seat. His name was Burlane. Gold gleamed and winked in the firelight at his ears and his throat, upon his fingers, and at his belt. He belched and chuckled and reached vaguely for his tankard again.

To his left sat a real dwarf, the worn and baggy leather of his breeches not a foot from Shandril's bent head as she scrubbed and scraped beneath the table. The breeches smelled of woodsmoke. The dwarf was called Delg, "the Fearless," as one of his companions had added mockingly, to everyone's amusement. Delg wore a dagger strapped to his leg just above his boot; its hilt shone enticingly inches from Shandril's face. Something rose up within her and, trembling a little, yet with infinite care, she reached out . . .

One of the veterans of the dale, Ghondarrath, a stern-eyed old warrior with a gray-white beard edging his hard jaw, was telling of the treasures of the ruined City of Beauty, Myth Drannor. Shandril had heard it before, but it was still fascinating. She listened intently, scarcely daring to breathe, as she took hold and pulled ever-so-gently. The dagger came free, cold and hard and heavy in her hand.

". . . So for many long years the elves kept all others away, and the woods grew over the ruins of Myth Drannor. The Fair Folk let it alone; not a harp or spellbook or gemstone did they take. There it all lies in the woods still, not a week's ride north of here. Waiting for the brave—and the foolish—to try for it, for it is guarded by *devils* . . . and worse."

The old man paused, his audience intent upon his every word, and raised his tankard. His free hand slid across his chest like a striking snake.

One of the adventurers, a thin man with short blond hair and a ratlike face, was passing behind him, and old Ghondarrath grunted and set down his tankard. He raised his other hand, and all could see the adventurer's wrist clasped within. In that captured hand was Ghondarrath's purse.

"Well," Ghondarrath said dryly, "look what I've found." The room fell silent, save for the crackle of the fire. No one moved. Shandril clutched the dagger fiercely in excitement. She knew she should creep away quickly, lest the dwarf reach for his blade . . . and yet, she couldn't miss this!

There was a flurry of movement; the thief whipped a slim dagger out of a sheath at the back of his neck with his free hand, stabbing downward. Ghondarrath jerked him coolly sideways, and he crashed helplessly forward onto the table. Ghondarrath's free hand came down upon the back of the thief's neck with a solid crash, like a tree falling. "Dead?" asked one of the other dalemen in a hoarse whisper. For a second more there was silence, and then with a roar the Company of the Bright Spear was on their feet.

"Get him!"

"Sword the graybeard!"

"He's killed Lynxal!"

The dwarf nearly took Shandril's nose off as he kicked back his chair and sprang to his feet, but Shandril jerked back just in time. Chairs overturned and men shouted. Adventure, she thought ruefully as she scuttled on hands and knees beneath the table, was upon her at last.

"They'll kill you, Ghondar!" said one of the old warriors, face white. Beside him, Ghondarrath stood defiant, his chair raised before him in his hands. He had no other weapon.

"I was never one to back down," he said roughly. "I know no other way. Better to die by the blade, Tempus willing, than grow old shamed and craven."

"So be it, graybeard!" said one of the company's warriors viciously, striding forward, blade out.

"Stop!" the old man bellowed with sudden force, startling all there. "If it's to be a fight, then let us go outside. Gorstag's a good friend to us all—I'd not see his house laid waste!"

"You should have thought of that a breath or two earlier," sneered another company member through the general laughter of his fellows. They surged forward. Shandril reached her feet just as Gorstag and Korvan pounded past her, the cook swearing, a cleaver in his hand. She turned in time to see two blades flash in the firelight as, catlike, the two ladies Shandril had noticed earlier leaped in front of the old man. One of those blades glowed and shimmered with blue-white fire. A rumbling gasp of wonder shook the room at the sight.

"I apologize to this house and to its master for drawing steel," said its silver-haired owner in a clear, lilting voice. "But I will not see butchery done by young fools with quick tempers. Put up your blades, company"—her voice twisted that into a shaming quotation rather than rightful name—"or die, for we shall surely slay you all."

"Or," her companion added pleasantly over the point of her own ready blade, "this can be forgotten, and all keep peace. The thief was caught and drew steel. The fault is his and his alone, and he has paid. That's an end to it."

With an oath, one of the adventurers plucked at his belt, meaning to snatch and throw a dagger. The man grunted and then cried out in fury and frustration, but his hand was held in a grip like unmoving iron. Gorstag said quietly, "Drop your blade. All others, put away your weapons. I will not have this in my house."

At the sound of his voice, everyone relaxed, the dagger clattered to the floor, and blades slid back into scabbards.

"Have I your peace while you stay at The Rising Moon?" the innkeeper asked. The company members nodded, said "Aye" in reluctant chorus, and returned to their seats.

Across the room, the silver-haired bard sheathed her glowing blade and turned to Ghondarrath. "Forgive me, sir," she said simply. "They were too many. I would not shame you." The chair trembled in the old man's hands.

"I am not shamed," he said roughly. "My friends sat all around, and when it came to the death, I was alone, but for you two. I thank you. I am Ghondarrath, and my table is yours. Will you?" He gestured toward a chair.

The two ladies clasped hands with him. "Aye, with thanks. I am Storm Silverhand, a bard, of Shadowdale."

Her companion smiled, too. "I am Sharantyr, a ranger, also of Shadowdale. Well met."

Gorstag passed them wordlessly, reached the bar, and turned. "The night is hot," he said to the crowd, "so the house gives you all chilled wine from far Athkatla." There was a general roar of approval. "Drink up," he added, as Lureene hastily started around with flagons, "and let this incident be forgotten!" He lifted the limp body of the thief, its head dangling loosely, and carried it away.

Across the room, Marimmar removed a restraining hand from Narm's arm. "Well done, boy," he said. "Continue to hold your peace, and life will be far easier for you."

"Aye," agreed Narm dryly. His master had certainly given him much practice in holding peace. All around them laughter and the clink and clatter of eating built up again. Tempers had been restored, and it was too soon to talk of the near-brawl. The company seemed in fairly good humor, as if the thief hadn't been liked much anyway. Narm looked about for the girl he had locked eyes with earlier, but she was nowhere to be seen. There was something about her. . . . Ah, well . . .

Narm turned his attention to the chilled wine the serving

girl had just brought, before Marimmar could forbid him to drink more. Now, if the old man would just take up his tale of the treasures of lost Drannor, and the city's ruin by devils again. . . .

But Ghondarrath, it seemed, had no more tongue for tales this evening. He sat talking quietly with the two tall, lithe ladies whose ready blades had saved his life. His eyes shone and his face was ruddy, and he seemed more alive than for many a long winter. Several of the locals called on him to resume his tale, but he paid them no heed. Finally, the calls became more general, floating across the taproom to the travelers from afar.

To Narm's quiet embarrassment, Marimmar cleared his throat importantly, squared his shoulders, and turned about grandly in his chair. Oh, gods, thought Narm despairingly, deliver us all. His eyes sought out the ceiling.

Before the Mage Most Magnificent could draw breath, however, one of the company of adventurers had turned to another and said, "Rymel! A tale! Give us all a tale!"

"Aye! A tale!" echoed other companions.

"Well, *I* don't know," Rymel began, but he was drowned out in a roar of protests.

"Tell you what?" Rymel asked. "What would you hear?"

"Wha—well, man, *you* know! Anything. Delg," the man added, turning to the dwarf, "you choose. You know more of the old days, and—"

"Odd things, aye," the dwarf of the company said sourly. "Odd myself, am I not?" He chuckled away their protests, hefted his drink consideringly, and said, "Well, Rymel, if you will, tell the tale of Verovan's last race. It's been awhile, and I would hear it again."

Narm noticed that Marimmar, who had been hemming and puffing in his seat, forgot his vanity at hearing the dwarf's request and leaned forward in interest. The two ladies who had defended Ghondarrath also fell silent and turned to listen. The bard Rymel looked about at all the attentive faces and said slowly, "Well enough then. It's a little tale, mind, not a great saga of love and battle and treasure."

"Tell on," the lady called Sharantyr bade him simply from across the room. Rymel nodded, and spoke quietly. Silence fell but for the snap of the fire as those in the taproom leaned forward to hear the better.

The bard was good, and his gentle words brought the tragic tale of the last king of Westgate to chilling life. All listened, in the cozy room where the old axe hung.

The mood of the evening had changed, the danger past and forgotten, Gorstag affably at ease again. Marimmar the mage never did tell his tale. . . .

* * * * *

The Company of the Bright Spear drank much and went up to their room late. Rymel, his lute left upstairs with their travel gear, had led the locals in a score of ballads with his fine voice alone. Delg the dwarf had lost his favorite dagger somewhere and was moody and suspicious. The burly fighter, Ferostil, was very drunk, and—as usual—trading coarse jests in voices loud and slurred, and the wizard Thail, grim and sober, was guiding him up the stairs with many a sigh and jaundiced look.

"Lend me a hand, Burlane," he pleaded, as Ferostil nearly fell back on top of him. "This lout is nearer your size."

"Aye," their burly leader said good-naturedly. "We've lost enough tonight." He leaned back to grab Ferostil's shoulder. "Come then, Lion of Tempus," he said, hauling hard. "Now, where's that room?"

"This one," the wizard said, and threw the door wide.

Within, all was as they had left it—packs strewn about, cloaks thrown over racks. A single lantern had been lit.

"My spear!" Burlane roared suddenly. "Where is the Bright Spear?" They peered all about, alert upon the instant, but there was no place in the room that could have concealed its flickering radiance. Their greatest treasure was gone.

"By all the gods!" Burlane bellowed. "I'll have this inn apart stone by stone if need be! That thieving bastard of an innkeeper! Delg—quick, run to demand it of him! Thail, look to our horses! Is anything else missing?"

"Aye," said the wizard thickly. His hands trembled above his opened pack. "All my spells." His face was ashen; he sat down on the bed suddenly and stared at nothing, dazed.

"Thail!" Burlane roared, shaking him. "Come, we must—"

"My axe also," the dwarf's sour voice cut through Burlane's rage. "I see no sign of our charter from the king, nor Ferostil's shield. Rymel?"

The bard was standing sadly by his pack. His shrug and empty hands told them his lute was gone as well. The men of the company stared at each other mutely. Everything dearest and of most value was gone.

Into the shocked silence came a knock upon the door.

Delg was nearest. Dourly he flung the door wide, expecting trouble. Over his shaggy head they all saw the pale, solemn face of a young girl with large, dark eyes. In one hand, she held their charter from the King of Cormyr. In the other, she gripped a spear that flickered with a pale blue light. She stepped calmly into the room past the astonished dwarf, cleared her throat in the tense silence, and said softly, "I understand you need a thief."

🌿 2 🌿

Wandering in the Mist

If discomfort and danger be always at hand, why then adventure? There is something in mankind that leads some always on to such foolishness, and the rest of us benefit by the riches and knowledge and dreams they bring us. Why else tolerate such dangerous idiots?

Helsuntiir of Athkatla
Musings
Year of the Winged Worm

The Company of the Bright Spear were six in number. The tall warrior Burlane bore the magical Bright Spear and led the company. A younger bladesman rode with him, the merry Ferostil. Delg, the dwarf, was also a warrior. His constant companion was the bard Rymel, probably the brightest of them all. The wizard Thail deferred to his younger, louder companions. Last and least of the company was the thief, one Shandril, a bright-eyed, soft-spoken waif in ill-fitting old breeches and a much-patched tunic.

They had nearly slain her when she had appeared with their missing gear, which she had slipped away and stolen while the ladies Storm and Sharantyr were facing down the company in the taproom. After their rage had subsided (under Rymel's laughter), only Delg had protested against her joining, but the fighter—with the same avid look in his eyes that Korvan got—was enthusiastic. So far, however, Ferostil had not bothered her.

Shandril had slipped out of the inn that same night to wait for the company in the trees on the edge of Deepingdale, leaving only a hastily scribbled note for Gorstag. She had spent anxious hours in the dark with small forest creatures rustling and scuttling unseen around her, afraid that the company would change their minds and ride off without her. Shandril's heart had leaped when they had come into view through the dawn mists, leading Lynxal's empty horse for her. She had trembled so with excitement that she could hardly speak, but she had gotten into the saddle somehow, though she had never before ridden a horse. She was relieved to discover the dead thief's weapons and gear strapped securely to the saddle, though she had no idea how to use them either. She would just have to learn . . . and fast!

She'd taken nothing from the inn but the clothes she wore, and the single nice gown that had been made for her. Robbing Gorstag seemed a poor way to repay him for his kindness, and Shandril was not a thief at heart.

She wondered that night if she'd be any good at thievery, with the company's eyes on her in judgment. Her arms shrieked stiffly from gripping at reins and saddlehorn. Her legs ached even worse. Places on her thighs had been rubbed raw, and when it rained and cold, lashing winds blew at the same time, Shandril wondered why she'd ever left the safe, warm household of The Rising Moon.

The next morning, her heart light and free, she knew why she'd left. All around her lay the green gloom of deep woods, where men said only elves had walked scant summers ago. Everywhere she looked she saw new, wondrous things. When Burlane had changed their course after a discussion in which Rymel and Thail spoke most, Shandril had been thrilled at the simple freedom of choice.

There was another reason she'd left to start a new life. For the first time in her life, she had friends around her. Oh, Gorstag and Lureene had been her friends, but they were always busy, always rushing off to do something that did not involve her. But now she had friends who rode with her and would fight with her and were there all the time. Hunger for freedom and friendship had pushed her to take that extra step, to steal up to the long room and knock on the door to face the Company of the Bright Spear. Even in the taproom, when it might have meant gruff old Ghondar-rath's death and they had been loud and mocking, even then it had thrilled her: the belonging, the trust.

One of their number had been endangered. As one, they sprang to aid him, daring all, heedless of rules or cost. Above all in the world they were companions, and each one raised his blade to defend the others, no matter how weak. That's what she was, the weakest of the company, the one with the least experience and with no magical weapons or magery to boast of. She was not even truly a thief. The weakest of the company, indeed.

But she was of the company, a full and proper member who darned her socks with the rest of them by the fire the next night in wild country and washed herself, fully clad, in an icy stream, as they did in the gray, misty morn that followed. Shandril had given up on her snarled, greasy hair, pulling it back into a simple tail with a broken strap of Delg's. Even if she was the only female and jests were often hurled her way as she scrambled, red-faced, out of the deep brush after relieving herself, she *belonged*. They were her companions, her family, and she would die for them.

* * * * *

The company had left Deepingdale and promptly turned north into the woods, heading for Lake Sember. From old records in Suzail, the wizard Thail had learned that the elves had lived on the shores of the Sember in great numbers for two thousand years or more. Even if nothing of value had been left behind, Lake Sember lay along their path to Myth Drannor, and scouting it would serve them as practice for when they reached the ruined city. The company had come upon good trails in the woods, and for days they had ridden steadily north. Game was plentiful. The forest was never quiet around them, but neither did they see men or other large, dangerous creatures. At last the trees thinned ahead, and they looked out over Lake Sember.

The waters of Lake Sember were deep blue and very still. Clouds scudding overhead were mirrored in the lake at their feet; by the shore, the water seemed as clear as crystal. Beneath it they could see the bottom of the lake falling away, a drowned tree's limbs long, dark, and silent, and the scuttling of a tiny crayfish bound for deeper waters.

The company fell silent as they looked upon Lake Sember. They all knew now why it had been so special to the elves. Far away down the long lake, a great gray heron rose from the near shore and winged silently across the lake. They watched in silence. The heron vanished into the trees.

The air had grown cooler, and Shandril shivered. Tall Burlane looked up abruptly and said, "We must move east. I hope to make camp where the Semberflow leaves the lake tonight. Let us go."

The company turned east along the shore, weaving in and out around the trees, but keeping the water always in view. It would not do to get lost and stray south again now. Mist began to gather in white curls along the water's edge as the air grew colder. Wisps drifted in under the trees, and the sky fell to silver-gray. Burlane hurried them on. Shandril found a cloak in the saddlebags and thankfully drew it on over her chilled arms and shoulders.

Somewhere ahead, a bird called amid the trees. The call did not echo, but faded away. Glancing around in the gathering darkness, Shandril noticed that Ferostil had quietly drawn his sword. The trees grew dense and the footing uneven, so they continued on foot.

"Sharp watch," Burlane commanded quietly. Blades were drawn all around him. Shandril drew her own slim longsword and clutched it firmly. Made for her predecessor, Lynxal, it was just a trifle too heavy. She felt no safer. The mist closed in around them.

Suddenly there came a high, weird, unearthly call, as if from a great distance. The horses snuffled and shifted uneasily. Looking at her companions, Shandril could see that they were puzzled by the sound as well. She was not the only frightened one, either.

By unspoken agreement, the Company of the Bright Spear waited in tense silence, but the call was not repeated. Shandril breathed a silent prayer for the kindness of Tymora, Goddess of Good Fortune. Finally Burlane ordered the advance again with a silent jerk of his head. Glad to be moving, they all shifted damp grips on weapons and reins and led the horses on through the thick white wall of mist.

"We should tarry until this mist passes," Rymel said, his bard's voice and gray eyes serious for the first time in Shandril's memory. Tiny droplets of mist hung in the curls of his short beard.

"Aye," Ferostil replied, his voice low and wary. "And yet— that cry we heard. If we wait, who knows what might hunt us? Surround and entrap us, and we not able to even see them until too late?"

His words left a deafening silence. Shandril met Burlane's eyes, trying to look calm. A trace of a smile crossed his lips as they traded glances, but his calmness was an act too. Shandril felt grateful, and suddenly she was less afraid.

Delg the dwarf spoke. "I second that. I cannot abide waiting a whole night through in this damp, doing nothing. I say push on, and we'll be the sooner out of it!" The light was growing dim. One of the horses snorted and shifted again, and Delg went to it and spoke soothingly.

"What say you, Thail?" Burlane asked quietly.

"It would be more prudent to stop and wait for morning and the lifting of this mist," the wizard replied calmly. "But I, too, would hate such waiting."

"Shandril?" Burlane asked in the same voice, and Shandril looked up in surprise, thrilled to be considered an equal.

"I'd rather risk stumbling into danger than waiting the night," she answered as calmly and steadily as she could. She heard several vigorous murmurs of agreement.

Burlane said simply, "We go on. Better to be all awake and expecting the worst than to be all asleep but two."

Suddenly, they heard a soft slithering sound, then a loud "plop," as something entered the lake nearby. Shandril's skin crawled. But the company could see nothing. Cautious minutes later they moved on, and soon they came to a place where the long grass was flattened in a wide swath as if by the passage of some great bulk, and flecked with trails of green-white slime. The horses shied from the area and had to be pulled across, snorting and rolling their eyes and lifting their feet as though surrounded by coiling snakes. The company hastened on as quickly and quietly as possible. Later they heard something scuttle away from their path, but again met no creature. They went on as night drew down.

At length, the sounds of wide waters moving before them could be heard, and Thail, probing with his staff, barred their way. "Open water," he said in a low voice.

"Either we have turned about and headed into the lake," said Rymel, "or the shore has doubled back before us, or—and this seems most likely—we have reached the Semberflow, where you intended to camp," he said to Burlane.

In the twilit gloom they heard their leader reply, "Aye, it is likely. I will look."

Pale light flared as he unwrapped the Bright Spear and bore it past them. The bard went with him, passing the reins of his horse wordlessly into Shandril's hands. She clung to two sets of reins in anxious silence, pleased to be so entrusted, and yet apprehensive. If something startled the horses, she knew she lacked the strength to hold them.

The two were a long time looking, and even Thail had begun to step about anxiously before the Bright Spear's radiance could be seen again in the thick violet and gray mist that enshrouded them. Burlane stepped back among them, looking pleased.

"It is the Semberflow," he announced. "We camp here. We cannot see to cross."

"A fire? Lanterns?" asked Delg. Burlane shook his head.

"We dare not. Double watch the night through—Shandril and Delg, then Ferostil and Rymel, and I'll see the dawn. Make no needless noise. Don't let the horses lie down—it's too damp, and they'll take the chill."

The band quickly unburdened and fed the horses, shared cold bread and cheese, and rolled themselves in cloaks and blankets. Shandril found Delg in the darkness.

"How can I keep watch if I can't see?" she whispered.

Delg grunted. "We sit down in the middle of everything, ladymaid. Back to back, d'you see? We give each other a pinch or an elbow now and then to keep awake. Three such, or more, quickly, means: beware, there's danger. You look, yes, but mostly you keep still and listen. Mist does funny things to sounds—you can never trust just where and how far away something you hear is—but listen hard to us and the horses first, mind you, and get to know the sounds, and then listen for sounds that aren't us."

Shandril stared at his red, gnarled face for a moment. "All right," she said, drawing her blade. "Here?"

The dwarf, already sitting on his cloak with legs outstretched, the axe in his lap warded from the dew with a fold of his cloak, rumbled affirmatively. Shandril sat down against his rounded, hard back, feeling the cold touch of his mail, and laid her own blade across her knees. She said no more, and around them the camp settled down into steady breathing, muffled snores, and the occasional faint, heavy thud of a shifting hoof. Shandril peered into the night, blinking dry eyes.

A long while passed in silence. Shandril felt a yawn coming. She tried to stifle it, and failing, tried to yawn in utter silence, but she felt the firm pressure of Delg's axe-butt driving against her flank immediately. Grinning in the darkness, she elbowed him back and was rewarded with a gentle squeeze of her elbow.

Shandril could visualize his stubby, iron-strong fingers pressing on the point of her elbow, and was reassured by the veteran's presence. His eyesight was far better than hers in the near-darkness, she knew, and she trusted his years of calm experience. What seemed like hours later, he squeezed her elbow gently again; she extended it in firm reply, grinned again, and so they passed the night.

Suddenly Delg shifted. "Sleep now," he said into her ear. "I'll wake Rymel and Ferostil." Shandril nodded automatically. The gruff warrior clasped her shoulder and was gone. Sleep now? she thought. Just like that? What if I can't?

Shandril rolled over, pulling her cloak up, and stared into the dank darkness. Where were they? How would she know which way to walk if she awoke and her companions were all gone? Suddenly she felt lonely and very homesick. Shandril felt the sting of tears, but she bit her lip fiercely. No! This was her decision, for the first time—and it was right! She settled her head on her pack and thought of riches and fame . . . and if not, an inn of her own, perhaps?

* * * * *

A gentle hand on her shoulder shook her slowly but insistently awake. Shandril blinked blearily up at Rymel. The bard smiled a wordless greeting and was gone. Shandril sat up in the dripping grass and looked around. The world was still thick, white, and impenetrable. She could see her companions as gray, moving shadows, and a larger bulk that must be one of the horses, but little else. By all the gods, was there no end to this mist?

The patient, gray-white cloak of vapor stayed with them as the Company of the Bright Spear followed the Semberflow's banks away from the unseen lake until Thail recognized a certain moss-covered stump and directed them to cross. The wizard stepped down into the dark river confidently, the water swirling around his ankles and then rising to near his bootstops. Rymel followed, just as matter-of-factly, leading his horse. But Shandril noticed that he kept his blade ready in his other hand and looked at the waters steadily and narrowly. Ferostil followed, and then Burlane waved Shandril to go next.

The water was icy. Shandril's boots leaked at one heel, and once she stepped into a deep place hidden under the water and nearly fell. Her firm grip on the reins saved her; her horse snorted his displeasure as all her weight pulled at his head for an instant, and then she recovered herself and went on.

The far bank seemed no different from the one they had left—tall, drenched grass, mist as thick as ever. The company gathered wordlessly to rub the legs of their mounts dry and peer about. The mist brightened still more as the unseen sun rose higher, but it did not break or thin. Burlane strode ahead a few paces and listened intently.

Then, quite suddenly, three warriors in chain mail advanced out of the fog with weapons ready. They bore no badge or colors, and behind them a fourth man led a mule. The mule was heavily laden with small chests securely strapped to a harness. Something metallic within the chests clinked and shifted at the beast's every step.

There was an instant of surprise, and then the three strangers rushed forward with an oath, springing to attack the company without so much as a greeting. The fourth turned from the mule to flee back into the mist.

Abruptly, Burlane's glowing spear hurtled through the air to pierce the runner at the back of the neck and bear him down. "At them!" the burly leader hissed. "Look sharp!"

Ferostil pushed roughly past Shandril to take a stranger's blade on his own, shove hard to rock the man back on his heels, and then, by a rapid succession of ringing, teeth-jarring blows, batter his way past the man's blade. The two men seemed evenly matched in strength. Shandril was shocked at the savagery of their hacking blows.

Even as she watched, Delg trotted past her and calmly launched himself into the air with a grunt. At the height of his leap, he cut hard at the side of the man's helm with his axe. There was a dull *crump* sound as the blade bit home, and the warrior reeled, then tumbled to the ground. Delg had already reached the next warrior, a burly man who raised his voice to roar a warning into the mist as he fell back before the blades of Rymel and Ferostil.

Shandril heard Burlane grunt in pain as the third warrior's blade bit into his shoulder. The man also swung a war-hammer, but the wizard Thail caught it on his staff before their attacker could drive it through Burlane's guard.

Shandril let go the reins of her mount and ran toward the Bright Spear, which flickered and glowed in a tangle of grass near the man Burlane had hit. She heard a strangled cry behind her but dared not look as she rushed over the uneven ground. Metal skirled and clashed again behind her. As Shandril reached the spear, she saw menacing shapes looming out of the mist. More warriors! She had no time to look down at its victim or behind her, for one of the new-comers was snarling at her, eyes glittering, a longsword reaching for her as he charged.

She saw the angry face of a second attacker before she could jerk the spear free and run, ducking low and turning, trailing the spear point down in the grass. The closest war-rior's swing clove the air, and she was away, stumbling in her haste. Delg grinned at her as he rushed past to meet the newcomers. Beyond him, Shandril could see the company advancing. All of their opponents had fallen.

She looked to Burlane, raising the spear, but he shook his

head, clutching his shoulder. "I cannot use it. Wield it well! More come!" Turning again, Shandril saw Ferostil and Delg closing with five warriors. Beyond, more newcomers loomed out of the mist, weapons gleaming.

The company was overmatched. Shandril hurried to Burlane's side, to guard his injured flank with the spear. It felt awkward in her hands, and he'd be close enough to shout directions for its use to her, if nothing else.

From Thail's hands burst three bolts of light, streaking through the air to strike at three foes. One stiffened and fell; another staggered but came grimly on. The third gasped and then roared a warning back into the mist, in a harsh, hissing tongue Shandril did not understand.

Then a warrior was rushing at her again. He had burst past or cut his way through the company's warriors and was closing quickly, a great sword clutched two-handed above his head. Shandril saw with sick fascination that its edge was dark with blood. It came toward her so smoothly, so quickly, swinging down, down—and then Burlane shoved her roughly from behind.

Shandril fell helplessly forward, dropping the spear as she crashed into the man's legs. He toppled and came down hard on her shoulder.

Red pain exploded in Shandril's arm as she fought for breath. She sobbed and then rolled desperately away. Her shoulder burned. The arm below felt numb. Shandril came dizzily to one knee in the grass and saw Delg calmly hew another foe down into the grass a little distance away. She turned wildly and saw Burlane regarding her gravely across the body of the warrior she had faced. He had tripped over her or gotten tangled with her and the spear long enough for Burlane to cut his throat.

The Bright Spear blazed in Burlane's grasp. He held it out to her. "Never freeze in a fight," was all he said. As he raised his head to look past her, Shandril noticed the white line of an old scar on his neck that she had not seen before.

The mist had lifted enough to reveal, trampled in the grass, the still bodies of fallen enemy warriors. Before them stood the company's warriors, leaning on their weapons and panting. Thail looked worried as he turned to Burlane.

"Perhaps I can use the art to drive some of them to slumber," he said, "but too many remain—far too many."

Shandril knew he was right. The strangers had drawn back from the company's blades to gather their strength and attack as one. Shandril counted nearly twenty men, clad in leathers or chain mail. None bore any sigil or blazon; all were armed. They seemed to be led by a stout warrior who wore a dark helm. At his gesture, his men had spread out in a long crescent, curving around the company, advancing slowly to either side.

Shandril turned to Burlane to warn him to pull back, to run *now*, but as her eyes saw his face—calm and bleak and a little sad—the cry died on her lips. Where was there to run to? She turned back to look at their foes. So many, so intent on her death. Beyond their grim, slowly advancing line, more men held the reins of a score of mules, all laden as the first one had been. There was no escape. Shandril, her shoulder throbbing, gripped the Bright Spear firmly, determined to please the war god Tempus even if Tymora, the Lady of Luck, had turned her face from them. She should never have left Gorstag and The Rising Moon. . . . But she had, and she was going to see this through. She hoped she would not run.

"Clanggedin!" Delg roared hoarsely, as if to the ground at his feet. He flung down his axe. "Battle-Father, let this be a good fight!" He drew the warhammer at his belt and brought it down hard on the axe with a ringing sound—a sound that thrummed and echoed around them before rolling away. To Shandril's amazement, Delg began to sing. The axe at his feet glowed and shimmered and then lifted slowly into the air before him.

The whole company and their foes alike stood amazed. Delg, his weathered face wet with tears and his voice cracking as he sang on, extended one stubby hand and the axe rose into it, winking with a light that had not been there before. Delg seemed to grow and straighten. His beard jutted defiantly, and the warhammer he held began to glow faintly. Its radiance pulsed and grew as he sang, until it matched the sheen of the axe in his other hand.

The dwarf stepped forward, then, singing old ballads in

his rough voice. Pride and awe and gratitude rang in his songs as Ferostil and Rymel stepped forward to join him.

Shandril looked to Burlane and whispered, "Does he do this every time? I mean—" She stopped, embarrassed at the twinkle in his eye. Suddenly, Burlane roared his laughter aloud and clasped her to him, and she felt foolishly happy. *Ah, but if one is to die,* she heard the voice of an old wandering priest of Tempus who sometimes stopped at the inn, *it is best to die in a good cause, fighting shoulder to shoulder with good friends.*

That thought brought a sudden chill, and Shandril raised the Bright Spear's glowing point before her and tensed. Across the trampled grass, the enemy warriors exchanged a few barked commands and replies and began to trot forward, blades raised to slay. Delg sang on.

The gleam of the dwarf's weapons grew dazzling and then died away suddenly as the mist parted.

In the sudden morning light there was movement. Between the two warring bands walked two newcomers. One was tall and handsome, clad in forest green. A great sword was scabbarded at his hip, and a gray hawk rode on his shoulder. He strode easily, obviously slowing his stride to match that of his companion.

The companion was an old and long-bearded man whose eyes shone with keen intelligence and good humor. He wore plain brown robes with a tattered gray half-cloak, and the stains of spilled food and wine were dry but copious down his front. He spoke to his companion in a voice of aged, crotchety distinction, and, as the two stepped nearer, Shandril could make out the words.

" . . . Silverspear distinctly *told* me, Florin, that if there were elves left to meet us anywhere in the Elven Court, they would meet us *here,* and I've never known elves . . ."

His companion had noticed the two groups of combatants in the mist. Darting swift glances about, he made to draw his sword. But the old man beside him walked on.

" . . . to be untrustworthy, *or* forgetful, mark ye. Never. I doubt overmuch that they've been either this time, say others what they may. Five hundred winters have I known them, and . . ."

The tall warrior plucked gently at his companion's shoulder. "Ah, Elminster . . ." he ventured, hand on his hilt, eyeing the score of charging warriors on their left and the waiting six on their right. "Elminster!"

". . . though that be but a short time to an elf, it is long enough for these eyes and ears to take the measure of—eh? Aye then, what?" Irritated, the old man peered about, following the warrior's swift pointing finger to right and left.

He peered at the Bright Spear in Shandril's hands and then seemed to pause and nod as he saw Delg. He stopped and nodded to his right. The warrior the old man had called Florin obediently turned toward the company, half-drawing his blade. It glowed with its own blue-white light. He did no more, but stood watchfully, wary eyes raking them all. Shandril thought that here was a man other men would follow to the death and obey with loving loyalty. The company stood unmoving.

The mage called Elminster was chanting as he drew two items too small to be seen from his robes and brought them together, his hands moving with a curious, gentle grace. Abruptly, he drew his hands apart violently. Light pulsed between them, and the items were gone. Elminster faced the charging warriors, flung his hands wide, and spoke a last quiet word.

The warriors came to a halt just short of the old mage, blades flashing; then they wavered and backed away. Trotting awkwardly as they turned and roared their bafflement, they gathered speed. In wonder, Shandril watched mules, warriors, and all charge away as fast as they could, crying out in rage and frustration and brandishing their weapons. The mist swallowed them long before their cries died away.

The old mage walked on unconcernedly. The kingly warrior paused a moment, looking after the warriors Elminster had repelled, and then strode suddenly on to catch up with his friend, casting a last long look at the company. Shandril noticed that the green eyes of the hawk on his shoulder had never left them. Elminster looked again at the Bright Spear, made a "move away" gesture with the backs of his fingers at the company, and strode on into the mist.

"Now, as I was saying, she said I was to expect them on the banks of the Sember, and I've never known Silverspear to speak falsely. There's many a time . . ."

As the mists swallowed them both, the tall warrior cast his calm gaze at them once more, and Shandril could have sworn that he winked.

The company stood a moment in shocked silence, and then Burlane dragged Shandril with him to where the others stood. "Come on!" he hissed. "Delg! Enough! Clanggedin has heard! Let us go, before they return!"

"Who was that?"

"Go? Where?"

"Aye, while we can!"

"Did you see that? A wondrous thing!"

"*Later!*" Burlane said sharply, and the company fell silent. "Thank you, Delg. Let us not waste the good fortune Clanggedin has given us! Delg, check the bodies! Thail and Rymer, collect the horses! Be back here before I count six. Then we flee!"

"What? Af—"

"Later," Burlane said, and they went. No coins were to be found on the bodies, however, and the weapons did not measure up to their own. A few extra daggers and one good pair of not overlarge boots was their booty.

Burlane had sheathed the Bright Spear's glowing blade while the others searched. He and Shandril bound Ferostil's shoulder with strips of cloth. Rymel and Thail arrived back in haste with the horses, which had not strayed far.

Burlane pointed ahead and to the right. "We go this way," he said. "Quick and—at all costs—quiet. They'll expect us to flee. Men so strong in numbers and so quick to slay will not expect us to pursue them." He strode forward.

"What?" Ferostil hissed angrily. "Slink away with nothing to show for it? There was coin on that mule, maybe on all of them! Wha—"

"Later," said Burlane again, almost mildly, but Ferostil flinched as if a sword had struck him. "I've no wish to let slip treasure, nor let pass those who draw our blood without so much as a greeting. Our skulker can trail them. We'll follow and strike when death is not such a close and certain answer." He smiled down at Shandril as they pressed on over the grass. "Ho, little skulker. A task for you . . . most dangerous. Will you?"

Faces turned to her, curious, waiting, as they walked. Shandril flushed, then heeded the smile and ignored the danger warning to reply firmly, "Yes. Tell me what and how, and I will do it."

"Well said," Burlane said with a grim smile. "It is a simple thing, and yet it will be difficult in this mist. Hide—belly down was Lynxal's usual way—and lie near where we fought. Not close to the bodies, mind—they'll check those. Keep close and quiet. Follow us this way only if they haven't come back before you get hungry. I think they'll be back soon, and expecting us.

"You follow them, without being seen. Come back to us if they camp or night falls, or they go where you cannot follow. We will try to keep near, but I can promise nothing in this mist. No fighting, mind—just eyes and ears. Understood?"

Shandril's nod brought another pain-twisted smile to his face. "Good, then, enough talk. Pass me your reins, and wait here. May Tymora and He Who Watches over the Shoulder of Thieves smile upon you." Burlane did not name the god Mask. To any who did not worship the patron of thieves, the utterance of the god's name brought ill luck.

Shandril shivered a little at the thought of what the evil god's aid might be, as she watched the company hasten on until the mist swallowed them all. Better to trust in Tymora, Lady Luck, capricious though her luck might be. Suddenly remembering Burlane's instructions, she sank to her knees in the wet grass, ignoring the pain remaining in her shoulder. The dew made the grass about her glisten silver-gray. Shandril slipped the tail of her cloak in front of her and lay down upon it to wait. The unseen sun was brightening the mist, revealing the ground a few paces around her. Wet grass tickled her nose.

Shandril peered intently all around. She had not quite yet escaped death today . . . and there would be no Elminster to magically rescue her this time, if the twenty warriors saw her, with their treasure and all. She lay very still.

With heart-stopping suddenness, a warrior loomed out of the mist perhaps forty paces away. Another followed, and another, and they looked familiar to Shandril. The men whose names she did not even know were returning, free now of the mage's magic. They came carefully in the wet grass, weapons ready, close together, not speaking.

Shandril tried to keep count. She did not want to creep out behind them only to find others behind her. If she were caught, she thought with a sudden chill, a quick death might be a kind end. Adventure? Aye, adventure.

She tossed her head in silence and counted warriors. Like creeping shadows, they passed in front of her—sixteen, eighteen, twenty-one. Now the mules passed, all loaded with chests and canvas sacks. Shandril counted fifteen before the procession ended. She waited for the space of two long breaths, fearing a rearguard.

Her caution was rewarded when six silent bladesmen stalked into view, looking all about, swords drawn. One seemed to stare at her all the while they passed. Shandril kept still, hoping he would not be too curious or too diligent. He was not. The gods were with her. She drew a trembling breath and waited until she had drawn two more before she eased herself up and crept after them.

The mysterious warriors were heading roughly westward, close to Lake Sember. They were moving rapidly despite their wariness, as people do who still have a long way to travel. An occasional tree loomed up out of the mist as Shandril followed them, cautiously working her way closer on the higher ground and carefully dropping back in wet areas where one slip and splash might bring them all down on her. She was soon soaked and shivering.

So this is what Gorstag meant when he said adventure usually means pain and weariness, both conveniently forgotten later, Shandril thought, recalling a fireside talk. Grinning, she crept closer. She had seldom felt more alert, more alive, more excited. You never told me it was this much fun, she chided Gorstag mentally as she climbed a little rise and dropped to her belly in the tall grass.

It was well she did. The mist rolled away briefly, revealing six warriors, standing just below the brow of the hill on which she lay. Mules were being led up the hill beyond. The land was rising, and the men were taking their treasure west. These must be the rearguard, Shandril reasoned.

Shandril could hear the low mutter of their voices, but could not make out the words. She dared not crawl nearer. Three of them were deliberately peering her way.

The mist began to close in again. They were waiting here, probably planning some sort of trap for anyone following them. It would mean her death to come up over the ridge of the hill, even with the mist. Shandril lay still on the damp ground and thought for a bit. What should she do now?

Without warning, a man loomed up out of the mist no more than two steps away, strode past her with the wet grass whispering around his boots, and was gone, walking back the way she had come. He held a strung bow and a shaft ready in one hand, and wore a long knife at his belt, but no armor. He looked young and bleakly confident. After a moment, another archer followed, and then four more, passing farther away. Shandril gasped in horror. The archers were going back to slay the company!

In her mind she could see arrows leaping one by one from the mists to bring down Delg, Burlane, Rymel, Thail—one by one, convulsed and writhing in the grass, their slayers quickly gone. Any chase would run straight into a storm of arrows.

How to warn the company? Shandril doubted she could get around the archers without being killed. There was only one thing to do, she realized with a sick, sinking feeling. *Fun*, she reminded herself wryly as she rose out of the grass and turned, drawing Lynxal's blade—her sword now—and went off to war.

She hurried forward as quietly as she could, picturing the faces of her companions as she strolled up to them with dripping blade and tossed two heads at their feet. Her stomach lurched at the thought, and she stared down at the blade, cold and heavy in her hands, with real revulsion.

She looked around in the mist, feeling suddenly lost and helpless. A sharp blade is little comfort when you know you can't use it on anyone. Even less comfort once the anyone realizes that. She stopped for a moment to lean against a gaunt and bare tree. Sheathing her sword carefully, she looked over the tree. The wood was dead but damp; it broke with a dull sound, not the sharp crack she had feared. She held a curved, surprisingly heavy, twisted limb. Shandril hefted it a few times and then stalked on through the mist.

She came upon him quite suddenly. The archer who had passed close to her was now standing alone, bow ready, listening intently. He heard her and half turned. As his eyes met hers and his mouth opened in surprise, Shandril leaped forward, heart pounding, and brought the tree limb down as hard as she could across his throat.

The force of the blow numbed her hands and knocked her off balance. She slipped in the wet grass and slid right beneath him, getting tangled in his legs. He made a horrible gurgling noise, and his knee hit her forehead hard. Dazed, Shandril lay staring up at the mist for a moment, the breath knocked from her lungs, her back and bottom aching. Then she heard thudding footsteps.

"Bitch!" a man's voice snarled close by. Shandril rolled to one side and looked up. The other archer was charging at her, a long, gleaming knife drawn up to strike.

Shandril screamed in helpless terror as the knife leaped at her throat, so bright and so quick. She threw up her hands—the tree limb gone, her sword too slow to draw—and tried to jump aside.

Too late. The archer's grasping hand caught her left shoulder as she shifted to the right. The cruel force of his fingers drove her back and spun her sideways. His biting blade stabbed again and again at her shoulder and back. Shandril screamed again at the burning, slicing pain, as they fell together on top of the sprawled body of the first archer. Her shoulder felt wet and cold as the knife slid across it.

The man's angry face was inches from her own. Shandril struggled furiously to avoid his clutching hands and block the knife, clawing, biting, and driving her knees viciously into him. Somehow, she got both hands on his wrist and forced the knife past her, but he was stronger and he pulled it slowly around at her again.

Then the snarling face inches from her own gasped. The eyes darkened, and blood dribbled from the lips. Shandril felt his strength ebb away, and then strong hands lifted the man's weight from her. Through bleary eyes she saw the bright and terrible tip of a blade growing out of a dark, spreading stain on the archer's chest. His head lolled as he was lifted aside.

Anxious faces looked down upon her. Shandril smiled weakly as she met Rymel's eyes, and saw Delg, Thail, and Burlane behind him. She caught a shuddering breath, steadied her shaking hands, and said, "My thanks. I . . . think these two were . . . sent back . . . to slay you all with their arrows . . . I . . . had to stop them."

She winced as gentle hands touched her shoulder to raise her. Burlane murmured something comforting as Thail's fingers probed cautiously. The wizard took a flask from his belt with crimson, dripping fingers and said simply, "Drink."

The liquid was thick and clear and slightly sweet. It soothed and refreshed, and a delicious warmth spread from Shandril's stomach. "Thanks."

Her eyes sought Burlane. "I followed them," she said. "They went west . . . the land rises. Two hills away the rearguard split. Four swordsmen followed up the mules, and these two came back this way to slay any who pursued." She realized with sudden vigor that the pain had subsided, and with it her sick, dizzy feeling. "What was in that vial?"

"A potion," Thail said gently. "Can you walk?" He raised her gently to her feet.

Delg patted her hip and said, "Well done, ladymaid." Shandril looked around at the others: Ferostil, looking relieved as his eyes met hers and saw they were no longer misted in pain, and Rymel, who wordlessly held out to her the knives of the two archers.

"Can you use a bow?" Burlane asked her quietly.

Shandril shook her head, but took the knives and slid one down either boot. Rymel nodded approvingly.

Burlane laid a gentle hand on her shoulder. "Let us go," he said. "I would have this treasure we've bled for."

There was a general rumble of agreement, and the Company of the Bright Spear strode forward. Shandril looked once over her shoulder at the twisted bodies of the archers before the mist swallowed them. She had killed a man. It had been so quick, frighteningly easy. She stumbled on a clump of grass despite Burlane's arm—and paused in shock.

"Shandril?" Burlane asked quietly. "Are you well?"

"I—ah, yes. Yes. Better now." Shandril strode on, trying not to look down at the tunic that clung to her damply. It was dark and glistening with the blood of the man who had nearly slain her. Her skin crawled. She hoped it would not begin to smell too soon.

*　*　*　*　*

Far to the east the mist was thinner. Wisps of it curled about Marimmar as the Mage Most Magnificent led his apprentice through old, thickly grown trees. "This way, boy! Just ahead, and you'll lay eyes on what few have seen unless they be elvish for four lifetimes of men, and more! Myth Drannor itself! Who knows what art may wait there for you and me? We could wield magics unseen in these lands for many a long year, boy! What say you?" The pudgy mage fairly trembled with anticipation.

"Ah, Master . . ." Narm began, looking ahead.

"Aye?"

"Well met, lord of the elves," Narm said hastily, "and lady most fair. I am Narm, apprentice to this Mage Most Magnificent, Marimmar. We seek Myth Drannor."

Marimmar blinked in surprise and beheld a tall, dark-haired male elf who bore both wands and sword at his belt. The elven warrior stood beside a human lady of almost elfin beauty—dark eyes, a gentle mouth, and a slim, exquisite figure—who wore plain dark robes. They stood together in the middle of the old, overgrown trail Marimmar had been following and showed no signs of moving aside, though both wore polite expressions and had nodded courteously at Narm's salutation.

Marimmar cleared his throat noisily. "Ah—well met, as my boy has said. Know you the way to the City of Beauty, good sir? . . ." The elf smiled thinly.

"Yes, I do, Mage Most Magnificent." His voice, low and musical, was faintly sarcastic. His eyes were very clear.

Narm stared in wonder. This seemed an elven lord like the old tale spoke of.

"However," the elf continued, gently and severely, "I stand here to bar your way to it. Myth Drannor is not a treasure-house. It is today a sacred place to my people, even now that most of my kin have gone from these fair trees. It is also a very dangerous place. Devils have been summoned to the ruined city by evil men. They patrol the forest even now, not far beyond where we stand."

"I am not a babe to be frightened by words, good sir," Marimmar snapped. "We have come far to reach Myth Drannor before it is plundered, its precious magic lost! Stand aside, for I have no quarrel with you, and would not harm you!" Marimmar urged his pony forward.

"Back your mount, mage," the lady said calmly, "for we have no quarrel with it." She stepped forward. "I am Jhessail Silvertree of Shadowdale. This is my husband, Merith Strongbow. We are Knights of Myth Drannor. This is our city, and we bid you politely begone. We have the art to drive you back, Marimmar. Make us wield it at your peril."

Marimmar cleared his throat again. "This is ridiculous! You would tell me where to pass and where not to pass? *Me?*"

"Nay," Merith mocked the mage's florid speech. "We but inform you of the consequences of your choice in this matter, good mage. Your destiny remains in your hands." He smiled at Narm, who had backed his pony away.

Marimmar looked around and discovered he stood alone. He harrumphed and turned his mount. "Perhaps—ah, there is something to your warnings. I shall direct my quest for knowledge elsewhere for now. But know this! Threats shall not stay me—nor many others, who even now seek this place with far more greedy intent than I—from exploring Myth Drannor, when the opportunity proves more—ah, auspicious. My art may open me a way that you cannot gain-say!"

Merith smiled. "It is said that a man must follow where his foolishness leads," he quoted the old bardic saying mildly.

"Safe journey, Narm and Marimmar both," Jhessail added, her eyes alight with amusement. Narm could see no less than three wands at her belt. Marimmar saw them too and nodded curtly to the knights as he wheeled his pony.

"Until our paths cross again," he said loudly. The Mage

Most Magnificent spurred his mount into a canter, tearing past Narm like a whirlwind. His young apprentice turned and saluted the elf and the lady mage with courtesy and a smile, then trotted off in his master's wake.

The two stood and watched them go. "The old one is too much the fool," Jhessail said thoughtfully. "He will turn about and come by another way and meet his doom."

Merith shrugged. "One less arrogant fool to swagger his art, then. He was warned. I hope he doesn't drag the young one down with him."

Jhessail nodded. "If not for the devils and the beasts, Myth Drannor's population would have grown to rival Waterdeep's this past season. Why are these magic-seekers all such idiots?"

Merith grinned at her. "You should know well, my dear, that adventurers and idiots are one and the same."

Jhessail merely looked at him. Merith smiled again and gathered his wife up in an embrace. It was rare for an elf and a human to love so deeply and so simply, without high tragedy. Marimmar would not appreciate this, Jhessail thought with pity. But that young one might. . . .

* * * * *

"Here, then," said the Mage Most Magnificent, a short time later. "I can see towers through the trees . . . this must be that part of the old city where the mages dwelt." The confident words had scarcely left his mouth before a dark and grinning face rose from the underbrush just ahead. Narm, heart sinking, had not time for even a cry of alarm before the devil leaped, clapped batlike wings, and flew unhesitatingly at them, its fellows also rising dark and sinister from the brush. Marimmar's voice as he babbled a hasty spell quavered in fear. After that one terrible instant of realization, they were fighting for their lives.

❧ 3 ❧

The Gates of Doom

My fires ring my foe around, and my fangs and claws strike at her while she flees. Cruel, am I? Nay, for until now she has never really lived, now known the worth of the life she has used so carelessly. She should thank me.

Gholdaunt of Tashluta
Letter to all Sword Coast ports
on his hunting of the pirate Valshee
of the Black Blade
Year of the Wandering Waves

Mist rolled about them as the Company of the Bright Spear hurried westward over rising hills, quiet and as wary as possible. Bare rock appeared more frequently now as they passed, and the land rose gently. Somewhere ahead, hidden in the mist, the Thunder Peaks jutted like a great wall. The warriors who had attacked them so suddenly without challenge or banner hastened on before them, unseen but trailed in the tramplings of the wet grass by mule after mule laden with treasure.

Burlane was frowning. "What do you think, Thail? If their bowmen don't return, will they still be warned? Are we rushing into a trap?"

Thail nodded. "Aye. Yet we dare not turn aside and approach the peaks by another way. In this mist we would lose their trail, and knowing not where they lair, could well head into any number of traps. Best we continue close on their heels, or turn back altogether."

Burlane looked at them all. "Well?" he asked. "Do we press

on, turn back to Myth Drannor, or seek fortune elsewhere? This chase could mean our deaths, and soon."

"We face death every day," Ferostil said stoically, shrugging, "and treasure is guarded the world over." There were nods of agreement.

"We go on, then," Burlane said. "Weapons at the ready, and pick up the pace. We slow only where an ambush seems likely." They began to trot, tugging the reluctant horses into faster gaits. The hills climbed and rolled more steeply, and the company saw no sign of the warriors or their laden mules. The trail led on through scrub, upward into the mountains. Loose stones soon forced them to dismount.

"Who do you think we're following?" Delg grumbled, running hard on his short legs to keep pace. Burlane spread his hands; each bore a weapon.

"Who can say?" their leader replied. "No arms displayed, yet blades were ready, and they weren't slow to use them. They're outlaws, surely, but where did they come from with such booty, and where do they lair? Who can tell?"

"Cheery speech," Burlane grunted sourly. "We hasten to meet gods-only-know how many bandits, all well-armed and expecting us. And me without fresh bandages on my wounds!"

Rymel chuckled. Ferostil snorted. Delg grinned wolfishly.

"If it's fresh bandages you seek, longjaws," the dwarf said, "I could be seeing my way to providing you with fresh dressings—and fresh wounds to go beneath 'em, too!"

"Ahead!" Thail said quietly but sharply. All fell silent and looked. The trail they followed led up a rocky rise and between two pillars of bare rock. The place looked bleak and uninhabited. The company was leaving the mist behind, and they could see ahead a high, green, deserted valley. Mountains rose up on either side. Beyond the rock pillars the valley climbed to the company's right.

Burlane nodded. "A place to be wary. Yet I see no danger waiting."

"Invisible, by magic?" Ferostil suggested. Delg gave him a sour look.

"Waste all that art to hide from *six* adventurers?" the dwarf said derisively. "Are you foolish?"

"No, he's just a gloomthought," Rymel said, grinning. "Yet if we climbed a wall of that valley when we get inside, I'd feel safer. This looks like a gods-favored spot for a lookout, if not an attack."

Burlane nodded again. "Climb the right-hand slope, then, once we're through the mouth of the valley. Look sharp, everyone! I want no foes sounding an alarm or rolling rocks down on our heads. Understood?"

Everyone in the company muttered and nodded agreement as they trotted onward between the rock pillars. Shandril noticed Delg peering narrowly at the rock faces to either side. To her eyes, they seemed natural, not quarried. The valley beyond lay empty and quiet.

The trail grew harder to follow as they went on. The grass grew shorter, broken here and there by bare rock, moss, and weeds, but even Shandril's eyes could still find the tracks of the mules. The unshod hooves had left deep marks in the soft, muddy patches between the rocks. The trail led upward, and the company followed until the valley opened out before them.

In the clear light of highsun, the land before them lay green and rugged, walled in by mountains. It was not over-large, and the only trees were stunted and scraggly, huddled along the base of a steep rock face that formed the northwest wall of the valley. Water gleamed in little pools to the company's left. Rocks rose brokenly to their right. Nothing living met their eyes except one lone hawk, circling high above. There was no sign of warriors or of mules, only the faint trail running on.

The company swung to the right and began to climb. Burlane turned to Delg. "Stay with the horses. Bring them on only at my call." The dwarf nodded.

"Does something about this place feel . . . wrong to you, too?" Delg asked.

Burlane nodded. "Yes," he said, mounting a rock, "and until—"

At that moment a man in robes appeared on a rock above them, farther up the slope. He was broad and stout and thin-bearded, and he wore robes of dark burgundy.

"Who are you," he called angrily, looking down on the

company, "and why have you passed the gates without leave? Speak! Show me the sign forthwith or perish!" The man bore no staff or weapon. His eyes were black and glistening. Shandril thought she had never before seen a man who looked so cruel and *evil*.

"What gates?" Burlane called, climbing nearer. From where she crouched behind a rock, Shandril could see all of the company moving, weapons out, advancing on the man, shifting apart from one another. The black eyes darted coldly back and forth.

"The Gates of Doom," came the cold reply, and the mage's fingers moved as if they were crawling spiders. He chanted one rising phrase, and lightning leaped from the air before his fingers in a spitting, crackling bolt.

In the blue-white flash of the bolt, Shandril saw Ferostil raise his sword in a convulsive, jerking dance. The fighter's roar of agony died away faintly as his body blackened, tottered, and fell. Shandril was too shocked to make a sound. The warrior toppled forward out of view, down between two rocks.

Rymel threw a dagger as the company leaped to attack. The short blade flashed end over end toward the dark-eyed mage, but he ignored it, speaking something coldly as he pointed at the company. Before it reached its target, the knife seemed to strike some sort of invisible barrier, and it bounced suddenly away to one side.

Abruptly, nine streaks of light darted at the company from the mage's pointed finger. Shandril watched in morbid fascination as each glowing missile flew with frightening speed, turning in the air to follow her scrambling companions. She watched as Thail and Burlane were struck by two bolts each before there was a flash of light around the edge of her boulder and something cold and burning and almost alive hit her. Very hard. Such pain . . .

Shandril twisted in agony, crying out as she clutched herself, arms tight around the searing fire in her gut that burned up into her chest and nose and brought tears to her eyes.

It passed, finally, leaving her empty, weak, and sick. She was dizzy, and as she leaned against the rock, her hands were shaking uncontrollably. Shandril knew she should draw her blade and attack, but she could not. The world spun around her in gathering darkness as she wept and shook helplessly, dropping to her knees. Then she fell sideways against the rock, its cold stone hard against her cheek. Gods above! What had the wizard done to her? . . .

After what seemed most of a day, Shandril's eyes saw again. Pain from her stiff neck and bruised check roused her from where she lay slumped against stone. She looked up over the hillside to where the mage stood, his hands twisting in spellcasting, only feet above where Rymel grimly climbed. On the rocks between there and where she crouched lay the still, twisted form of Thail. Delg, obviously hurt, crouched beside Thail helplessly. Beyond, the radiance of the Bright Spear bobbed into view as Burlane leaned on it. He was climbing toward the mage, mounting a massive boulder slowly and painfully.

Shandril could taste blood in her mouth. She spat it out angrily as she watched Rymel's sword bloody the mage's hand and ruin another spell that might have slain them all. The mage struck aside Rymel's blade with his other hand. The bard drew back his sword to strike again, and the mage shouted a word in desperate haste.

An instant later he was gone. Rymel faced empty air, sword flashing as he spun about to look for his foe. Shandril saw him, suddenly, very near, behind all the company but herself. She cried out in rage and terror and drew her own blade, knowing even as she did that she was too weak and too unskilled to do anyone any harm.

Burlane heard her cry. With cool speed he took his balance, turned, and threw the Bright Spear all in one smooth motion. Shandril, her eyes fixed on the mage who stood grinning down at her, his hands moving again, saw only a flicker before the spear struck home. The mage, intent on her, did not see danger approaching.

Suddenly the spear's long shaft stood out of the mage's side, and he was thrown sideways by the force. As his knees buckled, he fell crumpled up around the spear's shaft, out of sight. Shandril clambered feebly over the first rock between them, peering anxiously. But even as hope grew and rose in her throat, the mage's shoulder and drawn, furious face appeared again.

He flung one hand into the air in a fist. On it he wore a brass ring that twinkled with sudden magical light. She ducked down behind the rock she had been about to climb, praying aloud to Tymora that whatever the ring unleashed would spare her. But after she had drawn two long, ragged breaths and nothing had occurred, she dared to look up again, slowly and warily, sword raised.

The mage had not moved. He leaned against a rock, clutching his side where the spear was still lodged. Burlane was climbing over the rocks toward him, brow bristling in fury, sword drawn. Ferostil and Rymel also clambered among the rocks to the attack, moving faster but coming from farther off. The mage raised bloody hands and began to cast another spell. Burlane cursed and flung his blade. The mage ducked and stepped back a pace, but did not cease his weaving of art, and the blade missed, clanging lightly on the rocks before it slid out of sight. Burlane cursed horribly and went on, staggering as he came down off a large rock and hurried to the next. He drew the long knife he carried at his belt as he climbed nearer.

Shandril remembered the knives in her own boots then and plucked one out, sheath and all. Carefully she judged the distance, drew off the sheath, and threw the blade.

She was too late. The mage finished his spell. Burlane was suddenly shrouded in a dark, sticky web of strands that held him fast among the rocks, his roar of baffled rage almost deafening even as he struggled. Shandril had the small satisfaction of hearing the mage cry out and curse, too. He glared at her in hatred, clutching the back of his left hand where her dagger had cut him.

Cold fear settled in her, but she raised her heavy sword and climbed toward the wizard. Only a few rocks separated them, but Rymel was near, climbing over the rocks in angry haste. The mage backed away, the spear quivering. Its end caught and scraped on a rock. The mage gasped and stopped, sinking down briefly in pain. Then he staggered to his feet and turned away from them all.

"Oh no, you don't!" Rymel roared, leaping wildly over

Burlane's webbed form and landing precariously on the rocks beyond. He drew back his arm to hurl his own sword—and then they heard the roar.

Shandril looked up. In the sky above the valley, turning ponderously as it emerged from between two frowning crags, was the vast scaled bulk of a green dragon. Its huge, batlike wings beat once, and then it dipped its great serpentine neck and dove down at the company.

Vast and terrible it was, and in its glittering eyes Shandril saw her death. Paralyzed with dragonfear, she could not even scream as the dragon spewed out a billowing cloud of thick, greenish yellow gas. Shandril heard screams, saw for an instant the mage laugh in triumph as Rymel's hurled blade missed, and then the shadow of the flying wyrm fell upon them. She could not breathe. Her lungs were suddenly burning, her eyes smarting. Shandril choked and coughed and choked again and fell hard to her knees, the searing pain spreading in her lungs. Darkness claimed her.

After drifting through shifting, blood-red mists, Shandril dreamed of dragons dancing. . . .

* * * * *

It was cold, and Shandril was lying on something hard and rough. The air itself was cold and smelled of earth and old dust and damp mold and decay. She opened her eyes, tensing herself against the pain—and was astonished to find she felt none. She was no longer hurt. How this was, she did not know—magic, most likely. Whose, and why so used, she had no idea—but she could move freely, without pain. Even her shoulder felt whole, she realized, touching it in wonder.

Shandril lay against a stone, and from beyond it, somewhere very close to her, two human male voices she did not know were speaking.

". . . No, I say your men shall not have her! Her blood is too valuable to use for that—valuable, mind, only so long as she is inviolate!" The voice was excited, imperious.

"How can you be sure of *that?*" an older, deeper, more sour voice snarled. "These days—"

Shandril listened no more. With frantic haste she scrambled up and began searching for a means of escape. The stone was cold under her bare feet. Someone had taken her sword, dagger, the remaining knife from her boots—and the boots themselves. She had been lying against a large stone which had evidently been rolled across the mouth of the cavern in which she stood.

The cavern was small, narrowing at one end into a crack impossibly small to pass through. There were no other visible doors, cracks, or side passages. Her prison was lit by a pale violet magical radiance which outlined a smooth, obviously carved stone block. The block lay horizontally in the center of the cavern, the height of two men or so in length and breast-high to her. Shandril was horrified to realize that the block was really a casket; she could see the edge of the lid. Two other, unlit caskets lay on either side of it. With growing despair, she wondered how, gods willing, she was going to get out of *this* tight spot.

She listened at the stone again but heard nothing; the men had left. She pushed futilely at the stone, felt around its edges carefully, heaved at it with all her strength, kicked at it and, in hysterical desperation, rushed at it and leaped on it. Nothing. Finally Shandril beat upon it with her fists. Still nothing.

Gasping for breath, she slumped down against the stone. It hadn't budged. Her blows had not even made any noise. She was trapped, and she was going to die. She shuddered at the memory of the voice speaking about not giving her to "your men"—and then her blood ran cold at the phrase "her blood is too valuable to us."

"I have to get out of here!" she cried aloud. She *had* to!

But there was no escape. She had looked everywhere, and there simply was no way out. The cavern was not large, and she had felt, beat upon, or run her hands over the floor and almost all of its walls that were within her reach. The cavern ceiling above her looked just as solid. She had looked everywhere. Suddenly her eyes fell on the black boxes in the center of the cavern.

She had not looked in the caskets.

Shandril stared at the lit one, sitting there in the cold gloom. It was huge, featureless, and silent. There were no runes or inscriptions cut into or painted on its sides or top.

It had been smoothed with great care and skill and then left unmarked. Dwarvenwork, most likely. Now that she had thought of opening it, she hardly dared do so for fear of what she might find. A fresh corpse, horribly mutilated and crawling with worms, her imagination whispered. Or worse, one of those terrible undead creatures—vampires, or ghouls, or skeletons that were dead and yet moved. Her skin crawled. She had nowhere to run if something in the casket reached for her. Why was only one lit? Would a spell be unleashed upon her if she touched or opened it? Or did something magical lair—or lie imprisoned—within?

For a long time Shandril stood staring at the caskets, trying to master her fear. Nothing stirred. No voices could be heard. She was alone and unarmed.

Trapped. At any moment she might hear the stone covering the portal begin to grate open, and then it would be too late . . . for anything. Shandril swallowed. Her throat seemed suddenly very dry. She heard her own voice again, as if from far away, saying softly to the company, "I understand you need a thief."

Briefly she wondered if they were all dead now: Delg, Burlane, and the others . . . then firmly she thrust such thoughts aside by concentrating on the casket. What if my friends, dead and bloody, are inside, shut in here with me? She screamed inwardly at the thought.

Then into her mind came Gorstag's kind, weathered face, smiling at her. Gorstag must have been in worse straits once or twice, and he was still around to tell the tales. . . .

Again Shandril turned to the lit casket. Swallowing the dry lump in her throat, she strode forward and stared at the glow and at the stone within it. There was no flickering in the radiance, no change, as she laid a hand on the lid.

Nothing happened. She was not harmed. Silence reigned. Shandril took a deep, shuddering breath and pushed. Still nothing happened. The stone lid was massive and old and did not move. Steeling herself, Shandril crouched beside the eerily glowing casket and put her shoulder to the lid, feeling nothing as the radiance played about her. Then, snarling with the effort, she gathered all her strength into a heave, bare feet slipping as she drove the lid sideways. It scraped and shifted, and she caught herself before her arm or head could dip into the open tomb.

She looked in. Nothing moved, nothing stirred. Bones . . . yellow to brown, scattered about inside the cold, black box. A human skull, a jawbone elsewhere. Peering carefully into the darker corners, Shandril made sure that there was nothing within but bones. She sighed, looking at the tumbled mess of bones. Someone had obviously ransacked this casket already; any weapons or things of value must have long ago been carried away. Why then the radiance?

Shandril stood in the cold, wondering who lay buried here—or rather, lay uncovered—bones scattered like so many rotten twigs on the forest floor. Idly she looked for certain bones in the tangle. There, a thigh bone . . . he (for some reason she thought of the pour soul as a he) must have been tall. . . . And then she noticed something odd.

There were three skeletal arms in the casket.

Just the one skull, and . . . yes, only bones enough, give or take a few, for one body. One body with three arms? She peered at those arms, one crumbling into separate bones, another almost intact, strips of withered sinew still clinging to the wrist and holding all together. And a third that was larger. . . . Curious, she reached into the tomb and touched the hand that did not belong.

Idiot! she thought, too late, the bones cold under her fingertips. *What have you done?* She froze, waiting for some magical doom to befall her, or the old bones to take her rash hand in a bony grasp, or a stone block to fall from the ceiling—something!

But nothing happened. Shandril peered around the cavern warily, and then shrugged and lifted out the skeletal arm. It dangled limply at the wrist. Small fingerbones dropped off into the casket as she raised the arm into better light.

Then she saw. Faint scratches caught the light along the armbone she held—writing of some sort. Shandril peered at it closely for the first time, wrinkling her nose in anticipation of a rotting smell that was not there as she brought the bones close to her face. The writing seemed to be only a single word. But why would someone scratch a word on a bone, then leave it here? What did it all mean?

Squinting, Shandril made out the word. "Aergatha," she mumbled aloud.

Suddenly, she was no longer in the cavern. The bones cold in her hand, she stood somewhere dimly lit and smelling of earth. She could feel cold air moving against her face. Shandril barely had time to scream as cold claws reached for her.

*　*　*　*　*

Narm, the mage's apprentice, swung his staff desperately, white with fear. The skull-like faces of the two bone devils he faced grinned at him as he backed away, trying to keep their hooks at bay and to flee from Myth Drannor as fast as he could. The devils were making horrible, throaty chuckling noises, tremendously entertained by his struggles. Thunder rolled overhead, and it was growing dark here under the trees.

Narm backed away desperately. Thrice they had tried to catch him between them, and only desperate leaps and acrobatics had saved him. By turns they would fade into invisibility, and he would swing wildly at the apparently empty air, hoping to deflect an unseen bone hook swinging for his throat or groin. Once, his staff did crash into something, but the devil seemed completely unaffected when it reappeared, grinning, just beyond his reach.

Twice now he had been wounded, and he was nearly blind with sweat. Magic as feeble as his own was useless against these creatures, even if he had been allowed the time necessary to cast anything. Magic had not saved Marimmar.

Narm had watched the pompous mage be overwhelmed after a few spectacular spells, then torn slowly apart with those bone hooks—the same bloody weapons that even now were tormenting the two screaming ponies. These two devils were only playing with him. The elf and his lady had given fair warning, and Marimmar had scoffed. Now the Mage Most Magnificent was dead, horribly dead. One mistake, only one, and now it was too late.

Suddenly Marimmar's severed head, dripping blood, eyes lolling in different directions, appeared before him in midair. Narm screamed as Marimmar's rolling eyes focused on him. The mouth opened in a ghastly, bloody smile, and the head moved toward him. Frantic, Narm swung his staff.

The wood cut empty air. The head was gone, gone as if it had never been there. Illusion, Narm realized in helpless anger, as the hissing laughter of the bone devils rose around him.

Around him! They had gotten on both sides of him! Desperately, Narm turned and charged at one, swinging his staff wildly, trying to batter it down and win free. It danced aside, still hissing, its scorpionlike tail curling at him. Narm sprawled in the dry leaves and dirt, rolled over, heart pounding, and jumped up to his feet with staff flailing about. . . . He was dead, dead anyway . . . he'd never escape . . . if only he and Marimmar had turned back!

Then there was a blinding flash and the world exploded. Narm hit something, hard. Putting out a hand, he felt bark, felt his way up the tree, realizing that he still held his staff in the other hand.

Abruptly he heard a dry female voice close by. "He lives, Lanseril. If your bolt had been a couple of hands closer, mind . . ."

"Your turn, remember?" a light male voice replied, pointedly. Then both voices chuckled.

Narm blinked his dazzled eyes desperately. "Help," he managed to say, almost crying. "I can't see!"

"Can't think either, if you planned on storming Myth Drannor armed with nothing but a sapling," the female voice said to him and then hissed a word. Narm had the impression that something brightened, suddenly, to his left, and raced off in a spray of separate moving lights. But he could see nothing more—everything looked like a white fog. A hand fell on his arm. He stiffened and swung his staff up.

"No, no," the male voice said in his ear. "If you hit me, I'll just leave you again, and the devils'll have you after all. How many companions had you?"

"J-just one," Narm replied, letting his arm fall. "Marimmar, the—the Mage Most Magnificent." Suddenly Narm burst into tears.

"I take it that he is no more," the female voice said gently. A hand took his sleeve, and then Narm was being led rapidly over the uneven leaves of the forest floor.

"Aye," the man said by Narm's shoulder. "I've seen pieces of him. Mixed up with two horses. Can you ride, man?" Insistently he shook the sobbing Narm, who managed a violent nod, and then added, "Good. Up you go." Narm felt a stirrup, and then he was thrust up onto the back of a snorting, shifting horse. Narm clutched the horse's neck thankfully, and from one side heard the female hiss a word that he had heard earlier.

The male voice spoke again. "Tymora spit upon us, they're persistent! There's another flying at us now! Ride! Illistyl, lead him, will you?" Narm heard a sudden flutter of wings. He struck out at it wildly, blindly, with his staff.

"Mystra's strength!" the woman said, and Narm was jerked roughly to one side. "Strike down Lanseril? Idiot!" A small, strong hand clouted him under the jaw and then jerked the staff from his grasp. Narm heard it clatter against something off to his right.

"I beg pardon!" he said, clutching the horse's neck as it gathered speed. "I meant no harm—devils flying, he said!"

"Aye, they are, and we're not—as they say in Cormyr—out of the woods yet, either. It might help if you held the reins and let the horse breathe and turn its head by loosening your hold on its neck," she suggested flippantly. "I am Illistyl Elventree. Lanseril Snowmantle flies above us. He may forgive you by the time we reach Shadowdale."

"S-Shadowdale?" Narm asked, trying to remember what Marimmar had told him of the dales. He could see dark things moving . . . no, he was moving past them. Trees . . . his sight was coming back! "What—how did you save me? I was—was—"

"Trapped, yes. Lanseril nearly caught you in the lightning he called—it wouldn't have been the first time. Can you see yet?"

Narm shook his head, trying to clear the white mist before his eyes. "Trees, yes, and the horse before me—" he turned his head toward her voice—"but I fear I cannot see you, yet." His voice shook a little, and then steadied. "How came you to find me? . . . And—and—"

"We are Knights of Myth Drannor. Those who venture here for treasure often meet with us. The unlucky visitors such as yourself and this mage—your master, I take it— encounter the devils first."

"We . . . we met an elf first, good lady. Strongbow, he gave as his name, and he stood with a lady mage. They warned us back. My master was very angry. He was determined to find the magic that remains and so went around by another way. He is—was—proud and willful, I fear."

"He stands in large company both in life and death, then. You were apprentice to him?"

"Aye. I am but new come to the art, lady. My spells and cantrips are not yet of any great matter. They may never be, now." Narm sighed.

"What is your name, wise apprentice?" the woman asked.

"Narm, good lady."

"Nay, that I'm not. A lady, yes, when I remember, but I fear my tongue prevents my being called 'good' overmuch, save in courtly politeness. Slow your mount a bit, Narm—this next stretch is all roots and holes."

"Yes, but the devils?"

"We are largely clear. They seem to be under orders as to how far they may venture. If we are beset now, I have time enough to call on Elminster."

"Elminster?"

"The Sage of Shadowdale. He has seen some five hundred winters, and he is one of the most powerful mages in Faerun. Mind your manners to his face, Narm, if you would see the next morning as a man and not a toad or worse."

"As you say, lady. This Elminster—is he in need of an apprentice?"

Illistyl chuckled. "He enjoys having a 'prentice as much as coming down with a plague, as he has often put it. But you may ask."

Narm managed a grin. "I know not if I dare, good lady."

"A man who fights bone devils with a stick of wood, afraid to ask a question of Elminster? He'd be most flattered to hear of your trepidation." She chuckled again, the full, throaty chuckle few women allow themselves, and leaned over to lead Narm's horse by the bridle through a narrow passage between two trees and then sharply to the left, around the lip of a large pit.

Narm could see her clearly at last. To his astonishment, she was a tiny wisp of a girl, no older than he, clad in a simple, dark cloak over the earthen-hued tunic and breeches a forester might wear. Her boots, he noticed, were of the finest leather and make, although their swash-topped cuffs were plain and not of fancy cut or ornament. She felt his gaze and turned in her saddle with a smile.

"Well met," she said simply. Narm smiled back as she turned away and spurred down a slope in the path, and then blinked. How powerful were these knights, that one so young might, with but one companion, calmly contend with devils? And what would become of Narm in the hands of ones so powerful?

With dull despair Narm realized that he had lost all of his books of magic—worse, all he owned but a knife, a few coins, and the clothing on his back. He now had no home, no master, and no means of earning coins anew. What need would Shadowdale have of an apprentice worker of the art with the likes of Elminster and Lady Illistyl in residence?

Narm set his jaw and rode on with a heavy heart. Illistyl saw and said nothing, for some things must be faced and fought alone.

They rode on, and the day waned and grew dark beneath the trees. Suddenly a great eagle swooped down from the sky to join them in a clearing. Writhing before their eyes, the eagle became a lively eyed man in the simple robes of a druid. Narm bid a grave greeting to Lanseril Snowmantle.

Lanseril returned it gravely and asked him if he cooked meals or washed up afterward. There was laughter, and the darkness within Narm lightened.

Nothing disturbed their camp that night, but in his dreams Narm died a thousand times and saved his surly master a hundred times and slew ten thousand devils. He awoke many times screaming and weeping, and each time Illistyl or Lanseril sat close to reassure him with words and hand-clasps. As Narm lay down again he would shake his head wearily. He knew it would be a very long time before his dreams would be free of grinning, hissing devils.

* * * *

The next day, riding westward through the vast wood with Illistyl while Lanseril flew above, Narm knew that he must return to Myth Drannor. Not to avenge Marimmar or to try to recover lost spellbooks that would doubtless have been seized by now anyway, but to be free of the taunting devils of his dreams. Half-asleep, he slumped in his saddle and wondered if he would live long enough to see the ruined city itself. They rode on toward Shadowdale.

They rode at last through a beautiful dale of busy farms and gardens and well-loved trees to a keep on the banks of the river Ashaba, at the base of that bald knob of rock known as the Old Skull. Illistyl nodded to the guards and turned their mounts out into a meadow, into the care of an old and limping master of horses and three eager youths, and led Narm into the Twisted Tower.

Watchful guards within nodded to Illistyl as she turned left in the great hall that led back from the doors. She nodded back and went through massive arched inner doors into a vast chamber where an expressionless man in elegant finery sat on a throne and listened to two farmers argue over the ownership of some hogs, stemming from a broken fence. Lord Mourngrym's moustache hid his mouth. One finger repeatedly traced a chased, sinuous design of stags and hunters worked into the gold scabbard of the slim long-sword he wore.

Illistyl led Narm to a bench at the front of the nearly empty hall. The stolid faces of the guards flanking the throne watched Narm and Illistyl steadily. Looking about the room, Narm saw that huge tapestries hung behind the throne. A balcony curved across a corner of the room to the right, high above them. A guard stood there, too, and Narm noticed the front of a loaded crossbow resting casually on the balcony rail.

"Enough," the lord said then, and the argument stopped immediately. "I shall send down men to repair the fence this day. You are to obey them as you would me. One of them will see you divide all hogs living on both farms into two equal groups, one to each. You will eat together tonight, both families, with my men and the wine they'll bring, and I expect you to drop hard feelings, put them behind you, and be true friends again. If any trouble over the fence brings you here again, a hog each it will cost you."

He nodded then, and both farmers bowed and walked out wordlessly. But no sooner had they passed into the hall than their voices could be heard breaking into argument again. Narm thought he saw a smile steal briefly onto the lord's handsome face. Illistyl rose and tugged at his arm.

"Come," she said simply and led him to stand before the throne. Narm started to bow hesitantly. Illistyl's hand on his arm jerked him upright. "Narm," she said, "this is Lord Mourngrym of Shadowdale. He will ask questions; answer him well, or I shall regret having aided you." Smiling, she turned to address the man on the throne. "We found him beset by devils in Myth Drannor, Grym."

Lord Mourngrym nodded and turned clear blue eyes upon Narm. "Welcome," he said. "Why came you to Myth Drannor, Narm?" His gaze held the youth as if at the point of a gentle sword.

Narm was silent a moment, and then his words came out in a rush. "My master, the mage Marimmar, sought the magic he believes—believed—the city holds. We rode out of Cormyr and up through Deepingdale to the ruined city, just the two of us.

"There we met Merith Strongbow and Jhessail Silvertree of the knights, who warned us back. My master was angry. He thought that they were trying to keep him from the city's magic, so we went southeast and turned again to reach the city. We were set upon by devils, and my master was killed. I would have died, too, had not this good lady and the druid Lanseril Snowmantle come to my rescue. They have brought me straight here."

Mourngrym nodded. "Their patrol was ended. Here you stand; what will you do now?"

Narm paused. "A night ago, lord, I would not have known. But I am resolved. I will go back to Myth Drannor, if I can." He saw devils in his mind again and shuddered. "If I run," he added softly, "I shall be seeing devils forever."

"It could be your death."

"If the gods Tymora and Mystra will it so, then so be it," Narm replied. Mourngrym looked to Illistyl, whose eyebrows rose in faint surprise.

"What say you? Let a man go to his death?"

Illistyl shrugged. "We must do as we will, if we can. The hard task, Grym—decreeing who can do as they will—is yours." She grinned. "I look forward to observing your masterful performance."

Mourngrym's moustache curled in a tight smile. He turned to Narm. "You lack a master; do you also lack spells?"

"Yes, lord," Narm replied. "If I return from Myth Drannor, I would seek a mage of power to study my art. I have heard of Elminster. Are there others here who might stand in welcome to an apprentice?"

Mourngrym smiled openly this time. "Yes," he said. "The lady who stands beside you, for one." Narm looked at Illistyl; she was smiling faintly, eyebrows and gaze raised to the rafters high above. Mourngrym continued. "Her mentor, Jhessail Silvertree, for another. Other, lesser workers of art in the dale may also welcome you."

He inclined his head. "Illistyl trusts you. You have the freedom of the dale and are welcome, here in the tower, to our table and a bed. May the gods smile upon you when you return to Myth Drannor."

Narm bowed and placed his arm firmly on Illistyl's. "Thank you, lord," he said to Mourngrym and turned to go. "My lady?"

Illistyl nodded, winking at Mourngrym. "Adventurers and fools walk together, eh?"

"Yes," Mourngrym agreed. Only Illistyl saw a sparkle glimmering in his eye. "But which is which?"

🦋 4 🦋

Many Meetings

Always we hurry through our lives, we who travel. Only folk tied to the land wait for danger to come to them. All others blunder ever onward, swords at the ready, through many meetings—and each may be the last, for in the wilds only the dragon waits for his meals to walk into him. The wolf, the orc, the gorgon— these hunt and smile much when they meet dinner. What is more dangerous even than these? Why, any man you meet.

Jarn Tiir of Lantan
A Merchant's Tale
Year of the Smoky Moon

Shandril flung herself desperately to the floor, landing with bruising force. Moaning aloud, she scrambled on hands and knees away from those terrible claws. She recognized the creature from a carved chest that had once been carried through doors she held open. Gorstag had pointed them out to her: gargoyles.

This was a gargoyle. Shandril wished briefly she was back in The Rising Moon washing dishes, as she leaped to her feet and ran full-tilt out of the glowing circle she had appeared in, down the dark cavern toward the far end. Ahead there was another area of glowing light, a doorway outlined in dim radiance.

Behind her she heard leathery wings snap as the gargoyle leaped from where it had been crouching and swooped after her. Whether it was guarding the magical gate that the bones had taken her through or was just waiting to attack anyone using it, she neither knew nor cared. The bony hand clutched in her fist flopped and bounced as she sprinted precariously down the uneven cavern floor. Tiny finger bones broke free and clicked on the stones about her as they fell. Shandril slipped on one and righted herself only with an agonizing wrench. The gargoyle was eerily silent behind her.

Panting, Shandril knew as she ran that she'd never be able to get the door open before the gargoyle caught her. She was sobbing for breath when she got close enough to see the place where she would die. The cavern ended in a narrow cleft choked with bones and fallen rock.

In midair before her was an oval of radiance, standing upright and flickering slightly. There was no door at all, only the empty air of the cavern and this strange frame of light. Shandril had no time to turn aside or even slow, as she felt a plucking at the already torn back of her old tunic. She ran straight at the magical radiance, hoping it was some way out, even as the next rake of the gargoyle's claws cut across her back. Shandril fell through the glowing doorway screaming, burning wetness across her back.

She was elsewhere again, landing hard on her knees and forearms on a stone floor littered with dust and rubble. Dim sunlight crept in from somewhere off to her right. Shandril rolled over and got up hastily to look behind her.

She was alone in a vast, high-ceilinged chamber or hall. No gargoyle, no doorway of light. In the dust she could see the marks of her landing. She had simply appeared here, wherever here was. Shandril could see nothing living in the chamber, although its far end was lost in gloom. She had no desire to explore at the moment. Instead, she sank to the floor, cursing softly at the pain as she bent her back, and sat still, catching her breath.

The inscribed bone was still clutched in her hand, although most of the other bones of the hand had fallen off. Shandril dropped it in her lap and sighed. Here she was, lost and alone, penniless, unarmed, even barefoot, in pain, somewhere reached by art. Moreover, she was very thirsty and badly in need of relieving herself. Food would be nice, too. Shandril sighed again, brushed sticky, tangled hair out of her eyes, and got up. Adventure, hah. Unending pain, fear, and discomfort were nearer the mark.

That, she reflected, looking warily about as she loosened her breeches, and never relaxing, not even for an instant. She was not surprised to see something moving high up in the darkness at the far end of the hall, flapping toward her.

There were three creatures, all alike, she saw, as they flew closer. Ugly things with pointed, curving beaks and barbed, clinging claws reaching for her. Bat-shaped wings covered with rusty brown, dusty feathers flapped nearer. Small yellow eyes glittered nastily at her.

Shandril sobbed a curse, struggled to her feet, laced and belted her breeches with hasty fingers, and ran weakly across the hall in the direction of the daylight, dodging blocks of fallen stone. It's not like this in travelers' tales, she thought ruefully as she slipped on loose stone and twisted her knee painfully. "Come to think of it," she said aloud, shocked to hear how very close to tears her voice sounded, "I've not seen a single gold coin yet." She clutched the bone that had brought her to this place and ran on.

The sunlight came from two high windows in the far wall of the great hall in which she ran. Beneath them she could make out the arch of a small doorway, a wooden door carved with some sort of beautiful flowing design. Then she realized in horror that she could see no pull-ring, knob, or even keyhole. Wings flapped close behind her.

She reached the door, ran desperate fingers around it, tugged vainly at the ridges of the carving and the edges, and finally hurled her shoulder against the thick, polished wood, gritting her teeth against the impact.

There was a dull crash and she was through the door, its rotten wood collapsing into splinters and pulpy dust. She twisted helplessly in empty air, falling in daylight, down, down into a well far below. Shandril glimpsed huge trees and vine-covered stone towers. Where was she now? Wild, helpless laughter choked her as she fell, and from a nearby stone spire a woman with wings sprang into the air and flapped in her direction. Shandril had a brief glimpse of dusky naked flesh, cruel eyes, and a dagger flashing as the wings beat. And then she struck cold water with a crash that shook her very bones.

She plunged deep; only the icy water kept her from passing out. Shandril struggled weakly as she rose slowly to the surface.

"Lady Tymora," she gasped as her face broke water. "Please! No more!" Overhead, through darkening eyes, she saw the winged woman gleefully swooping and darting, dagger flashing, gutting the three little horrors who had flown after her. From the stories she had heard, the little things were probably stirges, and the woman . . . the woman was some sort of devil.

A devil. She knew from the tales that devils were denizens of ruins. And the nearest ruins, she remembered the talk from her last few nights in *The Rising Moon*, were those of Myth Drannor, the splendid, ancient city of the elves. Gods preserve me!

Weakly Shandril splashed her way to the edge of the well and crawled out. Her arms felt leaden. The magical bone was gone in the dark water. At least, she thought slowly, crawling away from the well with fading strength, there's nothing waiting for me in the well.

Then she heard splashing behind her.

Rolling over to look back, Shandril saw great tentacled arms reaching up from the waters she had just crawled from. A cluster of eyes goggled about on one dripping stalk. The others looked like giant squid tentacles. They were coiling about and slapping at the winged devil.

Shandril watched as the female devil was overmastered, breasts heaving for breath, feathers flying, long-fanged teeth snarling, and saw her finally drawn down. She was still striking feebly with her dagger when the tentacles rolled over her and sank, leaving only bubbles, and slowly darkening water, behind. Shandril turned away, feeling sick. She crawled toward some bushes at the base of the building.

When the stones beneath her gave way before she reached the wall and Shandril fell into musty darkness, she was too weary to care.

Tymora, it seemed, had answered her prayer. Shandril sank into oblivion, wondering what she had landed on that was so hard. Whatever it was shifted under her with a metallic slithering, for all the world like coins. Perhaps she would end up a rich adventurer, after all. . . .

* * * * *

"Have a care, sot," Torm said affectionately to Rathan, kneeing his horse's flank to come closer. "Else you'll be right off your beast and head-first in the mud!"

The florid, red-eyed cleric clamped large fingers onto the rim of his saddle and fixed Torm with drunken, baleful eyes. "Tymora love thee for thy ill-placed concern, sly and thieving, bootlicking dog!" He belched comfortably, adjusted his budding paunch in a small disagreement it was having with the front of the saddle, and wagged a finger at the slim, mischievous thief. "So I like to drink! Do I fall from the saddle, despite thy cries? Do I disgrace the Great Lady whose symbol I bear? Do I yip and yap incessantly in a double-tongued, fawning, untruthful manner, like some thieves? Aye?"

Narm, riding between them, wisely said nothing. They were traveling in the deep wood, moving steadily eastward toward Myth Drannor. The horses evidently knew the trail, for the two Knights of Myth Drannor spared little attention to guiding them. Since they had left Shadowdale, days ago, the sharp-tongued Torm had spent his time needling Rathan, and the big cleric had spent his time emptying skin after skin of wine. The two pack mules that followed his mount had resembled huge ambulatory bunches of grapes when they had started out, bulging with full wineskins; now they merely looked heavily loaded. The pack mules behind Torm carried all the food.

Mourngrym had lent Narm the mount that now snorted and grumbled beneath him. He had also suggested that if Narm were so tired of living he ride back to the ruined city in the company of two Knights of Myth Drannor leaving for a patrol there. Narm, somewhat overwhelmed by a magnificent feast and a comfortable canopied bed in the Tower of Ashaba the night before, as if he were visiting nobility and not a penniless ex-apprentice, had accepted. Several times since, he had questioned the wisdom of that decision.

Torm's thin moustache quirked in a smile. "Lost in

thought, good Narm? No time for that, now, not once you're an adventurer! Philosophers think and do nothing. Adventurers rush in to be killed without a thought. A single thought as to what they're facing would no doubt have them fleeing just as quickly!"

"Not so," Rathan rumbled, wagging that finger again. "If ye worship the Lady Luck, Tymora the True, luck will cloak thee and walk with thee, and such thoughts but mar thy daring."

"Yes, *if* you worship Tymora," Torm returned. "We are both more prudent men, eh, Narm?"

"Ye worship Mask and Mystra between ye and speak to me of prudence?" Rathan chuckled. "Truly, the world rears strangeness anew with each passing day." He leaned forward suddenly to point into the dimness. "Look ye, loosetongues! Is that not a devil in the trees?"

Narm froze in his saddle. His hands suddenly felt like ice. He tried not to tremble. Torm had turned his mount, slim longsword out. "Do they wander so far, now? We may not be able to wait for Elminster's or Dove's return before we raise all against them, if they are grown so bold!"

"It's but the one, oh bravest of thieves," Rathan said dryly, standing in his stirrups to get a better look. "And there's something awry . . . see how its flame scorches not and it passes through brush without disturbance, without so much as a leaf crunching or a twig cracking? Nay, 'tis an illusion!" He swung about to fix Narm with a stern eye, the silver disc of Tymora shining in his hand. "This would not be your work, Narm Not-Apprentice, would it now?"

"No," Narm said, spreading honest hands. Indeed, the knights could see he was white with fear. Both turned back to peer at the woods around suspiciously.

"Why an illusion, but to draw us away?" Rathan said in a low voice.

"Yes," Torm replied softly, "but into a trap, or to get us off the trail and away from someone who wants to pass without meeting us?"

"Hmmph," Rathan said and rose in his saddle again, holding his holy symbol aloft. His hands traced empty air around the disc, following its curves. First he used one hand, while the other held the disc, and then he switching hands, all the while chanting gently, "Tymora! Tymora! Tymora! Tymora!" The disc began to glow, faintly at first, and then gradually more brightly, until at last it shone with a bright silver radiance. Torm scanned the woods ceaselessly, blade ready. Abruptly Rathan released his hold upon the glowing disc. It did not fall, but hung silently in midair. Rathan said to it:

"By Tymora's power and Tymora's grace,
Be revealed now wherever I face,
All lives and things that evil be
Unveiled truly now before me!"

The cleric took hold of the disc as his words ended; the disc flared with silvery light, and then the radiance slowly faded away. Rathan, holding the disc before him, was already peering ahead down the path, eyes keen. "Aha!" he said, almost immediately. "Six creatures on the trail, moving this way!" He dragged a long, heavy mace from his belt and whacked his armored knee lightly, swinging his arm to limber up his shoulder. "Ready, Torm?" he asked. "Narm, watch the rear, will ye?"

"Six?" Narm asked. "What if they're devils?"

Rathan Thentraver stared at him blankly for the space of a breath and then shrugged. "I do worship the Lady of Luck," he replied, as if to an idiot child. "Torm?"

The slim thief slipped back into his saddle, and grinned. "It's your head, oh smeller-of-evil. The mules are hobbled."

Rathan nodded briefly and jerked his horse's reins. His mount reared, pawing the air. The cleric clipped the disc onto his shield with practiced ease, mace held in the crook of his arm. When the horse came down, the mace was in his hand and he leaned forward, bellowing, "For Tymora and victory! The Knights of Myth Drannor are upon ye! Die!"

Narm gulped as the horse and the roaring man atop it tore away through the trees at full gallop. Torm was right at Rathan's heels, waving his longsword in circles. Far ahead he heard yells echoing in the forest and then the slash and skirl of steel upon steel. There was a short shriek, quickly cut off, much thudding of hooves, more steel, and then a few scattered yells.

Narm wondered uncomfortably what he should do with the mules if the two were slain. He had no wish to be thought of as an enemy of Shadowdale, or a thief, but . . .

He heard crashing on the trail ahead, nearer than the sounds of battle, and he nervously drew his dagger.

"Ho, Narm!" Torm's voice came floating through the trees cheerfully. "Haven't the mules eaten all the leaves on that stretch yet?" The thief rode into view with a cherry wave, eyed the dagger Narm was sheathing without comment, and swung lightly down from the saddle to see to the mules. "Adventurers out of Zhentil Keep—priests of Bane, and a worker-of-illusions out to make a name for himself," he explained briefly.

"Dead?" Narm asked.

Torm nodded. "They weren't willing to surrender or flee," he said mildly, holding the reins of the mules firmly as he thrust the hobble-ropes through his belt and swung up into his saddle again. Narm shook his head. "Eh? Why so?" Torm asked, eyeing him. Narm grinned weakly.

"Just the two of you," the ex-apprentice said, "and Rathan bellowing war cries . . . and three breaths later you come back and tell me they're dead."

Torm nodded. "It's what usually happens," he said, deadpan.

Narm shook his head again as they walked their horses forward. "No, no," he said. "Mistake me not . . . How can you just ride forward like that, knowing you face six foes, and at least one a master of art?"

"The war cries and all? Well, if you're risking death, why not have fun?" Torm replied. "If I wanted to risk death without having fun, I'd be a tax collector, not a thief. Come on—if we're much longer, Rathan'll have finished *all* the food and wine, and we're not even there yet!"

* * * * *

Where was she? The smell of earth and old, dank stone hung around her in the darkness. Shandril lay still on something hard and uneven and collected her wits. Her mouth was dry, her head ached, and her back and shoulder throbbed. Oh, yes . . . she had fallen into this . . . while crawling away from a well. She was in a large ruin in a forest, inhabited by devils and other fearsome monsters. It was probably Myth Drannor, and she would probably neither get out nor survive. Shandril rolled over; metal slithered and shifted under her. Oh, yes. Coins! She clutched one in her hand and rolled onto her knees. It was too dark to make out what sort of coin it was. Overhead, faint light could be seen through the gap where the stones above had collapsed. She could not reach the opening.

Tymora spit upon all! If this was adventure, perhaps it was worth Korvan and unending drudgery at The Rising Moon, after all! Shandril looked about her helplessly. It was too dark to see anything. She would have to blunder around in the dark, feeling for a way out . . . if there *was* a way out. Shandril sighed. The Lady of Luck smiled indeed. . . .

Then, above her, she heard a shout. Running feet, screams. More shouting, and the clang of weapons. A horrible groan, more running feet, and then, suddenly, someone hurtled down from above Shandril in a shower of dirt and paving stones. Shandril slid down the heap of coins desperately. A stone fell on her foot, already half-sunk in coins, and another glanced numbingly off one elbow. There was a great crashing and slithering among the coins, and a rough male voice said triumphantly in the darkness, "Ha! Got you! Thought you c—"

"*Ilzazu!*" hissed a second voice, and there was a blue-white flash and a crackling, sizzling sound, followed by a horrible, dying moan.

This was just about enough, Shandril decided, and fainted again.

*　*　*　*　*

When she knew the world around her again, the light overhead was much brighter. Shandril found herself lying at the edge of the pile of coins, feet up on the slithering riches, head down and aching. She felt weak and dizzy; it seemed like days since she fled from that gargoyle.

She got up and looked around. The coins—thousands of them, rusty-brown with age and damp—looked to be all copper. Sigh. Above her, atop the heap, lay two bodies on their backs, feet entangled, both human. One wore armor, much blackened; about him there still clung a faint reek of burned flesh. The other wore robes, and clutched the crumbled fragments of a stick of wood. A sword protruded from his rib cage, and a small shoulder bag lay half-crumpled beneath him. Shandril clambered up the mound of coins again. Food? Perhaps one carried water, or wine?

The armored corpse was cooked black; Shandril avoided it. The other had a dagger, which she took quickly, boots—too large, but her feet had bled enough for her to take any boots over no boots—a skin of water, which she drained thirstily, and the shoulder bag. She tugged it free of the body and examined the scraps of wood curiously. The thickest piece, from the butt end of the stick, bore the word 'Ilza-zu,' but nothing happened when Shandril cautiously said it aloud. She scrambled down the heap again.

The bag proved to contain hard, dark bread, a wheel of cheese sealed in wax, another half-eaten wheel speckled with mold (Shandril ate it anyway, saving the other for later), and a small book. Shandril opened it cautiously, saw crawling runes and glyphs, and slammed it again. There was also a hopelessly smashed hand lamp, a flint, and a metal vial of lamp oil. She put everything but the flint and oil back into the bag and slung it on her shoulder. She crawled back to the dead magic-user again and tore off what she could of the man's robe, doused it in oil, and wearily struck the flint against coin after coin, and finally upon the scorched armor of the other corpse to strike sparks onto the soaked cloth, until at last it began to smolder. Then she gingerly borrowed the blackened sword from the fallen warrior and lifted the bundle on its point. It flared up, and she clambered hastily down the heap of coins, looking for a door or stairs or anything that might lead out of here.

Above her was a stone rack that ran along the ceiling, supported by arches between the squat pillars that held up the ceiling itself. Upon the rack lay three huge barrels. From each hung a dusty, cobwebbed chain. With a shiver, Shandril realized that a fourth barrel had hung over the heap of coins; looking back, she saw the shattered wooden ribs of the fallen barrel. And at the base of the heap on this side, where she had not ventured before, the rusty end of the chain projected out of the heap beside a pair of skeletal legs. Trembling, Shandril opened her mouth to scream and then shut it again. Soon the cloth would all have burned, and she would be unable to see in the full darkness away from the hole again.

She hurried on, through a chamber as vast as the hall that must be above it. She had come far enough, Shandril realized, to be well beneath that vast hall. She knew there were no stairs nor door in the top level she had arrived in except perhaps down at the end she had not investigated, where the stirges had come from. She turned in that direction, the daylight growing dim behind her.

The flickering, feeble light of her flame revealed a stone stair spiraling up from the floor, without railing or ornament. It looked impossibly thin and graceful to bear her weight. Shandril hesitated, looking around—and then the cloth burned through and fell from her blade in a small shower of glowing shreds. Larger scraps flickered on the floor, but proved too small to balance on her blade. Shandril sighed and shrugged. In the last of the light she slid the blade through her belt and grimly started to climb the stairs on hands and knees.

When she reached the floor above, she was in complete darkness. This should be the ground floor, she reasoned, and if there were a door, it would probably be over in *that* direction, somewhere. That is, if the floor doesn't give way and dump me into the basement again, she thought grimly. Holding the sword out crosswise before her to fend off any obstacles, she advanced forward gingerly. Slowly, slowly she went, lifting her feet gently and quietly, listening tensely for any unusual sounds. Nothing.

On into the dark she went until her blade scraped on stone. She probed, carefully, and then felt her way around the stone. A pillar. She drew breath and went on.

Once she heard dry bones crackling underfoot, and another time she stubbed her toes on a large block of stone that had fallen from above. Carefully she went on, until her blade found a wall, a wall that ran on in both directions for at least six paces. Left, she decided arbitrarily, scraping the wall and feeling it barehanded a foot or so behind her prob-ing blade until she found a corner.

Having mapped out that section of wall in her mind, she retraced her steps. Quite soon she found a wooden door, intricately caved, from the feel of it. She felt for a pull-ring, but found none. Feeling desperate, she stepped back and ran full tilt at the door, driving her shoulder into the wood as she had done before.

There was a dull thud, much pain, and Shandril found herself on the floor. "Tymora *damn* me!" she said exasper-ated almost to tears. Would nothing go her way? Was this the gods' way of telling her she should have stayed dutifully at The Rising Moon? Growling a little in her throat, Shandril got up and pushed and pulled at the door. Solid as stone and as unmoving. She felt for catches, knobs, latches, and key-holes, both high and low. Nothing.

To the right, she decided abruptly. Look for another door.

She found one right away and, surprisingly, it opened on the first try, leaving her blinking foolishly, but happily. It made no sound, this door, and swung as if it had no weight. She peered at it curiously, and then growled at herself for being a fool and stepped quickly through, into sunlight.

Another mistake. Not two hundred paces away across the tilted stones and crumbling pillars of Myth Drannor, six warriors were fighting a losing battle against three more of the winged she-devils. Shandril stepped back into the door-way again, and then changed her mind and slipped out, sword drawn. She ran across the tumbled stones to the nearest trees. Crawling under a thorny bush, she peered out to look across the courtyard where the well lay, decep-tively placid, and watched the men fighting for their lives.

The battle was eerily silent. The flapping and beating of wings, the grunts of warriors taking blows on their shields or swinging a heavy sword two-handed, the scrape of shuf-fling feet, and the occasional metallic ring of dagger on blade was all that could be heard. There had been two more adventurers, she saw; both lay motionless a short distance behind the fight. The men were trying to keep moving and find cover.

Even as she watched, one of the men ran a few steps,

abandoning his protective crouch, and one of the winged devils swooped. Shandril caught her breath, but the run was a ruse. The warrior turned and swung his blade with two hands, beheading the devil with a triumphant grunt. Shandril saw the black, smoking blood run down the edges of the warrior's silver blade as he turned and cut the body apart. The body began to smolder, greasy black smoke curling up in snaky wisps.

He dared not try to take up the devil's fallen dagger, for two more were swooping down with screams of anger, uncoiling ropes in their hands. The warrior looked from one to the other and suddenly turned and fled in terror, sword waving wildly. The devils flew wide to take him from two sides. Shandril swallowed and looked away.

From the reactions of the party, the warrior must have been the leader. As the devils tore his body apart, his fellow adventurers ran in all directions, crying and cursing. The devils circled, teeth gleaming, and Shandril decided to flee before the battle was over and she risked being seen.

She crawled into the trees, hoping she was heading out of the city. Judging by the sun, she was probably heading south, but she had no idea whether she was near the edge of the city or not.

Twenty minutes of clambering and skulking later, she decided she definitely was not near the city's edge. Tumbled stones and gaping, empty buildings were everywhere. Gnarled trees had broken through marble and anything else that got in their way as they grew, rending once-beautiful spires and high, curving bridges. Most of the bridges had cracked and fallen; a few were intact, though choked with creepers, trailing vines, and old nests. Shandril stayed low and tried to avoid open spaces, for here and there in the ruins she saw devils—some black and glistening, some blood-red, barbed and scaled, and some mauve or yellowish green. They perched on crumbling spires or battlements, or sprawled at ease on bridges or atop heaps of tilted stone. A few, mainly the winged devil-women, but some horned, spine-tailed, and scaly horrors, too, flew in lazy circles around the ruins. If this was Myth Drannor, it was a wonder any of the dales still existed. What was bringing them here—and what was preventing them from flying in all directions, murdering and wreaking havoc?

It did not matter now. Shandril wanted only to know how to escape. She lay huddled under the edge of a slab of stone carved with a very beautiful scene of mermaids and hippocampi, now forever shattered. Her large boots were rubbing her calves raw as they flapped at her every step, and her borrowed blade was too heavy for her to lift quickly in a fight. Against these devils, she dared not try to fight. Not even the whim of Tymora could save her against even one amused devil, and one devil could call, given time, on all she had seen here. She shuddered at the thought, and it was a long time before she dared leave the shelter of the stone slab.

The sun cast long shadows as the day gave way to dusk. Grimly, Shandril knew she had to act soon, or be trapped in the ruins after dark. She set off past more cracked and tumbled buildings, dreadfully afraid she might be moving aimlessly in circles, merely postponing the inevitable.

The ruined city seemed endless, though she saw more trees among the stones than she had earlier. Perhaps I *am* nearer the edge of the ruin, Shandril thought hopefully. She sighed and looked all around cautiously for perhaps the thousandth time. It was then she saw them.

In a place of tilted piles of stone, where all the buildings had toppled and fallen, there stood two figures confronting each other across a wasteland of rubble. A sharp-eyed man in wine-red robes stood on the cracked base of a long-fallen pillar, facing a tall, slim, cruel-looking woman in purple standing on what was left of a wall.

"Die, then, Shadowsil," the man said coldly, and his hands moved like coiling snakes. Shandril crouched low and kept very still.

The woman's hands were also moving. Shandril wondered briefly if everyone in all Faerun would arrive in Myth Drannor before she could get out of it.

From the man's hand burst sparkling frost, a white cone that spread, roaring as it closed on the beautiful woman. She stiffened, arms shining with frost, but already from her hands four whirling balls of fire had burst forth, flashing through the fading cone of frost, trailing winking sparks.

Shandril scrambled on hands and knees around the pile of rubble and behind the corner of a building that wasn't there anymore. It was well she did so, for an instant later there was a flash of flame and a roar, and a wave of intense heat passed over her face.

When she peered cautiously around the rubble again later, the man was gone. There was a large, blackened area on the rocks, and the woman in purple was walking triumphantly across mountains of jagged stone to where her foe had stood. The cracked stone creaked as it cooled; the woman turned on her heel to stare levelly all around. She saw Shandril's head immediately and stared. Shandril scrambled hastily back to the corner again and fled down a ruined street. At its end she ducked around a corner, blood hammering her brain in fear. Biting her lips to silence her panting, she dared not believe she had escaped so easily.

Suddenly, the air before her shimmered and the lady in purple stood before her. "Who are you, then, little one?" she asked softly; Shandril shivered. The lady was very beautiful. "I am Symgharyl Maruel, called The Shadowsil."

Shandril held her blade up in silent answer. The lady mage laughed, and her hands moved deftly. Shandril rushed at her, but knew before she started that the woman was just too far away. She was staring in fear and anger at the mage, still yards distant, when her limbs locked in midstride and she froze helplessly.

The purple robes swished nearer. The lady undid a rope from around her waist as she approached.

Tymora, aid me, Shandril thought desperately as the mage placed the rope gently around the wrist of the hand in which the immobile, straining thief held the sword. She looped it also about Shandril's neck, drawing it tight across her throat, and said, "*Ulthae*—entangle." The would-be thief's scalp prickled in horror as she felt the rope slithering of its own accord across her skin, tightening about her arms and neck and knees, pinning her securely. When it was done, Shandril was bound tightly about, truly helpless, and a short length of rope led from a great knot at her waist to the languid hand of the lady in purple.

At least, Shandril thought, that means she'll take me out of here . . . although with the luck Great Lady Tymora has shown me thus far, devils will show up to slay her, leaving me as a ready meal for anything that happens by. She had a brief memory of the thing in the well, and shuddered . . . and then, in sinking horror and despair, found that she could not shudder. Her own body was her prison.

Symgharyl Maruel jerked on the rope that bound her, and Shandril fell over helplessly to crash upon the broken stones that had long ago been a pleasant winding lane of the City of Beauty. The side of her face scraped painfully on the rock, grit making her eye water, and her blade fell out of frozen fingers. It was left behind as the lady in purple dragged her away.

"I don't know who you are," Symgharyl Maruel said with lightly mocking malice to her helpless bundle between tugs which bumped Shandril silently over the jagged, heaved stones. "You remind me of someone . . . you may well be the one those stone-heads of Oversember let slip away. Are you, hmmm? The girl who was with the Company of the Bright Spear, but whose name did not appear on their charter? You'll tell me, girl. Yes, you'll tell. Their lost one or not, the Cult will value you highly for your blood, dear, if you are a virgin." Again the tinkling, mocking laughter. "But you shall be my present to Rauglothgor in any case. So pretty . . ."

Shandril could not even weep.

*   *   *   *   *

Narm took his leave of the two knights on the forest trail where he and Marimmar had met the elf and his lady. Narm was surprised to see who stood in the very same place they had, though: the two ladies who had been in the inn in Deepingdale. The ones who had faced down the angry adventurers when the thief was killed. Narm nodded to the women during Torm's introductions to Sharantyr and Storm, not thinking they would remember him.

To his surprise, they both smiled at him with careful eyes. The younger of the two clasped his arm and said, "Yes, we've met. At The Rising Moon in Deepingdale, although you were under the heavy eye of—was it your master of the art? A strict man."

Narm nodded. Yes, Marimmar had been that.

The silver-haired bard also remembered the young man now that Sharantyr had placed him. Torm rapidly explained Mourngrym's decision to let Narm into the city. They shouldered their bags and harp and took their leave with the horses and mules.

As they mounted, Storm leaned down and said to Narm, "Until next we meet. I think our paths will cross again soon, good sir. Fare well in Myth Drannor." With that, she and Sharantyr rode away.

"Will you go into the city after all?" Torm asked, after they had watched the ladies disappear amid the trees.

"Yes," Narm said, grinning weakly.

"May Tymora smile upon thee, then," Rathan grunted. "With being such a fool and all, ye'll need the full favor of the Lady's luck to see even this day out. Don't forget how to run for thy very life, now. The devils are the ones with wings."

"Most of them," Torm agreed with a smile. "Though they can be hard to see if blood is pouring into your eyes."

"Aye, that is very true," Rathan agreed gravely. Narm grinned and waved good-bye to them, shaking his head. A merry life the other knights must lead, indeed, in the company of these two jacks! He set off down the path quickly before his fear could slow him or turn him back.

The ruined city of Myth Drannor rose out of the trees before him. Alone now, Narm did what he wanted to do, free of rules and restraints. He was going to see devils. He was going to look at them again and somehow survive. By Mystra, he was going to do *something* on his own, now that Marimmar was gone.

Cautiously, Narm went on. Off to his right he could see a leaning stone tower, its needle-shaped spire still grand. Much heaved, tilted pavement choked with shrubs and clinging vines lay ahead. He saw steps leading down in a broad sweep from the street into unknown depths. A slim woman in purple robes was dragging someone thin and long-haired along the ground by a rope. The hapless captive was completely entangled in its coils. Narm heard tinkling, mocking laughter as they descended from view down the dark stair.

By the time he reached the stair, nothing was visible below. Narm hardly stopped to think before he followed. The art! Strong magic, undoubtedly. Just what Marimmar had wanted to find in this place!

The underground way led on fairly directly to a place where Narm could at first see only a fitful glow. He walked quietly and cautiously in the dimness toward it, until he could see that the cellars had opened into a natural cavern. Within it, the lady in purple and her captive stood before the source of the light. An oval of glowing radiance hung like a doorway in midair. Magic, indeed.

The woman in purple was stronger than her slim frame suggested. By main strength she was holding her captive upright. It was a girl, who was struggling violently. The rope that bound her seemed to move by itself to fight her. She managed to tear its coils free of her face and throat. Narm could scarcely believe it—he knew her!

She was the girl from the inn. That beautiful face had stared at him from the shadows. The kitchen-slut, Marimmar had dismissed her. But he had been wrong. Narm knew that, even then. But how came she to be here?

The woman in purple let go of the rope, laughing mockingly, and the girl fell hard to the cavern floor, still struggling. Seeing her face so set as she battled the rope made anger burn within Narm, and he raised his hands and pointed at the woman in purple and spoke the word of the spell Marimmar had forbidden him to study, the spell he had studied while his master slept. The magic missile burst from his finger like a bolt of light and flashed at the lady.

It struck her, and she turned, startled, and then laughed, her hands already moving. Narm dodged aside, thinking how feeble the rest of his art was. The mage stopped her casting and locked her fingers in Shandril's hair. As Narm watched in dismay, she dragged the struggling girl through the oval of radiance and vanished.

Then, with a shattering roar, the fireball exploded all around him.

❧ 5 ❧

The Grotto
of the Dracolich

*There in the darkness many a wyrm sits and
smiles. He grows rich and lazy and fat as the
years pass, and there seems no shortage of fools
to challenge him and make him richer and fat-
ter. Well, why wait ye? Open the door and go in!*
Irigoth Mmar, High Sage of Baldur's Gate
Lore of the Coast
Year of the Trembling Tree

The radiance faded and left her somewhere cold. She was
lying on stone again. Shandril sighed inwardly as she twisted against the ever-tightening, ever-slithering rope.

"Where are we?" she hissed at her captor, almost in tears.
The relief she had felt when the power to move her own
limbs had returned was gone.

The Shadowsil shrugged. "A ruined keep. Come." The
rope had shifted backward to more securely bind Shandril's
arms to her torso; she found she could get to her knees, and,
painfully, to her feet. The mage led her down a curving
stone stair, but not before Shandril got a good look out the
window. She saw mountains that looked cold and jagged—
and many days' journey from Myth Drannor. A snow hawk
glided across the scene, but she could see no other life
before she was dragged down a dark, curving, stone stair-
way. It was narrow and steep and littered with old feathers
and bird droppings. There was no sound or other sign of life
now. Shandril was propelled ahead down the stairs with a
firm hand.

* * * * *

"I *told* you he'd poke his nose into something straight away, and buy a swift grave before we'd even got to your next sausage!" said a familiar voice, swimming somewhere above Narm. "That's why I followed, *not* for treasure."

"Well, ye'd be the one to know about poking one's nose," said another. "By the gods, but he caught it squarely! Do ye think he'll live?"

"Not if you don't use some healing magic quickly, leviathanbelly! Don't wag your jaws—waggle your fingers! He grows weaker with each breath you waste. Look at the smoke coming off him; he smolders still! No, lie still, Narm. I can hear you."

Narm struggled through excruciating pain to tell them of the girl from the inn and the woman in purple, but all that came out was a twisted sob. Torm spoke gently in reply.

"Lie down, Narm. You want us to rescue the pretty girl bound in the rope of entanglement that the mage—with our good fortune she's an archmage, no doubt—just pushed through that gate. Well, lie still; rest easy. You're lucky enough to have found the greatest reckless fools in all of Faerun, and we'll do it for you. Oh, by the stars, don't cry! It gives me the shivers!"

"Hush," said Rathan. "How can I work healing when ye're blaspheming Tymora?"

"I never!"

"Ye did! 'Our good fortune,' I heard ye say in a slighting tone. Now hold this healing potion; he'll be able to drink it after this." There was much murmuring, and through the watery red haze before his eyes Narm saw a flash of radiance. Then sweet coolness spread slowly through his limbs, banishing the shrieking pain. He fainted.

* * * * *

They descended the crumbling stairs for eight or more turns around the inner wall of the tower, and then the stonework gave way to natural stone scarred with tool marks. "What is this place?" Shandril asked wearily, but the mage behind her made no reply. She dared not ask again, as the rough tunnel about them opened suddenly. It joined other passageways in a small, slope-ceilinged cavern.

Symgharyl Maruel pushed her firmly toward the largest opening, which led steeply downward into darkness. Shandril came to a stop. "I can't see!" she protested. The Shadowsil chuckled softly behind her.

"You do nothing in your life, little one, that you cannot first see where it may lead?" She laughed again, gently, and said, "Very well." She did something unseen in the darkness, and light appeared. Four small globes of pearl-white, pale radiance grew from nothing before Shandril's eyes and then drifted apart in midair in stately silence. One moved to hang at her shoulder. Another drifted well ahead, dimly outlining the rough ceiling of the tunnel, which descended sharply from where she stood. The other globes moved behind her for Symgharyl Maruel's benefit. Shandril stood motionless and peered about. There was stone all around and cool air wafting toward her. Suddenly, something struck her bottom hard, and she fell to her knees.

The Shadowsil had kicked her.

"Up and on," came the cold voice. "My patience grows short." Shandril struggled to her feet in the tight coils of the magical rope, in angry silence.

Up and on. Under her feet as she descended, the uneven ramp became broad stairs cut out of the solid rock, and the air grew cooler. There was some sort of dim, scattered light ahead, beyond the pale globes. Shandril turned to find the left wall and descend with it, but Symgharyl Maruel twitched the rope that bound her sharply, and she turned back to her original course with an inward sigh. The twinkling lights were farther away than they appeared and were all about when the stair ended.

A great open cavern lay before them. Its walls were studded with the fist-sized, sea-green gems which Shandril recognized as the fabled beljurils, for at odd intervals one or more would give forth a silent burst of light just as the storytellers had said. Shandril could tell by their light that the cavern stretched away to her right, but of its true size she had no idea. It was big, she knew—and suddenly she shivered in the twinkling darkness. Would the mage slay her here, leave her in a cage to be tortured later, or killed or deformed by magic in some experiment or other? Or did something lair here? Shandril could hear only the soft sounds of the mage behind her and the noise of her own passage as she descended into that winking display of lights. Where in the Realms was she?

"Halt, little one, and kneel." Shandril did as that quiet voice bade her; the rope was already tightening about her knees to reinforce the order. The pale globes winked out. Behind her, Shandril heard The Shadowsil chant something softly, and then there was light all about, and Shandril could see clearly the rough walls of the huge cavern around her.

The floor descended in front of her, and its lowest reaches were heaped with things that gleamed and sparkled in the light. There were gems, and coins beyond number, and here and there statuettes of ivory and of jade. The gleam of gold also caught her eye, and there were many other dazzling things beyond Shandril's knowledge.

Then a great voice boomed and echoed around them, freezing Shandril in terror. It spoke deeply and slowly in the common tongue of humans, and to Shandril the voice seemed old and patient and amused—and dangerous.

"Who comes?" it demanded. Something moved deeper in the cavern, beyond the mage's light, and then Shandril saw it. Her dry throat tightened, and she would have fled if the rope's coils had not held her firmly where she stood. As it was, her struggles caused her to fall sideways on the stone, where she lay face-down and did not have to see.

"Symgharyl Maruel Shadowsil stands before you, O mightly Rauglothgor. I have brought you a gift: a captive, gained among the ruins of Myth Drannor. Its blood may be valuable to you. But the followers of Sammaster would question it first. It may be one who escaped them at Oversember, and they would know how that was accomplished."

The lady faced the great night dragon calmly and spoke with respect but in tones that held no fear. Shandril peered sidelong up at it. She dared not meet its eyes again; she shuddered at the very thought. But the thief of Deepingdale saw its great skeletal bulk advance across shifting treasure toward them, vast and terrible. By its great wings and claws and tail it was a dragon, but except for the chilling eyes, it was only bones. Its long, fanged skull leered down at her.

Shandril knew it could see her looking at it and knew further, with a stirring of defiant anger, that it was amused.

"Look at me, little maid," it rumbled, the creature's voice echoing in Shandril's head. She shook her bonds in terror. She would not look at the creature! Tears blinded her. She sobbed as the ropes tightened about her, pulling her to her knees again, pulling her brow and throat to turn her head up. Through a mist of tears, Shandril looked, and she saw.

The cunning eyes held hers, like two tiny images of the moon reflected in mica panes, like two candles set at the head and foot of a shrouded corpse. Shandril shivered uncontrollably as she looked, and she felt those eyes boring into her very soul. She looked back as deeply herself, and she knew much.

It had been old, this sly and gnarled giant among dragons, when men first came to the Sea of Fallen Stars and fought with elves and the tribes of bugbears and kobolds of the Thunder Peaks, the mountains that the elves called Airmbult, or 'Storm-fangs.' Rauglothgor had been the fangs amid the mountain storms often. Rauglothgor the Proud, dragonkind had called the creature, for its presumption and quickness to take offence or pick quarrels.

In cunning and malice it had sought out weak, old dragons and slain them, often by trickery, to seize their lairs and treasure. Hoard upon hoard had fallen into the dragon's claws, and it had piled them up in deep and secret places beneath the Realms known only to it—for other creatures of all sizes who ventured therein were slain, from peryton to centipede, without mercy or patience.

Years passed, and Rauglothgor grew and devoured whole herds of rothé in Thar and buckar on the Shining Plains and more than one orc horde coming down the Desertsedge from the North. Rauglothgor became strong and terrible, a giant among dragons. It thrust aside pretense and prudence and slew all dragons as it met them; in air, on land, and even in their lairs, slaying with savagery and skill, and adding hoards anew to its own.

Yet in its dark heart the old red dragon grew afraid—as it grew older and escaped clever traps set for it and slew more dragons—that one day its strength would fail and some younger, greedier dragon would drag it down as it had served its elders, and all its striving would have been for naught. For years such worries ate at the creature's old heart, and when men came with offers of eternal strength and wealth, the dragon slew them not, and it listened.

By the arts of the Cult of the Dragon, the great and evil red dragon became, in time, a great and evil dracolich. Dead it was and yet not dead, and the years touched not its vigor and strength, for it had become only bones and magic, and its strength was of the art and could not be diminished by age.

The years passed, and Faerun changed, and the world was not as it had been. Rauglothgor flew less often, for there was little left to match its memories, and few lived that it had known, and willing men of the cult brought it treasure to add to its dusty hoard. The dracolich grew moody and lonely as kingdoms fell and seas changed and only it endured. To live forever was a curse. A lonely curse.

Shandril could not look away from those lonely eyes. "So young," said the deep voice, and abruptly the bony neck arched up and the eyes closed and she was alone, shivering.

"Well met, Great One," Symgharyl Maruel said. "By your leave, I would question this one before I leave her with you."

"Given, Shadowsil," Rauglothgor replied. "Though she knows little of anything, yet, I deem. She has the eyes of a kitten that has just learned to walk."

"Aye, Elder Wyrm," said the Shadowsil, "and yet she may have seen much in the few days just past, or even be more than she seems." The lady in purple strode around to stand before Shandril. At a gesture, the rope slithered slowly from Shandril and left her free. Shandril gathered herself to flee, but Symgharyl Maruel merely smiled down at her in cold amusement and shook her head.

"Tell me your name," she commanded. Shandril obeyed without thinking.

"Your parents?" the mage pressed.

"I know not," Shandril replied truthfully.

"Where did you dwell when younger?" The Shadowsil continued quickly.

"In Deepingdale, at The Rising Moon."

"How came you to the place where I found you?"

"I . . . I stepped through a door of light that glowed in the air."

"Where was that door?" the mage continued, a note of triumph in her voice.

"I . . . I don't know. In a dark place—there was a gargoyle."

"How came you there?"

"B-by magic, I believe. There was a word, on a bone, and I said it. . . ."

"Where is the bone now?"

"In a pool, I think—in that ruined city. Please, lady, was that Myth Drannor?"

The dracolich chuckled harshly. The Shadowsil stood silently, eyes burning into Shandril's. "Tell me your brother's name!" she demanded abruptly.

Shandril shook her head, confused. "I—I don't have a brother."

"Who was your tutor?" The Shadowsil snapped at her.

"Tutor? I've never had—Gorstag taught me my duties at the inn, and Korvan about cooking, and—"

"What part of the gardens did the windows of your chamber look upon?"

Shandril flinched. "Chambers, lady? I—I have no chambers. I sleep—slept—in the loft with Lureene most nights . . ."

"Tell the truth, brat!" the mage in purple screamed, her face contorted in rage, eyes gleaming. Shandril stared at her helplessly and burst into tears.

The deep chuckle behind the mage cut through both angry threats and sobs. "She speaks truth, Shadowsil. My art never lies to me." Shandril looked up, startled.

Symgharyl Maruel dropped her rage like a mask and regarded the disheveled, tearful Shandril calmly. "So she is not the missing Cormyrean princess, Alusair," she said aloud. "Why then is she such a sheltered innocent? She is not simple, I believe."

The dracolich chuckled again. "Humans never are, I have found. Ask on; she interests me."

The Shadowsil nodded as she moved forward to confront Shandril. Her dark eyes caught and held those of the young thief; Shandril prayed silently to all the gods who might be listening that she be free of this place and these two horrible beings of power.

Symgharyl Maruel regarded her almost sympathetically for a time and then asked, "Were you a member of the Company of the Bright Spear?"

Shandril lifted her head proudly and said, "I am."

"'Am'?" The Shadowsil laughed shortly. Shandril stared at her with mounting fear. She had secretly hoped that Rymel, Burlane, and the others had somehow escaped the great dragon. She covered her face at the memory of the vicious attack, but she knew the truth now. The mage's cold laughter forbade her to deny it any longer. Tears came.

"You were taken by the cult and imprisoned in Oversember. How did you escape?" The Shadowsil pressed.

"I—I . . ." Shandril's face twisted in fear and grief, and mounting anger. Who was this cruel sorceress, anyway, to drag her here and bind and question her thus?

The dracolich's deep, hissing laughter rolled around Shandril again. "She has a temper, Shadowsil. Beware. Ah, this is good sport!"

"I found the bone and read what was on it," Shandril answered sullenly. "It took me to the place with the gargoyle. I know no more."

Symgharyl Maruel strode toward her angrily. "Ah, but you do, Shandril! Who was that fool who attacked me before we took the gate here?"

Shandril shook her head helplessly.

"My name, witch,"—a new voice echoed over them all in answer—"is Narm!" There was a flash and a crackling in the air, and Shandril saw the mage stagger and almost fall, face contorted in pain and astonishment, as a swarm of small bolts of light struck her body.

Shandril looked behind her as she rose from her knees. High above, at the mouth of the cavern, were six humans. Two in robes stood before the others. One of them, also the one who spoke, she recognized from those last seconds before Symgharyl Maruel had forced her through the gate. He was young and excited. The other, a woman whose hair was as long as The Shadowsil's, stood with hand outstretched. She had been the one who had just hurled magic at the purple-robed sorceress.

Shandril had no time to see more before the cavern rocked with Rauglothgor's roar of challenge. The dracolich reared up to face the newcomers, eyes terrible, bony wings arching. Shandril hurled herself at The Shadowsil, who sprang away and hissed a word of art—and vanished before Shandril could grab her. Rauglothgor spat a word that echoed in the grotto around her, and a fiery streak lashed high over her head and exploded flame in all directions.

Shandril dove flat and looked around wildly. The newcomers were leaping down the sloping cavern floor toward her, apparently unharmed by the fireball. She saw the purple-robed sorceress appear on a high ledge behind them all.

"Look out!" Shandril screamed, pointing above them. A man in plain robes glanced up and back, and there was a winking of red light from a circlet he wore. From it burst a thin red beam that struck The Shadowsil. The sorceress stiffened, hands faltering in their spell-weaving, and then she slumped back against the rock wall, holding her side and screaming curses of anger and pain.

The dracolich roared again, and the long-haired woman lashed out in reply with a bolt of lightning. As it crackled overhead, the lightning outlined a tall man in blue-gray plate armor and the young man as they scurried down the slope toward her. The man in armor held a drawn blade.

The young man called out to her. "Lady! You from The Rising Moon! We come to aid you! We—"

His words were lost in the roar of the dracolich's second fireball, bursting just behind the two running figures. Shandril turned in panic and ran downslope, slipping on coins, hard jade, and shifting bars. Behind her there was a cry of pain, the hissing laughter of the dracolich rolled around her, and the light abruptly faded in the cavern.

Shandril's feet slid again in slithering coins. She caught her balance with a painful wrench and leaped onto rocks. The silent winking of the beljurils grew ahead of her as she neared a wall. Behind her there was another flash and the metallic clinking sound of running feet on the heaped coins.

But the feet did not sound as if they were following her.

Shandril gasped for breath as she climbed rocks with bruising speed. Light sprang into being again, and she dove forward into a cleft between two boulders. The dracolich roared again.

And I haven't even a blade! Shandril thought, rolling to her feet, banging knees and elbows in the process. She peered back across the cavern at the battle.

Symgharyl Maruel stood upon a high rock, hands moving—but she was not spellcasting. Rather, she was slapping at something very small. Insects!

The slim and beautiful newcomer in robes was casting a spell, facing the dracolich across the grotto. Knee-deep in coins at the dracolich's feet stood the man in armor, chopping and slicing at the skeletal form that towered over him. Another warrior was racing down the slope to join him. An elf! This one, too, bore a glowing blade. The blade's radiance was briefly overwhelmed by a roaring blast of flames from the dracolich's bony maw.

Rauglothgor turned his head toward Shandril as he rose up from a gout of flames he'd launched at the warriors. Shandril turned in panic and scrambled up the cavern wall, praying that the dracolich would not overwhelm her.

"Lady!" came that voice again. The young man was still pursuing her, but she dared not stop. She clambered up over rocks and loose rubble. The dracolich, Symgharyl Maruel, and these powerful newcomers all stood between her and escape, she decided, and she doubted if the gods cared enough about Shandril Shessair to save her. Better to flee while they were busy slaying each other!

The flickering glow of another burst of flame reflected off the rocks before her. Shandril heard a man roar in pain as the fire died away. Behind her, much closer than she expected, she could hear the young man chanting rapidly. Was he trying to trap her with a spell, too? She scrambled away.

Suddenly, she slipped and fell hard, knocking the wind from her lungs. The favored of Tymora, as usual, she thought, gasping for air.

Shandril looked up in time to see the young man who'd been pursuing her land softly at her side. She jumped to her feet to run away, raising an arm to fend off attack.

Narm grabbed her hand and pulled her back down. "Lady!" he panted. "Keep down. The sorceress . . ."

Abruptly, there was a flash and a deep, rolling explosion, and small stones clattered and fell about them.

"She is free of the insects!" the young man gasped, looking around them frantically. "Oh, gods!" he cursed.

Shandril followed his gaze up the purple-robed form of Symgharyl Maruel, who appeared before them with a triumphant smile.

But the smile was knocked from her face as a slim, dark figure leaped at the sorceress, somersaulting in the air. The figure's feet struck The Shadowsil with bruising force in the shoulder and flank. The two figures hurtled clean out of view behind rocks.

"Well met, witch!" a merry voice said from behind the rocks. "I am Torm, and these are my feet!"

Back down below, however, Rauglothgor hissed and roared, and Shandril saw its great bony form twisting and rearing. Next to her, the handsome young man chanted, "By grasshopper leg and will gathered deep. Let my art make this one"—he touched Shandril's knee—"leap!" He thrust something small into her hand. "Lady," he hissed, "break this, turn, and leap up there. The sorceress!"

Shandril, goaded into fearful scrambling, fumbled with the wisp, broke it, and jumped. The art took her high and far in one mighty bound. She landed on a ledge in the heights of the cavern. Behind her she heard The Shadowsil chant high and shrill, and then there was a flash. Shandril landed lightly on tumbled rocks. Whatever art the sorceress had hurled had missed her.

Shandril glanced down—and met Symgharyl Maruel's glittering, angry eyes. She was casting yet another spell, arms moving in fluid motions. Again the acrobatic figure in dusty gray sprang at her from the side. But The Shadowsil crouched at the last second, turned with a laugh of triumph, and hurled the spell meant for Shandril at the somersaulting Torm. But from his hands flashed two daggers, blades spinning end over end through the air.

Shandril turned and ran on without waiting to see who would die. A dull, rolling boom sounded from far behind her, and stones shook beneath her feet. The floor of the cavern, rising still, was scattered with riches. The faces of long-dead kings carved from cold white ivory stared at her as she pushed past, shuddering at the thought of how large the beasts who yielded those tusks must have been.

Shandril was feeling her way past a curtain of strung amber, the toothed ceiling of the cavern low overhead, when there was yet another mighty blast behind her. Dust swirled as small pieces of rock rained down around her. Shandril heard the hasty, sliding steps of someone running across loose rocks and coins behind her. She hurried on, stumbling for the hundredth time, hands outstretched to break her fall. The steps behind grew closer.

"Damnation!" she cursed aloud. "I can't keep running anymore. When will this nightmare end?"

And the gods heard. There was an ear-splitting crash from the cavern behind her. Shandril was flung violently forward amid a helter-skelter of rocks, coins, gems, gold chains, and choking dust. Over the din, the thief of Deepingdale heard the dracolich Rauglothgor give an anguished, bellowing roar that rose and fell, then died away in hollow echoes.

Then came three short, sharp explosions. Shandril screamed and held her ears. The deep rolling did not die away, but seemed to be coming from all sides. Small rocks struck her like stinging rain. Then loud booms sounded again, and larger slabs and pillars of rock broke free and fell. Refusing to be entombed alive, Shandril crawled desperately on into the darkness. She heard faint, despairing shouts far behind in the dark, but the words dissolved in the never-ending echoes.

When chaos finally died into stillness, Shandril was alone in the drifting dust. Her ragged breathing was deafening in the sudden silence. She lay still, aching from bruises and scrapes, covered by sweat and dust and small stones.

Suddenly, she noticed a pale glow from the rubble below. Shandril stared at it as her eyes slowly adjusted to the gloom. The glow came from a sphere of crystal. Its curves were glossy-smooth, and it was a little larger than a man's head. The steady white radiance came from within it, and by its light Shandril could see that it lay among a pile of treasures.

She picked her way to the sphere. When she nudged it cautiously with a toe, the glow did not flicker. She watched it for a time, waiting for any change, peering closely to see if anything might be hidden beneath it. Finally, she reached down and touched it. She ran her hand lightly over the cold smooth surface, then stepped hastily back, eyeing the sphere narrowly. But nothing flickered, nothing changed. Shandril crouched down and gently lifted the sphere. It was light, and yet somehow unbalanced, as though something were moving inside. But she couldn't feel, hear, or see anything inside.

Holding the sphere up like a lamp, Shandril looked around. The jagged ceiling of the cavern hung close overhead, stretching away perhaps twenty paces, to meet the broken and rubble-strewn stone floor. She swung around slowly, gold coins and other treasures winking as the radiance met them. She was at a dead end. The roof of the cavern had fallen in, and she was trapped, far underground!

Panicking, Shandril scrambled forward. There must be a way out! The whole wide cavern can't have been blocked, just like that! "Oh, please, Tymora, whatever has gone before, smile upon me now!"

And then the light she bore fell upon an outflung arm.

The young man who had been chasing her across the cavern earlier lay face-down, silent and unmoving. A pile of stones half-buried his legs. Shandril stared down at him for a moment and then knelt carefully amid the rubble and gently brushed the hair from his face.

His eyes were closed, his mouth slack. She knew him now. He was the man whose eyes she'd met across the taproom of The Rising Moon, the same man who'd defiantly hurled magic at Symgharyl Maruel before the gate in Myth Drannor.

He was handsome, this man. And he had tried more than once to help her. Abruptly, he moved slightly. Before she knew it, she had set the globe down and was carefully lifting and cradling his head.

He stirred and worked his jaw. Pain and concern lined his face, and he spoke suddenly. "More devils! Is there no end? No—" His hands moved, and he caught at her. Shandril found herself dragged down onto the rock beside him.

"Must . . . must . . ." he hissed weakly.

Shandril grunted and struggled against his grip, reaching for a weapon she no longer bore. And then, inches from her ear, she heard a surprised "Oh." The pressure on her shoulders eased, and his hands became suddenly gentle. Shandril looked up into his eyes, now open and aware. They met hers in wonder, and in them she saw dawning hope, and confusion, and regret.

"I—pray your pardon, lady. I have hurt you." His hands fell away, and he scrambled to rise, rocks rolling all about. He fell back weakly.

Shandril put her hand out to him. "Lie still! Rocks must be moved first. Your feet are covered. Do they hurt?" She clambered past him as she spoke, wondering to herself if it would be safest to leave him helpless, unable to reach her. But no; she could trust this one. She must trust him. The rocks lifted easily. They were many, but small.

"I—can feel nothing. My feet seem . . . a little bruised, but no worse, I hope." He smiled wanly. "Lady, what is your name?"

"I—Shandril Shessair," she replied. "What do they call you?"

"Narm," he replied, moving one foot experimentally. It felt intact, so he rolled over to help her free his other foot. "How came we here?"

Shandril shrugged. "I ran. The fight went on, and—was that you following me?"

"Yes," he replied, grinning.

After a moment she grinned back. "I see," she said. "Why?"

Narm looked down at his empty hands for a moment and then into her eyes. "I would know you, Lady Shandril," he said slowly. "Since first I saw you at the inn, I have . . . wanted to know you." Their eyes held for a long silence.

Shandril looked away first, reaching to take up the glowing globe and cradle it in her arms. She looked at him over it, eyes in shadow, long hair veiling her face. Narm opened his mouth to tell her how beautiful she looked, and then closed it. She was looking at him steadily.

"The cavern fell in upon the others," she said abruptly. "We have been buried, walled off."

Narm sat up, heart sinking. "Is there no way out?"

Shandril shrugged. "I was looking for one when I saw you," she said. "Can your art open a way?"

Narm shook his head. "That is beyond me. But I can dig, gods willing," he said with a nod. "Where did you leave off looking?"

Shandril went forward with the globe. "Here," she said. Slowly, carefully, they moved along the stones, shining the globe high and low. But they found no gap. Together they continued on around the walls of their prison. Reaching their starting point, they straightened wearily.

"What now?" Shandril sighed.

"I need to sit down," Narm said. He selected a large, curving boulder and sat, patting the rock beside him. Slowly, Shandril moved to join him. Narm swung a battered sack from his shoulder and pulled it open. "Are you hungry?"

"Yes," Shandril replied. Narm handed her a thick sausage wrapped in oiled cloth, a partially eaten loaf of round, hard bread, and a leather water skin.

"What is it?"

"Only water, I fear."

"Good enough for me," she said, taking a long swig. They ate in silence for a time.

"Who was that sorceress?" Narm asked suddenly.

"She called herself Symgharyl Maruel, or The Shadowsil," Shandril said. She told him of the Company of the Bright Spear, and of finding herself imprisoned in the cavern, of how the bone had brought her to Myth Drannor, and The Shadowsil to this place. She stopped her speech suddenly and eyed Narm. "Your turn."

Narm swallowed a lump of bread quickly and shrugged. "There is little to tell. I am an apprentice of the art, come from Cormyr with my master, Marimmar, to seek out the lost magic of Myth Drannor. When we reached the ruined city, we met several Knights of Myth Drannor, who warned us away from the city, speaking of devils. But my master thought their counsel false, and he tried to enter the city by another route." Narm paused and took a pull from the skin. "Marimmar was slain. I would have died as well, had not another pair of knights rescued me. They took me to Shadowdale, where Lord Mourngrym lent me an escort back to Myth Drannor. I came upon you and was nearly killed. The knights healed me, and I . . . persuaded them to come through the gate with me to . . . rescue you."

They looked at each other.

"I thank you, Narm," Shandril said slowly. "I'm sorry I ran from you and led you into this." Their eyes met. Both knew they would probably die here. Shandril felt a sudden, raw regret that she had found a man so friendly and so attractive too late. They had met just in time to die together.

"I'm sorry I drove you here," Narm replied softly. "I am not much of a warrior, I fear."

Wordlessly Shandril passed him the bread and clasped his forearm as the company clasped those of their equals. "Maybe not," she said after a time, desire stirring within her, "and yet I live because of you."

Narm took her hand and raised it slowly to his lips, eyes on hers. She smiled, then, and kissed him on impulse.

It was a long time before they parted and looked at each other. "More sausage?" Narm asked hastily.

And then they both laughed nervously. They ate sausage and bread, huddled together in the gentle light of the globe. "How came you by this globe?" Narm finally asked.

Shandril shrugged. "It was here," she said, "with the other treasure. I know not what it is, but it has served me as a lamp. Without it I wouldn't have found you."

"Yes," Narm said, "and my thanks for that." The look in his eyes made Shandril blush again. "You asked about the dracolich. This is the first time I've ever seen one, but my master told me of them. They are undead creatures, created by their own evil and a foul potion, just as a fell mage becomes a lich. A depraved cult of men worship such creatures. They believe that 'dead dragons shall rule the world entire,' and they work to serve these dead dragons so that they will be favored when this prophecy comes to pass."

"How does one serve a dragon, save as a meal?"

"By providing the potions and care it needs to achieve unlife," Narm replied. "After that, they provide spells and treasures. Servants also provide a dracolich with information and much flattery when visiting."

He fell silent as they ate. After a time, Shandril asked quietly, "Narm, how great is your art?"

Narm shook his head. "Feeble, lady. Too feeble. My master was a capable mage, though 1 have never seen him hurl magics as the Lady Jhessail of the knights did, back there." He nodded at the darkness where the rocks had fallen to wall them in. "I know a few spells of use, a few more that are but tricks or little things used to hone the will or the nimbleness of mind and fingers, and the names of a few who may tutor me further. My master is no more, and as a mage, I am almost nothing without him."

"Something more than nothing rescued me," Shandril countered. "You did, and your magic was strong and swift when I needed it. I—I will stand with you and trust in your art."

Narm looked at her for a time and laid his hand on hers. "I thank you," he said. "It is enough, indeed." They embraced, holding each other fiercely in the near-darkness. "We may die here," Narm said abruptly, in a low voice.

"Aye," Shandril said. " 'Adventure,' they call it."

Abruptly, from the back of the cavern, they both heard clearly the click and clatter of a falling stone. They fell silent, listening, but there were no more sounds of moving rock. They exchanged worried glances, and then Shandril picked up the globe and held it high. Its radiance fell across the rocks but revealed nothing. Narm stepped carefully toward the wall of rock, dagger in hand. He walked about for some time.

"Nothing, my lady," Narm said, returning. "But I found this for you." He held out a pendant of electrum wrought in the shape of a falcon in flight, set with garnets for its eyes. She took it slowly, smiled, and hooked it about her neck.

"My thanks," she said simply. "I can only give you coins in return. I am sitting on a heap of them, and one at least has fallen into my boot."

"Why not?" he said. "If die we must, why not die rich?"

"Narm," Shandril said very softly, "could you not gather coins later?"

Narm turned and looked at her. Shandril held out her arms toward him. When he knelt by her, he found she was shaking. "Lady?" he asked, holding her.

"Please, Narm," she whispered, dragging him down atop her, her hands moving with sudden urgency. Narm, surprised, found that she was very strong. His discarded pack fell across the globe, and they spoke no more for a very long time.

* * * *

Later, they lay face-to-face on their sides in the darkness, Shandril's breath warm upon Narm's throat and chest. Even cold coins and rock could make for a comfortable bed, he decided. Shandril held Narm gently, thinking he had drifted off to sleep, but he spoke to her then.

"Lady," he said roughly. "I know it has been but a short time since we met, but I love you."

"Oh, Narm," she said. "I think I have loved you since our eyes first met in The Rising Moon, and that *feels* like so very long ago—a lifetime at least!" She laughed, hugging him tenderly. Her expression turned thoughtful. "It's strange, but I'm not afraid to die now. It's not so terrible to die here, if we die together." Narm's arms tightened about her.

"Die?" he said. "Who knows but that a little digging might win our freedom? The dracolich's grotto is too big to be completely filled with rock . . . I hope."

"We'll dig, then," Shandril said, "if you'll let me up." They rolled apart and uncovered the globe. Its radiance showed them each other, shadowed and bare, and Shandril snatched up her tunic automatically to cover herself.

"Lady," Narm said gently, "may I not even see you?"

Shandril laughed in embarrassment, and her laughter became tears. Narm held her and soothed her as her sobs died away. He murmured gentle support and reached over her shoulder to catch up her tunic. "We're not dead yet," he whispered.

They sat together for some time in silence, arms about each other, summoning strength. Then Shandril began to shiver, and they both dressed and got up to walk around for warmth. Narm gathered gold enough to fill both their pouches and found another treasure for his lady.

He handed Shandril a ring and bracelet joined together by fine chain, so that it covered Shandril's forearm from finger to elbow with curved plates and worked hoops of chased electrum, chain and all being set with many sapphires.

For himself, he found a dagger, with its brass pommel worked into the snarling head of a lion, and two rubies inset as the lion's eyes. He passed over many splendid treasures, but he managed to put one bar of gold in his pack before he heard Shandril's hiss of surprise.

Something moved on the rocks beyond Shandril, approaching her from the tumbled rockfall. Something black and scaly, and about as long as a shortsword. It scuttled soundlessly over, around, and through the stones toward them. It was some sort of long-necked, long-tailed lizard. Narm stepped forward hastily to blast the creature with his art if it attacked. Without slowing, the creature crested a rock five paces from Shandril, who raised the globe to see the creature more clearly.

Suddenly, the creature began to grow. It continued down the rear side of the rock, boiling, shifting, and growing taller. The black surface flecked off. Beneath was purple cloth. Rising tall, and stretching slim arms out, Symgharyl Maruel smiled at them triumphantly.

"So we meet again," the sorceress said with soft menace. "Cower there, dear," she told Shandril, "while I deal in art with this young lion of yours." Her hands were moving like gliding snakes. Shandril looked back at Narm. His hands were also moving, but she saw in his face the brave despair of one who has no power left to hurl magic.

The Shadowsil hissed a word of power, then took the time to laugh. Shandril felt red rage boil up within her, and she leaped forward. At least she would have the satisfaction of seeing the sorceress surprised before she herself died.

❦ 6 ❦

Death in the Dark

*On facing magic: Run, or pray, or throw stones;
many a mage is a fraud, and you can win the
day even while your heart trembles. Or you can
stand calm and mumble nonsense and wiggle
your fingers. Some few workers of the art are
such cowards that they may flee at this. And as
for others, at least when men speak of your
death in days after, they'll say, "I never knew he
was a mage; all those years he kept it secret. He
must have been a clever fellow." Of course,
some who listen may disagree.*

Guldoum Tchar of Mirabar
Sayings of a wise and fat merchant
Year of the Crawling Clouds

The glowing globe was in Shandril's hands. Without
thought, she swept it up and smashed it with all her
strength into The Shadowsil's face.

The sharp singing of its shattering was lost in Symgharyl
Maruel's rough shriek. Darkness fell.

Shandril dropped the fragments she still held and drove a
foot hard into the purple-robed belly. The screaming ended,
and Symgharyl Maruel sat down suddenly.

Narm was running toward Shandril. "My lady! Are you all
right? Shandril?"

At his words, the sorceress drew a shuddering breath and
fixed one glaring eye on Shandril through the blood now
running down her face. Symgharyl Maruel's hands began to
move.

"Oh, gods!" the young man moaned in fear. Shandril stood frozen an instant. But with The Shadowsil caught up in spellcasting, Shandril seized a rock and smashed it again into the sorceress's face. The rock struck with a horrid, wet thud, and Shandril drove it down again.

"Leave us alone, you bitch!" Shandril screamed at the sorceress, as the rock rose and fell yet again.

The Shadowsil struggled to block Shandril's attack. She fell backward until she lay full-length on the rocks, bloody and unmoving.

"Shandril?" Narm whispered anxiously, as he clambered over the jagged rocks to reach her.

Shandril stared down, the rock falling from bloody fingers, and she burst into tears.

Narm held her with a fierce tenderness and stared down at the sorceress. Neither her spell nor his cantrip had taken effect. Perhaps Shandril had spoiled The Shadowsil's spell with her rock attack, but Narm doubted it. Certainly nothing had spoiled his casting. A twinkling cloud of light around Narm was all that let him see the fallen sorceress in the darkness. Symgharyl Maruel lay still and silent. Was it that easy to kill so strong a wielder of the art?

Shandril mastered her sobs and held tight to Narm. As they stood together they heard the distinct scrape and tumble of rocks beyond the rockfall. Hope leaped in them both.

Shandril looked up through the twinkling mist. "Do we shout to tell them we're here?"

Narm frowned and shook his head. "I think not. We may not want to meet the diggers. Let's shout only if they stop digging."

"Well enough," Shandril said, "if you stay with me."

Narm held her tight. "Think you, fair lady, that I am a rake?" he asked in mock anger.

"A lady cannot be too careful," she quoted the maxim back at him.

He grinned. "Please make known to me, Lady, when this carefulness of yours begins."

Shandril wrinkled her nose and blushed with embarrassment. Then her attention was caught by the twinkling cloud surrounding Narm.

"What's that?"

"I don't know." The young man tried to dust the glowing mist away from him, but it clung close. "Strange . . ." he said, but then the rocks grated again. They stood and watched warily for the rocks they could see to move. Once there was a louder, rumbling clatter, and a surprised male voiced a cry.

Suddenly, a glimmer of yellow light appeared, flickering between two rocks. The light grew as more rocks were lifted away.

"We should hide!" Shandril whispered, drawing Narm down into a crouch among the stones.

Torchlight blazed at them before they could move. "Narm?" a voice came from the darkness. "Lady?"

"Florin?" Narm replied eagerly, rising and drawing Shandril to his side.

"Well met!" came the glad reply, as the man scaled the rocks toward them. Shandril recognized him as the kingly warrior who had walked with Elminster in the mists between the company and the mysterious men who guarded the mules. "I heard screaming," he said. "Is all well with you?"

"We're fine," Narm replied, "but she who screamed—the sorceress—is not. She will work her art no more."

"Aye? So it is," Florin's face was impassive. "Danger sought, danger found. You did well. Our foe lies buried, but may yet live." He stopped for a moment to squint at Narm. "Hold, what's that?" he asked. "A balhiir!" he exclaimed, drawing back in alarm. But he was too late.

The swirling, sparkling cloud around Narm boiled up like the plume of a campfire when wind draws it into long flames. The cloud struck at the ranger's blade.

"A balhiir!" Florin gasped again, swinging his sword away. But the mist was already swirling around his blade in cold silence. The weapon grew heavier in his grasp as its magical blue light twinkled once and then dwindled away. The twinkling mist remained and seemed a little brighter.

"Whence came this balhiir?" the ranger asked.

"Is that what it is? I struck down the sorceress with a crystal sphere," Shandril told him. "The sphere broke, and this came out."

The ranger gazed at his blade in consternation, and then smiled. "By the bye, I am Florin Falconhand, of Shadowdale, and the Knights of Myth Drannor. Might I know you?"

Smiling, she said, "Shandril Shessair, until recently of Deepingdale and the Company of the Bright Spear, though I fear the company is no more."

"Your servant, Lady," Florin said with a bow. "You have loosed an ill thing on the world. This creature feeds on magic. Only the one who loosed a balhiir can destroy it. Will you aid me in this task, Lady?"

"Is it dangerous?" Narm asked, feeling his anger rise.

"Your lives both bid to be filled with danger," Florin replied gently, "whether you kill this creature or not. Striving for something worthwhile and going to your graves is better than drifting in cowardice to your graves, is it not?"

"Fair speech, indeed," Shandril replied, meeting his eyes. "I will aid you," she said firmly, calming Narm. "But tell me more of this thing."

"In truth," the ranger told her calmly, "I know little more. Lore holds that the one who releases a balhiir is the only one who can destroy it. Elminster of Shadowdale knows how to deal with such creatures, but like all who use the art, he dare not come near something that drains magic. Items of power all seem to fare poorly against the creature; it foils spells, too."

"Well," Shandril asked, "why should such a creature be destroyed? Doesn't it leash dangerous art?"

"Fair question," Florin replied. "Others might answer you differently, but I say we need art. There are prices to be paid for it, but the shrewd use of the magical art helps a great many people. The threat of art rising, unlooked for, keeps many a tyrant sword from taking what can be taken by brute force."

Shandril met his level gray gaze and slowly relaxed. She could trust this tall, battered man. At her side, Narm stirred.

"The balhiir was about me for some time. It drained both my cantrips and the sorceresses' spells. Do you know if I will be able to work the art again?"

"Indeed, so long as the balhiir is not present. It will move to absorb unleashed magic if it can." Even as Florin spoke, the twinkling cloud stirred about his blade, spiraled up, and left him. In a long, snakelike mist of lights, the balhiir drifted back the way the ranger had come. Florin started after it. "Follow me, if you will. If not, I'll leave the torch."

The two hurried after him. Shandril glanced back once at The Shadowsil lying among the rocks, but all she could see was one foot jutting upward. As they passed through the escape hole Florin had dug, the foot seemed to move in the dancing torchlight. Shandril shivered despite herself.

The cavern where the dracolich had laired was much changed. The ceiling had broken away and fallen. The gleam of treasure was gone, covered by rubble and dust. There was a mighty rumbling and clattering of stones to their right, as the eternal dracolich rose slowly from under a castle's worth of fallen rock. Far across the wide chamber, a woman was raising her hands in magical passes.

Bright pulses of magic burst from her hands as Narm and Shandril climbed over the rocks. They saw magic missiles streak across the chamber and strike the dracolich. The winking cloud of mist streaked down hungrily.

Rauglothgor roared anew in pain and fury. Its deep bellows echoed about the cavern. The battered dracolich rose up and hissed, "Death to you all! Drink this!"

There was a flicker of the art, but nothing else occurred. The balhiir had reached Rauglothgor. The dracolich roared again in surprise and rage. Its great claws raked huge boulders aside as a cat scrapes loose sand. "What is this?" it raged. Its hollow neck arched, its jaws parted, and flames gouted out in a great arc.

Fire rolled out with terrifying speed and washed over the lady on the far slope. The air was filled with the stench of burning. As the flames died the lady still stood, apparently untouched, her hands moving in the casting of a spell. About her the sparkling mist danced. The balhiir had ridden the fire across the chamber.

"Jhessail," Florin called. "A balhiir—the art is useless!"

"So I see," Jhessail calmly replied, ignoring the roars of Rauglothgor across the cavern. "Well fought, Narm. How is your companion? She looks worth our trouble."

Shandril found herself smiling. "Well met, Lady Jhessail."

Jhessail came up and hugged her. "You show a good eye, Narm. Let us proceed elsewhere now, lest we not see another meal to get acquainted over."

Florin and the elf, Merith, stood with drawn blades facing the dracolich. The mist swirled away from Jhessail and moved toward the elf's weapon.

"Your blade," Florin warned.

"If drained, then so be it," Merith's merry voice came back to them. Both of the fighters charged the skeletal monster.

Again and again the elf avoided the raking bones of the dracolich, with Florin also rolling and leaping in the same dance of death.

Shandril and Narm looked about in time to see a gray streak of motion; a slim, fast man leaped down the rocks toward them.

"Beware!" Jhessail shouted.

There was a sudden flash, and a roar, and the ground leaped to meet all of them.

* * * * *

Someone was shaking him. "Up, Narm," Jhessail said firmly. "We cannot stand in this place longer."

"I have Shandril," Lanseril's voice said from somewhere. "She's heavier than I expected."

Narm struggled to move, to rise. A warm hand was on his shoulder. "The dracolich?"

"Rauglothgor lives." Jhessail's voice was rueful. "The balhiir hampers both sides in this struggle. The dracolich's lair has traps and harbors creatures subject to its will. It has moved to block our escape to the upper caverns."

"Are you not its match in art?" Narm asked, then he realized what he had said. "Oh, my pardon, La—"

"None needed," Jhessail replied, guiding them around tumbled boulders. "I doubt it, here in its lair. Alone, spell to spell, perhaps. My spells are more numerous and stronger, but its are unusual and suited to defense."

They climbed up one side of the cavern toward where Merith stood waiting. His drawn sword no longer glowed. "Well fought," he said, kissing Jhessail.

"Where is Torm?" Narm asked, politely waiting until the kiss was done.

Merith and Jhessail exchanged glances and chuckled. "We think he used something from a little bag of tricks he carries to teleport out of here when he saw the balhiir, no doubt to save all of the magic he carries. I hope he also went to tell Elminster of what has befallen us, and we shall see some aid," Jhessail explained.

"And if aid doesn't come?" Narm asked.

"Then our inevitable victory will be a little harder," Lanseril said. "If you don't mind saying, what art do you currently command?"

Narm grinned. "I am but an evoker, lord. I have left one cantrip of little use."

The words had scarcely left his lips when there was a great crash and a roar of moving rock. Suddenly, the world was falling down on them again.

* * * * *

She hurt all over. Why had none of the tales of adventure ever mentioned the constant pain and discomfort? Shandril rolled over, slowly, feeling many aches and twinges. Stones must have fallen on her. Nothing seemed broken, thank the gods. It was dark, and it felt as if she were somewhere underground. She could tell by the cold flash of the beljurils around her that she was still in the dracolich's grotto. Where was Narm? Then a gem flashed nearby, and she saw a hand inches from her own. Narm!

Helpless tears blinded her. The hand was cold, lifeless. Then another flash of the magical balhiir showed the hand—black hair, thick fingers. It wasn't Narm. In relief and revulsion, she let go of the dead thing. Where to go? What to do?

There was the faintest of scraping sounds to her left. Someone was moving quietly over the stones. "Who's that?" Shandril demanded of the darkness, feeling for her dagger. "What do you want?"

"Molesting you sounds good" a broken voice croaked at her elbow.

Shandril jumped, startled.

The voice took on a gentler, more human tone in the darkness. "Well met. I am Torm, of the Knights of Myth Drannor. No noise now. It is best that no one think you still live. I will be your eyes and ears and hands until we can leave this trap. Wait here."

Shandril felt hope leap within her. She reached out only to feel rapidly receding cloth. "Thanks to you, Torm. Why would you aid a stranger?"

The answering voice was fainter as it moved away. "I have a weakness for fair ladies who reach for boot daggers and face the unknown. Now hush, and wait."

She sat down on the most comfortable stone she could find and composed herself to wait.

After a long time there was a stirring in the darkness.

"Torm?"

"Rauglothgor's spells search for us even now." Torm whispered in her ear. "Your Narm lives and is unharmed. I will take you to him as soon as the dracolich settles down. For now, we must abide here."

They both sat, and Shandril again felt the dead hand. "Torm, there's a dead man beside me." She took Torm's hand and guided it down in the darkness.

"Gods!" he hissed. "It must be Lanseril. Jhessail told me it was Lanseril carrying you."

Torm slipped around her and Shandril heard him grunt in effort. He began moving rocks. "I'll help. If you roll the rocks to me, I can stop them here and you won't have to carry them as far."

"Dangerous," she heard him hiss through set teeth.

Then, in a gem-flash, she saw another man crouching with a dagger. "An enemy!" she hissed.

Behind her there was a sudden grunt and then a gurgling moan. Torm spoke aloud, "A dragon cultist, no doubt. Now quite dead. Now, Lady, I need you to help. We must get Lanseril's body quickly. Never mind the noise; the time for quiet is past."

Torm handed Shandril a hooded lantern and slapped a dagger in her hand. He moved Lanseril's body onto his shoulder, and they moved quickly through the boulders.

Their route rose and fell in the rubble. They heard the

sound of battle several times but never encountered an enemy.

Soon they saw torchlight, and a voice from beyond bawled out merrily, "Where in the Lady's name have ye been?"

"Around and about," Torm called back. "I found Shandril and she found Lanseril, but he needs help. Have you spells left?"

"Aye, if the accursed balhiir stays elsewhere," Rathan rumbled, striding towards them. Jhessail was at his back, and Merith, and—Narm!

Wordlessly, Shandril rushed forward to embrace him, passing Torm like the wind.

He smiled and said, "I raced back to tell you that some seventy riders are coming up to the keep above us; dragon cultists, most likely. Shall we hit them with spells or take them by surprise down here?"

"No magic remains to us that we can trust," Florin told him grimly.

"Well"—Torm grinned—"I hadn't planned on dying of old age, anyway."

Shandril and Narm held each other, feeling that they could take on anything as long as they had each other to count on.

Torm tapped Narm on the shoulder. "If you ever find yourself tired and need someone to stand in for you, just call my name."

The look he got made him roar with laughter. Somehow, Narm didn't see anything funny about the offer.

"The only place the few of us can defend against so many is that dead-end where Florin found you both. Let's move," Jhessail said.

The torches flickered as they hurried through the twisting tunnels in wary silence. They saw no living creature. There was no sign of the balhiir. Finally, they reached the dead-end and readied their weapons.

"I presume you returned to Shadowdale to stow away your magic," Florin asked Torm. "Did you ask the aid of Elminster?"

The thief grinned. "Yes, but he always suspects me of

youthful overexcitement. I know not how serious he thinks
our situation. I did mention the dracolich and that ought to
intrigue him into putting in an appearance."

"Done," Rathan rumbled, getting up from the healing of
Lanseril. "He'll live a little longer."

Lanseril sat up with a sigh and locked eyes with Shandril.
"Permit me to introduce myself, good lady. After all, if one
must die, it is best to do so among known friends. I am Lanseril Snowmantle, of. . . of. . ." The druid's words trailed
away and he fell back with eyes closed.

"Is he dead?" Narm asked in alarm.

"He's fine; just needs sleep. One must sleep to heal. But
enough of imprudent druids . . . let us speak of the chosen of
the gods—clerics. Myself, for instance." He drew himself up
grandly, girth and all. "I am Rathan Thentraver, servant of
Tymora."

"Well met," Narm said politely.

Rathan was bending to bring Shandril's hand to his lips.
"Lady, with all this running and butchering, there's scarce
been time to get to know each other. Although I dare say ye
two have managed it. I know what it is to be young, and in a
hurry."

"I must ask—you are a cleric," Shandril said, "yet you seem
so—forgive me, ah, normal, much like the men I knew who
came into the inn each night. Does worship of the Lady
Tymora not change one?"

Rathan nodded at her question. "We do not all live the
stuff of rousing tales. For all the glory of victories and treasure won there are painful days of marching hurt, lying
wounded, or swinging swords or maces in weary practice.
The Lady helps those who help themselves. She doesn't ask
for change, she just asks for our best."

"Yes," Merith said, working on his blade with an oily rag,
"the gods are strange. Those who come against us now worship the monster that nearly slew us all."

"The Cult of the Dragon," Shandril said slowly. "Why
would anyone want to worship a dead dragon?"

"Don't worry about them," Torm boasted. "I keep around
me a few magics that should . . . damn!" The sparkling mist
swirled around him. "Well, I had some magic," he finished

ruefully.

"Why did it leave us before?" Narm asked curiously, watching the coiling mist rise again above Torm, drifting along the ceiling over them all. It seemed larger and somehow brighter.

"I think it went to the greatest concentration of magic," Rathan said, his eyes not leaving the balhiir, "either the dracolich's hoard, or the spells of Rauglothgor. Seventy cultists, you said?" The cleric grunted.

"And a dracolich. Let us not forget the dracolich," Merith added dryly.

"Enough. Something comes!" Florin said sternly. The ranger rose, lifting his two-handed sword as though it was a thing of feathers. At his back, the knights snuffed out lights and readied themselves for battle. Merith, striding catlike over the rocks, joined Florin. Jhessail moved behind the rocks in line with the entrance. Rathan moved to shield Lanseril, saying gently, "Wake now."

The druid's eyes flickered. Shandril heard him whisper, "Weapons out?" as Torm took her by the hand and led her and Narm to the left. The druid became a blur, and the balhiir moved toward the vanishing form. A small gray bird appeared where the druid had been.

Torm took the couple to a pile of hand-sized stones. "A thrown stone can spoil spells and aimed arrows better than the strongest art." The thief of Deepingdale noticed that the balhiir had drifted above Jhessail in an incriminating, winking cloud.

"Not too quick with those stones now," Torm whispered. "If they don't see us at first, we'll let them come ahead until there are some to slay in the midst of our ring. Strike when they first notice us, not before."

Beyond the entrance, a bobbing sphere of radiance could be seen floating in the air, moving nearer as it danced and played about like a curious firefly. The balhiir gathered itself like a snake, then plunged forward along the roof of the cavern in silent haste, toward the light.

The light shone on the dark-robed shoulder of a man wearing some sort of large hat. He seemed to be alone as he clambered over the rocks of the entrance. He was white-bearded, and bore a long, knobbly staff of wood a head taller than himself. Then the balhiir reached the glowing globe that hung at his shoulder. The globe's radiance flared into the twinkling cloud, and then died.

"Put away that overlong fang, Florin, and light me a torch," said a somehow familiar voice, disgustedly. "Ye have a balhiir indeed. Young Torm managed to keep to the truth for once."

"Elminster!" the ranger said in calm, pleased greeting.

"I know, I know . . . ye're all delighted to see me, or will be if ye ever manage to make a light to see anything by."

Light flared up as the ranger relit his torch. Elminster stood in the flickering light looking at Shandril and Narm. "A fine dance ye've led me on, ye two . . . Gorstag was in tears when I left him, girl; nearly frantic, he was. Ye might have told him a bit more about where ye were going. Young folk have no consideration, these days."

Then he winked, and Shandril felt suddenly very happy. She cast the stone in her hand so that it crashed at the old mage's feet.

"Well met, indeed," Elminster said dryly, "O releaser of balhiirs. We may as well get to know each other before the dying starts."

❧ 7 ❧

To Face the
Bright Danger

*Tell ye of the balhiir? Ah, a curious creature,
indeed. I hear it was first—the short version, ye
say? Very well; ye are paying. The short version
is thus: a curious creature, indeed. Thank ye,
goodsir; fair day to ye.*

> The sage Rasthiavar of Iraiebor
> *A Wayfarer's Belt-Book of Advice*
> Year of Many Mists

"I expected to see the cultists here long ago," Torm said,
slipping lightly up onto a high, flat rock. "Or at least to see
something of the dracolich. Why so long?"

"Fear of us," Rathan said with a grin. Florin remained alert
by the entrance, obviously expecting an attack.

"I'm so scared I can scarce stand still," Shandril said, "and
you talk calmly of strategies and jests! How do you do it?"

"We always talk before a fight, lady," Rathan answered.
"One is excited and among friends and may not live to see
the next dawn." The fat cleric shrugged. "Besides . . . how
better to spend the waiting? Much of what a bard calls
'dashing adventure,' at least for us, is a little fast and hard
running and fighting and lots and lots of waiting. We would
grow bored wasting all that time in silence."

"Hmphh!" said Elminster. "All this jaw-wagging's the mark
of minds too feeble to ruminate in solitude." Torm chuckled.
Jhessail rose from the rocks, the sparkling and glowing
balhiir moving above her. She went to Shandril, and took
her hand.

"Elminster," the magic-user said, turning from Shandril to

the ancient wizard, "there will doubtless be time for chatter later. After the battle, most likely. Tell us now of the balhiir. That thing floating in the air above us has not approached you since destroying your globe, so I know you bear no magic item. It will rob you of your spells, as it has done me, if we do not deal with it. What say you?"

"Yes, yes," Elminster said severely. "I am not so addled that I forgot the lass or"—he indicated the shifting mist above the two women with the head of his staff—"that." He took off his battered hat and hung it upon the staff now cradled in the angle of one arm. He then leaned back against a massive boulder and cleared his throat noisily.

"The balhiir," the old sage began in measured tones, "is a most curious creature. Rare in the Realms and unknown in many of the pl—"

"Elminster!" Jhessail protested. "The short version. Please."

The sage regarded her in stony silence for two long breaths. "Good lady! This *is* the short version. It would do ye good to cultivate patience . . . a habit I have found useful these last five hundred winters or so." Pointedly he turned his head away to speak solely to Shandril.

"Listen most carefully, Shandril Shessair." The young would-be thief tensed at the old mage's serious tone. "In this place, we lack all means for banishing or destroying this balhiir, save one, and ye alone can master it. 'Tis a dangerous affair for all of us, but for ye most of all. However, there is no other answer. Are ye willing to attempt it?"

Shandril looked around at the adventurers who had become her friends. Then she gazed up at the strange, magic-eating, glowing wisp above her. Letting out her breath in a long, shuddering sigh, she said, "Yes. Tell me."

She met the old sage's eyes squarely, holding them with her own. Gently she disengaged herself from Narm's encircling arm and stepped forward.

The old mage bowed to her solemnly. This drew surprised looks from the knights who watched. He then asked, "Narm, ye retain a cantrip, don't ye?" His twinkling blue eyes, grave and gentle, never left Shandril's.

"Yes," the apprentice magic-user replied.

"Then cast it while touching thy lady," he said, "and we shall stand clear. This will draw the balhiir to ye both. Shandril, thrust both hands into the midst of the glow. Try not to breathe in any of it, and keep thy face—eyes, in particular—away from it. When Shandril touches the balhiir, Narm, ye must flee from her at once, as fast as ye can. All here, stand clear of Shandril from then on. Her touch will probably be fatal."

The great sage went forward to clasp the determined but trembling Shandril by the arms. The balhiir coiled above them both.

"Child," Elminster said then, voice gentle, "thy task is the hard one. The balhiir's touch will tingle and seem to burn. If ye would live, ye must keep thy hands spread within it and not withdraw. You will find you can take the pain—a cat of mine once did. Use the force of your own will to draw the fire into thee, and it will flow down your arms and enter your body. Succeed and ye will hold the balhiir's energy.

"Ye must then slay its will or perish in flames. Ye will know when ye have destroyed it. Master it as quickly as ye can, for the fire within thee will burn more the longer ye hold it. Ye can let it out from thy mouth, thy fingers, even thy eyes. However, beware of aiming the blasts carelessly. Ye could easily slay us all." Shandril nodded, dark eyes meeting his.

"Ye must go out through the entrance, if the dracolich or the cultists have not attacked us by then. Seek them out and blast them until ye have none of the balhiir's energy left. Let go of it all, or it may slay ye." Their eyes held for a time longer, and then he bent slowly to kiss her brow. His beard tickled her cheeks, and his old lips were warm. Her forehead tingled, and she felt somehow stronger. Shandril drew herself up and smiled at him.

"We shall be nearby," he said. "Narm will follow thee, and we shall guard ye both. Are ye ready?"

Shandril nodded. "Yes," she said, lips suddenly dry. "Do it now." She hoped the effort of keeping her voice steady did not show on her face. She raised her hands over her head as Elminster bowed again and drew back. Narm stepped forward reluctantly. The balhiir winked and swirled overhead, closer now, as if it were waiting for her to destroy it.

"Forgive me," Narm said, coming to her side, "but the cantrip I have will make you—uh, belch."

That struck her as so incongruously funny that her helpless laughter rose and rang out across the silent cavern. She was laughing as the magic was cast and the balhiir descended upon her. She saw nothing, heard nothing, knew nothing but the curiously coiling sparks and wispy mist which smelled ever so faintly of rain upon leather, as the balhiir enveloped her.

The pain began. Elminster had spoken the truth and Shandril wondered, only briefly, if he had ever done this himself. He must have, mustn't he? She could feel the sparks, the fire, the energy somehow flowing into her, stirring. She bent her head back to gasp a breath, found herself staring at the dark rock above her, heard her own voice sobbing, moaning, crying out. . . . It hurt. By the gods, *it hurt*!

The tingling grew with the rising, burning pain, until her whole body was shaking and twitching. She had to fight to hold her hands out. She wanted desperately to pull back and clutch herself in pain as the fire spread down her arms and across her chest.

Shandril sobbed. Blue-purple fire was licking up her rigid outstretched arms. Narm rushed toward her, some part of his mind noting as he screamed at her to stop that the flames were not touching her hair or her clothes.

"No!" he cried, reaching out desperate arms to her. As the young apprentice rushed past, Elminster extended a long, thin arm of his own and clutched his shoulder.

"No!" the great mage said in his turn. "Keep back, if ye love her!"

Narm scarcely heard the words, but the hand gripped him like iron, and he could not break free of its grasp. Shandril's sobs rose into a raw, high shriek. "Gods have mercy!" she screamed, and flames leaped from her mouth. Elminster waved imperiously at the knights watching in amazement to get down and seek cover.

The fire raged down Shandril's arms and flared up from her shoulders. She could not see; flames of blue and purple rose from her nostrils and mouth. She could feel energy rolling restlessly around her arms and breast, coiling and

flaring, drawing in . . . drawing all in. She could feel burning
anger rising within her, too, crawling behind her throat and
forcing her to roar and snarl.

Flames rolled before her nose. Startled, she stopped, cast
a burning gaze at Jhessail, saw the flames reflected back
from the mage's beautiful, anxious face, and waved an apology as she looked away again. Her veins were boiling; her
body shook.

Something scuttled and writhed snakelike within her,
awakening fear. She couldn't control it! She would bring
death to these new friends, to Jhessail, to Florin, to the great
Elminster, to Narm . . . *No!* The flames rolled away, and she
could see Narm's face, the reflected flames dancing on it, his
eyes meeting hers and darkening instantly in pain. Then
they were gone as Elminster stepped in front of her love,
grave eyes meeting hers, steadily, urging her on. How like
Gorstag's those eyes were. She thought of Gorstag, kind and
jovial, roughly wise and knowing. She closed her eyes and
clenched her teeth to fight the coiling thing within her. The
heat and the pain rose suddenly and sharply, squeezing her
heart in a blazing grip.

And then she was through. Sharp pains pierced her knees
as she fell hard onto the rocks, white heat building within
her. She was burning still, but she could master it.

Exulting, Shandril rose, and saw Florin and Merith, their
blades flashing, fighting many men in the narrow mouth of
the cavern. Her heartbeat was deafening thunder in her
ears and she barely heard Elminster's shout. The elf and the
ranger drew aside, steel flashing. Florin raised his blade in
solemn salute as she rushed past them.

Shandril knew she was shouting. White lightning lanced
from her hands, mouth, and eyes, and crackled ahead of
her. Wherever she looked men burned and died. She heard
screams, and drowned them out with a long, triumphant
shriek of her own, rising high as men were swept away in
flames. Then the cavern mouth was empty, blackened. Men
lay still, blades smoking in crisped hands.

Oh gods, what have I done? Six, seven . . . twelve . . . how
many? Was there no end to them? Shandril recoiled in horror, fighting the fires raging within her. As she stood there,

hands spread and smoking, a long skeletal neck swung down into the cavern opening, and two chilling eyes stabbed at her. Rauglothgor the Undying opened his bony jaws, and the world exploded in flame.

Shandril moaned, pain atop pain raged within her. Tears blurred the wall of flames; then she could see again, and Rauglothgor's horned skull-face was still before her. The dracolich's evil eyes met hers, and she was afraid.

Those eyes laughed down at her with all the arrogance and strength of cold centuries and dragonfire, and she was suddenly angry. This skeletal creature was laughing at her, secure in the knowledge that she was a girl, unskilled and unwise in the ways of battle and magic.

She felt her anger grow. A rock—a mere rock!—had felled Symgharyl Maruel, in all her pride and cruel mastery of magic. Oh yes, she faced a dracolich now, but now she had the means to strike back! Burn, then, oh-so-mighty Rauglothgor, burn and know how it feels, you who burn us like so many flies scorched in torchfire . . . *burn!*

Shandril flung her arms out as if she could stab the undead dragon with her fingertips, and from them crackled lightnings anew. Rauglothgor burned. A sullen radiance pulsed white within his bones. The dracolich reared up high and roared in pain and fear. Stones raked from the cavern ceiling by his horns fell in a shower about him, and his great claws convulsed. He raised bony wings and writhed, until finally the great undead dragon sank down, bones blazing with white, blue, and purple flames.

So passed Rauglothgor, Night Dragon of the Thunder Peaks. His bones blackened, split, and burst asunder. All that remained crumbled as the flames died.

Shandril stumbled into the darkness, fire still raging within her. The cavern beyond was dark and large, and there were torches flickering below her, glimmering and dancing on drawn swords. More cultists, just come, scrambled to meet her, blades raised—easy prey stumbling blindly, undoubtedly fleeing the great Rauglothgor beyond.

Easy prey, indeed. Shandril opened her mouth and screamed as they came, and flames gushed forth. She raised her hands and smote them with spellfire, hurling blasts again and again, until none stood against her. Shandril stumbled on, exulting, fire still blazing within her. Less, now—she could see and hear that the knights followed her.

"Shandril!" Narm's anguished voice broke through the roar of her fire.

She shook her head and motioned him back. Fire from her hands fell harmlessly against Elminster's ready barrier of force, and Narm stayed silent as Shandril ran on. Still the fires raged within her, and she feared to bury herself and them all by blasting at the rocks around her. So she ran across the cavern and up its far slope, seeking the outside—and any more cultists who might lie ahead.

She found them, laden with treasure; though they soon enough dropped it to find their blades when she blasted the first of them. Some raised arms to hurl spells, but magic missiles curled past her and struck them down before the art could be unleashed. It was too late for them to run or fight. In the face of her spellfire, they only had time to die. As Shandril climbed past them, she thought that they did that very well. More cultists met her in the cavern above, and more died.

Shandril climbed up through the tunnels to the keep, and daylight. As she moved up the crumbling steps, blue flames licking the old stone where her boots touched it, Shandril saw the mountain slopes below. No cultists were upon them, and the sky was clear and cloudless. She turned, flames blazing around her swirling hair, and screamed, "Get back!" And the knights fell back. Elminster, his barrier still up, restrained Narm. Shandril turned to the sky and stones about her and spread her hands.

She threw back her head and screamed her pain and exultation, loud and long, and flames rolled forth. Stones cracked and fell around her, the shards cutting her, and she laughed. Daylight grew as the walls fell and stone crumbled. She backed down the stairs of the shattered keep as it fell away around her.

"Back! Back!" she cried to the knights behind her, and hurled spellfire forth again. Pillars of broken wall stood like huge teeth against the sky before they too toppled. The keep was gone, completely fallen, and still the fires raged.

Oh Tymora, release me! Will this never end? And yet, look, you gods! Such power! Nothing stands against me—not the dracolich, not his worshippers, not the stones themselves—not even this mountain!

Shandril laughed. Her blazing fingers found the throat of her tunic and ripped it open. From her bared breast poured out spellfire as she backed down the tunnel. Rock cracked and burst into fragments.

The fires were less now. Shandril could feel herself shaking as the energy raced through her, pouring out of her breast and mouth. She was on her knees again, amid the scattered gold of the dracolich's treasure. Above her the ceiling of the great cavern was breaking away and falling. Spellfire crackled and spat.

Suddenly Shandril felt very tired, and she swayed on her knees. Her gaze fell to her hands. The ring and armlet of electrum and sapphires still gleamed and sparkled. She managed to bring her arms up before her as she fell forward, shivering, onto the cold stone.

The fire was gone, and she was so cold, so numbingly cold.

"Shandril!" Narm screamed, slipping out of Elminster's grip at last. He crashed full tilt into the old mage's unseen wall of force, clawed his way along it in helpless frustration, and screamed at Elminster, "Let me go to her! Is she dead?"

The sage shook his head, understanding and pity in his eyes. "No. But she may not live. I had no idea how much art that balhiir had absorbed. Careful now." And the barrier was gone. Narm stumbled forward, falling twice on his way to Shandril.

"Gods," Florin said simply, as he followed. Beyond the place where Shandril lay, the mountain had been blasted open into a vast crater. They stood now in daylight.

" 'Rare in the Realms,' you said," Torm noted to Elminster as he came past. "And a good thing, too!" The other Knights of Myth Drannor had already joined Narm, kneeling beside Shandril's body. As Elminster walked up to them, the young apprentice raised a tearful face and asked the mage, "Can I . . . will it hurt her if I touch her?" He gulped and bit his lip. Shandril lay before him face down and motionless, her long hair spread out over her back like a last lick of flame.

Elminster shook his head. "No. No, it cannot. And yet . . . Rathan, can ye heal yet?"

The cleric nodded. "I've only a little favor of the Lady, I fear," he rumbled. "I used most on Lanseril, back there."

Elminster nodded. "Use what you can then. Narm?" The tear-tracked face lifted, almost challengingly. "After Rathan heals thy lady, carry her back to the cavern where ye waited for me. Haste matters more than gentleness. I shall go to Shadowdale at once for healing scrolls left hidden by Doust Sulwood, when he was lord, and then meet ye at that cavern." Rathan was already chanting softly, kneeling by the fallen girl.

Narm nodded, slowly. "Yes." Then, roughly, he burst out, "You knew it would kill her! You knew!"

Elminster shook his head. "No, Narm. I feared it might but saw no other way." He turned away. "Do not delay me now, or Shandril may die."

Rathan touched Narm's shoulder. "I am done, lad. Let us get her moved—if Elminster counsels haste, ye may be sure haste is the thing."

Narm nodded slowly, tore his eyes from the old mage's back, and sighed. "Yes. I trust him. Sorry." He looked down and burst into tears.

"Look," said a voice by his other ear, "stop blubbering and lift your lady by the shoulders. I'll take her feet. Jhessail, hold her head as we carry." Narm found himself looking at Torm, who nodded at Shandril. "Come on. Haste, the man said."

"Aye." Narm reached out a tentative hand and fumbled at the open front of her tunic.

"Leave it," Torm said firmly. "I promise you I won't look— much."

Narm shouted at him, a raw torrent of words that made Torm broaden his grin and finally break into a chuckle. Seething, Narm stopped when he realized he had no idea what he was saying.

They climbed up over broken rocks, Rathan at Narm's elbow, Jhessail hip-to-hip beside him cradling Shandril's head. Shandril's eyes were closed, her lips parted. She looked so beautiful. Narm started to weep again. Through the tears, he saw the elf, Merith, guiding Torm through the tricky entrance to the smaller cavern beyond where he and Shandril had been trapped together. The smell of burned flesh was strong around them. Narm looked down at Shandril in disbelief. He had seen it, yes. How much force had it taken? How much had she held? And how in the name of all the gods could she survive it?

"The scrolls—is Elminster back yet?" he asked frantically as they stumbled forward into the now-familiar, low-ceilinged cavern. Lanseril, in his own form again, sat against a wall with lit torches on either side of him.

"I felt the mountain shake," he said. "Was it Shandril?" At Torm's nod, he said nothing but only shook his head. And then a thought struck him. "Bring her over here. No, not straight across—Elminster might teleport in right there—around this way."

"Good thought, but unnecessary, as it happens," came a familiar voice from the back of the cavern. "Rathan—scrolls enough for both Lanseril and Shandril." Elminster held out the rolls of parchment to the cleric as he came forward, set aside his staff, and bent down. "I only hope the force within her did not damage her overmuch."

"Damage?" Narm asked.

"The spellfire burns inside," Elminster said gently. "It can burn out lungs, heart, and even the brain, if held overlong." He shook his head. "She seemed to be master of it at the last, but she held more than I have ever known anyone to bear before, without bursting into flames and being entirely consumed on the spot."

"Cheerful, isn't he?" Torm put in lightly. Narm stared at him in horror, then burst into tears and started to tremble. Jhessail held his shuddering shoulders and looked at the thief levelly.

"Torm," she said in a cutting tone, "sometimes you are a right bastard."

Torm indicated Narm with one hand. "He needed it," he said soberly.

Jhessail held his gaze for a moment and then said, "You're right, Torm. I'm sorry. I mistook you." She enfolded Narm in her arms, and he uncontrollably sobbed out his relief into her breast.

"You and the rest of the world," said Torm mournfully. "Most of the time."

"And with no cause at all," Merith added innocently. "Now shut your clever lips and help me spread my cloak over her."

Rathan nodded that he was done as they approached and got up wearily to see to Lanseril.

"A hard day of healing?" the half-elven druid asked wryly as the cleric knelt beside him. Rathan grunted.

"Hard on the knees, anyway," he agreed, rolling open the next scroll. "Now lie there, damn ye. It is hard enough convincing the Lady that healing an unrepentent servant of Silvanus like thyself is a devout act, without ye squirming around."

"True enough," Lanseril agreed, settling himself. "How does the young lady fare?"

Rathan shrugged. "Her body is whole. She sleeps. But her mind? We shall see."

Across the cavern, Narm looked down from Jhessail's arms at the softly breathing form. "Why does she not awake?" he moaned. "She's healed, the priest said. Why does she sleep?"

"Her mind heals itself," Elminster said from near at hand. "Do not disturb her. Be calm, Narm . . . a fine mage ye'll make, indeed, with all this weeping and shouting! Come away, and eat something and rest."

"I'm not hungry," Narm said sullenly, as Jhessail rose and pulled him up, her slim arms surprisingly strong.

"Oh, aye," Elminster said in obvious disbelief, handing him a sausage and producing a knife to saw at the hard piece of bread on his lap. Narm stared at the sausage and thought of Shandril and himself and sausages, and burst into laughter. Tears came again as he rocked helplessly back and forth.

"Stable fellow, isn't he?" Elminster inquired of the world at large. "Eat," he commanded, thrusting Narm's arm toward his mouth with a flick of his fingers and the quick saying of an unseen servant spell. The wood and string in the mage's hands melted away into nothingness, and suddenly Narm was sobbing on sausage, then eating ravenously. Elminster, shaking his head, used the spell to convey a flask from where it lay by Torm through the air to his own waiting hand. Torm discovered its theft, but snatched for it much too late.

Merith, who had been carefully examining the chamber with Florin, came over to Narm in his customary silence and touched the young mage's elbow. Narm surfaced from his sausage slowly. "Yes? Oh, sorry."

"No, lad. Don't be sorry," Merith told him. "If you would, point out to us where this mage your lady felled with the balhiir-globe and a rock lies now." The elf's eyes were serious and wary.

Narm blinked at him. "There, among the rocks." He pointed, but his hand moved uncertainly when he could not see Symgharyl Maruel's feet.

"Aye," Merith agreed soberly. "We thought so."

"She's gone?" Narm asked, astonished.

"She is nowhere in this chamber," Florin said quietly. "Not even among the bodies at the entrance."

"Then . . . where is she?" Narm asked, his mind still on Shandril and spellfire and sausages.

"I'm afraid," the battle-leader told him, "we'll find out soon enough."

*　*　*　*　*

Her jaw ached abominably. That little bitch had broken it, and her arm and probably her cheek, too. The cheek was so swollen that her left eye was almost shut. Symgharyl Maruel was still able to hiss spells and command words, though, and it would not be long before that wench would pay. Pay dearly, too; burn off her legs with the fire of Symgharyl Maruel's favorite wand, and then her arms, and then set to work with a knife. Oh, she'd whimper and plead—until her tongue was cut out. Symgharyl Maruel chuckled in her throat and winced at the stabbing pain this brought to her jaw. Gods spit upon the little whore!

Symgharyl Maruel found her feet wearily and unsteadily crossed the cave that was her refuge. Too unsteadily. Gods, the pain! She leaned wearily against the shelves which held her grimoires, arbatels, and librams. It was no use. She could not study art in this pain. Where were those thrice-damned potions?

The chest! Of course. She clawed her way along the shelves in frantic haste, fell upon her knees by the chest, and fumbled it open with her good arm. Careful, now; the right ones . . . She searched among the many vials for a certain rune. It would not do to make a mistake now. She'd never thought to need these, carefully gathered here so long ago. But if one plays with fire, she thought ruefully, one must expect to get burned. But a mere nothing of a girl, and with a rock! She snarled through the blood in her mouth and winced at the result. The pain! Would it never end? Never, indeed, if she didn't drink the potions! Gather your wits, Symgharyl Maruel—who knows but one of them might follow here. A spell-sealed cave, yes, but not to one with a tracer spell.

There! That one. And that one. Carefully she drew the precious vials out and, cradling them firmly against her breast, wormed her way across the floor to a heap of cushions where she was wont to lie and study. At last!

The liquid tasted clear and icy on her tongue, with a tang of iron and an odd, faint scent. Symgharyl Maruel lay back and felt the potion's gentle balm spreading down in a tingling, delicious, slow wave through her breast and shoulders and arms. The stabbing, sickening pain in her arm sank to a dull throbbing. Ah, good. Now the second one. Her long-ago mentor was a sentimental fool, but he knew a few tricks. It had been he who had insisted she cache these potions—potions not used until now.

Well, even if he came to Rauglothgor's lair and stood against her, he could save neither the little thief, nor the powerless lacklore of a dweomercraefter who had tried to protect her. There'd been another in the cavern—a druid, by his garb—when she had come to her senses, and the two of them gone, with the stench of burned flesh at the cave's mouth. Doubtless Rauglothgor had cooked some of the reckless adventurers who'd attacked him. Perhaps the wench was dead, too, but not likely. She'd interested Rauglothgor. Well, too bad, Symgharyl Maruel thought savagely. The dracolich could be interested in her corpse.

The pain was almost gone. She could think again, and plan. She rolled up from the cushions and found her feet, noting her torn robes as she did so. Breeches and boots, yes, and a half-cloak. She'd be dragonriding, if all went well. Wands, rings, and potions too. Adventurers were trouble unless you brought art enough to overmaster their every attack. They'd give her no second chance.

Symgharyl Maruel began the complicated ritual of passing the magical and monstrous guardians of her main cache of art. Blood would spill, indeed.

* * * * *

Far away, in a high cavern within a mountain, another dracolich sat upon much gold, and before it knelt three men in armor. Its voice was a vast hiss that held the echo of hammers upon metal and the whistle of high winds through great leathery wings. It regarded the men before it through eyes that glowed chilling white as they floated in dark eyesockets. Otherwise, it appeared as a gigantic blue dragon, vast and terrible, its scales gleaming in the guttering light of the torches the men had brought with them.

"'Treasure, yesss, good treasure," it said. "As alwaysss. But I can only play with treasure ssso much. Pile it here, pile it there . . . as with all, I grow bored. Bored beyond waiting. You never entertain me! What newsss in the world without?"

"A dracolich's lair is despoiled!" rang out a new voice. "The cult needs your great strength, O Aghazstamn!"

The dragon reared its spike-crested head with a great hiss. "Who comesss?" it enquired. Swords flashed as the cultists before it scrambled to their feet and turned to search out the intruder.

They had not far to look. Upon a coach of iron with chased gold and ivory panels, half-buried in a sea of gold coins, stood a woman in black and purple. She stood beautiful, proud, and alone, for all the world as if she had appeared there out of thin air. Of course, she had.

Nonetheless, the warriors of the Cult of the Dragon came toward her to slay, gold coins slithering under their feet. She raised a hand, and before them flashed the image of the dracolich Rauglothgor, its huge skeletal wings spread from wall to wall of the cavern. Aghazstamn hissed involuntarily, and spread its own wings with a mighty clap of air that scattered treasure like drops of rain and startled one warrior into a fall among the deeply sloped piles of coins. The image spoke in a deep, booming voice. "The Shadowsil, mage of the Cult of the Dragon, stands before you and would serve you. She seeks aid for one who is not used to asking for it; I, Rauglothgor, of the Thunder Peaks. I am beset by thieves, and they have loosed a balhiir that confounds my spells. Will you aid me? Half my hoard is yours, Aghazstamn, if you come speedily! Let the lady ride you. You can trust her." And then the image slowly faded away.

Symgharyl Maruel stood calmly silent, arms crossed upon her breast. Her art had shaped the image that her ring of dragons had called into being. She knew not how Rauglothgor would take losing half his treasure, nor did she care, so long as the wench died.

The cult warriors had halted, awed, at the image's speech, and now looked to the dracolich for direction, swords glittering in the torchlight. Aghazstamn's wings lowered slowly; its head sank, snakelike gaze remaining fixed upon the mage. "That wasss not real," it said finally, "and yet I know thee, sssmall and cruel one. You came to me before, not long ago. Did you not?"

"Aye, great Aghazstamn. I brought you treasure fourteen winters past. One of my first duties in the cult." Symgharyl Maruel's crossed hands both rested upon the ends of the wands she wore sheathed on her hips. Her eyes darted continuously from the warriors to the dracolich and back, but her voice and manner were relaxed and at ease. Symgharyl Maruel had come a long way to stand where she did in the cult and had risen far and fast; fear and timidity were luxuries she seldom had time for. She waited, now, because it was the best thing to do.

"Ssso." The dracolich put its great head to one side and regarded her, considering. It had been proud and great in life, and very curious. It had thought much on the intricacies of the art, and on death, and so had accepted the cult's offer to die and become undead.

Aghazstamn had accepted young and missed many years of high flying and dealing death upon lesser creatures, of battling other wyrms in the clear air, and of mating in roaring silence, gliding together in the chill upper air. It regretted the losses. Now here was a call to war. To leave its safe lair and its rich hoard, to face enemies . . . enemies, hah! Puny humans, even as these at its feet were, waving their tiny steel fangs and making much outcry and commotion. To ride the high winds again, to see the lands spread out below, feel the cold bite of the air about as lesser creatures fled in terror, far below . . .

"Kneel to me, Ssshadowsil, and pledge to turn not against me nor aid Rauglothgor in altering the ssstated bargain. Do that, and I will accept."

Symgharyl Maruel knelt among the coins, on the ornate top of a coach that had once carried young princes of Cormyr to hunt in the high country, before some forgotten wyrm had seized it, horses, royal blood, and all, and flown off. Hiding her smile in a low bow over the coins, she was rewarded by the great voice sounding again. "Mount, then. Warriorsss of the cult! Attend! Guard well my hoard in my absssence, and let not one coin be missssing when I return, nor any of you gone, or all will answer for it! Bow and pledge your obedience in thisss!"

The cult warriors, with frightened looks at Symgharyl Maruel, did so, and she wasted a flight spell in bravado (or rather, she told herself, began it a little early; she intended to have its protection about her when on Aghazstamn's back, in case of a fall in aerial battle or treachery on the part of the great dracolich). She flew past them, skimming over the heaped coins, trade-bars, gems, and inlaid armor to reach Aghazstamn. She paused before the dracolich's broad head and bowed again, eyes lowered—for it is not safe to meet the wise old eyes of a dragon, even if one is a great mage. Even less safe is it to peer into the awful floating, flickering orbs of a dracolich. She flew slowly up and around in a smooth arc to settle lightly upon a bone of its spine, between the wings.

"My thanks, great one," Symgharyl Maruel said, as she drew gauntlets from her belt, settled the wands on her thighs for rapid drawing, and nestled herself in behind a fin she could grasp once her gloves were on.

"Nay, little one," came the hissing reply. "My thanksss." The great wings gathered above them as the dracolich leaped upward in a great bound into the darkness. The shaft from its lair twisted and bent back upon itself to entrap and discourage flying intruders, but Aghazstamn knew it well. The great wings beat twice, precisely in the rare spaces where they could spread. Suddenly there was daylight, and they burst out into it in a great roaring glide that curved up and became a climb. The great dracolich let out a roar that echoed back from the surrounding peaks, and it wheeled out over the Desertsedge and back again through the Desertsmouth Mountains, where of old had been the realm of Anauria before the Great Sand Sea swept its greatness away, and gained the name Anauroch.

"Where is thisss lair we ssseek? In the Thunder Peaksss?" the great voice hissed back at Symgharyl Maruel. She did not try to shout into the wind ripping past her ears, but used instead her cult ring to speak to Aghazstamn's mind: Yes, great one. On the eastern flanks of the range, above Lake Sember.

"Ah, yesss! Fried Elf Water! I know it."

The Shadowsil winced but managed to stifle her giggle. 'Fried Elf Water'? No doubt. And there had been an elf among the adventurers who had attacked when she'd been questioning the wench before Rauglothgor. Well, who knows what the future holds and the gods see?

Upon the back of the mighty blue dracolich, she rode back toward the lair of Rauglothgor, to deal death upon them all. Die, all, and let The Shadowsil rise up on your bones!

She did not realize she had cried that aloud until she heard Aghazstamn chuckle.

❧ 8 ❧

Much Mayhem

A woman, or a man, may come to hold many treasures in life. Gold, gems, a good name, lovers, good friends, influence, high rank—all of these are of value. All of these most covet. But of them all the most valuable, I tell ye, are friends good and true. Have these, and ye will scarce notice the lack if ye never win aught else.

The adventuress Sharanralee
Ballads And Lore of One Dusty Road
Year of the Wandering Maiden

"Treasure! Aye, treasure for all, and to spare!" Rathan's voice rolled heartily out over the newly daylit crater where many of the knights stooped and gathered treasure. "More even then ye can carry, Torm Greedyfingers!"

"Hah," came Torm's reply from beneath a pile of rubble. "Change your tone, faithful of Tymora?" The thief rose up in his dusty gray, and in his hands was a gleaming disc of polished electrum. Six handwidths across.

"For love of the Lady!" Rathan gasped delightedly. "Good Torm, may I h—"

" 'Good Torm,' now, is it?" the thief answered mockingly. "Good Torm Greedyfingers, perhaps?"

"Shut your yapping maw, Good Torm Greedyfingers," Merith said from behind him. "Or else some good dale farmer will mistake thee for a nimble shrew and marry you."

"Some nimble dale shrew did marry you," Torm told him in return, "and look whaaa—!" His words ended in the roar of a crock full of gold coins being dumped over his head.

Narm watched in amazement as the air suddenly filled with small pieces of treasure, as it was pitched about from knight to knight with enthusiasm. "They're like children!" he exclaimed at last in astonishment.

"Sir Evoker," Jhessail said to him with a gentle smile, "they are children."

"But they are the famous Knights of Myth Drannor!" Narm protested mildly, matching her smile.

"We are all in the hands of children," she answered. "Who else would ride into danger with enthusiasm and swing swords against fearsome enemies far from home and saner pursuits?"

"And yet you are a knight," Narm pointed out. The lady mage spread empty hands.

"Did I say I was not a child?" she answered mildly. "Dear me." She rose in a shifting of skirts and threw a set of knuckle-claws of wrought brass set with small carbuncles hard and accurately at Torm's back. She favored Narm with an impish grin as she sat down demurely and turned to check Shandril. Behind them both, Elminster chuckled, as Torm let out a roar of pain and spun about, seeking his foe.

Amid the tumult, Narm's lady lay motionless, eyes still closed, breathing shallowly. She looked peaceful and young and very beautiful, and Narm's heart ached anew. "Will she—?" he asked helplessly. Jhessail patted his arm.

"It's in the hands of the gods," she said simply. "We will do all we can." Elminster nodded and took the pipe out of his mouth. Coils of greenish smoke and small sparks continued to drift from its bowl.

"She held and handled more power than I have ever seen come out of a balhiir," the old sage said. "More, I think, than this creature had in it." Jhessail and Narm both turned to stare at him in surprise.

"What, then?" Jhessail asked, but Elminster shook her question aside with his head.

"Too soon," he told them both. "Too soon for aught but idle chatter . . . and idle chatter will help no one and could well upset our young friend."

Narm fixed eyes upon him and said, "With all respect,

Lord Elminster, I am upset already. What do you fear?"

But Elminster was lost in chuckles. "I fear most, boy, being called 'Lord Elminster.' Now grip thy temper and thy grief and master them. There are good reasons not to talk on this now. If it makes ye feel better, I am amazed and awed at what thy Shandril has done."

"Oh?" Narm urged him on, trying to speak calmly.

"Aye. The most common way to destroy a balhiir requires at least three mages, and at best, five or more. They must hold the balhiir between them by force of art, opposing their telekinesis to offset its wild movements and struggles. They then tear it apart, each absorbing what he or she can of it. It is a spectacular process to watch—and," he added dryly, "it kills a lot of mages."

"Yet you sent Shandril alone up against the thing?" Narm protested, his frustration changing suddenly to rage. Elminster's gently sad gaze stilled his tongue against further, more bitter comments.

"I had not five mages," the sage said simply. "We still faced a dracolich and could not turn away from that even if we wanted, lest we and all our friends perish. If ye had tried to stand as one of those mages, Narm, ye would be dead now. Hold thy peace, I bid thee, for thy lady's sake. High words will not help her now."

"Are you always right?" Narm asked, but his tone was weary, not angry. "Is the good and true way always so clear before you?"

Jhessail shook her head warningly, but Elminster was chuckling again.

"Ah, slay me, but thy tongue is as sharp and as busy as Torm's!" The mage sucked upon his pipe once and turned within the smoky haze it produced to regard Narm gravely. "In tavern-tales the hero is always high and shining and his foes dark and dastardly," Elminster said with a smile. "It would be simpler if life were like that, each one knowing if he were good or evil, and what each should do and could expect to achieve before his part in the Great Play ends. But think on how boring it would be to the gods—everyone a known force, events and deeds preordained or at the least easily predictable—and so things are not so.

"We are here to amuse and entertain the gods, who walk among us. They watch and enjoy and sometimes even thrust a hand or quiet words into daily life, just to see the result. From this comes miracles, disasters, religious strife, and much else we could do without."

Narm met his eyes for the space of a breath and then nodded soberly. "You do think and care, then. I had feared you swaggered about serenely blasting with your art all who opposed you."

"That's just what he does do." Torm's voice broke in as he approached, arms full of gold. "Wizards! Wherever one sees battle in this world, there's some fool of a dweomercraefter jabbering and waving his hands. Honest swordswingers fall doomed—slain by a man who would be too craven to stand an instant against them, could they but reach him! Less art about would please me well! Then the brave and strong would rule, not sneaking old graybeards and reckless young fools who play for sport with the forces that give light and life to us all!"

"Aye," said Elminster with a smile. "But rule what? A battlefield covered shoulder-deep with the rotting dead, the survivors dying of hunger and disease. There would be none left to help the sick, or to harvest, or sow seeds. It is a grand king, indeed, who rules a graveyard." He drew on his pipe. "Besides, 'tis no good complaining about what is and cannot be changed. Art we have. Make the best of it."

"Oh, I intend to," Torm replied with a wolfish grin.

"Are you finished, Torm?" Jhessail asked sweetly. "Or have you something else upon your tongue that needs spewing forth?"

"Yes," replied the thief, irrepressibly. "Look you, old—"

"Enough talk!" Florin snapped from behind them. "Heads around, all! A dragon comes!"

* * * * *

"They sssee usss, little one!" the great voice boomed back at her. "Why ssso amazed?"

From the dracolich's back, Symgharyl Maruel gazed upon the blasted mountaintop in shock. The keep! she thought wildly at Aghazstamn. Gone! The whole peak has been shattered and thrown down! We must turn away! We cannot face power enough to do that! She shook her head in disbelief, but the vast crater below remained, as the dracolich wheeled about it.

"Flee? Nay!" its voice roared at her, and the great neck arched around, nearly tumbling the Shadowsil off. She clung to the bony fin before her grimly and shouted aloud, "But the entire top of the mountain is *gone*! We cannot prevail against—"

"Ssseee to your wandsss, little coward! I fly free, to fight and ssslay after all these yearsss! And you want me to turn tail and abandon the gold and thisss challenge? Think again, weaver of weak art!" Aghazstamn roared and wheeled wide, climbing so as to turn and dive.

As the wind ripped around her ears, Maruel drew forth a wand and held it firmly across her breast. Peering down, she could see one in armor, an elf, and others below. There was no sign of Rauglothgor. Perhaps the old terror had destroyed himself somehow and wrought all this devastation. This handful of dare-alls looked incapable of such destruction.

Well, what did it matter? Slay, and wonder later. Aghazstamn had already turned and was plummeting down, ever faster, the wind beginning to whistle past her ears. The Shadowsil bent low and narrowed her eyes to slits so as not to be blinded. Carefully she aimed at the hastily scattering warriors below, and said clearly, "*Maerzae!*" And fire blossomed from the wand in a tiny ball that spun away, trailing sparks, to burst with a roar in orange-red flames below.

One man was hurled into the air, blazing, and fell among the rocks. Others were thrown too, but she could not see their fates. Already she was aiming again coolly at those below. Such battles were never as tales had them; mages trading spells formally, one after the other. He who struck first and hardest usually prevailed.

The wind whistled around her as Aghazstamn roared in triumph as it plummeted out of the sky, wings drawn up and bent back over its vast scaled bulk. From its maw, lightning spat in a long, blue-white bolt that crackled to the ground. A tiny figure jerked and staggered, outlined briefly in the blue-white fire. The Shadowsil unleashed her second fireball at two in robes who still stood on the right.

It blossomed into flames before it reached them, however, spreading out against some sort of invisible wall. Symgharyl Maruel hissed in anger as the dracolich beneath her swept down. Fast, indeed, by Mystra! Still, they couldn't strike back at her without sacrificing that wall. . . .

With a roar and a clap of its mighty wings, Aghazstamn levelled off just short of the tumbled rock where its victims scrambled and shouted. It swooped low, reaching with long cruel claws for two who stood with swords raised like tiny needles against it.

Symgharyl Maruel felt the jolt as the dracolich struck and then clapped its wings to rise in haste from the rocks where sharp steel slashed and thrust at it. The mage looked back over her shoulder in time to lock eyes with the druid who had been lying wounded in the cave earlier. His hands and lips were moving, coolly calling a spell down upon her.

Before she could do anything, Aghazstamn was turning away and rising. The Shadowsil slid the wand back into its sheath as they rose and turned to look back, tossing her hair out of her eyes. Steady, I pray you, Great One, she thought through her ring. I would cast a spell and need a breath or two of stable flight from you. A thunderous snort was her reply, but Aghazstamn spread its vast wings spread out a level glide and the roaring winds lessened.

Symgharyl Maruel rose up as far as she dared and turned to face the knights. Below, the two swordsmen still stood; the tall one in armor and the elf. Bodies lay sprawled among the rocks, but the two mages in robes still stood beyond. Well, they might escape, but all of their comrades would perish. Carefully Symgharyl Maruel cast a meteor swarm down upon them all.

Done, she told the dracolich in satisfaction as she sat down and watched eight balls of flame roll forth. Aghazstamn hissed acknowledgement, and the great wings began to beat again. The sudden heat and rolling, roaring sound warned Symgharyl to reach for her wand.

Involuntarily she turned to see, just as the air exploded in flames. Somehow those below had turned her great spell against her. Only one mistake . . .

* * * * *

"See to Rathan," said Elminster. "And Torm, too. Here! Hurry!" From under his robes he drew two metal vials and thrust them into Jhessail's hands.

"But, master," she protested. "The dragon! Wha—"

"I can yet speak spells," the old mage told her with some severity. "Now go." His eyes remained on the blackened body of the wyrm that had begun to fall from above, trailing flames. Odd, that a single such spell could slay so quickly. Dragons usually died slowly and noisily, with much—unless this was no dragon, but—

"Another dracolich!" the old mage said aloud. Narm turned anxious eyes upon him.

"What now?" the young apprentice asked. Elminster turned a hawkish eye upon him.

"Go and help Jhessail," he commanded. "There is nothing ye can safely do here." His eyes were on the dracolich again, the great wings rolling it over and over as it fell. On its back he could see The Shadowsil, struggling weakly. He almost lifted his hands to pluck her away with telekinesis, but she bore a wand ready in one hand. Even as he considered it, he knew it would be too late to save her. The sage watched expressionlessly as Aghazstamn crashed to earth.

The dracolich's body struck head and neck first, with a horrible splintering sound. It rolled forward onto one shoulder, and over until the great back crashed to the ground. It rolled, once, spilling the slim figure of The Shadowsil from its back, and halted in a smoking heap against a broken rock where Shandril's blasting had ended.

"Get her!" Lanseril shouted from behind him. Before Elminster could speak Florin and Merith had leaped past him, blades flashing. The elf's armor was torn and twisted crazily at one shoulder where a dragon claw had earlier caught it. Had not Merith jumped desperately upward into its closing grip to strike with his blade, the body below the armor would have been torn apart as well.

Elminster knew they could not hear him. He hissed words hastily, exerted his will, then vanished.

Florin could see The Shadowsil, struggling feebly on one elbow to roll herself over. The wand was still in her hand. She was snarling through the long hair. He raised his sword as he ran, in desperate haste. He did not hold with slaying women, but this foe could be the death of them all, were he not fast enough. Merith crashed along behind him, slipping and staggering among the scattered rocks and treasure.

Suddenly Elminster was before them, barring their path. "Stay back!" he commanded. "No more butchery is necessary." Wildly waving their swords, they skidded to a halt only feet from the old mage. They cast quick glances back to ensure that this was not some illusion of their enemy's. "Put the steel away," the old mage said wearily and went to his knees beside Symgharyl Maruel. "The time for all that is past." As he spoke, she collapsed on her face with a groan, the wand clattering away on the rocks.

Gently he took the broken body under the shoulders and turned it until The Shadowsil lay face-up in his lap. Florin and Merith watched in astonishment, the elf's blade still wavering uneasily in his hand.

Florin drew off his gauntlets as he squatted, facing Elminster across the body of the foe who had sought to slay them all but a breath or two ago. "Elminster," he asked gravely, "what are you about?"

Symgharyl Maruel opened her eyes at the sound of Florin's voice and stared dully up at them, as one who has traveled a very long way. She spat blood weakly, and her eyes found Elminster. "Master," she hissed, blood bubbling horribly in her throat. "I—hurt." The last word was almost a sob.

"Little flower," Elminster whispered gently as she drew a shuddering breath, "I am here." At his words, she coughed blood and began to cry weakly, the tears running down her cheeks as the knights gathered about in astonished silence. "If ye lie quiet," the sage murmured, "I shall see if I can find art enough yet in my tower to heal thee." He clasped her hand gently and began to slide out from beneath her. One feeble hand plucked at his sleeve, and the mage the knights had all hated or feared mastered her tears.

"No," she told him firmly, eyes burning upon his, "promise me you shall not bring me back . . . I am too set to change now. I cannot learn this 'good' you stand for." The Shadowsil's eyes closed; her head fell back wearily. Then her eyes flickered. "Promise," she hissed, hands trembling on his.

"Aye, Symgharyl Maruel, I promise thee," Elminster told her gravely, stroking her shoulder almost absently with one old hand. Symgharyl Maruel smiled.

"Good, then," she said, voice trailing away. "'Ware my belt . . . it has a poisoned buckle. One more thing," she added, voice a hissing ruin now. Elminster leaned close to the bloody lips to hear, and the failing hands gripped his robes until they grew as white as The Shadowsil's face.

The mage raised herself, her body shaking with the effort. Dark eyes shone defiantly once at them all, and then her head reached Elminster's shoulder. She clung there, shaking like a leaf in a gale, and then leaned forward to kiss his cheek, softly and yet fiercely. "I love you. I wish I could have had you." And The Shadowsil turned her head against his chest, smiled, then died.

There was silence for the space of many breaths while the old mage sat motionless, cradling the still body in his arms. The slim hands loosened their hold on him, but Elminster held her. No one moved or spoke. All stood waiting. From Elminster there came no sound.

After a time, the sage looked up, laid his burden gently upon the stones beneath, and slowly rose to his foot. Symgharyl Maruel's bone-white face was still smiling, but it was wet with the old man's tears. Elminster stepped back and waved the knights and Narm away from him, gesturing at them to draw far back. He then started to sing. The old mage's voice began scratchy and hollow from disuse, but gained in strength as he sang the leavetaking, until the last lines rolled out deep and clear.

> *The sun comes up and the sun goes down*
> *Winters pass swiftly and leaves turn brown*
> *Watching each day and at last it has found*
> *Another dream to lay under the ground*
>
> *Another name lost to the wind*
> *Wailing away north past ears of flind*
> *And all she has been crumbles away*

Of all that great spirit, can nothing stay?

Mystra, Mother, take your own
Skill and power now dust on bone
Good or bad, what matters now?
Her song is done, her last bow

Mother of art, I pray now to thee,
Take back her truename in mercy
And as her body is lost to flame
Greet your own Lansharra again.

Elminster's hands moved, he spoke a few quiet words, and fire burst from his hands to strike the still form of The Shadowsil. Flames burst straight upward in a many-hued pillar. Narm watched the old man, who stood staring into the greedy flames. Hesitantly, the evoker approached. When he stood behind Elminster's shoulder, he spoke.

"She called you 'Master.'" The flames roared and crackled before them.

"Aye," said Elminster. He smiled slowly, and there were tears in his eyes again. He turned and looked out over the waters of the Sember, far below, but he didn't see them. He saw things long ago and in another place.

"You knew her?" Narm asked quietly.

"I once trained her and rode with her." The mage's lips moved roughly, almost reluctantly. Then his white beard jutted defiantly. "I was much younger then."

Narm felt a rush of sympathy and turned to look at Shandril, lying so still upon his cloak. His heart nearly broke. "Does one often see friends die if one is a mage of power?"

"Aye," Elminster replied, almost whispering. Then he seemed to rouse himself and caught Narm's eye in a gruff, more familiar look. "That is why even one's enemies are to be honored. If it falls within thy power, no creature must die alone."

Narm stared at him for a long breath, lips white, and then nodded slowly. Then he rushed forward and caught the old wizard in a fierce embrace, and tears came. A startled Elminster held him awkwardly and patted his head and said gruffly, "There, there, boy. Shandril lives. It's not so bad as all that." The sobs under the young apprentice's encircling arms died slowly and the strong young grip lessened. The muffled voice, when it came, was hesitant.

"Lansharra . . . did you love her very much?"

"Yes," the sage said simply. "She was like a daughter. Had I been several lifetimes younger and she not quite so quick to cruelty . . ." His voice trailed away and, abruptly, he spun about and stood facing the dying pyre. His voice rolled out, rich and imperious. "Look all of ye!"

He raised his hands and gestured. It seemed that above the thinning smoke that rose there a form came slowly into being— the form of a young and slim woman, with long glossy hair and almost chalk-white skin. She was very beautiful and wore a simple robe of white and gold bound with a blue sash. She looked around at them with joy and wonder.

All the hardened veterans of the knights stood and watched in silence, the flames flickering in ruddy reflections upon their armor and ready swords.

In utter silence the image of a youthful Symgharyl Maruel worked a bluefinger cantrip before them all. When the blue radiance sparkled into being at her fingertips, she laughed in sheer delight and held it up in one hand to show it. She then tossed her hair back to see it the better, waved at them, and was gone. Elminster stood looking into the last of the flames, his old face expressionless.

"You did that, did you not?" Torm asked, awed. "That wasn't . . . her."

"Aye, I did it, though not alone, and aye, it was her. So she was one summer before any of ye here but Merith was born. Her spirit lingered. I shaped an illusion, and she came into it to bid me—all of you—good-bye." The mage turned to Rathan. "Thy holy water, good brother?"

Rathan nodded and stepped forward, unclasping a flask from his belt reverently. A scorched smell from The Shadowsil's fireball hung about his clothing and he moved with the careful stiffness of the newly healed. At the mage's gesture, the flames of the pyre sank and died, and Rathan doused the charred bones from head to foot. Gray smoke rose and slowly drifted away.

Then Elminster removed his cloak, and Florin and Lanseril stepped forward to lay the bones upon it as soon as they were cool. Jhessail joined her voice with the old mage's in a prayer to Mystra. When it was done, Elminster caught his cloak up in a bundle and said, "All well, friends? Rathan? Torm? Ye took it the worst, if memory serves."

"Well enough," the cleric replied, and Torm agreed with a terse, "Yes." Elminster nodded.

"Well, get thy treasure and let us see to Shandril. I would be gone from here as soon as she can safely travel—wyrms who are not as dead as they should be seem to have a distressing habit of showing up here to visit." With that, the old mage rose with his bundle and went over to Shandril, puffing on his pipe thoughtfully. "I wonder just who shall call upon us next?" he said aloud, looked down at the bundle he bore, and shook his head suddenly.

*　*　*　*　*

Outside, the afternoon sun was bright upon the towers and parapets of Zhentil Keep. Within the Tower High of Manshoon, lord of that city, all was dark save for a circle of glass-globed candles in a corner of the high-paneled feasting hall. No grand company had feasted there for twenty winters.

Beneath the tinted, flickering light was a small circular table and about it the high lords of the Keep sat in council. Lord Kalthas, general of the armies of Zhentil Keep north of the Moonsea, spoke at ease, purring from beneath his sandy moustache, flagon of amber wine comfortably by his hand.

"Defending the empty wastes of Thar is not the problem," he said smugly, "now that the lich Arkhigoul is no more. The Citadel is strong, and I see no need to weaken our forces by placing small garrisons here and there on various frozen rocks in the east. If something comes over the mountains from Vaasa, let it come. We can move in strength when any such foe has committed itself to a long journey and a particular target, and crush any invasion at our leisure. The riders of Melvaunt can slow down any major assault long enough for us to muster patrols in from all Daggerdale and the Teshen lands. Why defend a week's cold ride of barren rocks and snow? Any fool . . ." The deep boom of a bell echoed somewhere in the darkness above them.

There was a sudden squeal of wood as the dark-robed figure of Manshoon, first Lord of the Keep, who had been sitting in languid boredom on one side of the table, rose suddenly. Table, papers, ink and quills, crystal decanters, and ornate metal flagons all crashed together to the floor. More than one noble lord, chair and all, went to the flagstones with them.

"My Lord!" gasped Lord Kalthas in protest, wiping wine from his fur-trimmed doublet. His words fell into tense silence and died away as their speaker realized his peril. "What means this?"

But Manshoon was not even looking at him. White-faced, he stared into the air, his voice quavered. "Symgharyl Maruel," he whispered, blinking away a tear. Lord Chess gasped aloud; more prudent nobles gaped in silence. None had ever before seen Manshoon cry or show any sign of weakness (or as one lord had once put it, "humanity").

Then the moment passed, and a coldly furious Manshoon snapped, "*Zellathorass!*" At his command, a globe of crystal swooped into view on the stairs, danced sideways in the air like a questing bat, and darted over to spin in the air before him. Manshoon seized it and peered into its depths, where a light kindled and grew.

He was silent for a moment, and his handsome face grew as cold and hard as drawn steel as he saw something that the other lords could only guess at. Then he released the globe, which began to spin slowly, said "*Alvathair*" softly, and watched it vanish back the way it had come. His mouth tightened.

He turned to face them all. "Sirs," he said curtly, "this meeting is at an end. For your safety, leave at once." He crooked a finger, and horribly grinning gargoyles, hitherto motionless on stone buttresses overhead, flexed their slate-gray wings. The high lords of Zhentil Keep hastened to find their feet, and then their cloaks and swords and plumed hats, babbled and stammered their thanks and good-byes all together, and found the exit with comical haste. A patient golem closed the door they left standing open.

Manshoon then spoke to the gargoyles in a harsh hissing

and croaking tongue, and they began to glide about the tower on their leathery wings, watching in terrible silence for intruders. Their lord stood in the dark hall and spoke. The candles sank and died. They had scarce guttered into acrid smoke before he spoke again, and at his words this time a stone golem as tall as six men strode ponderously toward him from one corner of the hall. It waited there in the darkness to greet any visitors foolish enough to enter unannounced in his absence. Manshoon looked about and then raced up the stairs in the darkness. His ragged shout of rage and loss echoed back down the stairs behind him. "Shadowsil!"

As he stepped out into the chill air atop the Tower High, he spoke a certain word. There came a stirring, and part of the tower beneath him moved. A great bulge of stone shifted and humped. Vast wings opened out over the courtyard of the tower and the minarets of the walls. A great neck arched out and glimmering eyes regarded Manshoon with eagerness and quickening interest, and fear.

The massive bulk rose up the tower wall as huge claws caught and pulled. Somewhere a stone broke loose and clattered, unseen, far below. Then the wings beat in a lazy clap that echoed back from the rooftops of the city. Frightened faces appeared in the windows of temple spires and noblemen's towers, and vanished again in haste. Manshoon smiled without mirth at the sight and coldly locked eyes with the huge black dragon he had freed. Cold eyes looked back at him.

Few men, indeed, can retain sanity and will in the face of the full gaze of a dragon. The wyrm regarded him with vast age, and knowledge, and amusement. Manshoon merely smiled and held its eyes with his own deep gaze. The fear in the dragon's eyes grew. Then Manshoon hissed in the tongue of black dragons, "Up, Orlgaun. I have need of you." The great neck arched over the parapet for him to mount.

With a bound and flurry of beating wings the black dragon soared aloft from the city of cold stone and ready swords. Manshoon came with fire and fury to destroy the slayer of his beloved. Many have done so before, in more worlds than Faerun, and will again in days to come.

❦ 9 ❦

The Battle Ne'er Done

The worst trouble with most mages is that they think they can change the world. The worst mistake the gods make is to let a few of them get away with it.

Nelve Harssad of Tsurlagol
My Journeys Around the Sea of Fallen Stars
Year of the Sword and Stars

"I wonder," Torm said slowly, coins of silver and gold clattering through his fingers, "just how long this bone dragon had been gathering this stuff." He looked across a glittering sea of gleaming metal.

"Ask Elminster," Rathan said. "He probably recalls the day of Rauglothgor's arrival, what—or who—he ate at the time, and all." The cleric was methodically scrutinizing handfuls of coins, plucking out only the platinum pieces, and adding them to an already bulging purse. Nearby, Merith was shifting coins carefully with his feet, looking for more unusual treasure amid the coinage.

"Is this what we go through all the blood and battle for?" Jhessail said, coming up to him with her hands full of sparkling gems.

"Yes. Depressing, isn't it?" Lanseril replied from where he knelt with Narm beside Shandril. The onetime thief of the Company of the Bright Spear lay still and white, for all the world as if dead. Elminster puffed on his pipe thoughtfully as he stood looking down at her, but he said nothing.

Lanseril gave Narm a shove. "Enough brooding, mage. Get up and find some gems and platinum coins and the like

❦ 145 ❦

while it's still lying about for the taking." At Narm's dark look, he said more gently, "Go on. We'll watch her, never fear. You'll need the gold, you know, if you plan to learn enough art to see you both past all the enemies you've made these past days."

Narm looked at him again, doubtfully. Thoughtful eyes met for a time. The young man nodded slowly. "You may be right. But . . . Shandril . . ." He looked at her helplessly again. The druid laid a hand on his arm.

"I know it's hard. You do the best for her, and for yourself, though, if you get up and go on with your duties. The plans of gods and men unfold even while you sleep, as the saying goes. You can do nothing for Shandril sitting here. Go, lad, and play among the coins. You'll see few enough of them before you die, as it is." Lanseril pushed him again. "I'll keep your spot warm, here by her shoulder. I even promise to call you if she should awaken and want to kiss someone, or the like." He grinned at Narm's expression. "Go on."

Narm rose on painfully stiff legs and looked down at Shandril again for a moment. He traded quick glances with Lanseril and Elminster, nodded wordlessly, and hurried away. Lanseril sighed. "These younglings . . . their love burns so." He looked up suddenly as he realized Elminster was grinning at him.

"Aye, indeed, old one," the mage said gravely, leaning on his staff. The two friends looked at each other for a moment in silence and then spoke as one, the druid who had not yet seen thirty winters and the mage who had seen some five hundred.

"Well, when you get to be my age," they quoted the old saying together and broke into chuckles. Around them the knights were striding back and forth with small, clinking bundles, gathering Rauglothgor's hoard at a great rate. They could see Narm in the distance, peering curiously at a ruby in his palm. A fistful of gold coins was beginning to creep between the fingers of his other hand.

"Not much magic—damnation upon that balhiir," Torm said to Jhessail, a dozen brass rings spilling from his hand as he brought them within range of her detect magic spell. They did not glow with the radiance that betokens magic.

Jhessail spread her hands. "It is the way of balhiirs," she said simply. Then she smiled, eyes twinkling. "Poor Torm," she said in mock sorrow and commiseration. "You'll have to settle for mere gold, gems, and platinum . . . and so little, too!" She waved at the scattered riches that lay all around the knights.

Torm grinned. "Scant compensation, good lady," he said in courtly tones, "for the discomfort and danger attendant upon almost my every breath, these days. What good are coins to a dead man?"

"Precisely the thought that prevents most sane beings from taking up thievery," Jhessail replied mildly. Torm chuckled and bowed to her in acknowledgement of a point well made.

Lanseril looked beyond them to the broken ridge of rock that marked the edge of the devastation Shandril's spellfire had wrought. Florin stood there, watchful, bearing a special shield Elminster had brought back with the healing potions. The ranger's blade was in his hands. He was silent and alert, eyes flicking here and there over the cold gray peaks above and the tree-clad land below.

Elminster, too, was silent and intent, but his eyes were upon Shandril. Even as Lanseril looked down at her, she moved slightly and frowned, murmuring something so faint they could not hear it. Lanseril leaned forward to reach for her, and the long, knobbly end of Elminster's staff came down before him, warningly. The druid looked up its length at he who bore it and asked, "Do we tell Narm?"

Elminster smiled. "No need." A crashing noise, growing swiftly louder, heralded Narm's progress through the coins toward them. "Shandril!" he cried, and then met their gently silent gazes. "Is she—"

"She stirs, no more," said the sage. "If ye must shake her, do it gently, and only once or twice."

Narm threw him a frightened look and then fell to his knees beside his chosen's unmoving form, scattering coins in all directions. "Shandril!" he pleaded at her ear, laying a timid hand upon her shoulder. "Shandril! Can you hear?" He shook her gently. Beneath his hand, his lady moaned and moved one hand. "Shandril!" he said with sudden urgency, and shook her. "Sh—" and he broke off as Elminster's staff tapped him firmly on the shoulder.

"And how is she to heal her wits if ye awaken her with shakings and other such violence?" the sage asked gently. "Leave be for a time, and see how she does on her own." Lanseril nodded, but it was Elminster's face Narm was staring up at, throat tight and eyes very full, when Florin shouted. Elminster's head snapped up, his eyes lighting like lamps as he looked to where the ranger's blade pointed. "'Ware, all!" came Florin's voice, and all about them knights drew weapons, and looked.

Far off in the sky to the north a dark winged shape moved, drawing nearer. It was large and serpentine.

"Dragon!" Florin and Elminster said together, and the knights began to move.

"Gods' laughter," Torm muttered as he ran past, jingling and bulging with loot, "will this never end?" The adventurers scattered, seeking the cover of the larger boulders. Merith and Florin arrived on the run to where Narm and Lanseril sat by Shandril. Elminster stood over them, apparently unconcerned but watching the sky. Then he put his staff in the crook of his arm and quietly began to work a spell.

Narm looked up to him for guidance, but it was Florin who spoke. "We must move your lady," he said, and jerked his head toward a spur of rock far off to the right. "There, I hold that place best for protection. Stay with her there, unless you have spells up sleeves and down boots that we don't know about." His tone, for all its gentleness, was a command, and Narm made no protest as they gently lifted Shandril together and bore her in stumbling haste across the scattered rock and treasure.

Jhessail and Elminster were both casting spells. Rathan was quaffing hastily from a skin Torm was holding. The cleric held his mace ready in his hand.

"This is not a good time for us to fight a dragon," Narm said in helpless frustration, as they laid Shandril down gently in the lee of the rocks.

"Lad," Florin told him with rare humor, "it's never a good time to fight a dragon." The knights turned away from the young spellcaster quickly, Lanseril squeezing his shoulder for a moment, and were gone across the open rubble-pit, weapons flashing as they were drawn. A faint belch echoed in their wake. Torm turned once to wave and grin as the dragon roared down upon them.

Orlgaun came down out of the chilly heights in a long glide, great black wings spread stiffly. Upon its back, Lord Manshoon waved his hands and spoke grim words of magic. Eight balls of fire sprang from his fingertips, flashing past Orlgaun's black neck like shafts from a bow, trailing flame. Down they sizzled. Orlgaun arched its giant wings like sails to slow its dive.

There was a flash and a ground-shaking roar as the balls of flame exploded. Fire leaped briefly toward the sky. In the inferno Manshoon saw shapes staggering, yet standing against him. He drew a wand from his belt even as Orlgaun eagerly lowered its neck and spat blue-green acid. The spray sizzled as it struck dying flames and still-hot rocks. Orlgaun hissed triumphantly as one of his enemies fell. The dragon was turning and climbing steeply as the cold gray flank of one of the Thunder Peaks rushed up to meet it.

The great wings beat once, twice, and then there was a sudden, sickening shudder beneath Manshoon. The vast body faltered and twisted. Manshoon grabbed at a razor-sharp bony fin on the wyrm's neck to keep his seat and yelled, juggling the wand for a few anxious moments. Orlgaun convulsed again, and sheered off sideways in the air with breath-robbing speed, revealing their foe.

In the air behind them flew a human in full coat-of-plate, shield up before him, long naked sword reaching again toward Orlgaun. Manshoon snarled and blasted the fool with his wand. Magic missiles pelted the twisting man like a sudden rain, and he fell away as they swept on.

Manshoon hissed a curse into the wind as he felt Orlgaun's wingbeats come more slowly, and heard the joyous battle-roars of the great dragon no more. His wyrm was hurt already, and these people looked to be tougher than he had thought. He was readying a lightning bolt as Orlgaun swept around once more and he saw the old bearded man standing, alone now, on the rocks below. Beyond him there was a maiden in robes. Manshoon dismissed her as nothing as he bent his gaze on the bearded one and cast his bolt.

Lightning seared the air in its crackling descent, white and writhing. It turned aside mere feet in front of the old man and crawled harmlessly away, as if it had struck something unseen. The old man looked up calmly as he cast a spell of his own, and Manshoon recognized him with a shock: Elminster of Shadowdale. The old mage was not off on some other plane meddling, or fussing scatter-brained among scrolls and librams dusty and brittle with age, but here and alert and looking completely unafraid. Of Symgharyl Maruel there was no sign. Manshoon snarled, a little unsettled, and reached for another wand. Orlgaun would not stoop as low as last time; the great wings were lifting them already.

Then a great hand loomed in the air before Manshoon, and before he could even groan, Orlgaun's flight had swept him into it with stunning speed. The clap of their meeting was thunderous.

A broken wand and a dagger spun down out of the air as the dragon screamed shrilly and thundered past above them. Merith turned in the wind of its passing and said, "Now!" almost laughing, as he disspelled the protective barriers about the mage. Jhessail nodded, lifted a wand of her own, and breathed its word of command gently over it, her eyes on the mage. Magic missiles hissed forth, twisting and turning in the air to follow the slumped mage clinging to the back of the great black dragon. The huge disembodied fist hung in the air by his shoulder and moved with him. Elminster followed it with his eyes and frowned in concentration, but a smile was playing about a corner of his mouth.

Orlgaun swept around again, and Manshoon rose in his saddle, roaring his rage and pain as he spat the necessary word and the wand spewed lightnings. The fist struck at him again, and Manshoon was hurled back against Orlgaun's rough scales by the blow. He had a brief glimpse of the foe in armor flying up and at him, again, that long sword swinging . . .

Orlgaun saved him, striking out in fear with one wing at the darting creature that had so hurt it before. The point of

Florin's blade skittered harmlessly across the dragon's scales. It struck at him and then, with a flapping of wings, rolled swiftly away.

Far below, Jhessail said the last words of a spell of flight as she touched her husband's forehead. Merith kissed her before he sprang aloft, blade flashing, to join the fray.

As he knelt by the moaning forms of Torm and Rathan, Lanseril was calmly using his own art to summon insects to attack the enemy mage. Ten paces away, Narm stared at him helplessly as the battle raged overhead. The great dragon slashed at Florin with its claws, cartwheeling across the sky with mighty beats of its wings. Merith Strongbow was flying after it as fast as he could, while the uncanny fist struck again in midair and their beleaguered foe cast down lightnings once more.

Lanseril finished his spell, pointed at Manshoon carefully, and then turned his attention again to healing his companions. Jhessail raised her wand again and then staggered as the lightning struck. The ground shook as something the mage had hurled exploded in front of Elminster, and Narm shielded Shandril desperately with his own body as stones flew. A stone struck his shoulder, and then his back, with numbing force, and he had not even time to sag before something else hit him on the temple. His eyes saw red, deepening steadily into . . . darkness. . . .

*　*　*　*　*

Half a world away, Khelben Arunsun and Malchor Harpell, great mages both, looked at each other across the aged parchment between them as they felt roiling art echoing in their blood. With one accord they turned to the crystal ball that stood at hand. The room about them, high in Blackstaff Tower in the great city of Waterdeep, fell silent as the two mages stared intently into the crystal, and the great lords gathered there waited to learn what had occurred.

*　*　*　*　*

In Candlekeep, near the sea, the Keeper of the Tomes looked up from pages of stamped and burnished electrum as the soft glow of the runes of power they bore flickered.

The First Reader had seen it too, and fallen silent in his translation. The two men looked at each other in the dark, dusty round room that was the innermost and most sacred of the Inner Rooms, and then stared out, unseeing, into the darkness. The glowing globe that gave them light to read by dimmed where it hung at the keeper's shoulder, brightened, and then dimmed again.

"Great art, somewhere, contending with great art," the First Reader said quietly, and the Keeper nodded.

"Aye," he said grimly, "and what changes will it bring this time?"

The question hung unanswered in the room with them for a long time before they could begin reading again.

* * * * *

Orlgaun wheeled again, and Manshoon shook where he sat on the broad, scaled back from the aftereffects of the mighty disjunction he had worked. The hand that had nearly slain him was gone, as were the other, lesser magics that had assailed him—but below on the rocks, the old mage and the younger maid still stood calmly. Their hands moved again in the gesture of spell-weaving, and the elf and the ranger still flew after him, low and beneath Orlgaun's body where he could not reach them, one on either side.

Manshoon snarled in frustration and tore another globe from the necklace he wore as the black dragon dove again toward his enemies. Orlgaun moved more slowly and heavily with each pass. Both spells and steel had struck the dragon, and struck deeply. The black dragon had felt nothing worse than the sting of arrows for a long time. Nor have I met such resistance in a fair while, Manshoon thought darkly, as he hurled the globe he held. He then watched magic missiles rise up toward him in a bright dancing group of lights. He was powerless to stop them.

Behind him he heard Merith's triumphant song as the elf thrust his blade between two of Orlgaun's armored scales. Manshoon turned, raising his wand, but Florin was there, sword sweeping out. The blade burned across the lord's fingers like liquid fire, and Manshoon saw the wand whirl harmlessly away in the air amid droplets of his own blood just before the magic missiles struck.

The dragon rider's globe exploded with stunning force, showering everyone on the ground with a spray of dust and small stones. Larger fragments cracked sharply off the rocks they crouched behind. Only Elminster and a sorely wounded Jhessail still stood in view. The other knights lay still under the dust or crouched behind cover tensely. The earth's shuddering nearly threw the weary Jhessail to her knees.

Under Narm's heavy weight, Shandril was jolted into confused awareness of the tumult around her. Where was she now? Wearily she wriggled into the light, scarcely aware that she was pushing away a body, and completely unaware that it was Narm. She saw dust swirl everywhere. In the open pit of tumbled rocks and coins before her Elminster stood calmly, facing to her right and looking upwards.

Shandril peered upward, and saw a dark form approaching rapidly. It was Merith, blade in hand. He was flying somehow, and was hurrying. He seeks Jhessail, Shandril thought dully as she saw his dark, anxious face and where he was headed. Jhessail had just sagged down onto a rock, palm showing on her face.

But beyond the hurrying elf, in midair, Florin was flying with the aid of his shield, and as he hung from it he struck, again and again, at someone who was riding a gigantic black dragon. Whoever it was twisted this way and that under Florin's blows until suddenly he straightened with a roar of triumph and there was a flash. Florin was hurled end over end through the air like a husk doll. The dragon turned ponderously under its rider's urging, and thundered down out of the sky at Elminster.

The old mage stood alone. No, not alone, thought Shandril, as she felt roiling fire deep within her where there should have been nothing left. It glinted briefly in her eyes. Not while I live. She struggled to her knees, set her teeth, and pointed her arms at the mage on the dragon. She felt sick and as weak as a newborn kitten, and her head throbbed piercingly, but she could feel the fire flowing within her. Let it be as it was before, she thought. Whoever you are, evil one, burn! Burn! How dare you harm my friends!

She had screamed that last aloud, she realized dimly, as the last of the spellfire roared up out of her in a bolt of crackling fire that drained her utterly. Her knees gave way, and she could not even see if she had struck true as she fell on her face on the rocks.

Manshoon stared at the bolt in astonishment, an instant before it hit him. And then all he could do in the teeth of the blinding roar was scream.

Orlgaun fell away weakly, hearing its master cry out. The dragon drew back, uncertain. It dared not attack anything that had slain Manshoon—and if Manshoon was dead, there was no reason to tarry. It had hurts of its own, deep, raw pain that stabbed to the lungs at each wingbeat. . . .

But Manshoon yet lived, clinging to his wits and his saddle grimly, barely able to hold himself upright. He could not survive another blast like that—and it had not even come from Elminster. The old mage still stood waiting, calmly, and Manshoon knew he could not continue this battle and live.

Beyond Elminster lay the young maiden who had come crawling out from the gods only knew where to smite him with what must have been raw energy: Spellfire! Manshoon shuddered, looked around quickly to ensure that neither of those who had flown to attack him was near, and urged Orlgaun away northward. He tilted the dragon's body to shield himself from Elminster's gaze and foil any magic missiles the old mage might now unleash. An attack he could not hope to survive, Manshoon thought despairingly.

Behind him, the air crackled and there was a flash of light as one last lightning bolt struck. Orlgaun convulsed beneath him and fell, the great wings shuddering. For terribly long moments they dropped before the dragon caught itself and began, raggedly, to fly again. He had escaped alive. Not quite the achievement he had expected.

* * * * *

"Shandril!" was all Narm said. It was all he needed to say. They hugged each other fiercely and cried for a long time. Around them, the Knights of Myth Drannor used art to heal each other, and packed yet more treasure, and saw to their weapons, and laughed. In their midst, Elminster, who had cast another spell and now stared off northward with a frown of concentration, stood like a statue. At last, when all were as whole as could be managed, and heavily laden with coins and bars and jewels, Jhessail approached the embracing couple and touched Narm gently on the shoulder.

"Are you well?" she asked softly, as the other knights gathered around, Torm and Rathan grinning openly.

"Yes," Narm said thickly into Shandril's hair. "Right well." Then he disengaged himself from Shandril anxiously. "How are you, my lady?"

Shandril smiled back at him. "I live. I love you. I am most well."

Narm smiled in his turn, and then asked very softly. "May I take you to wife, Shandril Shessair?"

Jhessail turned away to seek out Merith's eyes and found his gaze already upon her. They shared a smile of their own.

The knights waited. Shandril's face was hidden in her hair, her head bent down. Someone—Florin—looked away in sudden dismay. Silence fell. Then Shandril's shoulders shook, and they realized she was crying. Her slim hands reached out and found Narm's shoulders, and she clung to him and pulled herself into his embrace and said brokenly, "Oh yes. Yes. Please the gods, yes."

The knights let out a great roar of pleasure and congratulation, and hands were pounding the shoulders of the young couple. Jhessail and Merith embraced, Rathan raised a wineskin, and Torm laughed and tossed a dagger high and caught it out of the air as it fell twinkling. Then the thief raced over to Elminster, who still stood motionless with his back to them all. Torm caught at his sleeve, tugged the startled mage around, and shook him in glee.

Elminster spoke mildly. Only his eyes glinted. "Ye've ruined the spell, and I've lost him. Ye'd better have a good reason for this, Torm, son of Dathguld."

Torm stopped in mid-laugh, startled. "You know who my father was?"

Elminster waved a hand in vague dismissal. "Of course, of course," he said peevishly. "Now, I asked thee thy reason for all this hooting and slapping me about and dancing up and down even now upon my very toes!"

"Oh." And for once in his life, Torm could think of little more to say, until his own feet were clear of the old mage's, and his hands free of Elminster's clothing. Then his joy and his purpose both returned to him in a rush, and he said grandly, "Narm and Shandril are to be wed! What say you? Wed, I say!"

The mage looked bewildered for a moment, and then cross. "Is that all?" he demanded. "Oh, aye—any fool could see that. Ye spoiled my spell and lost me my hook on Manshoon for that? Garrrgh!" He stamped his foot and turned away sharply in a swirl of dusty robes, leaving Torm to stare after him in astonishment. The thief recovered his customary grin when he saw that Elminster was heading straight for the laughing, still-embracing couple.

"Dolt," said Rathan affectionately, and pressed his wineskin into Torm's hands. "Come and sit, and have drink."

Torm shuddered. "I hate this swill!" he protested. "Can't we just play pranks on each other, instead?"

"I have wondered, friend Torm," came Florin's grave voice behind them, "just what you do when really happy . . . and now I know. Truly, wonders anew unfold before my eyes every passing day. But the message I bear is to your damp companion. Rathan, Narm and Shandril would speak with you and myself as soon as the gods will."

Rathan looked at him, momentarily surprised, and then nodded in understanding. "Aye. Of course." He thrust the skin into Torm's hands, and said, "Mind this for me then, Torm? Thankee." Two steps away, he checked, whirled about, and said sternly, "And no pranks, mind!"

Torm shrugged and spread his hands in mock innocence. "Is it my open, honest face? My kind, forgiving manner? My gentle disposition?"

"Nay," said Elminster dryly from behind him. Torm jumped, startled. " 'Tis the length of thy tongue." The old sage put his hand under the thief's elbow as he passed and drew him along. "Come," he commanded, simply, "thy presence is required."

Narm was looking up at Rathan, his arm about Shandril and a kind of light about his face. Yet out of his eagerness, he spoke gently and hesitantly. "I—I have no gift to give you, good guide of Tymora," he said. "But I—we—could you wed us two, and soon?"

Rathan grinned back at him. "Of course I will. But a gift indeed ye have." He gestured at the broken litter of rock about them, where coins still gleamed here and there amid the dust. "One of those, perhaps," he said gruffly. "Mind it's a gold one, look ye." Narm thanked him and clasped his hand and plucked up a gold piece. Rathan held it high, and said, "Tymora looks down upon us and She finds this good, and shines the bright face of good fortune upon this union. By the sign of her favor, I declare ye two handfast, and to be wed before nine days and nights are out. All ye who are here, cry, 'Aye.' "

And as the chorus of "Ayes" rang out, the sun above them shone with sudden brightness, and a beam of golden light touched the coin in Rathan's fingers. There was a flash, and it was gone. Narm, who had secretly doubted the stout cleric's sincerity until that moment, opened his mouth in awe. Rathan spread his empty hands in benediction, stepped forward to take one each of Narm's and Shandril's hands and clasped them together under his own. He stepped back and bowed, and then he was Rathan again, smiling and blinking and looking about for his wineskin.

"Our thanks, Rathan," Shandril said huskily, and he bowed again and said, "Tymora's will, but my pleasure," and made of the formal words the approval and joy of a friend.

Narm spoke then. "My lord Florin," he said to the tall ranger in the scorched and claw-scraped armor, "may we come to Shadowdale for a time, with you all? We have no home, and my lady—no, we are both weary of running and fighting and never knowing rest, or a home. It is much to ask, I know, but—"

"But no more drivel," said Torm unexpectedly. "Of course you will come to the dale . . . where else would you go?"

Florin looked at him sternly, and then grinned. "In truth, Torm," he said, "I could have put it in no better words myself . . . you are welcome for as long as you both desire it. I daresay you can study art better in Shadowdale's peace and quiet—relative though that may prove—than out here, as one mage after another hurls it at you."

"Study?" asked Narm faintly, staring at Elminster, who stood puffing his pipe expressionlessly.

"Yes, with Illistyl and I," said Jhessail. "He," she added, nodding at Elminster, "will be studying your bride. It's been a long time indeed since someone last mastered spellfire so ably—and survived its use so well."

* * * * *

Flames flickered red and angry orange in two braziers. They stood in a vaulted stone hall, and between them was an altar of black stone, polished glossy-smooth and shaped like a gigantic throne, forty feet high. At the foot of the Seat of Bane was a much smaller throne, and upon it sat a cold-eyed man with pale brown hair and wan features. His high-cowled robe was deep black and simple, and his hands gleamed with many rings. None living knew his truename, save himself; few knew his common name. He was the High Imperceptor of Bane, and he was very angry.

"Give me good reason," he said coldly to those who knelt before him, "why I should not put you to death. You have failed me. Manshoon was to have received our message at this meeting with his lords. We cannot move against the traitor Fzoul with Manshoon in the city, or we shall know certain defeat. You had the message; you delivered it not. What can you say to stand against this?"

"M-my Lord," said one of those kneeling, hesitantly, "the message was about to be passed on to Manshoon, in a believable manner—and for that, we needed those assembled to be on the topic, or he might well have smelled out our ruse. The meeting was scarce begun, and the fool Kalthas telling all grandly that garrisons across the northlands were wasteful and needless, when Manshoon stood up, all of a sudden, and upset the table and all. He—he began to cry, Dread Lord. He whispered a word, 'Maruel' or something similar, and then summoned a scrying-crystal. He was not even looking at us. He looked into the globe when it came to him—"

"The word of summoning!" the High Imperceptor interrupted sharply. "What was it?"

"Ah—a moment, Dread Lord, it began, 'Zell' . . . ah, it was *'Zellathorass'!*" the kneeling man said triumphantly. The High Imperceptor nodded.

"Rise, and continue," was all he said. Bowing, the man did.

"The—the word he dismissed the globe with, Dread Lord, was *'Alvathair,'* I do recall. He seemed furious after that and dismissed us. He said, 'Sirs, this meeting is at an end. For your safety, leave at once.' And he called down gargoyles upon us from above, and—and we fled."

"Did you see where Manshoon went?" asked the High Imperceptor eagerly.

"N-no, Dread Lord. He was not seen in the city all the rest of that day." The speaker spread his hands. "We came straight to you, leaving that night, for fear of delivering our message wrongly, once the chance you had directed us to take was lost."

The High Imperceptor nodded shortly. "Well spoken, well recalled. Rise, all of you." When the brief shuffling and rustling had died away again, he looked down at the line of men facing him. "Do any of you have aught else to report?"

One Theln spoke. "Aye, Dread Lord." He was gestured to continue. "I met with a merchant loyal to The Black Lord"— he bowed to the great throne—"who told me of a young girl now on her way to Shadowdale in the company of those who call themselves the Knights of Myth Drannor. This maid can by some means produce spellfire. He said this fire can strike through magical barriers and empty air alike, and is very powerful."

The High Imperceptor was leaning forward on his throne now, interested. At a subtle signal of his hand, an unseen upperpriest behind black tapestries nearby had cast a spell to detect any lies Theln might speak. "They take her to Elminster, no doubt. Very powerful, indeed. If we held this power, we could strike down those who stand opposed to our great Lord"—all save the High Imperceptor bowed again—"and those traitors who were once our brothers, alike. We must try for this spellfire, if this tale be true. This faithful—who is he, and how old his news?"

"One Raunel, a dealer in sausages from the Vilhon Reach. He spoke to me on my way to you, on the road very close. He said he'd spoken with a forester who'd seen the girl and all himself, near the Thunder Peaks, in the late morning yesterday. He met this forester, one Hylgaun, yestereve at a roadside fire they shared."

The High Imperceptor nodded agian, and almost smiled. "You have done well, Theln. You will be rewarded. Go you and call upon the priest Laelar to attend us at once. All of you, leave us."

The last to leave stepped from behind tapestries, bowed, and said merely, "No lies, Dread Lord," as he left. Good. That left only two possible liars in this matter: this Raunel and the one called Hylgaun. It felt true.

When he was alone, the cold-eyed, wan man looked thoughtfully across the empty chamber. "Maruel . . . Maruel. I know that name." He caught up the great black mace of Bane and hefted its dark and cruel length absently as he pondered. Why could he never remember such things? Why? It could well bring death one day . . . the wrong detail forgotten, the wrong precaution taken. The High Imperceptor sighed. It had not been a good day.

* * * * *

The black dragon flew heavily and raggedly. Often its wings faltered and it would sink down and to one side or the other, despite Manshoon's commands and curses. Orlgaun was sorely hurt, and might never bear him again. That thought burned in Manshoon's mind, atop his defeat, and he almost turned back in anger to slay with the art he yet held ready.

It was impossible. Orlgaun was flying on the last of its lagging strength now, lower than Manshoon would have preferred. The seemingly endless green of the great Elven Court stretched on beneath them as the dragon flew north and east. Manshoon thought back over the fray and concluded bitterly that he'd probably not slain a single one of those who'd stood against him. Elminster had shielded them at the first, aye, but few could survive he and Orlgaun both, even in passing. That cursed elf, and the ranger with his flying shield! He could feel their blades yet . . . they'd not live long, when he had that girl in his hands, even if they'd had nothing to do with Symgharyl Maruel's death.

The thought of The Shadowsil's passing made him feel dark and weak inside, and he rose out of that momentary sadness feeling savage. He clutched a wand fiercely and wanted badly to strike down something. Then he frowned.

The girl. Yes. Spellfire, it had been. He yet smarted where it had briefly touched him, despite all the healing potions he'd drunk since, emptying the belt he wore across his stomach. Gods, but it hurt yet! It had been fortunate she was so untutored and so unused to battle, or Manshoon the Mighty might well have fallen this day. Her power must be his own, and soon, before Elminster mastered it! Not such an old fool, that one. Not aggressive, but even stronger in art than he'd thought. No doubt he'd take a measure of killing—something best prepared in haste when back at—

Gods! They were flying among the trees!

Orlgaun had sunk lower and lower as Manshoon had pondered, the great wings moving more and more feebly, and suddenly its claws and belly were crashing and thrusting through the small uppermost branches of the tallest trees in the forest. Manshoon shouted, hauling hard on the fin before him and staring ahead. But the dragon did not respond, and the trees stretched on as far as the eye could see, with only a few gaps just ahead. Manshoon cursed feelingly as the dragon crashed further downward amid snapping and wildly whipping branches, rocking and buffeting its rider. The blows and crashes grew steadily harder as Orlgaun sank full into the trees, crushing them with its vast bulk and smashing them aside with the velocity of its fall.

More and more slowly they struck the next tree, and the next, and Manshoon crouched low and fended off flailing branches grimly as the great wyrm came down to earth. Orlgaun did not even grunt; perhaps its spirit had fled its torn and battered body in the air while still above the trees. Certainly this would be its last flight. Manshoon saw one wing smashed limply backward by a gigantic phandar that itself broke asunder, the trunk groaning as it parted, and then the dragon struck a stand of shadowtops head-on and the world itself seemed to shake and split asunder.

Manshoon found himself, when he could see straight

again, hanging head-down in a tangled ruin of shadowtop branches and leaves, Orlgaun's scaled back above him. The dragon lay belly uppermost among smashed and splintered wood, impaled and twisted horribly. The mage crawled and slipped about until he fell out of the branches to the leaf-strewn ground beneath, and moved out from under the vast carcass as soon as he gained his feet. He had lost the wand, though he still carried other items of power aplenty. Ahead, in the direction Orlgaun had been flying, the trees thinned into some sort of clearing. All about lay green dimness, still echoing with the last rustlings of Orlgaun's fall.

Manshoon took a step forward, and another, and then stared in shock at a bat-winged, horned, and tusked creature that had appeared out of the trees in front of him. A malebranche! Beyond it he could see another, and quick glances about told him that others were approaching. The devils of Myth Drannor!

The High Lord of Zhentil Keep cast a spell in grim haste, backing away, and then cursed loudly and feelingly as his lightnings struck down the nearest devil. He turned away from the clearing and fled as fast as his legs could go. The trees here grew too thickly even to fly! As he ran, Manshoon drew a wand of paralyzation from its holder at his belt and thought on how best to use the magics he had left. It had not been a good day.

☙ 10 ❧

Full Flagons

I have known high honor, proud fame, and great riches, and have drunk deep of good wine at feasts where my mouth watered and my belly was filled with delightful viands amid good fellowship and conversation . . . and I tell you that all these pale and drift away as idle dreams before the gentle touch of my Lady.

Mirt 'the Moneylender' of Waterdeep
In a letter to Khelben 'Blackstaff' Arunsun
in proclamation of his lover Asper
as his lawful heir
Year of the Harp

The knights had traveled swiftly into the woods, moving northward, after the retreat of Manshoon. The Thunder Peaks marched north on their left with them as they went, leaving Rauglothgor's shattered lair behind. They walked until night fell, rose with the dawn, and went on again until another nightfall.

In Mistledale, the knights purchased mules. Elminster let lapse the last of a succession of floating discs he had conjured up to carry Shandril, despite her protests. The others had walked.

A footsore Narm clambered up onto his mule, which favored him with an unfriendly look, and glanced enviously at the knights who still sprang about and vaulted up into their saddles and traded jests with unflagging enthusiasm. They were obviously all used to walking miles at a stretch, from aged Elminster to the Lady Jhessail. Narm's thighs were achingly stiff. He grinned as Rathan, who had begun a ballad that told of the glories of Tymora's favor, gave up helplessly under Torm's persistent needling. The thief had quickly parodied line after line as they plunged into a narrow, gloomy path in the woods. Rathan ceased with a sigh when they were barely out of sight of Mistledale's sunlight.

The green dimness of the woods was all about them now. Shandril leaned over to Narm and asked in a low voice, "How far away is Myth Drannor?" They traded sober glances, and Jhessail turned in her saddle and said, "Due east of us, several days distant. The river Ashaba lies between us and Myth Drannor at all times, this trip. That gate The Shadowsil took you through in the ruined city took you across half the Dalelands to the dracolich's lair."

The couple's involuntary shared sigh of relief was cut short by Torm's dry, sharp voice saying from where he rode watchfully behind them, "Ah, yes. We can head that way if you'd like. I hear one can have a devil of a time there, heh-heh . . ."

He smiled benignly at the chorus of dirty looks flung his way. Someone has to provide entertainment, after all.

* * * * *

It was late. The golden light of approaching sunset glinted on leaves ahead of and above them. Yet the knights pressed on. Riding beside each other except where trees in the trail forced them into single file, Narm and Shandril clasped hands reassuringly. Whatever happened, they were together. When it grew suddenly much darker, Jhessail and Merith conjured glowing motes of light that drifted along in midair with them, bobbing and floating about, occasionally darting to one side to illuminate this or that tangle of brush or dark thicket.

They rode on slowly amid the giant trees and smaller saplings alike, the soft singing of crickets all about them. The chorus would die away in front of them and begin again behind them. Off to one side or the other, particularly to the right, eerie gray-green and blue radiances—small and scattered glows that did not move—could be seen occasionally.

"What's that?" Narm asked, pointing. "Is it witchfire?"

Merith nodded. "Glow moss, witchfire, and the other fungi of the forest that shine at night. The elven name for all of them is, in Common, 'nightshine'." The elf lounged in his saddle, helm hung from its horn, very much at his ease. Of course, Shandril thought, feeling suddenly less awed and much safer, to Merith this endless wood is home. She relaxed, and very soon sank low in her saddle.

Jhessail saw her, and quietly worked a spell of sleep upon her and upon Narm, who rode, nodding himself, beside her. Merith took charge of the mules as his lady cast another floating disc. Torm chuckled softly as he boosted the sleepers from saddle to disc, and then yawned himself.

"Oh, no, you don't!" Jhessail warned him. "Get back on your mule."

Torm spread his hands in injured and very feigned innocence. "Why you think all these terrible things of me I don't know—I am grievously wronged, indeed, and—"

He staggered forward a step under the unexpected impact of a solid nudge in the back from his mule, and his friends burst into laughter all around him.

"Be an adventurer," he grumbled as he settled himself in his saddle again. "Become rich and famous, they said. Hmph."

"Famous, anyway," Merith assured him. "Why, I've even seen notices with your picture on them posted here and there. And of course all these men with knives keep calling on you . . ."

Torm made a rude noise. It was returned, with spirit, from where Elminster rode in stately dignity ahead of them all, startling everyone into silence. It all made no difference to the mules.

* * * * *

The sun was bright and high again when Narm and Shandril came slowly awake. Their arms had crept about each other in slumber, and they were drowsy and deep-rested. Narm looked up at the sun-dappled leaves overhead, heard the familiar creak of leather and soft thud of the mules' hooves, and relaxed, Shandril's warmth and weight on his left side. His left hand tingled. He wiggled his fingers to

ED GREENWOOD

bring feeling and strength back and felt her stir. Then he realized he was flat on his back, moving, with no mule bumping and shifting beneath him. He sat up in alarm.

He and Shandril were floating serenely along on a disc of firm nothingness, with Jhessail just behind them and Merith just ahead. Far ahead, over Elminster's shoulder, he could see Lanseril leading the way toward a brightening in the trees. Jhessail smiled reassuringly at him. "Well met, this morn," she said. "We are almost in Shadowdale."

As she spoke, and Shandril sleepily pulled herself up Narm's shoulder to see, they came out of the trees into a high-walled passage between two redoubts of heaped stones. The silver and blue banners of Shadowdale, showing the spiral tower and crescent moon, stirred in the faint morning breezes, and men in armor with Shadowdale's arms on their surcoats stood with pikes and crossbows.

" 'Ware!" called the guard formally, barring the way to the bridge beyond. The sight of the lords and lady of the dale had them bowing and standing aside in the next breath. The sight of Elminster made them more silent than usual, and Narm and Shandril passed over the mill bridge and into the dale without a word of query or challenge.

No escort rode with them as they passed by lush green fields. The dale opened out before them, the forest rising on either side like great green walls. Shandril looked about her happily. Narm, who had seen it before, asked Jhessail, "Lady, may we ride? I would feel—less the fool, I suppose. My thanks for the traveling bed, mistake me not—it's a trick I must learn one day, if you will. It moves where you will it to go?"

"It does," Jhessail said gravely, "although if you mind it not, it will follow twenty paces or so behind—and if you leave it where it cannot follow, it speedily passes away and is no more." She grinned. "But of course you shall ride—it would not do for you to look different fools than the rest of us."

They all rode up to the Twisted Tower together and were made welcome. Mourngrym came striding out with his cloak slapping around him, and said to Narm, "So here you are back, and I find that not only must you stick your neck into clear danger again and again, you must drag all my protectors and companions with you, even Elminster, and leave the dale undefended." His eyes twinkled. "And do I look upon the reason for your return to peril? Lady, I am Mourngrym, the lord who is left behind to sit the seat in the dale while his elders take the air, see sights, and enjoy their journeys. Welcome! How may I call you?"

"Lord Mourngrym, I am Shandril Shessair," Shandril said firmly, blushing only faintly in her shyness. "I am handfast to Narm." Her voice lowered in curiosity. "These are your comrades? You have ridden to battle together?"

Mourngrym laughed. "Indeed," he said, handing her down onto a stool one of the guards had just whirled into place. "No doubt you can tell from what you've known of them already how wild the tales of our adventures are." Merith clapped him on the shoulder in passing. Mourngrym grinned. "I'm afraid you'll have to wait until too much drink has flowed before I start telling any tales, though others here"—he looked meaningfully at Torm—"are weaker."

They went into the tower. "And how was your journey, Narm?" Mourngrym asked as they entered a feasting hall where the mingled smell of cooking bacon and a great spiced stew made mouths water.

"Oh," Narm replied mildly, steadying Shandril as they came to the table, "eventful."

* * * * *

"You are called to feast, lady," said the serving maid with a smile. Through the open door Shandril could hear soft harping. "One waits without to take you down. Shall I send him in?"

"Oh—yes. Yes, please," Shandril said, still gazing around at the beautiful bedchamber, with its hangings of elven warriors riding stags through the forest—the High Hunt of the Elven Court, a unicorn glowing in the trees far off at its head—and its round, canopied bed.

Shandril's gown, too, was a beautiful thing of Calishite silk overlaid with a finework tabard for warmth in the stone halls of the north. The tabard's beading was of interwoven crescent moons and silver horns and unicorns. On her arm she wore proudly her joined ring and bracelet of electrum and sapphires. It awed Shandril to see herself in the great burnished metal mirror.

Then in came Narm, in a grand great-sleeved tunic of wine-purple velvet, matching silk hose, and boots trimmed with fur. Hanging from his belt was the lion-headed dagger. His hair had been washed and trimmed and doused with perfume-water, and his eyes outshone the rings on his fingers.

He came in eagerly, mouth opening in a smile to speak— and stopped in awe. Eyes shining, he took a hesitant step forward. "My lady?" he asked. "Shandril?" His voice was very quiet. "You are beautiful," he added slowly. "As graceful as any high lady I have ever seen."

"And how many such ladies have you seen?" Shandril teased him. "It's still the same me, if I'm in plain gray robes or a man's tunic and breeches, hair washed or unwashed."

"Yes," Narm said. "But I fear even to touch you, when you are clad so—I could only mar perfect beauty." His voice was husky and serious. His eyes shone.

"Shameless flatterer," Shandril said reprovingly. "But if that is so, I'll have them all off, at once, and go down in my thieves' garb. I would much rather go on your arm in rags, than walk grandly clad and alone."

"No, no," Narm said, taking her arm. "I can conquer my fears—see?—only promise me you'll talk with me after all the hurly-burly, and in good light. I would not soon forget how you look now."

"Talk, and in good light? Let us go down to table, my lord. Your hunger is weakening your wits," Shandril teased, and led him to the door. Thus it was in the hallway outside, under the politely averted eyes of a guard, that the young mage turned Shandril about and kissed her. The soft horn fanfare that summoned all to first table sounded twice before they parted and went down the stairs. The guard kept his face carefully expressionless.

* * * * *

"Thank you, but no, Lord. Truly, I can eat no more," Shandril protested, holding up a hand in front of a platter of steaming boar in gravy. Mourngrym laughed.

"Well enough," he warned, "but the more you eat, the longer you can drink. When none of these here can eat a crumb more, you will find that they can yet find room to drink. It's a mystery to me why some who come to my table say they are come to a 'feast,' when what they do is eat a few bites and then hoist flagons all the night through."

"I—I should be sick if I tried, Lord," Shandril said simply. Mourngrym smiled again.

"Good, then. I am similarly affected. If the two of you can spare us a few words before retiring, my Lady Shaerl and I would be very happy to have your company in the bower upstairs. I believe you have met Storm Silverhand and Sharantyr. We will have other guests: Jhessail and Elminster, and possibly Illistyl. Go up when you cannot hear each other any more—oh, yes, it grows much noisier than this. If you will forgive me, I must walk among my people. When their tongues are wet and loose, I learn their true grievances and concerns." He nodded to them both and rose. Shandril and Narm exchanged glances.

All around them was tumult. Softly glowing luminescent globes of glass, enspelled earlier by Illistyl, lit the hall. At one end, a gigantic fire blazed merrily beneath spits of boar and ox, filling the room with aromatic smoke. The long board was crammed with platters of food and decanters and skins of wine. A harpist and a glaurist played almost unheard amid the din of sixty-odd people laughing and talking all at once.

Most of the knights were there. Torm was almost unrecognizable in dazzling, almost foppish finery of slit and puffed sleeves, fur-trimmed silks set with winking gems, and many fine chains of gold studded with large rubies and emeralds. A single giant king's tear hung in silky-smooth clarity upon his bared breast, encupped in a webwork of polished strips of electrum, the first that either Narm or Shandril had ever seen. The thief outshone Mourngrym and, indeed, all the bejeweled ladies in the room, and strode grandly about drinking from a massive chased silver tankard as tall as his forearm was long.

He caught Shandril's eye as she stared. He winked, reached into one sleeve, plucked out a silver-hilted dagger whose blade was needle-thin and dull black, tossed it casually into the air, caught it a breath later, winked again, and put it away as smoothly. Rathan, ruddy-faced and amiable, also looked resplendent in green velvet, the silver symbol of Tymora upon his breast.

Many of the diners were standing, now, and a few had begun to dance. Far across the room Narm caught sight of the commanding height and broad shoulders of Florin, looking every inch a king. Beside him stood a lady Narm had last seen on a forest trail near Myth Drannor, and before that in the taproom of The Rising Moon inn in Deepingdale, sword drawn and ready: Storm Silverhand. She wore a simple gown of gray silk, with only a broad black cummerbund and a silver-hilted dagger for ornament, but she looked so regal and beautiful that Shandril forgot all thoughts of what a fine gown and tabard did for herself.

"Look," she breathed, grasping Narm's hand and pointing with a nod of her head.

"Yes. I see," he replied, and turned to Lanseril, who stood near at hand talking to a burly, bearded man in amber and russet. The druid wore a simple brown woolen robe. Narm touched his hand. "Pray excuse my interruption, friend Lanseril."

"No excuse needed, Narm—it's what everyone does. My life is a series of interruptions," Lanseril replied with a warm smile. He bent his head near. "What is it?"

"The Lord Florin—is the Lady Storm his—ah, handfast to him, or—?"

Lanseril chuckled. "Florin is married to Storm's sister, the ranger Dove, who is soon to bear his child, and is for her safety presently elsewhere. Storm's man, Maxam, was killed this past summer. She does not speak of that, mind. Florin and Storm are friends who keep each other from being too lonely at dance and at table. Despite what Torm may slyly hint, they are no more than that."

The druid turned and touched the sleeve of the man he had been speaking with.

"May I introduce Thurbal, Captain-of-Arms and Warden of Shadowdale?" he asked politely. Thurbal, a man of weatherbeaten and plain features whose eyes were at once shrewd and kindly, bowed to them both.

"Lady Shandril and Lord Narm," he said, "I bid you my own welcome. Have you enjoyed the feast thus far?"

"I—I, yes, greatly," Narm replied, noting the great plain-scabbarded broadsword Thurbal wore at his side, despite his high-booted finery.

"It's the first feast I've ever been invited to, Lord," Shandril replied. "I-I am no high lady, I fear."

Thurbal frowned slightly. "My pardon," he said, "I assumed—ah, but no harm done if you will forgive me, for I am no lord, either. Lord Lanseril told me something of your importance. I hope you will not take offence if I seem to watch you closely while you're here; it seems my brawn is on the block, so to speak, if you are endangered when I might have prevented it."

"Endangered?" Narm asked, as Shandril paled. "Here?"

Thurbal spread broad, heavy hands. "We live in a world of magic, Lord. There are no safe defenses. All the might I can muster to hold steel to your lady's defense and your own cannot stop magic that finds a way through. I sometimes wonder what it would be like if all men had to stand or fall by their actions at the end of a sword, and there was no magic about. But then again, such a world might be in a worse mess than this one."

"But we have enemies?" Narm asked soberly.

Lanseril shrugged and replied, "Shandril, or the two of you together, can create and hurl spellfire, something known only in the histories of art; something very powerful indeed. Many would like to be the only one to control and wield it. You must watch the shadows, and expect trouble, even here."

"And get used to being 'lord' and 'lady'," Thurbal said with a grin. "All of the knights hold that title, and you stand with them until you declare and choose otherwise. My men will obey and aid you the better if they continue to think you are Lord and Lady of the Dale." He paused, and then added, "By the way, Lady Shandril. I have heard from the Lord Florin and the Lady Jhessail of how you put Manshoon of Zhentil Keep to flight. I bow to you. Even with art that the rest of us lack, that is no light thing to have done."

"Have you enemies, indeed?" Lanseril added. "Manshoon is no little one—I don't doubt that he yet lives." Shandril shuddered, and he patted her shoulder immediately. "But think no more of this. Enjoy this night, and let tomorrow look to tomorrow's problems."

"Hmmph—easy enough to say," Narm told him. "Not so easy to school one's mind not to think of something."

Lanseril nodded. "True, and I'm sorry I brought both your thoughts to this now. On the other hand—and think on this, mind; it is the most important training you can have for magecraft. You must be able to control your thoughts as an acrobat controls hands if you are to survive spell against spell. If you ever meet Manshoon to speak to at leisure, you will find him as cold and controlled as Elminster seems whimsical—but is not, underneath. If one is not controlled, one does not live to reach such power, unless one's art is never challenged." And then he smiled. "But enough. I must watch over these fools, while you speak with the more sober upstairs."

"You?" Shandril asked in surprise.

Lanseril looked at her. "Of course. Are these"—he spread both hands to indicate the revelers all around—"not creatures under my care here in the dale, even as the chipmunks and the farmwives' cats are?"

He left Shandril staring thoughtfully after him and strode over to where Torm stood laughing, each arm around a local beauty. Narm shook his head. "I don't know these people, really, yet," he said in her ear, "but they are good people—as good as any I've ever known."

"I know," Shandril whispered back. "That's why I'm so afraid we'll bring death upon them by being here."

Narm looked at her somberly for a long time. At last he said in a low voice, "We have to, Shandril. We will die without their protection—you know that."

Shandril nodded. "Yes. So I am here." Her eyes sought out Mourngrym and saw him walking slowly with Storm and Florin toward the doors. "We should follow on—they are going up now, I think."

Narm nodded amid the dancing and the deafening talk and laughter. Shandril noticed that Thurbal moved quietly to follow them, staying distant, eyes moving constantly.

Torchlight filled the hallway outside with light, reflecting off flagons and goblets all around. Many richly clad men and women, drinks in hand, leaned against the walls laughing and talking. Shandril heard a snatch of one story that was considered old even in The Rising Moon as she passed, on Narm's arm. They followed a regal lady in shimmering blue-green who wore a twinkling diadem up the stairs. When she turned at the top, they saw that it was Jhessail. She smiled.

"Such long faces," she said tenderly. "Do you like feasts so little?"

"No, it's not that," Shandril whispered back. "We fear to bring danger upon you all."

Jhessail shook her head as they walked on together. "Is that all? Do you not know that we here stand in danger at all times? Zhentil Keep attacks us every summer, at the least. The Cult of the Dragon and the dark elves beneath us are constant menaces . . . Myth Drannor's devils are a worry to us, as is the lawlessness in Daggerdale. Adventurers may move on, or even run from such problems—but we cannot move the dale. Once we accepted Shadowdale, we became targets, and remain so. Why else live so high as we have been tonight, as those below"—she gestured to the noise—"still do?"

She traded glances with the young couple. "I could be slain tomorrow . . . should I therefore be miserable today? Why not make the best of it?" She took Narm's free hand, and drew them both into the bower. "Come, let us talk of other things." Behind them, Thurbal came watchfully up the stairs.

Within, it was much quieter than below. Florin greeted them both with a firm armclasp, as one warrior to another. Storm smiled and kissed them both, saying, "It is seldom these days that I see two who have entered Myth Drannor leave again, alive."

Beyond her stood another lovely lady with long, silky hair who wore a gown of rich blue that left flanks and back bare, and had slit sleeves. It had been a long road from the taproom of The Rising Moon, and it took a moment before either Narm or Shandril recognized her.

"Sharantyr!" Shandril said when she did, and found herself in a warm embrace. At the same time, Narm was introduced to Mourngrym's wife, Lady Shaerl, by Illistyl—and then a sudden silence fell.

Atop a table that had been bare a moment before stood Elminster. Thurbal was coming in the door with sword halfdrawn before he saw who it was and halted, shaking his head. But the sage had eyes only for Narm and Shandril.

"Elminster!" Jhessail greeted him. "Well met!"

"Aye . . . aye," Elminster told her, "I've seen ye all before. It is with Narm and Shandril I would speak tonight." He turned to them where they stood, astonished, and said, "I fear I lack courtly graces and the patience for glib flattery and suchlike. So I'll just ask ye, Narm and Shandril. Will ye agree to a testing of thy powers this next night?"

Shandril nodded, her throat suddenly dry. Narm asked quietly. "Will it be dangerous?"

Elminster looked at him. "Breathing is dangerous, lad. Walking is dangerous. Sleeping can even be dangerous. Will it be more dangerous than these? A little. More dangerous than entering Myth Drannor alone? Nay, not by a long road."

Narm flushed and shook his head. "It would be a terrible thing, old mage, to fight you, both armed only with our tongues," he said dryly, and a muted roar of delighted laughter rose around him.

Elminster chuckled. "So, do ye agree?"

Narm nodded. "Yes. Where and when?"

"Ye shall know that only at the last," Elminster told him. "It's safer." Around them, talk began again. Elminster leaned close to them both. "Do ye enjoy the company of these folk?" he asked softly. Both nodded. "Good, then," he said. "Most will be at the testing." He patted Narm's shoulder absently in farewell and turned back toward the table. "Oh," he said, halting and turning in midstep. "I do grow forgetful. Shandril, what know ye of thy parents?"

Shandril almost reeled in surprise and sudden sadness. "I . . . I—nothing," she said, and burst into tears. Narm and Elminster looked at each other in bewilderment for a breath, and then the sage clapped Narm on the shoulder awkwardly. "My forgiveness, if ye will. I had no idea she'd be so upset. Comfort her, will ye? Ye can do it best of all living in Faerun." And with this cryptic remark the sage turned, muttered, "That explains much," to himself, stepped onto the table by way of the chair beside it, and was gone.

* * * * *

A guard touched Torm on his shoulder. "Lord," he said, voice carefully neutral, "it is the hour."

Torm looked up from the wench he'd been kissing and sighed. "My thanks, Rold." A sudden thought made him grin impishly. "Take my place, will you?" He rolled off the bed and to his feet, rearranging his clothing and adroitly bending to avoid the girl's angry slap. Rold held out his sword and belt for him solemnly.

"Me, Lord? It would be more than my life is worth."

"Aye," Torm said as they hurried out together. "I think you have the right of it." He halted in midstride, tore one of the chains off over his head, and handed it to the mustachioed veteran. "Give her this, will you, as a gift from me? My apologies, also, and I'll try to see her as soon as I can. My duty to Shadowdale must come first, and all that."

"Of course, Lord," Rold said, and turned back to calm Torm's angry companion. He found her sitting amid the disarray of the bed morosely, anger past, and dropped the chain into her hand.

"It's no fault of yours," he said, "that the Lord Torm is so young and ill-reared that he cannot give you a night when he is not called to guard duty. He gives you this by way of clumsy apology, and sends me to pour soothing words in your ear. I doubt he even knows we are kin."

"I could tell that," Naera said, taking her gown as he extended it to her wordlessly. "Are you angry with him, uncle?"

Rold shook his head. "Nay, lass, not for long. I have seen something of the road he walks. Are you?" He buttoned and adjusted with as much skill as any mistress-of-robes, and patted her behind fondly when he was done.

"Not after a breath or two. Where did he have to go in such haste?" She looked at the chain dangling in her hands.

"He patrols, outside, with the Lord Rathan. Elminster expects some trouble tonight . . . someone trying to get at our guests, no doubt."

Naera turned to him in astonishment. "The young lad and lass? What danger could they possibly be to anyone? They are not royal, or suchlike."

Rold chuckled. "Young, says Naera, who dallies with a man younger than herself, a—Oh? Did you not know? Yes, the lord's seen a winter less than you have . . . Don't look like that, now; was he any greater the monster for that?" He grew serious. "The young lass, as you rightly call her, defeated the High Lord of Zhentil Keep himself, the fell mage Manshoon. Scared him into flight, she did, and him riding a dragon, too! She holds some great power."

Naera stared at him in amazement. "And Torm is needed to guard that?"

Rold nodded. "Why else do you think I've never spoken ill to you of pursuing him as you have? It is a rare one you chase, for all his rashness and rudeness and dishonest ways. I'd not want to stand against him in a fight." He paused at the door and looked back, saying, "You'd do well to remember that, little one, when you're sending slaps his way. Come down, now, and we'll see what's left at table. You must be hungry after all you've been up to this evening."

Naera made a face at him, but rose to follow. She wore the chain proudly around her neck as they swept down the stairs.

*　*　*　*　*

In his chambers, Torm had torn off his fine clothing and jewelry like so many rags and pebbles and hurled them onto the bed, leaped around finding his gray leathers and blades, and burst back out the door like a lunatic, almost colliding with Rathan. The cleric stood waiting, arms crossed patiently, leaning on the wall across from Torm's door.

"Remembered, did ye?" the cleric said jovially. "I warrant ye had help. It's your short stature, I tell ye . . . with that small head ye carry upon thy shoulders, there's no room for a brain that can think, once ye've filled it with mischief until it runs out thy ears and mouth—"

His words were cut short by a shrewd elbow in the belly as they hurried down the stairs. Puffing for breath, the cleric leaned on a pillar by the door, thought a prayer to Tymora, and then bustled out the door into the night.

"Remembered, did you?" a mocking voice asked out of the darkness beside him.

"Tymora forgive me," Rathan Thentraver said aloud as he swept a pike out of the startled hands of a doorguard and rammed its butt end hard into the shadows. He was rewarded by a grunt. Satisfied, he returned the pike with a nod of thanks, and said kindly, "If ye're quite finished playing the bobbing fool this night, perhaps we can get going. It might interest ye to know, by the way, that the guard ye gave the chain to is the uncle of the maid ye were dallying with. Adroit, lad. Adroit."

"Oh, gods," came the softly despairing cry, out of shocked silence. "Why me?"

"I've often wondered that. Truly, the gods must have grander senses of humor than we do," Rathan replied, as they clapped hands on each other's shoulders in the darkness, and drew their weapons. "Now, let's get on with this, shall we?"

*　*　*　*　*

They had much wine and talked until late. At the last, Illistyl (she who had rescued Narm from devils not so very long ago) and Sharantyr were left in the bower, standing together, the ranger a head and more taller than Illistyl.

"We should say good-night, if we are to be fit for the testing on the morrow," Illistyl said wearily, putting down an empty goblet. "You have seen them both in battle, have you not? What manner of dweomercraefters will I be training?"

Sharantyr shook her head. "I never saw them fight. I cannot help you, I fear." She shrugged. "I think it better you should come to the task, if it falls to you, knowing nothing of them, and alert for all. What say you?"

Illistyl nodded and sighed. "You have the right of it." She turned for the door. "Good evening, sister-at-arms. I must seek my bed before I fall upon any bare stretch of floor."

"Good evening," Sharantyr replied, and they kissed cheeks

and parted. The ranger wandered down the stairs, a little dizzy, and nodded to the guards. Setting her goblet upon a table in the hall, she sought cool air to clear her head, and went out by the great front doors. One of the guards asked her, "Would you have an escort, lady?" He eyed her gown. "It is cold," he warned briefly.

"Aye? Oh, no, thank you," Sharantyr told him. "And it is the cold I seek," she added, putting the back of her hand to her forehead in mock-faintness. Both guards chuckled and saluted her.

"The Lady of the Forest and Tymora both watch over thee, Lady," they wished her, and she nodded. She went on past other guards and flaring torches and the last fading sounds of revelry, into the cool, dark night.

Overhead, Selûne rode high in the starlit night sky, trailing her Tears. Sharantyr stood for a long breath looking up at the bright moon, and then set off toward the river at a brisk walk. It would not do to catch a chill by remaining still too long—and, besides, no doubt her bladder would want to be free of much wine now she was out in the cold. The tall ranger looked about her without fear at the dark trees ahead. This was her true home, for all that she had come to it late. The dizziness was leaving her as she came out into the road with the dew of the tower meadow on her boots. She let fall the hem of her gown again and approached the bridge.

* * * * *

"Most will be drunk by now," the one called the Hammer of Bane grunted. "These Dalefolk are all alike. Too much to eat and too much to drink all at once, and they'll be as sluggish as worms in the winter until tomorrow eve, when they can do it all over again. The ones we want will be inside, you can be sure, and may be well guarded. But if we are quick enough that they cannot wake any mages, there should be few others they can call to their aid."

Laelar, the High Imperceptor's henchman priest, rose, in the darkness, and continued, "You two cast a spell of silence on that stone, and bear it with us as we swim across. Remain below, by the bank, until the rest of us have the rope up, and then stay at the bottom and deal with anyone who happens by. We'll up and do the grab. If we pull on the rope thrice, come up to us. Otherwise, stay where you are." There were nods, all around, and the curly-haired priest of Bane nodded. "Right . . . let's go. Cast your spell."

* * * * *

The guards on the bridge greeted Sharantyr with polite curiosity, but let her pass unchallenged. As she passed into the trees, she glanced back and saw them shrug to each other and smiled ruefully. Oh, well, no doubt they already considered all of the knights crazy. She walked on swiftly and quietly, past the temple of Tymora and into the deep woods, until she found a stump where she could sit and relax.

After a time, she heard unmistakable noises, and looked up with a frown. There were large creatures off to her right; men, most probably. Best to be quiet until she knew who they were, and why they were here. Then utter silence fell, very suddenly. Puzzled, Sharantyr rose and peered through the moon-dappled trees. Eight men were moving soundlessly down to the river Ashaba.

* * * * *

"Time to stop shivering here and make another round of the tower," Torm said. "Even anyone foolish enough to attack the dale in the first place knows that everything and everyone of value is in the tower. If they aren't creeping through these trees, they'll be over there on the other side of the river, in those trees."

"Think ye so?" Rathan grunted. "If they're as foolish as ye say, why don't they ride right up to the gates pretending friendship and then do their fighting? It'd save a lot of time and creeping around, would it not?" Torm chuckled. "Of that," Rathan noted, "ye can be sure. I may be reckless enough to please Tymora, but I'm not reckless enough to creep around as ye do." He peered ahead. "Look ye, down by the old dock . . . was that not a man, moving?"

Torm peered. "I see nothing," he muttered. "Get down, will you? They'll be well warned if some great giant with a mace and the sanctity of Tymora heavy upon him sails into their midst. Down!" Rathan grunted his way reluctantly to his knees and then to his breast in the dew-wet grass. "Now," Torm continued, "look along the ground and see if Selune above us lights them from behind as they stand above you." His tone changed. "There! Was that the place you saw before?"

"Aye, and there's another." The cleric rolled over and rose to his knees. Holding the disc of Tymora out before him by its chain, he chanted softly.

The silver disc seemed to sparkle for a moment, and then Rathan turned his head and said shortly, "Evil. Aye."

Torm nodded. "The prudent thing to do now would be to summon guards, create a big fray and much upset . . . Look, they have one of those magical ropes that climbs by itself. By the time we could rouse all, they could well have done much damage."

Rathan was already clambering to his feet. "Ye want to have fun, is what ye mean. Right, then; let's go." His mace gleamed in Selune's pale light as he raised it. "Don't fall, now," he warned. "It would not do for a priest of Tymora to rush upon them with the ferocity of a raging lion, but alone."

"Keep up, if you can," Torm replied, breaking suddenly into a run of almost frightening speed. Rathan shook his head and followed.

*   *   *   *   *

Laelar was third on the rope. He watched narrowly as the adept at the top looked cautiously in a window. If the alarm was raised now, before they could get proper footing within, things could go ill indeed. He belched to ease his taut stomach, knowing that the magical silence would cover the sound, for he carried a second stone that bore a dweomer of silence upon it. Utter silence reigned. Overhead, the moon shone uncaring.

There was a violent tug on the rope, and the warrior immediately above Laelar lost his hold and came crashing down upon the Hammer of Bane in a silence that could only be magical.

Torm rushed straight in at the two warriors. Blades swept

out to impale him, but he dove hard at the turf in front of them, rolled, and straightened his legs as he somersaulted to catch those blades and bring their points down. Rathan leaned over him, mace glinting in the moonlight, to strike a blow with all his weight behind it. The man he struck crumpled, neck shattered, and fell to the side, forcing his comrade to leap away or be struck and encumbered.

Torm, on the ground, scissored the man's legs between his own, and twisted around hard. The warrior toppled helplessly, arms and blade flailing, and Rathan dealt another heavy blow with his mace. He spun around to see if any of those on the rope were close enough to attack them, but the velvet silence had prevented any warning sounds. Only the man at the bottom of the rope was turning, startled. Torm slammed into him like a dark wind in the night, and swept him away from the rope into the wall beyond, knife flashing repeatedly as they fell together.

Rathan hurried to the rope, saw with satisfaction that only Torm was getting up, wrapped his hand around it securely, and hauled. He let go immediately and stepped back, not a breath too soon. Two mailed bodies crashed together into the space he had just left. Rathan attacked again with his mace. Tymora smiled, surely, or else it could never be this easy.

It wasn't. One of the two who had fallen still moved. Torm rushed in, catlike, with his dagger, and was struck by a black rod that seemed to come out of nowhere and shook him from teeth to fingertips. He staggered back soundlessly, and Rathan moved in.

Rod struck mace. Rathan felt the jolt up his arm, shuddered—magic! Gods' laugh, wouldn't you know it—and struck again. His blow was countered. The force of the counter-blow drove him back. Another was down the rope now, this one a warrior with a blade. Rathan and Torm went forward together, cautiously.

There was a flurry of blows, much shoving and twisting, and the foes reeled apart again. Torm threw daggers carefully at the curly-haired one with the rod, more to spoil any working of magic than to injure. They were struck aside, harmlessly. The other foe, the warrior, plucked something from his throat and threw it over Torm's shoulder.

The world burst into flames. Torm and Rathan were thrown forward in that terrible silence. Blistering flames raged over and past them. Those they faced reeled back against the tower wall at the searing heat. The rope, still standing upright by itself, was blackened but not burned. Torm stared at it as he sank to his knees in agony, face twisting in a soundless scream.

Laelar staggered grimly forward, his rod of smiting raised to strike.

Out of the night came something long and slim and feet first. The Hammer of Bane was struck in the neck and throat and flipped over backward like a child's toy, the black rod bouncing free of his weakening grasp as he hit the ground. Sharantyr, her wet gown plastered to her, landed on her shoulders after her devastating kick, and rolled over and up in time to face the warrior.

She stood, panting, hands spread but weaponless, facing that advancing blade. She suddenly realized that she could hear the wet grass slithering as her foe advanced and Torm groaning on the ground beside her. The spell of silence had been lifted. Light suddenly sprang into being all about them, and Sharantyr saw Rathan struggling to his feet out of the corner of her eye for an instant before the warrior of Bane charged. Someone—she had not time to see who—fell heavily out of the darkness above, and crashed to earth beside the rope with a horrible thud. The warrior was rushing at her.

"Die, bitch!" she heard him hiss under his breath, as he slashed down at her crosswise, a blow she could not hope to avoid. Sharantyr flung herself backward, and felt the very tip of his blade burn along her ribs as she fell. She cursed weakly, as she struck the ground, and rolled desperately away to her left—straight into Torm. Oh, gods, she thought, this is it. She twisted around, trying to raise her feet to kick away the killing blade.

But it never came. There was a solid, meaty thwack off to her right, grunts and the ringing clang of hard-driven metal upon metal, and crashing about in the grass. Then a very weak, whispering voice by her elbow said, "Good lady, I fear you are lying upon my arm. It's almost worth the pain, though, for the view." Sharantyr grinned in spite of herself.

"Sorry, Torm," she said, wincing, as she fell onto her side and rolled clear of him again. Across the beaten grass, a blackened and burned Rathan was thoughtfully picking up the black rod. Hefting it, he brought it down on the back of the warrior's neck, and then rapped the helm of the cleric with it smartly. Then he looked up.

Mourngrym was leaning out of the window above, Jhessail beside him, wand in hand. "All well?" he called. Mutely shaken heads answered him, and then guards and hastily-roused acolytes from the temples were around them.

"Don't kill that one," Rathan said faintly, indicating the cleric. "Mourngrym will want to question someone about this, and I'd rather it wasn't me." Then he fainted, laying aside his mace and all his cares for a time.

* * * * *

Dawn was clear and chillingly cold, despite the sunrise that shone brightly on the Thunder Peaks above. The small party of dragon cultists climbed the last reaches of a familiar trail and stared at the destruction before them. Where an abandoned but solid keep had stood, over the caverns that led to the lair of Rauglothgor the Undying Wyrm, there was now a vast, round basin of tumbled rock. Here and there gold coins glimmered in the bright, early light.

"May the Dead Dragons wake," Arkuel muttered, shocked. Malark ignored the blasphemy in his own amazement and gathering rage. It was even as those cowards had said. The girl—or others, but there was no reason to doubt their story now that he'd seen this—had blown the entire mountaintop asunder. The hallowed Rauglothgor, his treasure, the storage caverns, and all the spare weapons and provisions of the followers stored there were gone. This was magic such as the gods must have hurled about in careless might when the world was young. Oh, aye, a dozen archmages could wreak such a result on undefended, unmagical walls, given time enough—but one girl-child, untutored and alone, in the midst of a battle?

Malark drew off his gloves idly. A formidable foe, indeed,

if she could do this to great Rauglothgor. Yet she must die. The honor of the cult, of Sammaster First-Speaker, now dust in a ruined city, and of Rauglothgor, now destroyed, demanded it. The safety of us all who remain, he added wryly to himself, also demands it.

Malark, Archmage of the Purple, sat straighter in his saddle, slim and cruel, and looked around with cold black eyes. He gestured to the coins at their feet. "Pick those up—all of them. Recover the lost treasure of Rauglothgor." He dismounted, cloak swirling, and strode over to stare at the shattered stone. Gods above, he thought, shaken. The entire mountain has been smashed. He looked at the hand-sized pieces of rubble and recalled the tower upon its bare ridge of rock, as he'd seen it the last time he was here, and shook his head. He saw it, but he could still scarcely believe it. And yet he, Malark Himbruel, must stand against—and defeat— the power that had done this.

If he could not, who else? There were the liches, yes, but liches were chancy things. They served, really, only themselves, and were like the wine of Elversult—they did not travel well. There were other, lesser mages among the ranks of the followers, yes, but he dared not let such a one prevail against an important foe. His own standing in the ranks of the Purple might be threatened.

He was not loved, he knew. The others—who for the most part hated and feared magic that they could not control in their hands, magic not trapped in items they could wield and understand, or that which did not come from a god who laid down strict rules for its use—would not be slow to replace him if other, more controllable mages were at hand. Of course, they would discover that they had merely exchanged one dangerous blade with another—but by then it would be too late for Malark the Mighty. What would it be? Poison? A knife while he slept? Or a magical duel? No, the last was too risky, unless he were drugged or the duel was set against him by allowing his opponent items of power or protective art arranged beforehand; otherwise, Malark might win. The Purple would run red then, indeed.

There were ten non-mages in the Purple: the renegade priest of Talos, Salvarad, the most personally dangerous of them all; their warrior lord and leader, Naergoth; seven warrior-merchants, vicious clods, all; and the soft-spoken, slimy little master thief, Zilvreen. They'd be watching Malark Himbruel to see if he put a foot wrong in this affair. They'd all be watching. Malark thought silent curses upon the head of this mysterious girl and resolved to find someone who'd seen what she'd actually done in the fray. He had to know what the secret of all this power was!

Malark let none of this show on his hawkish face as he watched the men-at-arms scrabbling about in the rocks. "Enough, Arkuel," he called. "You and Suld, come with me. All others are to find all treasure, remains of the great Rauglothgor, and any other recently dead creatures who may be found where the lair was, and bear them to Oversember." Then he turned his back upon them all and began the casting of a Tulrun's tracer spell.

The girl who destroyed this place, Malark ordered firmly, and on a hunch he stood in the trail that led down the northern end of the rocky spur where the ruined keep had been. At once the air about him began to glow, and the radiance burst northward down the trail and into the trees below. Well enough. "Arkuel, Suld!" he commanded, and led his horse down the trail without looking back.

Looking back is a thing that one of the Purple cannot usually afford to do.

* * * * *

The Seat of Bane stood as empty as ever. The wan-faced High Imperceptor looked up to it in awe, as he always did, in case one day the Black Lord himself should indeed be sitting there. The head of the church of Bane sighed and took his own seat. He rang the little gong beside his throne with the Black Mace of Bane, wielding the great weapon with a delicacy that bespoke strength and skill surprising in one so thin and wan-looking. An upperpriest hurried in and knelt before the throne.

"Up, Kuldus," the High Imperceptor said. "The reports should be in by now. Tell me."

The priest nodded. "There is no report from Laelar yet, Dread Lord, or any who went with him," he began, "but

Eilius has just come from Zhentil Keep, and he says that
Manshoon has been absent from the city since the meeting
he dismissed, the meeting already reported to you! The other lords seek him, and that rebel Fzoul has been trying to
contact Manxam and the other beholders. The Zhentarim
are plotting and whispering like Calishites all this past day."

The High Imperceptor's smile lit up his face as if a lamp
had been lit within it. He rose from his seat. "Call in all the
upperpriests!" he ordered. "If Laelar reports with the girl,
well and good. If he reports and has not taken her, have him
forget all and return here at once. To Limbo with this maid
and her spellfire, while we have a chance at Zhentil Keep
and that traitor Fzoul! Go, speedily!" And he whirled the
great mace over his head as if it weighed nothing and
brought it down upon the stone altar with a crash that
shook the very Seat of Bane itself. Kuldus scurried out of the
room with the wild laughter of the High Imperceptor ringing in his ears.

*　*　*　*　*

The clear light of dawn laid a network of diamonds upon
the bed as it came through the leaded windows. Narm
awoke as it touched his face, reaching vaguely for a dagger
or something of the sort, and abruptly recalled where they
were—and where exactly he was now: in Shandril's bedchamber. But—he reached out his hand—where was she?

He sat up abruptly, which set his head throbbing, and
looked all about. The tapestries were beautiful, and even
the vaulted corners of the ceiling were impressive, but they
weren't Shandril. He looked the other way, past a tall,
arched wardrobe and a burnished metal mirror taller than
he was, to the door—which obligingly opened. Shandril
looked in and grinned.

"Ah, you're awake at last," she said delightedly. "Not feeling ill, I hope?"

Narm held his head for a moment, considered the nagging
ache within, and said carefully, "Not really, my lady. Is there
morningfeast? And—is there a chamber pot?"

Shandril laughed. "How romantic, I must say, my lord.
Morningfeast is an ask-in-the-great-hall affair that lasts until

highsun. The chamber pot is under there if you must, but behind that door over there is a water-bain—you flush with the jug after using it, or with the hand-pump—that all the ladies here have in their chambers. Was there not one in your room?"

"No," Narm said, vanishing through the little door to investigate. "Nothing like. It had only a bed and a clothes-chest, a wardrobe, and a little window."

"That," said Jhessail from the doorway, "is because Mourngrym and Shaerl figured you'd spend far more time here."

"Oh?" Shandril asked with lifted brows, "and how came they by that idea?"

"I suspect," Jhessail said innocently, "that someone must have told them." She chuckled at Narm's hasty reappearance to find the door-handle and pull it closed behind him as he vanished again. Then they both chuckled at his muffled complaint from within.

"It's dark enough!"

"Just like a cavern," Jhessail said encouragingly. "You'll get used to it . . . or you could light the night-lamp just within the door. Only mind you put it out when you leave, or the room will be a smoke-hole the next time you want to use it." She turned to Shandril. "Do you have plans for the day, you two?"

Shandril shook her head. "No. Why do you ask?"

Jhessail got up and paced thoughtfully over to the mirror. "Well, it is usual to see the dale, your first full day, and hunt or ride the countryside after highsun, with gaming and talk in the evening . . . but I'd like to advise a far less interesting alternative, if I may—Narm, the lamp, remember?—at least until after the testing this evening."

Shandril said simply, "Say on." She plucked up Narm's over-robe and, opening the jakes door, thrust it within.

"If you don't mind," Jhessail suggested, "Illistyl and I will bring your meals. You stay here in this room until tonight. Any of the knights will come to see you, or you could spend the day together, just the two of you . . ." The jakes door swung open and Narm emerged.

He grinned. "No words against that from this mouth."

"Nor from mine," Shandril agreed. "Only, why?"

Jhessail studied the rich rugs beneath her feet for an instant, and then raised solemn eyes to theirs. "Eight men tried to get into the tower last night, using magic. They were sent by the High Imperceptor of Bane, and they were after you, Shandril. They were to capture you for your power to wield spellfire. They were all slain, or are all dead now. They might well have succeeded except for Torm and Rathan, who were out on an extra patrol requested by Mourngrym, and Sharantyr, who went for a walk, unarmed, to clear her head."

Shandril's face had gone slowly white, and Narm had grown more and more angry, as she had spoken. "You mean," he burst out, "that enemies are going to be after Shandril for the rest of her life? I won't have it! I'll—"

"How will you stop them hunting you out?" Jhessail asked quietly.

Narm stared at her. "I . . . I'll master art enough to destroy them, or drive them away in fear of such a fate!"

Jhessail nodded. "Good. It's about all you can do. Once they get the idea you are powerful, as all know Elminster or The Simbul of Aglarond is, they will leave you alone—unless they have business with you, or with your tombstone, as the saying goes. But all of these who look upon you as weak and easy targets who have some power they can wrest or steal will fall away once you show Faerun that you are not to be so trifled with." She grinned suddenly. "But that time hasn't come, so stay in this room today, will you?"

Shandril grinned weakly and nodded; after a long moment Narm nodded, too.

Jhessail got up. "Good!" she said, and clapped her hands loudly. The door opened wide, and Illistyl came in, bearing a covered silver tray that steamed around the edges. With practiced ease she hooked a toe under a certain carving on the side of the bed, pulled it outward to reveal a folding pair of legs and a webwork of canvas attached to it, and set the tray on the table thus created. Shandril stared in open pleasure at the thought and construction of the bedside table, but Narm fixed Jhessail with a hard stare.

"You had it planned beforehand, did you not?" he said accusingly. "You would have given us no choice."

Jhessail shook her head. "No . . . if you had refused, Illistyl and I would have shared this morningfeast. I swear this, by holy Mystra." She grinned suddenly. "Elminster will tell you soon enough," she teased, "never force by magic anything you can trick a man to do for you. But know, please, that we will not force you to act as only we desire—ever. You can still change your minds; only tell us, please, so we can best arrange to guard you."

She got up, kissed them both fondly on their foreheads, and said, "Still, a whole day to spend together in bed—it's not something I'd pass up." She went to the door, where Illistyl had already gone, and said softly, "Fare you both well until tonight. We shall call for you then. Worry not about the testing; you are yourselves, and the whole affair is simply to know what that is, not change you. Illistyl and I have been tested by Elminster, when I came to the dale, and when she came to her powers. There is a guard outside; call if you need me." She went out slowly; between her feet a fast and silent smoky gray cat slipped in before the door closed, winked at her with Illistyl's eyes, and darted unseen under the bed.

The door closed and they were alone. "Well, my lord?" Shandril teased Narm challengingly. He grinned and reached for the tray deliberately.

"Morningfeast first, I'd say," he announced, and uncovered spiced eggs, scrambled with chopped tomatoes and onions, fried bread, slices of black sausage as large across as his hand, and steaming bowls of onion soup. "Holy Mystra," he said in awe. "I've had less than this for evenfeast at some inns!"

"Mourngrym told me yestereve," Shandril replied, reaching for the soup, "that in a prosperous dale, when one can, there is no better rule for a happy life than, 'Before all, eat well'."

"No disagreement here," Narm mumbled around his fork. "This is a fair place, indeed—at least, what we've seen thus far."

"Yes, it is," Shandril replied briefly, suddenly ravenous.

They ate in companionable silence for a time. Unseen, a long, slim centipede crawled in a tiny gap in the window-frame, and cautiously descended to the floor. Once there, it shifted and blurred and was suddenly a rat. It darted sleekly across the rugs and under the bed—and froze as it saw the wide-eyed cat watching it steadily, very near. The two stared at each other for a moment, and then the rat shifted and became a crouched cat just slightly larger than Illistyl, and they sat and stared at each other again.

Above, Narm pushed away his plate with a sigh of contentment, and looked at Shandril lovingly for a long time. "Well, my lady," he said slowly, "we still know only a little about each other. Will you trade life stories with me?"

Shandril regarded him with thoughtful eyes and nodded. "Yes, so long as you believe me when I say I know little enough about my own heritage."

"Oh? Is that why you were so upset when Elminster asked last night?"

"Yes. I . . . I have never known who my parents were. As far back as memory goes, I have lived at The Rising Moon. Gorstag, the innkeeper there—you saw him, that night; it was he who asked for the company's peace, and stopped the knife being thrown at old Ghondarrath—he was like a father to me. I never knew a time before the inn was his, and never saw the rest of Deepingdale. I still have not. I wanted to—to know adventure, so I ran away with the Company of the Bright Spear, who were there the night you were—and that is truly all there is to tell."

"How came you to Myth Drannor?" (Underneath the bed, both cats cocked an ear, but kept their eyes firmly on each other.)

"I know not—some magic or other. I read a word written on a bone, and was trans—tel—what do you call it?"

"Teleported," Narm said eagerly. "Like Elminster did, to fetch the healing potions for Lanseril."

Shandril nodded. "I was teleported to a dark place with another teleport-door in it, and a gargoyle that chased me. I was carried to Myth Drannor. I wandered about in the ruins for a long time, and then I was caught by that lady mage—Symgharyl Maruel. You saw me then." (More interest from beneath the bed. Both cats looked up, intently.)

"How, if you grew up only in the inn, do you know so

much of life, and of Faerun?" Narm asked curiously.

"In truth, I know little," Shandril said with an embarrassed little laugh. "What I do know, I heard from tales told in the taproom nights, by far travelers and the old veterans of the dale. You heard one, at least, I think. Splendid tales they were, too. . . ."

"Could Gorstag be your father?" (Tense interest, beneath the bed.)

Shandril stared at Narm, her face frozen upon the edge of a laugh, and then said, "No, I think not, although I am not as sure now as I was before you said that. We are not at all alike in face or speech, and he always seemed too old . . . but he could be, you know." She sat a moment in silence. "I think I'd like Gorstag to be my father," she said slowly. Time passed again. "But I don't think he is."

"Why did you never see Deepingdale? Did Gorstag keep you locked up?"

"No! It was just . . . there was always work. The cook would forbid me to do some things, and the older girls and chamber-ladies would forbid me others. Gorstag said that outside the inn and the woods just behind it, the wide world—even Highmoon—was no place for a young girl, alone. I was no one's special friend, except his, and I was not big or strong enough to fetch and carry as much as the older girls, so I was never taken along on any errands." She shrugged. "And so the days passed."

"What did you do in the inn?" Narm asked quietly.

"Oh, most anything. The chopping and washing and cleaning in the kitchen mostly, and fetching water, and cleaning the tables and floors in the taproom, and emptying the chamber pots, and lighting the hall-candles and the lamps in the rooms, and cleaning rooms, and helping wash the bedding. There are many little tasks in the running of the inn, too, things seldom done, like repainting the sign-board or redaubing the chimneys, and I helped with those. It was mainly the kitchen, though."

"And they worked you like a slave all those years?" Narm burst out angrily. "For what? You took no coin with you when you joined the company! Were you not even paid?"

Shandril looked at him in shock. "I—no, not a single coin,"

she said, "but—"

Narm got up, furious, and paced about the room. "You were treated little better than a slave!"

"No, I was fed, and given clothes, and—"

"So is a jester; so is a mule, if you count its livery! Before the gods, you were done ill!"

Shandril stared at him as he raged, and suddenly snapped, "Enough! You were not there and cannot know the right of it! Oh, yes, I got sick of the drudgery, and ran . . . and left my only friends—Gorstag, and Lureene, too—and I sometimes wish I had not, and I hated Korvan, but . . . but—" Her face twisted suddenly and she turned away. Narm stared at her back in astonished silence.

He opened his mouth to speak, not knowing what to say, but Shandril said coldly and clearly, as she turned about to face him, "I was happy at The Rising Moon, and I do not think Gorstag did me any ill. Nor should you judge him. But I would not quarrel with you."

Narm looked at her. "I would not quarrel with you, my lady. Ever." He looked away, then, and Shandril saw how white he was, and that his hands were trembling. She felt suddenly ashamed and abruptly turned aside as she felt her face grow hot. She got up hastily and walked toward the door. (Beneath the bed, two silent cats, who had watched all this, looked at each other and almost smiled.)

When she turned, Narm was watching her, and the look in his eyes made the last of Shandril's anger melt away into regret. She hurried back to him. "Oh, Narm," she said despairingly, and his arms tightened about her.

"I am sorry, lady," he whispered, head against hers. "I did not mean to upset you, or darken Gorstag's good name. I—I lost my temper . . ."

"No, forgive me," Shandril replied. "I should have let you yell, and not rebuked you, and there would be no quarrel."

"Nay, the fault is mine. Forgiv—"

"Disgusting," Torm's cheerful voice said loudly behind them. "All this sobbing and forgiving each other all over the chamber—and not even wed yet!"

The knight gave them no time to reply as he strode forward to pluck the food tray up from the table, saying, "Terrible stuff, isn't it? And such small portions, too! So, have you heard each other's life stories yet? Picked out any juicy bits to pass on to old, bored Torm? Pledged undying love? Changed your minds? Decided what you want to do next? Yes?"

"Ah, fair morning, Torm," Narm replied cautiously, rightly ignoring all the questions. "Are you well?"

"Never better! And you two?"

"Don't leer, it makes you look ill," said Shandril crisply. "I hear you prevented my capture, or worse, last night. My thanks."

"Ah, it was nothing," Torm said, waving tray, bowls, and all perilously in the air with one hand. "I—"

"Nothing, was it?" Jhessail challenged him severely from the doorway. "Three healing spells you took, and much moaning and complaining all the while, and it was nothing. Next time we'd do best to save the magic, and you'd appreciate your folly the more." She took him briskly by the arm. "Now come away . . . how'd you like someone to burst into your bedroom, when you are alone with your love?"

"Well, that would depend very much on who they were," Torm began, but Jhessail was propelling him firmly out the door.

"My apologies, you two," she said, over Torm's protests. "He's just come from his bride-to-be, Naera, and is in somewhat high spirits."

Torm looked at her, as if dazed. "Bride-to-be?" he gasped. "B-b-but . . ." His voice faded as he was marched out the door.

"Well met, Torm," Narm said dryly as the door closed again. He and Shandril looked at each other and burst into laughter. (Beneath the bed, both cats looked pained at Shandril's giggles.) When they subsided, the two embraced again, and sat in comfortable silence for a time.

"What do you think this test will be, love?" Shandril asked. Narm shook his head.

"I know not. Your spellfire, surely, will be put to the test, but how I cannot guess." Narm frowned. "But another thing occurs to me . . . this Gorstag must know who your parents are . . . and by the way he put it to you, Elminster may well know, too."

Shandril nodded. "Yes. I want to know, but I have lived all these winters so far without knowing. I would rather know you better, Narm . . . I do not even know your last name, let alone your parents."

"Oh, have I not told— Tamaraith, it is, my lady. Sorry. I didn't realize I had told you so little as that."

Shandril laughed. "We haven't exactly had overmuch time for talk, have we? You may have told me, and I've forgotten in all this tumult. All has been so confusing . . . if this is adventure, it's a wonder any soul survives it long!"

(Two cats exchanged amused glances. The one that was Illistyl pointed at the other with a paw, then spread its paws questioningly, and put its head to one side suspiciously. The other nodded and traced a sigil in the dust with one paw, saw that Illistyl had seen and recognized it—her feline head nodded, satisfied—and hurriedly brushed it out of existence again. The two cats settled down at their ease together.)

"Well said," Narm agreed. "I have not the love of constant whirl and danger that Torm does, that's one thing certain! Will we ever be able to relax and do just as we please, do you think?"

"I'd like to try," Shandril said softly, her eyes very steady upon his. Narm nodded and took her in his arms again, face set and serious.

"I would like that, too, yes," was all he said. (Under the bed, the strange cat shook its head, rolled its eyes, and yawned soundlessly.)

When their lips parted again, after a time, Shandril pushed Narm away a little, and said, "So tell me the tale of your life. Who is this man I am to marry? A would-be spell-caster, yes, but why? And why do you love me?" (Four eyes rolled, beneath the bed.)

Narm looked at his lady, opened his mouth, and shut it again. "Ah . . I—gods, I know not why I love you! I can tell you things about you that I love, and how I feel, but as to why—the gods will it, perhaps. Will you accept that answer? Poor it may be, but it is honest, and no base flattery, I swear." He paced, agitated. "I promise you this," he said finally, turning by the window, "that I will love you, and as I learn the whys, I will tell them to you. How's that?"

"My lord," Shandril answered him, eyes shining, "I am honored that you are so honest with me. Pray that we both remain so with each other, always. I approve, yes—now get on with your tale! I would know!" (Under the bed, two cats burst into soundless laughter.) Narm chuckled and nodded.

"Yes, I tarry. Know, then: I was born some twenty-two winters ago, in the far city of Silverymoon in the North. I don't recall it; I was still not a winter old when my parents journeyed to Triboar, and thence to Waterdeep, and—"

"You have seen great Waterdeep?" asked Shandril, awed. "Is it as they say, all bustle, and gold, and beautiful things from all Faerun in the streets?"

Narm shrugged. "It may well be so, but I cannot say. I was there but a week, and still not a year in measure, when my parents moved on. We moved about the Sword Coast North often, with the trade. My father was Hargun Tamaraith, called 'the Tall,' a trader. I think he had been a ranger, before he fell ill. He had the shaking-fever; he dealt in weapons and smith-work. My mother was Fythuera—Fyth, to myself and my sire—and her last name I never knew. They had been wed long before I was born. She played the harp and traded as my father's equal. I know not if ever she had been an adventurer. They were good people."

He stared into nothingness for a moment, and Shandril laid her hand upon his. His face was sad, but it was wistful, more than upset. "They are both dead, of course," he added calmly. "Slain in a sorcerous duel in Baldur's Gate when I was eleven—burned up in flames when the ferryboat they were on was struck by a fireball flung at the mage Algarzel Halfcloak by a Calishite archmage, Kluennh Tzarr. Algarzel flew out of the way; the ferry could not. All aboard who had no part in the dispute perished. Algarzel was slain later, or escaped into another plane, some in the city said. Whatever, he has not been seen since.

"Kluennh Tzarr left for his citadel in triumph. It is said that dragons serve him, and that he has many slaves. One day, if another does not get there first, I will be his death." His soft, cold tone chilled Shandril as he walked slowly around the chamber, arms swinging easily, eyes remote. Under the bed, the cats nodded approvingly.

"To defeat an archmage I needed magic—or at least, needed to know its ways. I knew not, then, that one cannot hope to separate them. So I tried to become an apprentice." He laughed, a little bitterly, at the memory.

"Imagine it, love—a ragged, barely lettered boy, alone and with no wealth to buy a mage's time or trouble, in Baldur's Gate where there are a dozen homeless boys on every street in the docks, pestering every mage that passes! I only escaped being turned into a toad—or just burned to ashes—by Mystra's will . . . nothing else can explain it.

"One day, two years after I started, a mage said yes. A pompous, sour mage—Marimmar, my master. His pride weakened him. He never worked to strengthen his art where he lacked spells or technique, in those places where he couldn't—or wouldn't—see that he was weak. But I learned much from him, perhaps more than from a smooth and masterful worker of the art. He had a temper, yes, and little patience—and he was perhaps the laziest man I have ever met, so he needed an apprentice to do all the drudge-work. You know the drudge-work," Narm added with a sudden smile. Shandril matched it ruefully.

"Marimmar disliked conflict, so he never fought mages to gain their spells—and he was obviously shining-proud that no mage ever challenged him. Those of real power saw him as a posturing know-nothing, with no spells worth seizing. Those of lesser power feared always that he must have something up his sleeve, he seemed so confident and fearless. His confidence killed him, in the end. He nearly took me with him.

"He saw the elves' abandonment of the Elven Court and Myth Drannor within it as his chance to become a great mage by seizing all the magic that he thought—as most mages seem to think—is just lying around in the ruins. I doubt there's much to be easily found. Anything that was has been seized already by the priests of Bane, or whoever it really was that summoned all the devils there.

"The devils slew Marimmar, and almost killed me, too. Lanseril and Illistyl of the knights rescued me—they are so kind, Shandril, I can scarce believe it, after all the swaggering heroes I've seen prancing down city streets—and here I am. I went back to Myth Drannor because . . . because I knew not where to go, really, and because I—I felt I owed it to the crusty old windbag, and because I could not sleep for fear of devils until I had faced them again. But by some miracle of Mystra, or the whim of Tymora or another, I was not slain, and I saw you. The rest you know." Narm turned thoughtful eyes upon her. "Forgive me if I have talked too long, my lady, or spoken bluntly or harshly of those now dead. It was not my intent to be rude or to upset you. I said what you asked, and now am done."

Shandril shook her head. "I am not upset, but much relieved. I had to know, you see." She rose and turned back the bed. "And now, my lord, if you will be so good as to drag that chest over in front of the door, we'll to bed." She smiled slyly. "The testing is to be late; I must have sleep first. Will you see me to sleep?"

Narm nodded. "Aye, willingly." One cat rolled its eyes again, and became a rat, and flashed over to the wall before Illistyl could even stretch. It dwindled and twisted and was a centipede again, and gained the sill while Narm was still heaving the chest toward the door, with many a grunt, and Shandril was hanging her robe upon a hook on one post of the canopy. An interested Illistyl saw a raven suddenly appear outside the window and fly soundlessly away. She nodded and curled up for a nap. Eavesdropping was one thing, but there were limits . . .

Narm finished with the chest, straightened up slowly, and caught sight of Shandril in the mirror. Two bounds and he was on the bed. Few delights come, it is said, to he who tarries.

❧ 11 ❧

Spells to Dust

*High magic is strange and savage and splendid
for its own sake, whether one's spells change
the Realms about or no. A craefter who by dint
of luck, work, skill, and the mercy of the Great
Lady Mystra comes to some strength in art is
like a thirsty drunk in a wine cellar—he or she
can never leave it alone. And who can blame
such a one? It is not given to all to feel the kiss of
such power.*

Alustriel, High Lady of Silverymoon
A Harper's Song
Year of the Dying Stars

Jhessail slipped softly into the bedchamber. Illistyl
straightened up from where she had dragged the chest
aside, and they shared a smile. "Worth hearing?" Jhessail
asked softly, and Illistyl nodded.

"I'll tell you later," the young theurgist replied quietly as
together they went to the bed. Narm and Shandril lay asleep
in each other's arms among the twisted covers. The two
spellcasters gently laid one of the bed furs over the sleeping
couple before Jhessail leaned close to Shandril and said, "It
is time. Rise, hurler of spellfire. Elminster awaits."

Shandril shivered in her sleep and clutched Narm more
tightly. "Oh, Narm," she murmured. "How it burns . . ."

The two spellcasters exchanged glances, and Jhessail
carefully laid a hand on Shandril's shoulder. There came a
swift tingling into her fingertips.

"She holds yet more power," Jhessail whispered, "and this

❧ 198 ❧

cannot be of the balhiir, not after so long a time and so much hurled forth. It's as Elminster suspected." She bent again to Shandril's ear. "Awaken, Shandril! We await you." The eyelashes below her flickered.

"Narm," Shandril said in a sleepy murmur, gaining strength. "Narm, we are called . . . ah . . . ohh. Where—?" Shandril raised her head and looked around. In the soft, leaping glow of the lamp Illistyl had just lit she saw the two ladies of art standing over her. She tensed involuntarily to hurl forth the spellfire within, then relaxed. "My pardon, Lady Jhessail, Lady Illistyl. I did not know you."

She shook her head as if to clear it and turned to Narm. "Up, love; arise."

"Eh? Oh. Gods, is it time already?"

"It is," Jhessail said gently. "Elminster awaits you."

"Oh, gods belch!" Narm said, rubbing his eyes and flinging back the fur. Hastily he pulled it up again. "Ah—my clothes?"

Shandril burst into weak, helpless laughter, and handed him his robe.

Illistyl smiled. "Jhessail and I will wait in the hall. Come when you are ready."

In the hallway, the theurgist said to Jhessail, "Tell no one yet, Jhess, but The Simbul came in by the window and listened, even as I did."

Eyebrows lifted, and then lowered again. "What did you both hear, aside from lovemaking?" Jhessail asked, lips twisted in amusement.

"The life-tale of Narm Tamaraith, full and open and unadorned. His mother, at least, may well have been a Harper," Illistyl replied, refering to the mysterious group of bards and warriors that served the cause of good in the Realms.

Jhessail nodded. "He thinks so?" Illistyl shook her head.

"The thought has not crossed his mind," she said. "It was the description."

Jhessail nodded again as the door opened, and the two hastily dressed guests of the dale stepped out. Narm looked at the two ladies curiously. "I mean no disrespect," he said slowly, "but is there a secret way into that room? I mean . . . that chest . . ."

"We workers of art have our dark secrets," said Illistyl

crisply. "I dragged it."

"Oh," Narm said, surprised. "I see. Uh, sorry." They went down the stairs, nodded to the guards and went out into the night. It was very warm and still. Selune shone brightly overhead. Merith and Lanseril waited with mules.

"Well met," the elf said softly.

"Where are we bound?" Shandril asked quietly, as he knelt to help her into the saddle.

"Harpers' Hill," Merith replied, and they set off. Shadow-dale lay dark around them. Looking about, Narm could see the watchful guardposts atop the tower and the Old Skull Tor behind them and upon the bridge and at the crossroads ahead. Silently the guards watched as the small party rode at ease through the dale and into the trees.

It was very dark, and the mules slowed to a walk on the narrow forest trail. Someone saluted Merith quietly. As they passed, Shandril saw a grim man in dark leather, with a drawn sword. "A Harper," Jhessail said simply. "There will be others."

The forest changed as they traveled on. The trees became larger and older, growing closer together. The darkness of their foliage, which now blocked the moonlight, became deeper and somehow quieter. Thrice more they passed guards, and at last came up a steep slope into a clear space. Torm and Rathan waited there, with others standing beyond. The thief and the cleric greeted them with quiet smiles and encouraging pats, and took their mules.

Merith drew Narm to one side, proffering a cloak. "Remove your clothes and leave them here," he said. "Cover yourself with this." Away along the bare hilltop, Jhessail was doing the same with Shandril. "Boots, too—the ground is soft."

"Will this be . . . dangerous?" Narm asked Merith.

The elf shrugged. "Aye, but no more so than spending your night any other way, if it's death you fear. Come, now."

Elminster stood in the moonlight at the center of the hill-top with Florin and Storm. As Shandril and Narm were brought to them, Elminster scratched his nose and said, "Sorry to get ye from bed for all this mystery and ceremony, but 'tis necessary. I need to know thy powers for certain.

Shall we begin, the earlier to be done?"

The knights embraced Narm and Shandril, and then left them alone on the hilltop with the old sage. He drew from his robes a small, battered book and handed it to Shandril.

"First," he said, "can you read this?"

The book was old, but upon its brown and crinkled pages were runes sparkling as clear and bright as if they'd only just been set down. Shandril stared at them, but she recognized nothing. Even as she looked, the runes began to writhe and crawl, moving on the page before her as if they were alive. She shook her head and handed the book back. "No," she said, rubbing her eyes. Elminster nodded, opened the book to a certain page, and extended it to Narm.

"And you? Only this page, mind—at the top; tell me the words aloud as ye can make them out." Narm nodded and peered in his turn.

"'Being A Means Both Efficient And Correct For The Creation Of—'" he began. Elminster waved him to silence, took the book back, and selected another page. Narm looked longer this time, forehead furrowed in concentration.

"I—I . . . 'A Means To Confound,' I think it says here," Narm said at last, "but I cannot be sure even of that; nor is a word more clear to me, anywhere upon this page."

Elminster nodded and said, "Enough, and well enough." He turned to Shandril. "How do ye feel now?"

Shandril looked at him with a little frown. "Well in head and body, or at least I feel nothing amiss, but there is in me a . . . stirring, a feeling . . . a tingling."

Elminster nodded slowly, as if unsurprised, and looked to Narm. "Have ye any spells or cantrips in thy head?"

Narm shook his head. "No. I—I have scarce had the time to study, since . . ." His voice trailed off under Elminster's grin.

"Aye, and good." From his robes, he drew forth a scroll, glanced at it, and handed it to Narm. "Read this," he commanded, "and cast it—at thy lady. 'Tis but a light spell; ye cannot harm her." He stepped back to watch.

Narm glanced around at the bare, moonlit hilltop, feeling the watching eyes he knew to be there in the trees. He took a slow, deep breath, and then cast the spell as carefully as he had done the first time ever. He turned and centered the art upon Shandril, who stood waiting.

Light flared around her, and then in a moment died. Elminster stepped near, looking at Shandril. Nodding at the fire in her eyes, he then produced another scroll. He gave this to Narm and said, "As before. It will not harm her."

Narm cast another light spell, and again it was absorbed. Shandril's eyes glowed brighter. A third time Elminster handed Narm a scroll, and he cast light. Shandril's body took it in. The old mage came near to Shandril and waved Narm away but did not touch her. He then said to Shandril, "Lady, do ye see that boulder, there? Shatter it with thy spellfire, if ye will."

Shandril looked at him, trembling a little, the fire leaping in her eyes, and said only, "Yes." Once again tingling fire coiled and raced within her, roiling about in her veins. She bore down on it with her will, thrusting it down one arm until it built to a soundless thunder.

From her hand burst forth spellfire in a long, rolling gout. The boulder was enveloped in orange flame, building to white intensity. The three could feel heat upon their faces, and there was a sharp crack as the stone shattered. Shards sprayed in a small shower upon the hillside as the flames died away. Silence stretched for long moments.

Elminster turned to Narm. "Stand back, now," he warned. "Over there, beneath that tree." The mage cast a light spell of his own. It, too, was absorbed. Elminster then cast two more. Then he created a wall of force to one side, and nodded toward it. Shandril raised her hands and hurled fire.

The flames clawed at the wall and raged, becoming a blinding inferno as Shandril fully bent her will upon the barrier. When at last she gave up and let her flame die, shrugging, the wall still stood. Elminster nodded again, and asked, "How do ye feel?"

Shandril shrugged. "A little scared, but I neither hurt nor feel strange in any way." She pushed with her will, letting flames leap up from her palms and then wink out in a little spurt, and added, "I hold more yet."

The sage nodded and said, "I shall raise a wall of fire there, before thee. When I nod, kneel before it and hurl spellfire through it, angling upward into the sky so as not to harm the forest. Only a little, mind thee. Cast it only for the length of a long breath, then cease."

Shandril smiled, flames dancing in her eyes, and said, "As you will . . . a short but steady burst of flame." Spellfire roared through the wall of flames as though it was not there, and roared onward, drawing the mage's flames with it. When the burst ended and curled away from the hilltop with a rippling, tearing noise of air, the wall of flames was gone. Flames dimmed and faded in the starlit sky above, and then all was gone as though it had never been. Shandril got up from her knees where she had been watching the beauty of the flames in the sky above her, and sighed.

"Are ye well?" Elminster asked, intently. Shandril nodded, and the mage said, "Right, then." He raised his hands and quietly cast a bolt of lightning at her.

It crackled and struck, and Shandril reeled. Narm cried out involuntarily, but already Shandril stood strong again, and the lightning was gone. The smell of the bolt hung in the air about her as she turned, bleeding a little from where she had bitten her lip, and smiled reassuringly at Narm.

"How are ye now?" Elminster asked.

"Well enough," she said. "I feel weary, a little, but not sick or strange."

"Good," the old mage said gently. "I shall cast more lightning at thee. Gather and hold it as long as ye can. If it starts to hurt thee, or ye feel it trying to burst out and ye cannot stop it, fair enough. Let it flow out at the sky or at the rock you struck earlier. Do not release it until then, so that I may roughly learn thy capacity. We have healing means near at hand. Be not afraid."

Shandril merely nodded and stood waiting, hands at her sides. When the sage's bolt struck her, she flinched but then stood quiet as Elminster hurled bolt after bolt at her. The air about the hill crackled and tingled upon the faces of those who watched. Narm trembled and twisted his hands about in the robe he wore, but could not look away.

More and more energy the delicate, aged fingers of the old mage poured into Narm's lady, and she stood silent and unmoving. At last she bent at the waist with a sob, threw her arms wide as she took a few steps to steady herself, and burst into a pillar of coiling flame.

"Mother Mystra!" Narm prayed hoarsely, in horror. Merith laid hands upon him quickly then, to prevent him running to his beloved—and a fiery death. Narm screamed Shandril's name and wrenched at Merith's grasp. He dragged the silent elf forward until Florin arrived to set his strength against the young spellcaster's. Narm struggled helplessly in their iron grip. On the hilltop above them a pillar of living flame writhed where Shandril had stood.

Abruptly, flames shot from it down the hill to strike the boulder. There was a flash, and those watching ducked as small red-hot chunks of stone showered down through the leaves around them. Jhessail hastily worked a wall of force from a scroll she had held ready, and Lanseril quenched those fires that started around them.

A smoking scar was all that was left where the boulder had stood. On the summit, a pillar of flame roared up as if to touch the glimmering stars. Elminster stood watching calmly, a cooling fragment of stone cupped in his hands.

Slowly, the roaring flames winked out. Shandril stood nude in the moonlight, sniffing curiously at the sharp smell of the scorched ends of her hair, which was otherwise untouched. Her cloak had burned away to nothing, but the flames had not marked her. Narm burst free of Merith and Florin's grasps and ran across the scorched rock, heedless of the pain in the bare soles of his feet.

Elminster moved to intercept him, but it was not necessary. Shandril herself backed away. "Keep back, love!" she warned. "I know not if my touch will slay, right now." Narm came to a halt barely a pace away. "I am well," she added gently. Her long hair rippled and stirred in the calm air as if with a life of its own.

"What can you do?" Narm asked Elminster in anguish.

"I will touch her myself, to end the test," the old mage replied firmly. "I am protected by potent spells, where ye are not. A moment, if you can contain yourself." He strode forward and took Shandril's hand in his own.

"Well met, sir," Shandril said with grave courtesy. Narm waited tensely.

"At your service, madam," Elminster replied, bowing. His

face was expressionless, but his eyes twinkled. Narm caught his gaze and shook his fists in impatience.

"Is she safe?" he almost pleaded. The sage nodded, and was fairly bowled over by Narm's rush to embrace his lady. He stepped back and waved at the trees. Harpers, knights, and guardsmen of the dale appeared from all sides.

Elminster looked at Narm and Shandril, smote his forehead suddenly and muttered, "Gods, I must be getting old!" and swept off his cloak to cast it about Shandril's shoulders. As he did, the stone he held suddenly twisted from his grasp and grew. In an instant he was facing a strange-eyed woman in dark, tattered robes, whose long silvery hair strayed wildly about her shoulders. All around, approaching Harpers reached for their blades.

"Well met," Elminster said calmly and turned to Shandril. "Shandril Shessair," he said formally, "I present to thee The Simbul, Queen of Aglarond." There was a murmur from those who approached, and then silence, as all waited for the infamous archmage to speak. Shandril gently freed herself from Narm, and bowed solemnly in greeting. The Simbul almost smiled.

"Impressive, young lady," she said, "but dangerous—perhaps too dangerous. Elminster . . . all of you . . . have you thought on this? Here stands a power you may have to silence. She may have to be destroyed." There was a babble of talk and then a hush. Shandril stared, white-faced, at the archmage, but it was Elminster who moved forward to stand between them and speak.

"No," said the old mage. He glared around at all on the hilltop with very old, sad eyes. "Ye," he said to The Simbul, "I, and all gathered here now, are dangerous. Should we then be destroyed out of hand because of what we might do? Nay! It is the right and the doom of all creatures who walk Faerun to do as they will; it is why we of the art frown so at those who charm often, or in frivolous cause.

"Not even the gods took unto themselves the power to control ye or me so tightly that we cannot walk or speak or breathe save at another's bidding! It is their will that we may be free to do as we may. Slay a foe, sure, or defend thyself against a raider—but to strike down one who may some day menace thee? That is as monstrous as the act of the usurper who slays all babies in a land, for fear of a rightful heir someday rising against him!"

"Aye. Well said," Florin agreed grimly, in quiet, deliberate challenge of the woman in black who stood among them. No other spoke. They waited in silence for the reaction of The Simbul.

The witch-queen stood in their midst, alone and terrible. They had heard of the awesome art she commanded, that held even the Red Wizards of Thay at bay, and hurled back their armies time and time again to preserve her kingdom. They knew the tales whispered of her temper and cruel humor and mighty power. Narm could smell their fear, there on the hilltop. Not a drawn sword moved.

The Simbul nodded, slowly. "Aye, great one," she said to Elminster, "you truly have the wisdom lore grants you in these lands. I agree. If others had not also agreed so, many winters gone, I would not have lived to stand here upon Harpers' Hill now." She stepped around Elminster, and he did not bar her way.

Narm, however, moved protectively in front of Shandril even as The Simbul advanced. She came to a halt and stood facing him. "I have trusted," she whispered. Her eyes were very proud. "Will you not also trust me?" Narm stared at her for a long, tense breath, and then nodded slowly and stepped aside. The Simbul glided up to Shandril and said, "My forgiveness, if you will take it. I wish you well."

Shandril nodded, swallowed, and said softly, "I—I hold nothing against you, great lady." She smiled, tentatively.

The Simbul smiled, too, and added, "A gift for you." Her hand went to the broad black belt about her waist and drew from it a plain brass ring. She leaned close until Shandril could smell a faint, strange, stirring perfume at her throat. Shandril had never seen eyes so steel gray, stern, and sad all at once. "Use this only when all else is lost," The Simbul whispered. "It will take you, and anyone whose flesh touches yours directly when you use it, to a refuge of mine. It will work only once, mind, and only one way. The word of command is on the inside of the band, invisible except when you heat the ring. Do not speak it aloud until you intend to use it.

Your spellfire will not harm this ring." Cold hands touched Shandril's and pressed the ring, strangely warm, into her palm.

"One last thing," said The Simbul. "Walk your own way, Shandril; let no one control you. Beware of those who stand in shadows." She smiled again and kissed the wondering Shandril gently on the cheek. Then she patted Elminster's arm wordlessly and turned in sudden haste. Her form writhed and rose, until a black falcon soared up among the stars and was gone.

Eyes watched in silence until she could be seen no more, and then everyone spoke at once. Amid the hubbub, Elminster said, "My thanks, Shandril. The test is at an end. Narm, take thy lady home, and sleep. Keep the spellfire that remains within thee until ye have need of it. It will not harm thee to carry it, I know now. Guard well thy ring. A gift from The Simbul is rare indeed." Behind them, Florin was quietly arranging a ring of guards to be about the couple as they returned to the tower.

"Think on this, and let us know when ye have decided," Elminster said as they went down from the hilltop. "Jhessail and Illistyl will train thee, Narm, if ye wish, and I shall show thee what I can of working together spellfire and spells. The cloak is thine to keep. It will protect thee in battle. It is old, and its magic is not strong, so beware not to drain its magic without intention. It is easy enough to do." The sage coughed. "Go now," he said, "and get thee to bed—where these old bones would be, if I had any sense. After all, you could be needed to save Faerun tomorrow, after highsun sometime, I suppose."

Shandril nodded, suddenly exhausted. "Thank you, lord," she said—Elminster winced at the title—"I must sleep soon, or fall down where I stand."

"Thanks, Elminster," Narm said with sudden boldness. "Good fortune this night and hereafter. After I get our clothes back from the knights, we shall go and think on your lords for a breath or maybe two before falling asleep."

They chuckled together, and then the young couple went down the hill, the guards closing in around them. Florin and Merith flew watchfully above, leaving the sage behind with

Jhessail and Illistyl.

"Satisfied?" the sorceress of Shadowdale asked her some-time master.

Elminster looked at the scorched marks on the rock at his feet. "I thought so," he said softly. "The power to unleash spellfire. Her mother had it." Both lady knights looked at him, startled, but Elminster merely smiled that distant smile that warned he would give no answer, and asked, "So what did ye hear of interest, Illistyl? Ye may edit such things as ye feel mine aged ears should not hear, out of consideration for my vulnerable heart."

"Well, then," Illistyl said, with an impish grin, "there is precious little to tell."

* * * * *

The mist was still streaming through the trees when Korvan from The Rising Moon, arrived at the butcher's shop. "Morning," said a stooped man the cook had never seen before. The stranger leaned upon the yard fence by the door, the mud of much travel on his boots and breeches.

"Morning," Korvan replied sourly. He had come for meat, not a lot of talk. Since that little brat Shandril had run off, he'd had to get his meat earlier, at a time of the day when he'd rather be abed yawning and dozing.

"Buying lamb? I've thirty good tails in the pen there, just down from Battledale." The sheepherder jerked his head at the muddy yards behind him.

"Lamb? Well, I'll look . . . if I can find two good hand-counts among them, I might do business with you," Korvan said grudgingly. The herder stared at him.

"Two hand-counts? Have you a large family?"

"No, no," Korvan said sourly as they went in. "I buy for the inn, The Rising Moon, down the road."

"Do you? Why, there's a tale I have for you, then!" the herder said, with sudden interest. "It's about that young girl who worked at the inn and left."

"Oh?" Korvan said, turning his head sharply in sudden interest. "Shandril, her name was."

"Oh . . . pretty, that," the herder replied, nodding. "I saw her in the mountains only a few nights back. I was chasing two lost sheep."

"The Thunder Peaks?" Korvan asked, nodding at the wall where, beyond, they knew the gray and purple mountains could be seen above the trees.

"Aye, near the Sember. I came upon a great crowd of folk, with weapons and all. They were all standing about, asking this girl of yours if she was all right, after she'd unleashed 'spellfire,' they called it . . ."

"Spellfire?" Korvan said, astonished.

"Aye. I hid—there were gold coins all over the place, and they had swords out. I wasn't sure that a guest who came uninvited would be left alive to walk away again, if you take my meaning—"

Korvan nodded. "Aye . . . but who were these people?"

"Shadowdale folk, they were. That old sage, and the ranger who rides about the Dales with their messages—Falconhand, is it?—and the elf-warrior who lives there, and a priest, I think. They were all excited over the girl . . . seems she burned up a dragon or suchlike with this spellfire. There was something about someone called Shadowsil, too. They walked about so that I couldn't rightly hear it. Never found the sheep, but I got their price and better in gold coins by keeping hid and coming out after they'd gone."

"She went off again, then?" Korvan asked. The herder nodded.

"North, down into the forest. Toward Mistledale, I suppose . . . and Shadowdale, beyond."

Korvan sighed. "Too far to follow," he said with feigned sorrow. "Anyway, if she wanted to come back, no doubt she'd have headed home by now." He shook his head. "Well, my thanks for your story," he said, looking past the butcher to the yard door. "Now, you had some sheep I'd do well to buy? The faster I buy from you, the faster I can be smoking and hanging."

* * * * *

Shandril must die, Malark of the cult decided. Not yet, but after these altruistic fools here had trained her to full powers. Somehow she had destroyed Rauglothgor and the dracolich's lair, slain or escaped The Shadowsil, and, if the talk hereabouts could be believed, had also somehow escaped—and driven away—Manshoon of Zhentil Keep. She had been lucky. It would be simply impossible for a slip of a girl to defeat the gathered mages of the Cult of the Dragon.

Malark cursed as the wagon crashed and rocked through a particularly deep pothole. Arkuel, in the leathers of a hired guard, turned and grinned apologetically through the open front door of the wagon. Malark snarled wordlessly and rubbed his aching shoulder. He collected his wits and considered how to separate this Shandril from her protectors in the tower of Ashaba. The Twisted Tower, they called it. Obviously, Malark would have to get into the ranks of the tower guards. Perhaps it was too soon.

There was a loyal cult agent already in the guard—Culthar, his name was. He could strike at Shandril later, when the time was exactly right. To try and take her now would be too risky. Malark did not trust his underlings to saddle a horse unsupervised, let alone do what would be necessary to make such a capture and escape, given the art and the swords that would come against them.

On the other hand, the longer the cult waited, the more likely it was that someone else would try to take the source of spellfire for themselves—the Zhentarim, certainly, and perhaps the priesthood of Bane.

Perhaps that would be for the best, though. With all the confusion that would ensue if one of those foes did make an attempt, Malark could storm in then and prevail, for the greater glory of the followers.

The archmage was jolted roughly out of that pleasant daydream as one wheel of the coach struck a pothole, bounced and sank, and then another wheel pitched sharply down into an even larger pothole. The wagon came back upright just as its rear wheels skidded sideways alarmingly on loose stones. The gods alone knew how fat little merchants managed this, day in and day out—and this was judged one of the better roads in the North! Malark questioned the wisdom of his own plan for the forty-third time, as the wagon slowed for the guardpost that would let him, a traveling merchant who dealt in love philtres, medicinal remedies, and special substances for use by distinguished practitioners of the art, into Shadowdale.

* * * * *

The bright light of morning made the bare, fissured rock of the Old Skull briefly a warm and pleasant place, despite the whispering wind that all too often made it the coldest, bleakest guardpost in Shadowdale. The three who stood there looked down over the green meadows to the south, and the grim and defiant Twisted Tower to their right.

"The gods help us if the Red Wizards of Thay hear of Shandril before she and Narm are both grown wise in the ways of battle and art," Storm said. "Without my sister, the defense of this little dale falls upon a few knights, and upon Elminster. And for all his art, he is but one old man."

"Things will get bad enough with just the Zhentarim, if Manshoon raises them against us," Sharantyr replied. "You miss Sylune very much. She must have been special indeed. They still speak of her often, and wistfully, in the inn below."

Florin smiled. "She was special—and she fell while defending the dale against a wyrm of the cult, a danger we may soon face again, with Shandril here. Even now, the cult must be searching for her—and with the testing, it will not take them long to learn that she is here."

Storm smiled, almost ruefully. "Elminster plays a deeper game than we do. He did that in front of everyone quite deliberately. . . . I trust him completely, and yet I confess his doings often make me uncomfortable. We will all have to deal with the consequences."

"You think such a public display was unwise," Florin said with a smile. "I, too—and yet I thought then, and still feel, that Elminster was like an actor in the streets of Suzail. He plays to a larger audience than those standing around him, hoping to attract the eyes of those who pass, perhaps a noble or even a ruler. Our sage is no fool, and not feeble in wits from age, unless there is some feebleness that affects the judgment but leaves one able to perfectly work art and develop new magics."

"There is such a thing," Sharantyr teased. "But it strikes the young, too—it makes us adventurers when we could stay safe at home in fields or forests, doing dull, honest work and acquiring respect as we grow gray and bent."

"Well said," Storm noted. "But I think Elminster has some purpose, though not clear to us yet, in displaying Shandril's power so dramatically."

"Is this 'us' we three here?" Sharantyr asked, "or the Harpers? Answer me not, if you'd rather not speak of them."

Storm shook her head. "I have not spoken formally with others of the fellowship, but I can tell you that most who saw the testing were of like mind. It is the act of a rash youngster."

Florin nodded, turning his gaze thoughtfully to the top of Elminster's small, rough fieldstone tower, just visible over the foothills of the tor below them. "Shandril is a danger to him, more than any other in the dale, for she brings spells to dust. If ever she moves against Elminster, or is duped into foiling him, the old mage can be destroyed—and our defense against Zhentil Keep will be gone. Those who would work such a deed are only too many."

"Aye," Storm said, her silver hair stirring with the rising breezes. She looked to the tower where they knew Shandril to be, and her eyes were very dark as she looked back at the two rangers. "So it must not happen."

* * * * *

"A lot of folk have died here, it seems," Shandril said, her voice showing fear. The young theurgist Illistyl was showing her the tower.

Illistyl sat down on a cushion and waved at Shandril to do the same. Shandril sank down as Illistyl answered calmly, "A lot of people have died, indeed. Zhentil Keep has attacked the dale twice since the knights came here. Almost half the farmers I grew up with are dead now. So are more adventurers who came to the dale than you could cram breast-to-breast into this room. It is real life; people die, you know.

"It is not all tavern-tales and fond memories. Ten levels beneath us, in the crypts, I know at least three of the knights who sleep forever. It is a price some of them, no doubt, never intended to pay—but pay it they did, most without choice. Think on this before you become an adventurer.

"The life you choose may well take Narm from you, or cripple one of you beyond art that you can command or hire to put right. Once you have power, though, you have very little choice—you become a foe and a target for many, and must become either an adventurer or a corpse."

"How did you come to be a knight?" Shandril asked curiously. "You are younger than Florin and Jhessail, and your art is . . ."

"Lesser? Aye, so it is. There was a lycanthrope here in the dale a few years back—not long ago, though it seems long enough to me now. The knights took a census, so that their art could be used to try and detect the weretiger. It was poor Lune Lyrohar, one of the girls at Mother Tara's.

"They found that I had powers of the mind, and Jhessail took me to study under her. I lost all my folk in the wars, so I came to live at the tower." She smiled. "Much of the time thus far has been spent raising Jhessail's and Merith's daughter; most of the rest, studying art. One has little choice once it begins."

"So I fear. Yet it was my choice to leave the inn. All else has followed on that. I suppose there is no other choice now." Shandril smiled. "Yet I do not regret any of it, for it has brought me Narm."

"Hold to that," Illistyl said, almost fiercely. "Do not forget that you have felt so. Hard times lie ahead, I fear. Your power, if wielded with deliberate intent, is a menace to all workers of art in this world. Few are stupid enough not to realize that. All who have the inclination will attempt to destroy you or control you as a weapon against others.

"You will see spellcasters enough to sicken you before long, and yours is an endeavour in which no matter how mighty one becomes, there is always someone more powerful. Learn that very quickly. The lesson is usually a fatal one if ignored. It can happen to you, too, Shandril—something of art may well be able to counter spellfire, perhaps something as simple as a cantrip most apprentices know."

Shandril nodded, soberly. "Sometimes I think I cannot do it . . . and yet it feels so good, even with the pain—when I let it out, that is. I see Jhessail, too; how happy she is with Merith, and both of them are adventurers. Even if she is not slain, Merith, as an elf, must know his lady will die hundreds of winters before he does. Yet they married, and seem happy. It can happen."

Illistyl nodded. "It is good you see that. It takes much work and patience, mind. Look—how does Jhessail seem? Her character, I mean."

"Warm, kind, yet strict and proper . . . understanding. I can say little more; I barely know any of you."

"Indeed, yet I would say you've seen Jhessail well enough. But there is more. Her control is so great that one does not notice that which won her Merith, which underlies her warmth. She is passionate—not just romantically, but spiritually—and strong-willed.

"Jhessail and the cleric Jelde were lovers when I first came to the tower. There was a great fight between Jelde and Merith over Jhessail. Jhessail decided she loved Merith more, so she set out to win him, before all the Elven Court and mindful of her brief span of years. She seeks longevity by her art, always, but she has never thought to outlive even his youth.

"That sort of control is required to master all but the simplest art. It is the sort of control you will need to stand at Narm's side through all that will come against you both. Hear and heed, Shandril, for I would be your friend for more than a few years, if I can." The theurgist grinned suddenly. "I seem to be one for long speeches this day."

Shandril shook her head. "No, no, I thank you! I've never had someone my age—or close, you know—that I could talk of things to, and not have to curb my words. Even Narm . . . especially Narm."

Illistyl nodded. "Yes," she agreed. "Especially Narm." She glanced around. "Remember the places I'm going to show you now," she added, as they got up. "One day you and Narm may be glad of a place to hide away in, together.

"One day soon," she added warningly, and Shandril could only agree.

* * * * *

Night had fallen, deep and dark, before Rozsarran Dathan rose from his table in the Old Skull's taproom, waved a wordless good-night to Jhaele, and staggered to the door.

Behind, the plump innkeeper shook her head ruefully as she went to mop up the table where two of Rozsarran's fellow guards slumped senseless and snoring in their chairs, dice and coppers alike fallen from their hands. They were like children sometimes, she thought, lifting one leather-clad sleeve out of a pool of spilled ale and adroitly avoiding the instinctive yank and punch its sleeping owner launched vaguely at her. Good lads, but not drinkers.

Outside, in the cool night air, Rozsarran reached the same conclusion, albeit slowly and less clearly. Hitching up his swordbelt, he began to walk hastily back toward the tower. An overcast sky made the night very dark, and a brisk walk might make him feel less rock-witted before he reached his bed. Late duty tomorrow, praise Helm. He could use the sleep. . . .

A silent shadow rose out of the night clutching a horse-leather knotted about a fistful of coins. He tipped Rozsarran's helmet sharply forward to expose the back of his head, and gave sleep to him.

The guard slumped without a sound. Suld caught him under the arms before he reached the ground and heaved him up. Arkuel caught hold of his booted feet, and they hurried him into the trees.

There Malark worked magical darkness and commanded Arkuel to unhood the lamp. In its faint light the cult archmage cast a spell of sleep upon the guard and then studied him carefully. "Strip him," he ordered briefly. When it was done, he studied the mage's face and hair intently and had his underlings turn the body, seeking birthmarks. None. Right, then. He cast yet another spell, slowly and carefully. His form twisted and dwindled and grew again, and a double of Rozsarran stood where Malark had been moments before. The disguised archmage dressed hastily, ensured that his concealing amulets were still upon him, and said coldly, "Wait here. If I do not return by dawn, withdraw a little way into the woods and hide. Report in Essembra—you know where—if I come not back in four days. Understood?"

"Aye, Lord Mage."

"Understood, Lord Malark."

"Well enough. No pilfering, no wenching, and no noise! I don't plan to be long." And Malark was gone, adjusting his swordbelt. How did they even lift such blades, let alone swing them about as if they were as light as wands? This one was as heavy as a cold corpse. He felt his way back out of the trees and the magical ring of darkness to the road.

There he found two guardsmen weaving slowly toward the tower. They were half asleep, irritable, and smelled strongly of drink. "Aghh, it's Roz!" one greeted him loudly, nearly falling. "Bladder feel the better for it, old sword? Fall over any trees?"

"Arrghh," Malark answered, loudly and sourly, thinking it the safest reply. He deftly ducked and rose up between their linked hands, putting an arm about the shoulder of each. One of the guardsmen gave at the knees and almost fell. Malark winced at the weight dragging at his shoulder.

"It is good you came back," the collapsing guard rumbled as he hauled himself up Malark's arm and rocked on his heels a moment before catching his balance again. "I need your shoulder, I fear. Gods, my head!"

"Arrghh," Malark said again, stifling a grin.

"Urrghh," the guard on his other arm agreed sagely, and they stumbled on. Ahead, the torchlight at the tower gates grew brighter and closer, step by bobbing step. Elsewhere, Malark might have crept or flown in the shape of a bird or vermin to a window and dispensed with all this dangerous foolishness, but not here. Not with Elminster about, and all these knights who could call on his aid. "Best I ever drank was at The Lonesome Tankard, where the roads meet in Eveningstar . . . 'at's in Cormyr, old sword."

"Uhh," Malark agreed.

Somehow he got the three of them through the guards and inside. He let them stumble slightly ahead of him to guide him, and they went straight down a long, high hallway to the guardroom. There luck was with Malark. Culthar, his spy, was one of the two watchmen, waiting in the guardroom until a bell rang on the board before him, calling him to assist of another guard elsewhere. The other was just rising, with an oath, to answer a bell three floors up.

"Why can't Rold relieve himself before he takes up his post?" he growled as he made for the back stairs.

Malark's companions stumbled around the room, catching at the table for balance. They made for the door to the bunkroom. One began to sing—under his breath, fortunately—as he went. "Oh, I once knew a lady of far Uttersea . . . she'll never come back, now, no never come back to me . . ." The door banged, and there came a fainter crash on the other side of it. Culthar cursed.

"He's always falling over that chair. It'll be broken now, sure, and we'll have to fix it again because"—Culthar's voice now rose in vicious mimicry of the guard—"he's not too good with his hands, and all." At that moment, the other guard who had come in with Malark heaved and shuddered, and made a sickening gulping sound. "Oh, gods!" Culthar cursed. "Quick, get his face into that bucket! Hurry! I should have known Crimmon would drink himself sick!" Malark scooped a leather bucket from its peg and did as he was bid, just in time.

When the retching was done, Crimmon roused himself blearily and walked toward the bunkroom almost normally, saying, "No more for me, I think. I'd best be getting back, Jhaele," back over his shoulder.

"Yes, dearie," Culthar said in disgusted mimicry, and they both waited. An instant passed in silence, and then there was another splintering crash from the bunkroom. Malark chuckled helplessly, and after a moment, Culthar joined in, as Crimmon's curses faded in the bunkroom. Malark put down the bucket and closed the bunkroom door. He turned to face Culthar, who frowned and said, "And how much have you had to drink?"

Malark let his face shift back to his own features for two slow, deliberate seconds and said, "Nothing, Culthar. Sorry to disappoint you." When he grinned, an instant later, it was Rozsarran's own lopsided grin.

Culthar stared at him in astonishment. "Lord, why are you here?" he whispered. "Is Roz . . . ?"

"Sleeping. I have little time for talk. Take this." He pressed a ring into Culthar's palm. "Hide it well, on your person, and do not part with it. It has magics upon it to conceal it from normal scrutiny by one of the art, but wear it only when you intend to use it. Speak its command word, which is the name of the first dracolich you served when you joined the followers, and it will instantly take you and one other creature whom you are touching flesh to flesh to Thunderstone—specifically, a hill above that town where one of our group lives as a hermit. His name is Brossan. If he is not there, go to . . ." Several more instructions followed. Then—

"One thing more. I may appear to you and give the sign of the hammer, or a redcrest may fly into this guardroom—it may be but an illusion, mind. These both are signals that you are to try and take this Shandril Shessair and escape with her by means of the ring if you see any opportunity, however scant. Otherwise, you are to take her when you think best—you guessed the task before I said it, did you not? Good. You will do this?"

"Aye. For the greater glory of the followers," Culthar whispered. Malark nodded and picked up the reeking bucket.

"Before your fellow watchmen return," Malark said, "I shall go to be sick outside." Holding the bucket before him, he staggered out and down the hall, once again every inch the drunken Rozsarran. It was a white-faced and thoughtful Culthar who drew off his boot and ran the brass ring onto his little toe where he could feel its presence reassuringly at every step.

It was a loudly and realistically sick Rozsarran who staggered out through the guards at the gate and into the night. It was a coolly efficient nightcat who loped from where the bucket and clothes had fallen, heading for a certain spot in the trees. There the nightcat became a rat, crept close to the the waiting cultists, and listened.

"Do you hear anything?" Suld asked suspiciously, peering into the night.

"Probably the master, coming back," Arkuel said. "Just sit quiet, now, or we'll both catch it."

"Sit quiet, yourself, cleverjaws. It wasn't me who bought a wagon whose front seat was so full of splinters it was like a carpenter's beard."

"Pierced your wits, did they? You shouldn't carry them so low down," Arkuel said smugly.

"You say a lot of clever things," Suld responded darkly. "I hope the scant wits you have about you work half as well for more useful work."

"Well met," said Malark dryly, stepping from the darkness in a spot neither of them was facing. "I'm glad to hear you both so happy and good-natured." He pointed at the sleeping Rozsarran. "Take up our sleeper, and come. Cover the lantern and I'll carry it."

When the light was hidden, the mage dispelled his darkness and set off back toward the tower. There he raised darkness again and within it they dressed Rozsarran and left him with the bucket in his hands, for the other guards to find. "Back to the inn," Malark commanded simply, banishing his darkness again.

The mage raised his arms and his fingers flowed and grew, then branched and branched anew. In the space of a breath or two, Malark's upper body looked like a large bush. A mouth opened high on one of the branches and said, "Come! And stay behind me." Together they crept through the night to the back of the stables.

"The dogs sleep," Arkuel whispered.

"Yes, but the stablemaster does not," Malark hissed back, and withdrew slightly, becoming himself again and muttering the phrases of a spell while Arkuel and Suld stood guard, swords drawn. Malark rejoined them and eyed the blades with contempt. "Put those away," he muttered angrily. "We're not carving roasts."

"The stablemaster, then?" Arkuel asked, as his blade slid back into its sheath. Somewhere off in the hills to the north, a wolf howled.

"He has something to watch, over by the well," Malark said. "Dancing lights. Come, now—quickly and quietly, to the wall." He strode across the innyard, his underlings at his heels.

At the base of the wall, the archmage's body shifted shape again, rising into a long pole with broad rungs; it gripped the windowsill of their rented room with human hands. The pole sprouted two eyes on stalks that peered back across the innyard. The stablemaster stood, axe in hand, watched the bobbing lights suspiciously.

"Hurry," commanded a mouth that appeared on the crossbrace Arkuel was reaching for. He flinched back and almost fell from the ladder.

"Don't do that," he pleaded, catching himself.

"Move!" the ladder responded coldly. "You too, Suld. Our luck can't hold all night." But they all reached the chamber and closed the shutters without incident.

Malark wondered, as he erected a wall of force between himself and his underlings, just what would go wrong when the time came. Everything had gone smoothly, yet he could feel in his bones that the secret of spellfire was not fated to come within the grasp of the followers.

Such hunches had given him sleepless nights before, but this time he fell asleep before he could fret. Soon he was falling endlessly through gray and purple shifting mists, falling toward something he could not quite see that glowed red and fiery below. "Horsecobbles," he said to it severely, but the scene did not go away, and he went on falling until he reached morning.

* * * * *

"I would speak with the cook," the traveler said. "I eat only certain meats and must know how they are prepared. If you have no objection—?"

"None," Gorstag rumbled. "Through there, on the left. Korvan's the name."

"My thanks," the dusky-skinned merchant said, rising. "It is good, indeed, to find a house where food is deemed important." He strode off, leaving Gorstag staring after him in bemusement. After a moment, the innkeeper caught Lureene's eye and nodded at the kitchens, pointing with his eyes. She nodded, almost imperceptibly, and straightened from a table where a fat Sembian merchant was staring at her low-laced bodice. Turning with her hand on her hip in a way that made Gorstag snort with amusement, and the eyes of every man at the Sembian's table involuntarily follow her, she glided toward the kitchen.

The stranger was suddenly at Korvan's elbow. "What news have you for the followers?" a silky voice said in Korvan's ear. The cook froze. He then turned from a pan of mushrooms sizzling in bacon fat and reached for the bowl of chopped onions, his long cook's knife still in one hand. He nodded briefly as his eyes met the merchant's.

"Well met," he muttered, as he turned back to the pan and dumped the onions in, tossing them lightly with his knife. "Little news, but important. A herder saw a girl who used to work for me here, a little nothing named Shandril who ran off a few tendays back, in the Thunder Peaks with the Knights of Myth Drannor and Elminster of Shadowdale. She had just wielded spellfire, and burned 'a dragon or some-thing;' Rauglothgor the Undying, I fear. This man said he heard The Shadowsil's name mentioned, and that there were gold pieces all around—"

"There will be, indeed, Sir Cook, if you do the boar just so," the merchant replied smoothly. Korvan, looking up with knife in hand, saw Lureene gliding into the kitchen behind him. He glared at her.

"What keeps you, girl?" he growled. "Can't you seduce patrons as fast as you used to? I'll be needing butter and parsley for those carrots, and I need the fowl-spit turned now, not on the morrow!"

"Turn it, then," Lureene said crisply, "with whatever part of you first comes to hand." She swept warming rolls from the shelf above the stew cauldrons into a basket and was gone with an angry twitch of her behind.

The merchant chuckled. "Well, I'll not keep you. Domestic bliss, indeed. My thanks, Korvan. Is there anything more?"

"They all went off northward, the herder said, from where he saw them, near the Sember. Nothing more." The onions sizzled with sudden force, and Korvan stirred them energetically to keep them from sticking.

"Well done, and well met, until next time," the silky voice replied, and when Korvan turned to reply, the merchant was gone. On the counter beside Korvan were three gleam-ing red gems, laid in a neat triangle. The cook's eyes bulged. Spinels! A hundred pieces of gold each, easily, and there were three! Gods above! Korvan snatched them in one meaty fist and then stood, eyes narrowed in suspicion. What if this was some trick? He'd best not be caught with them about the kitchen.

The kitchen door banged. Outside, Korvan glared all around until he was satisfied that no one watched. With a grunt, he put his shoulder to the waterbarrel just outside the back door. Ignoring the water slopping down the far side, he tipped it so that he could lay the gems, and a dead leaf to cover them, in a hollow beneath the barrel's base. Carefully he lowered the barrel again and straightened up with a grunt to look about again for spying eyes. Finding none, he rushed back into the kitchen again where the smell of burning onions greeted him.

"Gods blast us!" he spat angrily as he raced across the kitchen. Lureene stuck her head in at the door from the hall that led to the taproom and grinned at him.

"Something burning?" she inquired sweetly, and withdrew her face just before the knife he hurled flashed through the doorway where her smile had been, and clattered off the far wall.

Korvan was still snarling when Gorstag found the knife, minutes later. "How many times have I told you not to throw things?" the innkeeper demanded angrily. "And a knife, man! You could have killed someone! If you must carve something to work off your furies, let it be the roast! The taproom is filling up right quickly, and they'll all want to eat, I doubt not!" Gorstag tossed the knife into the stone sink with a clatter and went out.

Lureene, seeing his face as he went behind the bar to draw ale, sighed. He smiled all too seldom, now, since Shandril had run off. Perhaps the tales in Highmoon all these years had been true: Shandril was Gorstag's daughter. He had brought her with him as a babe when he bought the inn, Lureene was sure. She shrugged. Ah well, perhaps someday he'd say.

Lureene remembered the hard-working, dreamy little girl snuggling down on the straw the other side of the clothes-chest, and wondered where she was now. Not so little, anymore, either . . .

"Ho, my pretty statue!" the carpenter Ulsinar called across the taproom. "Wine! Wine for a man whose throat is raw with thirst and calling after you! It is the gods who gave us drink—will you keep me from my poor share of it?"

Lureene chuckled and reached for the decanter she knew Ulsinar favored. "It is patience the gods gave us, to cope when drink is not at hand," she returned in jest. "Would you neglect the one in your haste to overindulge in the other?" Other regulars nearby roared or nodded their approval.

"A little patience!" one called. "A good motto for an overworked inn, eh?"

"I like it!" another said. "I'll wait with good will—and a full glass, if one is to be had—for Korvan's stuffed deer, or his roast boar!"

"Oh, aye!" another agreed. "He even makes the greens taste worth the eating!"

He fell silent, suddenly, as his wife turned a cold face upon him and inquired, "And I do not?"

Ulsinar (and not a few other men) laughed. "Let's see you wriggle, Pardus! You're truly in the wallow this time!"

"Wallow! Wallow!" others called enthusiastically. The wife turned an even stonier face upon them all.

"Do you ridicule my man?" she inquired. "Would you all like your teeth removed, all at once and soon?"

The roars died away. There were chuckles here and there. Gorstag strode over. "Now, Yantra," he said with a perfectly straight face, "I can't have this sort of trouble in The Rising Moon. Before I serve all these rude men who have insulted you and your lord, will you have the deer or the boar?"

"The boar," Yantra replied, mollified. "A half-portion for my husband." Gorstag stared quickly around to quell the roars of mirth. The innkeeper winked as he met the eye of Pardus, who, seated behind his wife, was silently but frantically trying to indicate by gesture and exaggerated mouthing of words that he wanted deer, not boar, and most certainly not a half-portion.

"Why, Pardus," Gorstag said, as if suddenly recalling something. "There's a man left word here for any who makes saddles of quality that he'd like a single piece, but a good one, for his favorite steed. I took the liberty of recommending you, but did not presume to promise times or prices. He's from Selgaunt and probably well on his way back there by now. He'll call by again in a few days, on his way out from

Ordulin to Cormyr. Will you talk with me, in the back, over what I should tell him?" He winked again, only for an instant.

"Oh, aye," Pardus said, understanding. There was no Sembian saddle-coveter, but he would get his half-portion of boar out here, in the taproom, and as much deer as he wanted in the back, with Gorstag standing watchful guard, a little later. He smiled. Good old Gorstag, he thought, raising his flagon to the innkeeper. Long may he run The Rising Moon. Let it be long, indeed.

* * * * *

Late that night, when all at last were abed, and the taproom was red and dim in the light of the dying fire, Gorstag sat alone. He raised the heavy tankard and took another fiery swallow of dark, smoky-flavored wildroot stout. What had become of Shandril? He was sick at heart at the thought of her lying dead somewhere, or raped and robbed and left to starve by the roadside . . . or worse, lying in her own sweat and muck in slave-chains, in the creaking, rat-infested hold of some southern slave-trader wallowing across the Inner Sea. How much longer could he bear to stay here, without at least going to look? His glance went to the axe over the bar. In an instant the burly innkeeper was up from his seat—the seat where unhappy Yantra had sat— and over a table in a heavy but fast vault. He soon stood behind the bar, the axe in his hands.

There was a little scream from behind him—a girl's cry! Gorstag whirled as if he was a warrior half his age, snake-quick and expecting trouble. Then he relaxed, slowly. "Lureene?" he asked quietly. He couldn't go—they needed him here, all these folk . . . oh, gods, bring her safe back!

His waitress saw the anguished set of his face in the fire-light and came up to him quietly, her blanket about her shoulders. "Master?" she asked softly. "Gorstag? You miss her, don't you?"

The axe trembled. Abruptly it was swept up and hung in the crook of the old innkeeper's arm, and he came around the bar with whetstone, oil-flask, and rags with almost angry haste. "Aye, lass, I do."

He sat down again where he'd been, and Lureene came on silent bare feet to sit beside him as he worked, turning the axe in his fingers as if it weighed no more than an empty mug. After a long minute of silence, he pushed the tankard toward her. "Drink something, Lureene. It's good . . . you will be the better for it."

Lureene sampled it, made a face, and then took another swallow. She set the tankard down, two-handed, and pushed it back. "Perhaps if I live to be your age," she said dryly, "I'll learn a taste for it. Perhaps."

Gorstag chuckled. The metal of the axe flashed in his hands as he turned it again. Firelight glimmered down its edge for an instant. Lureene watched, then asked softly, "Where do you think she is now?"

The strong hands faltered and then stopped. "I know not." Gorstag reached for the brass oil-flask and stoppered it. "I know not," he said again. "That's the worst of it!" Abruptly he clenched his hand; the flask in his grasp was crushed out of shape. "I want to be out there looking for her, doing something!" he whispered fiercely, and Lureene put her arm about him impulsively. She could tell Gorstag was on the edge of tears. He spoke in a tone she'd never heard from him before. "Why did she go?" he asked. "What did I do wrong that she hated it here so much?"

Lureene had no answer, so she kissed his rough cheek, and when he turned his head, startled, stilled his sobs with her lips. When at last she withdrew to breathe, he protested weakly, "Lureene! What—?"

"You can be scandalized in the morning," she said softly and kissed him again.

❧ 12 ❧

Shadows Creep

The hawk circles and circles, and waits. Against most prey he will have but one strike. He waits therefore for the best chance. Be as the hawk. Watch and wait, and strike true. The People cannot afford foolish deaths in battle. War to slay, not to fight long and glorious.

Aermhar of the Tangletrees
Advice before the Council
in the Elven Court
Year of the Hooded Falcon

"I—I am too tired, lady," Narm said apologetically. "I cannot concentrate." Jhessail nodded.

"I know you are. That is why you must. How else will you build the strength of your will to something sharper and harder than a warrior's steel, as the old mages say?"

Jhessail's smile was wry. "You will find, even if you never adventure from this day forth, that you will almost never have quiet, comfort, good light, or space enough to study as you are taught to do. You will always be struggling to fix spells in memory while over-tired, or sick, or wounded and in pain, or in the midst of snoring, groaning, talking, or even crying. Learn now, and you will be glad of it, then."

"My thanks in advance, then, good lady," Narm returned as wryly. Jhessail grinned.

"You learn, you learn," she said. "Well . . . why are you not staring at the pages before you? The spells will not remember themselves, you know."

Narm shook his head, a half-smile of frustration on his

face, as he said, "I simply can't! It's not possible!"

"So says the warrior when told to learn spells and become a great mage," Jhessail countered, sitting suddenly in a smooth swirl of silver-gray robes. "So, too, the thief. But you already cast spells! I have seen you . . . the smallest cantrip you work says you can. 'Can't' died when you read your first runes, lad! You sit there and lie to me with open face and open spellbooks both? You can do better than that!"

"Aarghh!" Narm answered in frustration, striking the table with his fist. "I cannot think with you talking to me, always talking! Marimmar never did this to me! He—"

"Died in an instant because his foolishness was far greater than his art," Jhessail replied. "I expect more of you than that, Narm. Moreover, you must expect different ways of mastering art whenever you seek a different tutor. Question neither the methods nor the opinions freely given, even if they make you flame within, and do not belittle the knowledge imparted. It will shut off, as one shuts off a tap, and you will get no more for all your pleading and coins. You would be a mage, and know not what sort of pride you will have to deal with, yet? I know well—I'm dealing with your pride, right now!"

"I—my apologies, Jhess—Lady Jhessail. I have no wish to offend you. I—"

"—can avoid such offense by looking to your pages and trying to study through my jabber, and not wasting my time! I am older than you by a good start, lad. I have less left to me than you do, by far, if you have the wits enough to live to full growth—an increasingly doubtful prospect, it is true, but one that I will cling to nonetheless."

Narm tossed up his hands in wordless despair and bent his head to the spellbook open in front of him. Jhessail grinned again. "Well enough. Remember—no, don't look up at me. You know I'm beautiful, and I know it, too, but the art of Mystra is far more beautiful. Its beauty lasts where mine will wither with the years. Remember that I have learned some art from Elminster himself—" Narm looked up in surprise. Jhessail scowled and pointed severely down at his book again. "—and I'm fast running out of severe things that he said to me, to parrot back at you. So for the love of Mystra, Narm, look down at your spells and try. That way I can lecture you on the kings of Cormyr, or the court etiquette of Aglarond, or recite the love songs of Solshuss the Bard, and not have to tax my wits so."

"Aye, I-I'll try. One question of you if I may, lady, before I do." Narm looked up at her. Jhessail smiled and nodded. "Elminster spoke so to you? Why?"

"Because he considered it necessary, as I do, at this stage in the training of one who wields the art. Your Marimmar obviously never knew such discipline. Illistyl, who wields far less powerful spells than he did, has known it, and is the better for it. Elminster considered his tutoring remiss if a mage did not know such frustration.

"The art is a thing of beauty in itself, and it can also be helpful and creative. Too many spellcasters neglect such facets of art in their haste to gain wealth, and influence—and enemies—by mastering fire and lightning. Remember that, Narm. In years to come, if you forget everything else I taught you, remember that. You saw The Shadowsil's death. Elminster trained her for a long time. You saw what a fascination with power, and power only, can do."

"Aye . . . but why else become a mage?"

"Why? Why!? Why become anything other than a farmer, a hunter, or a warrior? Those three professions the world forces upon any born here, if they try to scratch out a living for themselves in the wilderness. All else—carpentry, painting, weaving, smith-work—one does because one has the aptitude and the desire.

"If power is all you want, become a warrior—but mind you always strike at the weak and unprotected. Your arm may grow weary with all the slaying, but power you'll have and power you'll use over others—until, of course, you fall before the greater power of another. Keep up questions of this ilk, Narm, and you'll find I can keep up the testy temper of Elminster! Why aren't you looking at your books?"

"I—aye. Sorry, Lady Jhessail." It was Jhessail who threw up her hands in despair this time.

"Gods above," she sighed. "To think that I once behaved as this one does! It is a wonder, indeed, that Elminster did not deem the form of a slug or a toad would do me more fittingly, to end my days! Patience, above all, patience! Pity the poor student of art; he still has this lesson ahead of him! Pity the little leucrotta, indeed!"

Narm looked up, alarmed. Jhessail winked, and then screamed, "Again you allow meaningless noise to distract you! You call yourself a magic-user!?

"Have you ever seen a rat? Oh, they'll crouch back to avoid a stick—but if you run about yelling, and they are eating in the grain sack, they'll go on eating as long as they can. If they must run, they'll run with mouth full, and fully intending to return! Have you no more brains than a rat? Study, boy, study! Kings are born to their station; rats are born to theirs, too. All the rest of us must work for it! Study, I say!"

The door opened and Illistyl peered in. "Quite a performance," she remarked mildly. "Now, if you could only imitate Elminster's voice . . ." She closed the door again hastily as Jhessail hurled a quill stand in her direction.

After the crash, the door popped open again, and Illistyl looked in again, rather anxiously. "You don't have any more of those at hand, do you?" she inquired, looking down at the unharmed brass at her feet. Jhessail grinned at her.

"Unfortunately not," she said. "He's using it."

"Using it? Whatever for? He hasn't written a line all this time. He seems to have been otherwise occupied," Illistyl declared, with exaggerated innocence. Her eyes found Narm, staring up at them both in astonishment, and she grew a head taller upon the instant. Her hair rose about her head, and her eyes grew the size of thumbs. "What's this? A few words we exchange, and this student breaks off his studying? Is he weak-minded? Is he a prankster? Or is he just wasting his teacher's time?"

All this time, as she shouted, Illistyl was rushing toward a frightened and dumbfounded Narm, until she was only inches away. Whereupon she smiled sweetly, and added in a normal voice, "Narm, how are you ever going to advance your art if you can't concentrate as well as any three-year-old playing in the mud?"

Narm looked as if he was about to cry, and then burst into helpless laughter. "I've never learned art like this before!" he said, when he managed to speak again.

"You must be used to a lot of ponderous dignity and mystical mumbling," Illistyl said. "Now look down at your book again . . . you can't read runes while you're looking at me."

Narm sighed loudly and feelingly, and bent to his books once more. "Mystra aid me," he muttered.

"She'll have to. But give her a little help in the task, eh?" Illistyl responded. She turned to Jhessail. "Well, it's nice to know I wasn't the only one to climb stone walls in my frustration at this stage of your teaching."

Jhessail raised an eyebrow. "You think I didn't, in my turn? Elminster continuously threatened to spank me with an unseen servant spell while I studied. Then he threatened to force me to battle him with the spells I'd managed to memorize through all of that."

Illistyl chuckled. "You never told me that! Did he make it any more than a threat?"

"No. I learned to study through nearly anything, with astonishing speed."

"Think he'll do as well?" Illistyl asked quietly, nodding at Narm's bent head. Jhessail shrugged.

"For himself, aye. But as protector and mate to one who will be attacked day after day because she can wield spellfire—that's less certain. Are you listening again, Narm?"

Narm looked up. "Sorry, did you ask me something?"

"Much better," Jhessail replied. "See that you apply yourself in this, Narm. Your life—and your lady's life—will certainly depend upon it."

* * * * *

Shandril looked around the cavern in awe. It was vast, and dark, and littered with rubble. Elminster saw her eyes moving about, and said, "An accident, long ago. Be ye ready, little one?"

"Aye," Shandril answered dryly. "What now?"

Elminster looked grave. "A few more tests. Things better learned before thy life depends upon it." He walked a few paces away from her. "My art shields this chamber against prying magic," he added. "First—hold thy hand up, like so . . . now the other."

Shandril looked at him, a little afraid. "Do you want me to

turn my spellfire upon myself?"

Elminster nodded slowly. "We must know," he said, "but mind ye do it very gently. Stop at once if it affects thee."

Shandril nodded in her turn, and bent her will to the task. The thought of burning herself made her feel sick. She set her teeth, looked up at the mage, and then stared at the hand which would receive the flames. Spellfire blossomed from her other hand, and writhed out in a small, delicate tongue to lick at her unprotected hand.

No pain, but a tingling in her limbs that built in intensity as she continued to envelop her hand in flames. She withdrew it from the raging, blistering heat, found it unmarked, and plunged it in once more. The flames roared; her uncontrollable shuddering grew.

Abruptly she felt something grasp her hand and draw it from the flames. Another hand took its place, and almost immediately she heard Elminster grunt, "Urrrgh," and draw away. He touched her shoulder, and then, slowly and deliberately, her bare cheek. No flame erupted from that contact. He patted her on the shoulder. "Enough."

The flames died. Elminster stood facing her, working the fingers of one blackened hand with a frown of mingled interest and pain. "Well, then. It does not burn thee, but the force may harm thine innards, circling back in. It does burn another, regardless of defences of art. When ye are not so full of energy that it burns in thine eyes, it harms only where ye intend it, and not at any touch. Narm will last longer than I had feared."

Shandril giggled at his tone. "You will want to watch the two of us, then, to further your investigations?"

Elminster looked up past his brows at her disapprovingly, as he waggled his fingers. "It may not surprise ye to learn," he said gravely, "that in over five hundred-odd winters, I have seen such things a time or two before." He grinned. "I'd have seen far more, too, if I'd had the courage to keep my eyes open at a younger age than I did."

He turned, in a swirl of robes. "But enough of such unsuitable topics for an old man to be discussing with a young lady when they are alone in the dark. Turn thy spellfire here, upon this wall—nowhere else, mind; this cavern may not be entirely stable! Let us see what befalls."

Again Shandril set her will, and spellfire flamed out from her hand. It struck the wall with a hollow roaring and burst in all directions, sparks and tendrils of flame leaping among the rocks. The cavern wall held, despite Shandril's fierce efforts to hurl all the heat and flame she could at it. When Elminster patted her on the shoulder again to desist, the cavern wall was red-hot and sooty black.

"How does it feel to hold such power in thine hands?" Elminster asked softly.

"Eerie, indeed," Shandril answered truthfully. "Exciting and fearsome. I—I never seem to be able to relax anymore."

"Could ye at the inn?"

"Well, yes. Short moments by myself, now and then. But it's not just the adventure . . . nor the spellfire . . ."

"It's Narm," Elminster said dryly. "Would ye try something else for me?"

"Yes . . . what is your will?"

"See if ye can hurl spellfire from thy knee, or forehead, or foot, or behind . . . or your eyes, again. See if ye can hurl it in a spray, or curve the flames around sharp bends, or hurl small balls or streamers of flame. Knowing the accuracy of thy aim would also be useful."

"How long do you—never mind. How shall we proceed?" Shandril mopped her sweating forehead with one hand; her fire had made it hot in the cave. Elminster held out his pipe wordlessly. She pointed one finger and pushed, just a little, with her will, and a tiny spurt of flame shot out. The mage sucked on the pipe and turned its bowl adroitly all at once to catch the flame, puffed contentedly, then nodded to her.

"Aye . . . we'll start so . . ."

* * * * *

It was quiet in the hall that night, despite the gathered band of knights. They sat at the trestle table that stretched at least thirty paces down the center of the room. It was warm and smoky, and the remains of a good feast were still upon the table. The guards who usually lined the walls and the servants always scurrying between table and kitchen were absent, barred from the chamber by Mourngrym.

Mourngrym and Shaerl sat at the head of the table. At the foot sat Elminster. Down one side of the long board, from the head, sat Storm Silverhand, Shandril, and Narm. The knights lined the other side. All other places were empty.

Jhessail was on her feet, addressing the assembled company. "My lords and ladies," she concluded, "Narm Tamaraith has advanced his art considerably since first he came among us. He lacked not aptitude or dedication, but merely suffered from poor and insufficient prior training." She smiled, and to Narm's intense surprise continued, "He was a joy to train. Illistyl and I have no hesitation in presenting Narm before this company as an accomplished conjurer. It is my understanding that Elminster wishes to examine and train Narm yet, to further him for the special task of art required in supporting the unique power of his betrothed. I yield to my master."

Elminster rose, even as she sat smoothly, and said, "Aye. I will talk to Narm of that before long. But I am here tonight in answer to Mourngrym's request"—His subtle emphasis on the last word brought a smile to the edges of the Lord of Shadowdale's mouth. "I will report to ye on what I have learned of the powers of Shandril Shessair, specifically that unique ability we call 'spellfire.' The power to wield spellfire has been known in the Realms in the past—"

"It is my duty this time, I fear," Florin interrupted, standing with a polite bow to Mourngrym and to the old sage. "Elminster—the short version, please. No disrespect intended, but we have not your interest nor patience."

Elminster eyed him sourly. "Patience seems in short supply these days. It is a lamentable state of affairs when things happen at such a pace that folk can scarce talk things over and grumble before the face of the land is changed again. Woeful days, indeed—" Here he forestalled several knights who had opened their mouths to speak. "But I digress. To the matter directly at hand: the Lady Shandril, betrothed to Lord Narm Tamaraith, both of whom sit among us.

"Shandril can now, without the presence of the balhiir that apparently began her use of spellfire, draw in spell energy without much personal harm—although some harm appears to be involved with some magic—and store it, for an unknown length of time and without apparent ill effects. She can subsequently send it forth, upon command and with some precise control, as a fire that burns despite most magical defenses, and affects all things and beings I have been able to observe it against thus far.

"Shandril has a finite capacity for such absorbed spell energy, but we are presently not entirely certain what it is. We know neither the precise effects of the spellfire upon Shandril, nor the limitations of the spellfire she wields.

"I can tell you what spellfire is: the raw energy that all workings of art are really composed of, broken down by Shandril's body in some unknown manner from a given magical effect—of spell or item—into the force necessary to create and enact such an effect.

"As The Simbul, distinguished ruler of Aglarond, pointed out at the testing, such a power is dangerous—dangerous to Shandril personally, and to those nearby. When Shandril's body holds so much energy that her eyes flash spellfire, her very touch can harm those around her with an unintentional discharge. She is also a threat to those who work magic everywhere in this world. Those who see this last threat will act to destroy Shandril, or to possess her to use her power against others.

"Certain fell powers undoubtedly already know of her abilities, and will act soon, if they have not begun already. There is much more to be said, but—hem—ye asked for the short version." The old archmage sat down again and reached for his pipe.

"So you are saying, then, that war will come to the dale again, because the source of spellfire is here?" the Lady Shaerl asked.

"Aye," Elminster replied, "and we must be ready. To arms and alert! We must defend Shandril's person with our swords, and raise the art at our command to defend against the many mages who will come for Shandril's spellfire. She cannot be everywhere to battle all of them, were she the most willing slayer in the world. Our spells we must also cast to Shandril, to feed her spellfire—it is this her man Narm does best. Days of blood, I fear, are upon us."

Mourngrym spoke then in challenge, rising to look at all

there assembled, and said, "It is hardly fair, you powerful and experienced adventurers, to drag these young folks into a battle that will almost certainly mean their deaths, just to use them as weapons against those who come here."

"They are in such a battle as we breathe now," Elminster said sharply. "We delivered them out of it once, as a knight drags a weary fellow out of the fray for a time to catch his breath, quell his pain, and set to again. It is the price of adventuring, such conflict. And don't tell me that they are not adventurers. One ran off with a chartered company of adventurers, while the other willingly returned to Myth Drannor, alone and unarmed, to 'seek his fortune' after the death of his master at the hands of the devils. We do not, lord, intend to 'use them as weapons,' but to see they know their powers fully."

The old sage glanced around at the knights, and added, "Why invite such peril? Why see a young maid become a threat to one's own powers? Why build her strength, and that of her consort, to make them an even greater menace? Because . . . because, after all these years, it still feels good to have helped someone, and accomplished something. This first fight, it is part of that, and we cannot avoid it. When it is done, it is our duty to let them go where they will, and not compel them or make their choices for them."

A large green glass bottle that stood upon the table, full of wine and as yet unopened, like many of its fellows, began to change shape. As all watched in astonishment, it grew and became The Simbul, kneeling atop the table with proud and lonely eyes. The witch-queen nodded to Narm and Shandril, and then looked to Elminster.

"You will let these two walk freely?" she asked. "Truly?"

The archmage nodded. "Aye. I will. We all here will."

"Then you have my blessing," she added softly. She turned into a bird and, with a whir of wings, she darted up the chimney and was gone.

The knights relaxed, visibly. "One day I suppose I'll be used to that," Torm remarked. "Old mage, can't you tell by art when she's near?"

Elminster shook his head. "Unless she actively uses art of her own, nay. Her cloak-of-art is as good as any greater archmage's—which is to say, well nigh perfect."

"Such as yours, perhaps?" Torm pressed him. Elminster smiled broadly, and suddenly he wasn't there. His chair was empty, without flash or sound. Only the faint smell of his pipe smoke hung in the air to say he had been present at all. Jhessail sighed and cast a spell to detect magic. She looked all about, keenly, and then shook her head.

"Faint magic, all about," she said, "and those things I know to be enchanted that we carry. But no sage."

"You see?" Elminster said, appearing at her elbow and kissing her swiftly on the cheek. "It is not as easy as it might seem, but it works."

"Now that's a trick I'd give much to learn," Torm said delightedly.

"Much it will cost ye," Elminster replied. "But enough of such tricks. Be thankful, all of ye, that The Simbul favors our desires in this matter. If she did not, all of my time would be spent thwarting her and my art would be lost to you. Who knows what foes we may yet face in this matter? Ye may have need of me."

"We always need you, old mage," Mourngrym answered, a twinkle in his eye. "Is there anyone else who would now speak on this? Narm and Shandril, you need not make speeches if you do not desire to do so, nor are you expected to answer any queries put to you." There was a brief silence.

"I would speak, Lord of the Dale," said Storm Silverhand softly. She rose, silver hair swirling gently about the dark leather that clad her shoulders. She looked directly at Narm and Shandril. "We who harp are interested in you," she said. "Think on whether you might want to walk our way."

Eyebrows lifted in silence all around the table. Rathan looked all about, then asked noisily, "Is all the formal tongue-work done, then? Can we enjoy ourselves now, and let all the others back in? Lord?"

Mourngrym grinned. "I think you have cut to the heart of the boar, chosen of Tymora. Open the doors! Let us feast! Elminster, do not go, I pray you!"

The old sage had already risen. "I am old for all the babbling and flirting that goes on at your feasts. I keep looking down at all the comely lasses, and see only the faces of those

I met at feasts long ago, in cities now dust—truly, Mourngrym, I enjoy it not. Besides, I have work to do. My art stands not still, and more things unfold under the eyes of Selune than just this matter of spellfire, ye know. Fare ye well, all." He strode forward and crouched before the fire. Suddenly Elminster became a great, gray-feathered eagle, and was gone up the chimney, as The Simbul had gone.

"Show-off," Jhessail said affectionately, watching him go.

Shandril looked at Rathan, who held a bottle in either hand, as she leaned across the board to speak to Jhessail. Her tutor bent her head obligingly, hair falling almost into a dish of cheese-filled mushroom caps.

"Lady," Shandril said in a low voice. "Wh—"

"Call me Jhess!" Jhessail responded fiercely. "This 'lady' business keeps me thinking there's some noble matron behind me, disapproving of my every move!"

"Jhess, then; forgive me. Why does Rathan drink so much? He never seems to get drunk, at least that I have seen, but . . ."

"But he drinks a goodly lot?" Jhessail agreed. "Yes . . . you should know. It was what our companion Doust Sulwood gave up his lordship of this dale for."

"Rathan's drinking?"

"No, no—I meant, they both faced the same problem. A good priest of Tymora must continually take risks—reckless ones, in the eyes of most others. Worshipping Tymora truly and trusting in the Lady's luck causes a problem if you are also sensitive to what your recklessness does to others, or are by nature cautious or considerate. The life of trusting to luck does not sit well with the life of contemplating the consequences of one's actions, or wishing for the security and comfort of routine and prudence. You see that?"

"Yes." Shandril nodded. "But how—?"

"Ah. Well, Doust as lord of this dale had to make decisions that affected the lives of the dalefolk. Concern for their safety was his duty, if you will. He could not do well by them and serve the Lady of Luck well. In the end, his calling proved the stronger, and he gave up the dale rather than rule poorly. I wish that more who fought such a battle within themselves between office and belief recognized their dilemma, and reached the right choice."

Jhessail looked fondly across the room at Merith. "As my lord, too, has done—but that is another story." She looked at Rathan. "As for that buffoon, his jesting is but an act. He is very sensitive and romantic, easily moved to tears. He hides it, and overcomes the barbs of his closest friend, Torm, with his 'drunken sot' act.

"He drinks because he is sensitive and prudent—and must, he knows, favor luck more and live in danger. To do so, he steels himself with drink. Because he does not want to become falling-down drunk, he eats like a starving wolf. This makes him fat, as you can plainly see, and in turn makes him able to take in more drink without staggering about and slurring his jests. Do not think him a drunkard, Shandril; he is not. Nor is he a lecher or a fraud, but a true servant of Tymora. I am proud to ride with him."

"You have given me different eyes to see him by, lady," Shandril said slowly, looking at Rathan, who was roaring with laughter at a jest of Storm's.

"Jhess, remember?" Jhessail said softly. "If you will listen to some advice, know that the most valuable thing I have learned from Elminster, in all these years, is to look at all things, and folk, however strange they seem, from all sides.

"Neglect not to act as you must, but try to think as you act. You will see things as others do, as well as the way you are used to thinking. If you walk with the Harpers," she added, nodding across the noisy room toward Storm, "they will tell you the same thing, dressed up in much grander words."

The room was filling up around them, as the good folk of Shadowdale and the staff and guardsmen of the tower all crowded in to the large, high-ceilinged hall. There was much laughter and chatter. Narm joined Shandril in the tumult, kissing her.

"They seem to party with a right good will here, I'll say that," Shandril greeted him.

"Aye," Narm agreed. "I swear some of the guards had wine-headaches this morning."

"No doubt," Jhessail said to them. "They drink, and love, and laugh, and eat, as if they may be dead tomorrow, for death hangs over them."

"What?" asked Narm, taken aback.

"Zhentil Keep threatens us daily—their armies could sweep down upon us any morn. Hillsfar has a new ruler, his intentions unknown, and devils walk in Myth Drannor to one side and in Daggerdale on the other. Now you are here, and they know powerful foes may attack at any time, seeking to slay or capture you. Some know a duty to defend you; some merely fear they will be caught in the way when great might is unleashed. They fear you, too, Shandril, no little bit. Your spellfire upon the hilltop is a scene told often, and vividly, in the taproom of the Old Skull."

The two stared at her, stricken. "We should leave," Shandril whispered. Jhessail caught at her sleeve and smiled.

"No! Stay here. The folk of the dale accept you, and will fight for you as for any guest before their hearth, kin or stranger.

"Who can follow adventure, or even stand up strong in these Realms, without finding foes on all sides, often more than it seems one can handle? You are welcome, truly. Besides, you will upset Elminster terribly if you run off now. He's not finished with you. But I flap my tongue and jaws worse than the old mage himself! Come, let us dance, you two and Merith and I!"

"But—I—"

"We've never learned—"

"No matter   Merith shall teach us all a dance of the Elven Court. We shall all be new to it. Try it and you can do courtesy to any elf you meet! Come!" And the long-haired magic-user pulled them out into an open space and let out a birdlike trilling call. At once Merith looked up, smilingly excused himself from two fat farmwives, and joined them.

"Storm!" he called out. "Will you harp for us?"

The bard nodded and smiled, and took up the harp of the hall. It was made of blackwood inlaid with silver, and hung on the wall among the shattered and rusting shields of past, long-dead lords of Shadowdale.

As Jhessail told the couple that the harp had been a gift from the elves of Myth Drannor, Merith reached them.

"You will be wanting to dance, my love?" he asked fondly.

"Of course . . . one of the gentler tunes, my lord, one that

human feet can follow. Narm and Shandril, and you and I
. . . may we?"

Merith bowed. "Of course," he said, as Storm joined them.
"What say you to the frolic that of old we danced on the
banks of the Ashaba? Storm, you know the tune. . . ."

*   *   *   *   *

It was late, or rather very early. Revelers saw stars glittering coldly in the clear dark sky from each window as they
went up the stairs together, footsore and happily sleepy.
"Elves must be stronger than I'd thought," Narm grunted as
they mounted the last flight to the level where their bedchamber was. The Twisted Tower was quiet around them.
Far below, the revelry continued unabated, but no sound
carried this far. The guards stood silent at their posts.

At the head of the stairs, Shandril stripped off her shoes
and set her aching feet upon the cold stone. The chill on her
bare flesh roused her somewhat from drowsiness. She
slipped out of Narm's grasp and, laughing, ran lightly ahead.
Wearily, he grinned, shook his head, and made haste to follow. They were both running when the blow fell.

Shandril heard a dull thud behind her, as if something
heavy and made of leather had been dropped. It was followed by a thumping and scrabbling sound, as if someone
had fallen. "Narm?" she called, turning as she reached their
door. "Narm? Did—"

She saw a grim-faced guard almost upon her and running
hard, the mace that had felled Narm raised before him in
one mailed fist. Shandril saw the blood upon it and realized
she had no time to dodge or fight. She let go the ring of the
door and ran.

She fled on bare feet down the long, dimly lit hall, and saw
the guard Rold, stationed far ahead under a flickering
torch, turn and look at her. A wild rage grew in Shandril out
of the shrieking fear for Narm's life. She looked back
through her streaming hair and saw a mailed hand only
inches away, reaching. Without thought, she dove sharply
to the rugs of the hall and rolled.

There were sharp, numbing blows on her back and flank
as armored boots struck her. A startled curse rang out

above her as her assailant tripped, landing in a crash of metal as he fell heavily upon his arms. Shandril rolled free and up to her knees even as the guard, who was fast and well-trained, spun about with his legs kicking in the air and drew back his mace to hurl at her.

Their eyes met across too little space, and fire exploded from Shandril's raging glare. The guard yelled in fear and drove his large and dark mace at her. It smashed aside her hastily raised fingers and struck her hard on one side of the face. Shandril slid into a yellow haze of confusion and down into darkness.

Rold struck Culthar from behind without mercy, war-hammer crashing down upon his helm even as he demanded, "Are you mad? You are sworn to protect her!"

Culthar, slumping limply aside with blood running from nose and mouth, said nothing. He crumpled against the wall and was forgotten as Rold scrambled over him to reach Shandril. He recalled that her touch was said to be death when she hurled spellfire, but his hands did not hesitate as he drew off a gauntlet and gently felt her temple.

He wiped away the blood there, then got up with a curse to fling his gauntlet at the nearest alarm. Wrapping her shoulders in his half-cloak, he held her close and drew a silver disc on a fine chain from his belt.

"Lady Tymora," he prayed hoarsely as the hollow singing of the gong died away, "if you favor those cursed to be different from most folk, aid this poor lass now. She has done no wrong within these walls, and needs your blessing now most dearly. Hear me, Lady, I beseech you! Turn your bright face upon Shandril. Tymora, Bright Lady, please hear!" And the old soldier held Shandril in his arms and waited for the sound of running feet, and prayed on.

* * * * *

In a turret that curved out from the inner wall of Zhentil Keep, there was a small, circular room without a window, and in that room, Ilthond waited with scant patience. The time was come; Manshoon still did not come back to the city of the Zhentilar. If Ilthond held spellfire in his hands and knew how to wield it, such a return would not have to be feared overmuch.

The young magic-user paced before his crystal. The eagle that had to be Elminster was even now coming to earth by the door of the little tower wherein the old mage dwelt. In another instant, the eagle became Elminster, pipe, battered old hat, and all, and went into the old, slightly leaning tower of crumbling stone. Ilthond waited an instant more, and then drew forth a scroll from a tube fashioned from the hollow wing-bone of a great dragon. A teleport spell, set down by the mage Haklisstyr of Selgaunt. Since his bony back had met with a dagger, thoughtfully poisoned by the ambitious Ilthond, he wouldn't be needing it anymore.

The mage rolled out the scroll on the table beside the crystal and set coins, a dagger, a candlestick, and a skull at the corners to hold it open. He fixed in his mind a clear picture of a certain blanket room on the third floor of the tower of Ashaba in Shadowdale, and began to cast the spell.

From below him, from another room of the turret, came the faint piping of a glaurist blowing the mournful melody of an old ballad:

> *Good fortune comes, fleeting, and then it is gone*
> *But the heart heavy with weeping must carry on*
> *Ill luck comes and stays like winter's cold snow*
> *Always you must weather more than one blow . . .*

Ilthond spread his hands in a grand flourish to finish the spellcasting and vanished. The floating, disembodied eyeball of a wizard eye spell that had been watching him from beneath the table winked out and was also gone.

* * * * *

"Of course she'll live, if ye get out of my way for a breath or two!" Rathan roared. "Lanseril, stay here to work healing magic! Rold, ye saved her; ye stay by her, too. Florin, bring Narm over here . . . be he awake yet? All others, get ye hence! Below stairs, the lot of ye! Mourngrym, ye and Shaerl may stay, of course. The rest—clear out! Get ye gone!"

"Narm stirs," Jhessail reported tersely. "We shall take this guardsman, if Rold has not quite slain him, and learn the whys of this." She gestured with her head to the gathered guards to move Culthar's body, and then added, "All others—back to your posts, please. Our thanks for your haste in coming." The guards saluted her and left.

A group of gawking servants and pages drifted back a pace or two at Rathan's words, but remained to watch. Florin laid Narm down gently upon a hastily found sleeping-fur, letting his bruised head down with care, and looked up at the onlookers. After a few moments of his silent, steady gaze, the gawkers began to shuffle away.

"How is she?" he asked, looking at Shandril's still face.

"Well enough," Rathan replied, "considering the blow to the wits she got. I only hope that it has not somehow harmed her ability to wield spellfire, now that half of Faerun seems to be attacking her to gain it." He and Florin exchanged a sober glance.

"Why would just one guard attack her?" Mourngrym muttered, frowning.

"One seemed to do well enough," Shaerl replied, gesturing at the two still forms at their feet.

"No, love; I meant I would expect to find other attackers near at hand."

The Lord of Shadowdale turned. "Rold, I want this tower searched, forthwith, this floor first. Jhessail, will you rouse Illistyl and stand guard over our two guests, here? I shall remain also." He drew his slim, jeweled sword, set it point down before him, and leaned upon it. Shaerl nodded and knelt by Narm, who had begun to moan faintly.

Florin knelt on one knee beside him, and was ready with gravely strong arms when the young conjurer suddenly surged up, arms flailing. "Where's—? Shandril! Danger! Beware! Danger!"

"Aye . . . aye," Florin agreed gently, holding him. "Danger it was, indeed. Stay still now, and we can see to your lady."

"Shandril? How—"

"Quiet and still, please. If you will heed, you will learn. She lies behind you; Rathan and Lanseril tend her."

"I—yes, I shall." Narm sank back, wincing as his head came to rest again upon the furs. "What happened?"

"Narm lay quiet and still as he was bid, that's what happened," the Lady Shaerl said severely.

Narm grimaced, and then he heard Shandril say softly, "I

thank you. Narm was hurt; have you seen to him?" His heart knew peace and he was asleep within a breath, not even hearing Rathan's reply.

* * * * *

It was dark in the blanket room and close, smelling of pomander and moth-mix. Ilthond stifled a sneeze, nodded in satisfaction at his accurate teleporting, and listened. He could hear nothing. Well enough. To work, then.

The mage worked invisibility upon himself, then cautiously eased the door open a crack. The corridor beyond seemed empty. He stole forth and looked about.

Better and better, he thought. Ilthond muttered a spell of flight and rose high to drift unseen along the corridor and search. No guards . . . why? Was Shadowdale truly so lax and careless a place as all that? No, there must be some strife or alarm. . . .

Around the corner came a dozen guards with drawn swords and forbidding, intent glares. Ilthond moved over and past them in careful silence. Where might the young maid be? The tower's mortar was mixed with substances to prevent scrying, but he was sure he'd find her anyway.

Perhaps she was up in the plainer but more secure rooms of the levels above, or down below, as befitted a guest of importance. The greater risk probably lay downward—but so, too, did almost all chances of learning who was where, and doing what. Ah well, a short, risky road leads fastest to the top, they say. . . .

Ilthond reached the stairs and headed down, keeping near the sloping stone ceiling. Carefully and quietly he went, like a silent shadow. He searched, nosing through rooms and along halls, flitting back and forth with patient care not to be brushed against or seen by those who might be able to detect him.

He had come down a long hall where the torches burned every twenty paces, and there at one end humans in rich garb stood or knelt near two who lay side by side on the ground. Ilthond came closer slowly, silently, straining to hear from afar.

"How d'ye feel?" Rathan growled. "Better, I trust?"

Shandril nodded, slowly. "My head still aches. But my thanks, indeed, good Rathan. Again I am in your debt for healing me when I lay stricken."

"Not in my debt," Rathan corrected. "The Lady it is whom ye owe." He traced a circle about the disc upon his breast with the middle finger of his right hand.

"Yes, I shall not forget the Lady's favor," Shandril replied. "How is Narm?"

Rathan looked over at Narm. "He sleeps. Best to let him sleep on. But you must try your spellfire," he said gently.

Shandril had come up to her elbows. She now drew her legs under her and extended her hand. From her spread fingers spellfire spat, crackling down the hall in a long tongue of flame. She ended it almost immediately, and it died away, curling into air. "As before," she said briefly. "I can still—"

A pain-wracked groan came out of empty air down the hall. Florin and Mourngrym drew blades instantly and stepped in front of Shandril to shield her. Shaerl drew her dagger and reached out with its pommel to pound a gong close at hand.

Its echoes had barely died away before the form of a robed man with hawkish features and glossy black hair came into view in midair. His face was twisted with pain, his robe still smoldered, his shoulder and breast were burned bare. He hissed the word that unleashed the power of the wand in his hand.

Lightning sprang into being and a forked bolt struck both Florin and Mourngrym. The Lord of Shadowdale staggered aside and fell heavily, blade clattering. Shaerl cried out and ran to him. Florin, too, fell, driven to his knees by the energy hurled against him, but he was struggling up into a weak charge, face black with pain and effort. Shandril stood up and lashed out in heartsick anger with spellfire.

"Wherever I go!" she said bitterly, on the verge of tears. "Always, beset! Always friends and companions hurt! You come seeking spellfire? Well, then—have it!" Spellfire roared out of her in a tumbling inferno that lasted for but a breath but raged down the hallway in a blistering wall that swept over the flying mage like a wave crashing over rocks in a storm.

Narm had awoken, looking dazed. He struggled to his knees to work art, to protect his lady from this new menace. His hands halted in midair as he gazed at the blackened, crippled thing that the spellfire left behind on the scorched rugs of the hall.

Shandril raised a hand again as the man moved weakly and twisted cooked lips in hissing words of art, but she did not unleash her flames. The head sank down between smoking shoulders that shook with pain. The mage vanished, gone as though he had never been. Only the smoldering of rugs showed where he had lain.

"Wherever we go," Shandril said wearily, turning to Rathan, "your healing services are needed. I hope you will not grow tired of it all before this comes to an end."

"Lady," Rathan said as he hastened to where Mourngrym lay. "This never ends, I fear. Worry not about my patience—it is what I walk these Realms for." He knelt by the Lord of Shadowdale, and looked back at her over one shoulder. "You do a most impressive job, I must say," he added with the barest trace of a grin.

Jhessail arrived then, robes held high as she sprinted along in the forefront of a large group of guards. "Shandril?" she cried. "Florin? Mourngrym?" Merith was at her side, blade out.

"Healing, we need," Rathan said. "The time for blasting and all that is past." He looked up. "Send ye four guardsmen for Eressea at the temple . . . I have no more power to heal now, and Mourngrym yet needs it." Jhessail spun about to relay his orders and then back to face them all.

"What happened?" she asked.

"Another mage. Flying about, this one was, and invisible. Shandril touched him with spellfire purely by chance when I asked her to test her powers. He struck Florin and Mourngrym with lightning from a wand. Shandril burned him but did not slay him. He teleported away," Rathan explained. Jhessail looked at Shandril and then sighed.

"You slew him not?" she asked.

Shandril nodded, eyes on hers. "I could not," she said. "It was . . . horrible. Who knows? He may have meant me no harm at all."

Jhessail nodded. "I cannot fault you," she said slowly. "Yet I bid you remember this: when you fight, art to art, seek to slay—and mind you finish the job. An enemy who escapes will return for revenge."

"Aye," said Shaerl, eyes hot. "A man who dared to strike down my lord lives yet! I blame you not, Shandril. It must be terrible to hold such death within you, always knowing you can slay. Yet, if that man were within my grasp right now, I would not hesitate to strike and slay. One who would harm my Mourngrym does not deserve to live."

As she spoke, they heard the sounds of running feet. A guardsman reached the head of the stairs, yelling, "Lord Mourngrym! Lady Shaerl!"

Shaerl turned. "Say on."

"My lady, the prisoner is gone! We had him in the cell, and his hands were bound—yet he vanished before our eyes!"

"The man Culthar?" Shaerl asked. "How could this happen?" She turned to Jhessail, and then back to the guard at Jhessail's calm-faced nod. "My thanks. I hold you blameless. Return to your post, with our thanks."

The guard nodded, bowed, and hurried off.

Jhessail shrugged. "A teleport ring, perhaps, or even a rogue stone. There may be other ways of art Elminster and I don't yet know. All would require outside aid. The Zhentarim, perhaps, or the priests of Bane. He was the eyes for someone, here in the tower." She spread her hands with a ghost of a smile. "All the ravens are gathering."

Shaerl sighed. "Yes, I'm growing tired of it."

Rathan looked up. "Ye're growing tired of it! What of we who heal?"

"Ah, but you have divine aid," said Mourngrym weakly from below him. "Mind you see to Florin, too," the Lord of Shadowdale added. "I need him healthy and alert."

The man who had declined the lordship of Shadowdale, and led the knights from their early days, was leaning against a wall in pain-wracked silence. "Florin?" Jhessail hailed him tentatively, as she drew near. "Are you badly hurt?"

"As usual." Florin's voice was rueful, and he lowered it so that only she could hear his next words, so faintly that she almost missed them. "I fear I am growing too old for this constant battle, Jhess. It's not the thrill it used to be."

"Oh, no, you don't," Jhessail said briskly, putting a slim arm about his great shoulders. "Not now. We need you." Awkwardly she drew him down until he was sitting against the wall. "You'll feel much better once you've been healed." Merith joined them. Florin nodded gratefully to them both, and then quietly fainted.

Jhessail let his head rest heavily on her shoulder and said to her husband, "My lord, please run to the strongbox for one of our potions. He's hurt worse than I thought."

Shandril, watching this, turned her face to the wall and leaned her forehead upon her arm. "I—I—we must leave you. You are always hurt for our sake, one attack upon another. You are my friends! I must not do this to you, day after day, mages attacking and all . . ." She burst into tears.

"Must we have all this weeping?" Rathan complained. "It's as bad as all the fighting! Nay, worse—ye can stop the fighting by slaying your foe!"

Narm rose to defend his lady, but Rathan pushed him down again with two strong fingers. "Don't start! Ye're not fully healed yet, not nearly. I'm not having ye rushing around getting hurt and dispensing worldly sage-speech and crying all about the place, yet. D'ye hear? Just lie back down and wait. We'll see if there's time for me to spare to listen to such foolishness later."

Merith went to Shandril then, and tickled her gently under the ribs on one side, until in irritation the young lady turned from the wall. Then he swept her up in his arms and kissed away her tears. "Nay, nay, little one, you need not be ashamed or upset on our account. It is a hard road you walk, an adventurer's road. Would you not walk it together, with us? It is not so lonely or hard, with friends."

"Ohh, Merith," Shandril said, and sobbed upon his shoulder. Merith carried her over to where Florin and Jhessail sat, and sat her down upon his own lap before them. Jhessail and Florin both looked at her with smiles.

"You must not cry so," Jhessail chided her. "Does the hawk weep because it has wings? Does the wolf howl because it has teeth? We do what we can with our art or our skill-at-arms. Is your spellfire so different? Use it as you see fit, and don't hold yourself responsible for the attacks others make on you, or this place. We do not blame you for them."

She reached over and patted Florin's knee. "Let's all go down to the great hall as soon as Eressea has done her healing," she said, "and see if there's aught to eat or drink. Violence always makes me hungry."

* * * * *

In a turret that curved out from the inner face of the walls of Zhentil Keep, in a small, circular chamber, Ilthond lay on a familiar floor. He lay upon the painted circle that he had practiced teleporting to over and over again, and groaned in pain. None were there to see or hear; he was alone behind three locked and hidden doors. The pain wracked him in waves of red agony, like a man struggling through the breakers upon a beach. Ilthond crawled forward between waves, seeking the cabinet where he kept his potions. He wondered dully if he'd make it in time.

* * * * *

"'That's quite enough of this foolishness," Elminster said peevishly. "I leave ye and within half a dozen breaths ye're fighting yet another mage trying to steal spellfire for himself! Well, then, I'll not leave ye again . . . ye'll stay in my tower, ye two, with my scribe Lhaeo and myself.

"To draw off all who are snooping about hoping to seize spellfire for themselves, Illistyl and Torm will impersonate ye, and will stay in a tent with Rathan upon Harpers' Hill. Merith, ye and Lanseril will keep a watch upon them. Now pass that wine ye're curled so lovingly about, Rathan, and let's have no argument or endless clacking of tongues; the matter's settled."

"I'm glad of that," Florin said dryly. "Have you no task for Jhessail or myself?"

"Eh? Gods' watch, man! Someone has to watch over the dale, and fight the armies of Zhentil Keep if they come calling! You two ought to be able to manage that!"

There were dry chuckles, and then a yawn. Shandril's eyes were nearly closed. "Love," Narm said gently, shaking her. "Are you sleepy?"

"Of course I am," she replied faintly. "We were going to bed when this uproar started, remember?"

"To bed, then!" Elminster said gruffly. "All of us will go over to my tower together—and then mind the lot of ye all return here, except ye two. I don't want to be falling over a lot of snoring knights in the morning!"

"At this rate," Lanseril replied, "you're safe on that score. You'll be falling over a lot of snoring knights at highsun, instead." Amid chuckles they went out into the night.

*　*　*　*　*

"Keeping you awake, Rold?" one of his fellows grunted jovially at dawnfry that morning. The guardroom was strewn with gloves, helms, and scabbarded blades, as their owners lingered over the last of fried bread, tomatoes, and bacon. The old veteran yawned again.

"Glad I am, indeed," he said, "that the young lord and lady are out of the tower. No offense to them, mind you. It's just that I'll be more likely to sleep when I'm off duty."

"Less of sinister mages and assassins skulking in every hall and chamber and peeking in at all the windows, you mean," another, sharp-voiced guard agreed, buckling on his sword.

"Aye, Kelan. Less art we cannot hope to fight . . . and less treachery from within." A little silence fell at the veteran's words. Then Kelan spoke softly to them all.

"Who d'you think got to Culthar? What did they offer him to chance such a reckless grab at one who could cook him to the bones in an instant?"

"Who can know another man's price?" Rold replied, as quietly. Several of the guards nodded. The veteran added, "I doubt that he needed much persuading. I think he was already loyal to someone or some group outside of the dale, and they merely told him to do this thing for them."

"What group?" came the blunt question, as swords were readied in sheaths, and belts settled about hips. Rold shrugged.

"That, I know not—or I'd be at Lord Mourngrym to let me go after them. Nay, do not laugh. It is always easier on one's temper, if not one's hide, to be moving and attacking, instead of growing weary and cold at a guardpost, never knowing where and when strikes a blade—or worse, art you cannot avoid or counter."

"Where did they go, then?" one of the younger guards asked; a late riser, still heavy about the eyes, dawnfry on a plate in his hand. Rold chuckled.

"Mind you aren't late for your own funeral, some morn, Raeth," he said. "The young lord and lady will be camping out by Harpers' Hill with Rathan Thentraver. Practicing hurling this spellfire where Lord Mourngrym's fine rugs won't be scorched. Most of the knights will be going off about the dale and elsewhere about the Dalelands at Elminster's bidding."

"Ah, things'll get a mite quieter for a few days, then," Raeth said with some satisfaction. Many of the older guards chuckled.

"Think you so?" Kelan asked him. "It's a long run through the forest, in full armor, to Harpers' Hill!" Rold was still chuckling as the bell rang and they hastened out to their posts. Raeth, mouth full of bacon, wasn't.

* * * * *

"This is a fool's plan," Rathan grunted. "One only Elminster could have come up with." The chosen of Tymora surveyed the tents sourly. "Lady, aid me," he prayed. "I am surely going to need all thy help."

"Cheerful, aren't you?" Torm answered him. "I'm enjoying this."

"Ye have weird enthusiasms," Rathan grunted. "Ye can't even enjoy thy lady when she must wear the form of Shandril every instant."

Torm grinned. "Oh? That's going to hamper me? How so?" He raised dark eyebrows. "Besides, I look like Narm for the the present."

"Shameless philanderer," Rathan growled. He looked at the trees all about them. "I wonder when the first attack will come?"

"While you're standing there," Torm replied, "if you keep yapping sourly about Elminster's wisdom and the danger you have so foolishly plunged headlong into. Go in, then, and pray to the Lady for healing art. No doubt we'll need it soon enough."

"Aye, there ye speak truth, I doubt not," Rathan replied darkly. "Is there no wine about?" He peered into the tents. Illistyl grinned back out of the depths of one, looking as if she were Shandril. She moved with the smooth innocence of Shandril, abandoning her own defiant strut.

"No," Torm answered the cleric brightly. "We seem to have left it behind at the tower. A tragedy, I agree."

"Indeed . . . well, one of the guards will just have to go back for it," Rathan concluded. "I can feel my thirst growing already," he added, squinting at the sun.

"Here, then." Torm passed him a flask. Rathan unstoppered it and sniffed suspiciously.

"What is it? I smell nothing."

"Water of the Gods," Torm replied. "Pale ale. Tymora's Tipple."

"Eh?" the cleric frowned at him suspiciously. "Ye blaspheme?"

"No," said Torm. "I offer you a drink, sot. Your thirst, remember?"

"Aye," Rathan agreed, mollified, and took a swig. "Aaagh!" he said, spitting most of it out. "It *is* water!"

"Yes, as I told you," Torm replied smoothly, and then leaped nimbly out of reach as the cleric reached for him.

The chosen of Tymora pursued his sly tormentor across the rocky hilltop, while Illistyl looked out of the tent and shook her head.

"Playing already, I see," she remarked, just loudly enough for Torm to hear. He turned and waved at her, grinning—and promptly fell over a stone, with Rathan on top of him. Illistyl burst into laughter before she realized that she couldn't recall what Shandril's laugh sounded like.

* * * * *

The little stone tower rose, leaning slightly, out of a grassy meadow beside a small pond. It was made of old, massive stones, and had no gate or fence or outbuildings. Flagstones led right up to a plain wooden door. It looked small and drab in comparison with the Twisted Tower, which rose large against the sky across the meadow. But it seemed somehow a place of power, too—and more welcoming.

Inside, it was very dark. Dust lay thick upon books and papers that were stacked untidily everywhere. The smell of aging parchment was strong in the air. Out of the forest of paper pillars rose a rickety curving stair, on up to unseen heights. A bag of onions hung over the doorway. Beyond an arch, faint footsteps could be heard.

"Lhaeo," Elminster called. "Guests!"

An expressionless face appeared in the doorway. "You need not do your simpering act," the old mage added. At that the face smiled and nodded. It was that of a pleasant, green-eyed man with pale brown hair and delicate features. He was about as tall as the elf Merith, very slim, and wore an old, patched leather apron over plain tunic and hose.

"Welcome," Lhaeo said then, in a soft, clear voice. "If you're hungry, there's stew warm over the fire now. Highsunfeast will be herbed hare cooked in red wine . . . that Sembian red Mourngrym gave us. I deem it good for little else. I fear I have no dawnfry ready."

Elminster chuckled. "Ye would have been wasted on a throne, Lhaeo. I've eaten no better fare since Myth Drannor fell than what ye cook. But I forget my manners, such as they are . . . Lhaeo, these be Narm Tamaraith, a conjurer who flourishes these past days under the tutelage of Jhessail and Illistyl; and his betrothed, Shandril Shessair, who can wield the spellfire." Lhaeo's eyes opened wide at that.

"After all these years?" he asked. "You were right to bring them here. Many will rise against such a one."

"Many already have," the sage replied dryly. "Narm, Shandril—I make known to thee Lhaeo, my scribe and cartographer. Outside these walls he is counted a lisping man-lover from Baldur's Gate. He is not, but that is his tale to tell. Come up, now, and I'll show ye thy bed—I hope ye don't mind, there is only one—and some old clothes to keep you warm in this place. We two don't feel the cold, but I know others find it chill."

"Keep him to one speech," Lhaeo added as they started up the stairs, which creaked alarmingly, "and I'll have tea ready when you come down again."

They went up through a thick stone floor into a circular, open room. Shandril cast an eye over the maps and scrolls littering a large table in the center of the chamber. She looked away quickly as the runes began to crawl upon the parchment. Over the table, a globe hung in midair, a pale ball of radiance that shone like a small, soft moon. By its light, they could see a narrow stair curving up into the darkness overhead. Books and scrolls littered the tops of chests and were piled high upon a tall black wardrobe.

The old, dark wooden bed, with a curved rail at head and foot, looked very solid and cozy. Shandril suddenly felt very tired after the battles and conferences and their long talk in the night outside. She swayed on her feet.

Narm and Elminster both put out a hand to her at once. Shandril waved them away with a sigh. "Thank you both. I really have been a burden since I left Deepingdale."

"Second thoughts?" the sage asked quietly, no censure in his tone. Shandril shook her head.

"No. No, not when I can think clearly. I just could not have lived through it alone." Then she noticed something, and turned to the sage. "There is only one bed. Where will you sleep?"

"In the kitchen. Lhaeo and I are rarely asleep at the same time; someone has to watch the stew."

Narm laughed. "The greatest archmage in all Faerun," he said, "or so I would deem you, and you spend nights watching a pot of stew!"

"Is there a higher calling, really?" Elminster replied. "Oh, speaking of pots, the chamber pot's by the foot of the bed. Aye, I know it looks odd—it is an upturned wyvern skull, sealed with a paste. I stole it from a Tharchioness's bedchamber in Thay long ago, in my wilder days.

"Come, have thy tea, and then ye can sleep. Ye will be safe here, if anywhere in the Realms. Do as ye always do together, so long as it does not involve a lot of screaming and yelling. A little noise will not bother us. If ye pry about, be warned that the art here can kill in an instant if ye put an eye or tongue wrong . . . on your heads be the consequences."

"Elminster," Narm said as the old mage started down the

stairs again, "our thanks for this. You've gone to much trouble over us."

"If I did not, what sort of greatest archmage in all Faerun would I be then?" was the gruff reply they got over the old mage's shoulder. "I'm stepping out for a pipe. Mind ye come in haste—Gond alone can guess what Lhaeo'll put in thy tea if you're not there to stop him. He thinks every cup should be a new experience." Below, they heard the door bang.

"By the gods, I'm tired," Narm said.

"Aye, too tired," Shandril agreed. "I hope we can sleep." Her hands, as she held them out to clasp his, were shaking. They went down to tea wearily.

When Elminster finished his pipe, he knocked the ashes from it out on the doorstep and came back in. "All well?" he asked.

Lhaeo came to the door with Narm leaning limply on his shoulder. The scribe's arms were clasped about the conjurer with casual strength.

"All well. They'll both sleep till tomorrow morning, with no ill effects, by the dose they had. I mixed it carefully, and they drank it all down."

"Good. I'll take his feet. A sound sleep will do them both great good, and I'll be able to have a look at the lad's spellcasting when he's rested and not worried sick about his lady love."

"How about her?"

"No training needed. She's already learned much precision. When we fought Manshoon, she was still at the stage of hurling it as a child does a snowball. Now, she can do more with it—uumph, mind this bit; the lad's heavy!—than many mages ever do with fire magics."

They laid Narm on the bed and went back for Shandril. "Hmmm . . . we have much that will fit the lad, but what of this little lady?" Lhaeo asked, as they went carefully up the stairs again.

Elminster looked wise. "I've already thought on that," he said. "Some of the gowns that Shoulree of the Elven Court wore, in the days of Myth Drannor. They're in the chest closest to the stairs. She, too, could wield spellfire, if the talk in the city then was correct. She won't mind."

"Walks she yet?" Lhaeo asked, as they laid Shandril gently on the bed beside Narm, and drew off her boots.

Elminster looked thoughtful. "I doubt she does . . . but perhaps some of the Elven Court who joined the long sleep years ago stir now. That would explain why the devils in Myth Drannor have not troubled us here more." He nodded. "Something to look into, indeed." Then his face split into a wide grin. "In my copious free time," he added.

* * * * *

"I know it is wisest and safest," Shandril said, "but I grow so bored, Lhaeo. Is there nothing I can do? I know I shouldn't pry about in the spellbooks; I'll only get hurt or changed into some ugly creature or other. I cannot tidy for the same reason!"

Lhaeo looked at her with his usual expressionless face. "Do you cook?" he asked. Shandril turned.

"Of course! Why, at The Rising Moon—" She stopped, eyes alight, and smiled. "May I cook with you?" she asked, delighted. Lhaeo bowed.

"Please," he said. "It is seldom I get to talk to others who spend much time in a kitchen. Few want to talk to someone who speaks thus," and his last words were spoken in a mincing lisp.

Shandril looked at him. "Why do you pretend to be— Elminster's companion?" she asked. Lhaeo looked at her soberly.

"My lady," he said, "I am in hiding. I will tell you who I am only if you never tell anyone—except Narm," he replied.

"I promise," Shandril said solemnly. "By whatever oaths you wish." Lhaeo shook his head.

"Your promise is enough," he said. "Come into the kitchen." The room, warmed by a small fire in the hearth, smelled deliciously of herbs and simmering stew and onion soup.

"Are you a lost prince?" Shandril prompted him as he waved her to a stool and went to inspect the huge pot of stew upon the fire.

"I suppose," Lhaeo said slowly, stirring the stew with a long-handled ladle, "you could say that. I am the last of the royal house of Tethyr. In happier times, I was so far from the throne that I never thought of myself as a prince or even as one of the court. But there have been so many deaths that I am, so far as Elminster and I can tell, the last left alive of royal blood.

"Why do you hide? You have no army to take back your kingdom. Why would anyone want to kill you?"

Lhaeo shrugged. "Because all who have seized power expect others to do as they would. Anyone of royal blood must want to wear the crown, they think. I live because they don't know that I still live. I fear that's all there is to tell. Not so impressive, is it? But it is a secret that must be kept, for my life hangs upon it."

"I shall not tell it," Shandril said. "What can I help you with, here?"

Lhaeo looked at her. "Cook what you like, and teach me as you go," he said. "Please?" They smiled at each other across a bag of onions. "And my thanks," he added.

"For keeping your secret?"

"Aye. It may not seem much, but each secret you carry has a weight all its own. They add up, secrets, to a burden you must carry all your days."

Shandril looked up from selecting onions, knife in hand. "You carry many?"

"Aye. But my load is nothing to Elminster's."

Shandril nodded, then looked down. "Whose gown is it that I wear?" she asked quietly. Lhaeo smiled.

"That is one of the secrets," he said. "I would tell you, but it is his to tell, not mine."

"Well enough. Do you have an old apron I might wear to cover it?"

"Aye, behind you, on the peg. Tell me of The Rising Moon."

She did. They serve others most who ask the right question, and then listen. The day passed, and they marked not the time.

* * * * *

The day passed, and Narm grew weary. He had grown used to the clear and careful teaching of Jhessail, and the practical tutelage of Illistyl. Elminster's methods were a rude shock, indeed.

The old mage badgered and derided and made testily impatient comments. The simplest query of him on this or that small detail of casting brought a scholarly flood of information in reply—a voluminous barrage that never seemed to include a direct answer. Elminster had worked on Narm's new spell, the flaming sphere, until Narm could have screamed.

Weary hours of study to impress the difficult runes upon Narm's mind, and then a sharp lecture on precisely how to cast the spell in view of the obvious shortcomings he had displayed last time were the grinding irritants. They were followed by a few moments of spellcasting, a ball of scorching flame rushing away—a thrill the first few times, but now Narm saw each one as a failure even before Elminster spoke—and then Elminster's scathing critique. The clumsiness or slowness of the casting, the lazy and inattentive formation of the sphere, and worst of all, the lack of precision in its direction, once formed, were all regular topics.

"Have ye not seen your lady hurl spellfire?" Elminster demanded, in acid tones. "Have ye not noticed how she can shape the flames—a broad fan or a thin, dextrous tongue— bend it around corners, pulse short spurts of flame to avoid setting her surroundings ablaze? I suppose ye couldn't tell me now the hue of her eyes, either!"

"Ahh, they're . . ." Narm hastened to reply, and found to his horror that an image of Shandril wouldn't come to his mind at the moment. Confused and badgered, he hurled fire angrily before Elminster bid him, tossing the ball of flames twenty feet before it landed and rolled.

"Temper, boy," Elminster admonished, watching it. "Too easily it can be thy death. Mages cannot afford it—not if it affects the precision of their casting. Here ye are, furious with me, and we've spent merely a morning together. Not good! Oh, that's all good enough for the lesser talents who swagger about throwing a few fireballs and bullying honest farm folk. I had hoped you would look for something more, in the service of Mystra.

"Ye can be a great mage, Narm, if ye develop just two things: precision in control of spell effects and imagination in applying your art. The latter ye will need more later on, when ye reach past most mages with whom ye would wish to associate in both experience and knowledge. The precision ye must master now, else thine every spell will have some waste about it. Thy art will lack that edge of shrewd phrasing and maximum effect that may mean the difference between defeat and victory, some day.

"As ye advance, ye will become a target for those who gain spells by preying upon other mages. If ye lack precision in a duel of art, ye will be utterly destroyed—then it will be too late for my lessons."

"But I cannot hope to win a duel now. How will spending all day throwing balls of flame about make any difference to that? If I win a duel, one day, surely it will be because I have stronger spells and more of them."

"Perhaps. Yet, know ye, a mage can do more with a few simple spells he knows back-to-front, and can use shrewdly, than with an arsenal hastily memorized and poorly understood from any spellbook he may look at. Do ye follow me?"

Narm nodded, slowly. "Good, then," the sage said. "I shall leave ye to thyself, if ye promise me to study and cast your flaming sphere at least four times more, here in this field, before ye rest for the day. Think on moving the sphere just where ye want it, and making it form in just the place ye choose. Think too on how ye can use such a weapon against, say, a running group of goblins who will scamper in all directions when they see it coming, but always try to get past it toward ye.

"Don't forget that only foolish and arrogant mages stand still after they have cast to admire the view. Move, or a simple arrow will soon make ye a dead mage, no matter how impressive ye were in life. Oh, and worry not about the stubble; ye're doing the farmer who owns this a favor by burning it off. Try not to take the fencing with it. It is harder to term that 'friendly help.' Do I have thy promise?"

Narm nodded. "Yes, and my thanks."

"Thanks? It is impatient ye are again, Narm! The task's not done yet. Save thy thanks until ye be master of this spell, at the least. Then thank yourself first. I can talk all day and only waste breath if ye do not heed, and work, and master the art."

Narm grinned. "You do," he replied. Elminster grinned back, only for an instant. The twinkle in his eye remained, though, as he became a falcon and flew away.

Narm stood in the field and watched him go, sighed, and reached for his spellbook. The sun was bright on the Old Skull. He sighed again and bent his head to the book.

When he stood up, much later, to cast his first flaming sphere, Narm drew a deep breath of satisfaction. At least he was alone and could work art without wisely watching eyes and a lot of sharp comments. He turned to look around at the stubble, enjoying the choosing of what he could burn at whim. It was then that he noticed a small boy had appeared from somewhere and was hanging upon the fence-rails watching him.

"Go away!" Narm said crossly.

"This your field?" the boy replied laconically.

"You could get hurt!" Narm said. "I'll be casting spells here!"

"Aye. I've been watching. But I won't be hurt unless you cast spells at me. You won't do that; there are no evil magic-workers in Shadowdale. Ma says Elminster won't permit it."

"I see," said Narm, and set his jaw. "Excuse me." He turned away to hurl fire again.

The boy watched fire roll away once and stayed glued to the fence. All day long he stayed, as Narm hurled fire, sat down to study, got up and threw fire carefully again, and then went back to his books.

Narm was weary when he finally went to the gate at evening, and very thirsty. The boy climbed down from the fence then, and fell into step beside Narm. "I wish I could be a great mage, like you," he said, almost shyly.

Narm looked at him and laughed. "I wish I could be a great mage," he said ruefully. "I know so little. I feel so useless."

The boy stared. "You?" He shook his head. "I saw you cast big balls of fire. You point them where to go, and they move at your bidding! You must be powerful!"

Narm shook his head, as they went on down the road. "Being a mage is a lot more than just hurling balls of fire about."

The boy nodded at him, slowly, and then waved a sudden

good-bye, ducked through a gap in a hedge off to one side of the road, and was gone. Narm shrugged and walked on. Ahead he could see a patrol of guardsmen on horseback, trotting toward him with lances raised. It must be nice to call a place like this home.

Elminster was sitting out on a boulder near his front step, smoking, when Narm came up the path. He put aside his pipe and regarded Narm thoughtfully. "Well?" he asked. "Can ye put a sphere where ye want to?" Narm nodded. "So are ye a mage, then?"

Narm shrugged. "I have a long road to go," he said, "before I am strong in art. But I can stand in most company, now, and know my art will serve me." He added proudly, "There will always be others more powerful, but I've truly mastered what I do know."

"Oh?" Elminster asked softly. "Think ye so?" His features suddenly blurred and shifted beneath the battered old hat, flowing and changing in a fascinating, rather frightening manner. Narm stared at the shrinking sage, and suddenly found himself facing the young boy who had watched his spell practice from the fence. The little face grinned; the little mouth moved, and in a perfect imitation of Narm's own voice said solemnly, "Being a mage is a lot more than just hurling balls of fire about."

Narm stared at him in anger, then resignation, and then sheepish amusement. "Elminster won't permit it, indeed," he said. "I can see that I'll have to rise early in the day indeed to get ahead of you."

Elminster smiled. "Ah, but I have five hundred years' start on ye. Come. Dinner is ready. Thy lady is a cook of rare skill. Ye have chosen correctly. See that ye serve her as well, boy, as she serves ye." With this last sage advice he knocked his pipe out on the doorstep and went in. Narm looked once at the stars, beginning to sparkle as the sky darkened, and followed him inside.

❧ 13 ❧

To Walk Unseen

The bards soon forget a warrior falling without
a great feat of arms. Would you be forgotten?
Face each battle, each foe, as though it is your
last. One day it will be.

Dathlance of Selgaunt
An Old Warrior's Way
Year of the Blade

The morning sun laid bright fingers upon the table where they sat in the audience chamber of the Twisted Tower. Shandril watched stray dust motes sparkle above the table as she and Narm waited for Elminster to come in from dawnfry in the great hall. Narm's hand found hers, and they sat together in contented silence, alone with the fading tapestries of Shadowdale's past and the empty throne. "I was brought here by Illistyl before we met in Rauglothgor's lair," Narm said quietly, "and spoke with Mourngrym. It seems an age ago, now."

Shandril nodded. "It seems long ago that I left Deepingdale, yet it is a matter of tendays, not months." She looked at the great painted map of the Dragonreach upon the wall. "I wonder where we shall be in a year?" she asked.

Narm never replied, for upon her words the doors opened and Elminster came in. Shandril had thought Mourngrym would be with him, but the sage was alone. He came toward them, slowly, and for the first time, Shandril thought, he really looked old. He sat down in a chair beside them, not on the throne, and fixed them with bright eyes.

"So quiet?" he asked. "Have ye both stopped thinking,

then?"

"No," Narm replied boldly. "Why say you so?"

The old mage shrugged. "The young are supposed to be always talking or laughing or fighting, they say. Ye two . . . surprised me." He took out his pipe, looked at it for a long breath in silence, and then put it away again, unlit. "I asked ye here to tell thee that I have watched, these past few days, and ye two are as well trained with art and spellfire as we here can presently make thee. It is up to thee, now, if ye would grow more powerful. More than that, it is time for the both of ye to decide what to do with thine lives."

"Do?" Narm asked, but not as one surprised. Elminster nodded approvingly.

"It is not good for ye to drift along under the influence of the knights and myself. Ye would be swept up into our councils and our struggles. Ye'd slowly grow embittered and empty, as ye lost the will and way to walk thine own roads and think for thyselves."

"But we have found friends here, and happy times," Shandril protested, "and—"

"And danger," Elminster interrupted smoothly. "I want to keep ye with me. One cannot have too many friends, and I grow weary of losing them all, one after another, with the years. But if I let ye stay, I would draw doom to ye, just as settling down together in the dale, or in a nice cottage somewhere by thyselves will."

"What? Living together will bring danger upon us?" Narm asked, bewildered.

"Nay—staying in one place will. With thy talent," Elminster said, pointing a long finger at Shandril, "one mage after another will seek to slay thee. Mulmaster, Thay, and the Zhentarim all must needs destroy anything that threatens magery. So walk ye out into the wide Realms and disappear. I can alter thine outward selves with magic, although to each other ye will look the same. Pass from sight, and thy menace will be forgotten in the struggles these tyrants of art have with one another.

"My advice to thee," Elminster continued, "is to wander, and hide. Ye will need friends who will raise sword or art to aid thee if needed. So walk ye with Storm Silverhand and her fellow Harpers, then find thine own way and thine own adventures again. Mistake me not—I would not be rid of ye. I think ye will soon be slain or stunted in art and spirit if ye stay here. Come back and visit, though." The old mage put his pipe in his mouth and puffed it furiously into life with fire that sprouted from his forefinger, and his eyes grew suspiciously misty.

Shandril and Narm looked at each other. "I—we both think you are right," Shandril said, reading Narm's eyes. "We would speak with the knights first however." Elminster looked to Narm, who nodded silently. "We do not want to leave this place, and our friends," Shandril added. "If we must, we would know where in the Realms it is best to go."

Elminster nodded. "Well said. If ye like, I'll tell Mourngrym."

Shandril nodded. "Please." She did not burst into tears until after he'd gone.

"He's right, you know," Narm said gently, arms about her. Shandril sniffled as she nodded.

"Oh, I know. That's not what makes it so sad. It's leaving friends. First Gorstag and Lureene at the inn, then Delg, Burlane, Rymel, and the others, and now the knights. I'll even miss Elminster, the crusty old bastard."

"Well, that's as polite and yet as honest a calling as I've had in a long time," the sage's unmistakable voice said dryly behind them.

Narm and Shandril broke apart, whirling. "You must have been waiting outside the door!" Shandril said hotly to Mourngrym. The Lord of Shadowdale raised calming hands.

"Everyone must stand somewhere," he said. "I lost five gold pieces at dice with the guards, if it's any consolation to you. The others'll be here in a moment."

He crossed to a tall cabinet. "In the meantime, shall we have a glass of wineapple? I strained it myself. It's not fermented; you cannot get drunk on it, Narm."

"Well, seeing as you have the cabinet open," Rathan hailed him from the door. Mourngrym sighed. "Is Torm with you? I thought as much . . . leave something drinkable in there that I can give to visiting gentles, will you?" He went and sat on his throne, flagon in hand.

"Well met, Jhess, Illistyl . . . where's Merith?" he called.

"Along in a minute, my lord," Jhessail said. "He was in the bath when Shaerl called."

"Ah, that's why she isn't back yet!" Torm said innocently to the glass he was raising to his lips. Mourngrym's empty flagon bounced off his head an instant later.

"My lord, if I may borrow your boot for a moment?" another voice said from the door, sweet and low.

"Of course, lady," Merith said politely, drawing it off and proffering it politely. Shaerl took it from him and threw it hard and accurately. Torm groaned and dropped Mourngrym's flagon with a clatter, amid general mirth.

"All here?" Mourngrym asked. At the door, Lanseril nodded as he set an ornate bar across the handles and snapped it down into place. "Good, then . . . Narm and Shandril have something to ask of you." Silence fell.

Shandril looked around at them all, suddenly shy, and nudged Narm. He looked at her uncomfortably, cleared his throat, and then lapsed into silence.

"Ye need no speech, lad," Elminster's calm voice came from his left. "Just say thy piece straight out, before someone else attacks the tower to seize thee." There were chuckles of agreement at this. Narm swallowed and got to his feet.

"Well, then," he said quickly. "Shandril and I think we should leave you, to have our own lives and adventures. We do not want to insult or upset anyone. You have been good friends and protectors to us, and my lady and I will be ever grateful. But as long as we stay, it seems Shadowdale will be an armed camp, as one evil group after another comes seeking us. We must go—but where, how, we do not know.

"We would talk it over with you, if you will, and then decide alone together after. We alone must live with what we decide, and with each other." He sat down suddenly, feeling foolish.

"Good speech," Illistyl said. "Well then, what would you know?"

Shandril spoke. "What are the Harpers? Not who, but what? What do they work toward?"

Florin answered her. "My wife is a Harper, lady, yet even

to me, they remain mysterious. They are secretive about their membership and their precise aims, but they do work for causes that we deem 'good.' The air of mystery they deliberately foster seems to be their defense against foes who are stronger at arms or art.

"When you see the device of a silver moon and a silver harp, you face a Harper. Storm Silverhand is one, you know, as is the High Lady of Silverymoon. Storm can tell you others, where it is not my place to do so. Many bards, rangers, and half-elven mages are Harpers. The Harpers oppose the Zhentarim, and those who cut trade routes into wilderness to mine and fell timber with no thought for those who live there—the merchants of Amn, for instance. We respect the Harpers, and aid them."

"Well enough, then," Narm said, sitting back. "Where should we wander, Harpers or no?"

"Somewhere where you can get filthy rich," Torm said with a grin. "And hide among the masses of people, and find any work you fancy—Waterdeep, for instance." Mourn-grym, whose family was of noble Waterdhavian stock, shook his head ruefully.

"Have you no honor?" Jhessail inquired wearily of Torm.

"Aye, indeed. I keep it at the bottom of my pack and take it out to shine it up and look at it on windy nights in the wilderness, by the fire. It looks grand, I tell you. But it is poor company, and doesn't keep one warm."

"Ignore him," Rathan said. "His ratlike city instincts lead his lips astray. Waterdeep is a good place to hide, aye, but it would probably prove more dangerous to thee than Shadowdale. It is full of prying eyes from half the lands in Faerun, and not a few who will take from thee what they can and leave the rest in a gutter."

"Aye," Lanseril agreed. "It is better to travel the wilds of the Sword Coast North, the high forests and the fair city of Silverymoon. The Unicorn Run is a place breathtaking in its beauty, with great trees that have stood there clad in moss since the world was young and man a fledgling southern race. It is worth the trip, I tell you."

"Aye, go where few tread, and where ye can see what few have seen and ye will always remember," Rathan agreed. "I shall envy thee thy journey, bring what perils it may—"

"Is every lord and lady among you going to philosophize pompously the whole tenday through?" Elminster asked in exasperation.

"Why not? It is our turn, indeed, after years of listening to your fulminations," Torm returned wickedly. A hush fell as all waited to see if he would forthwith become a frog.

Elminster merely chuckled and said, "True enough. My turn to listen and be entertained, then."

Florin and Lanseril were visibly disappointed that Torm was going to escape a transformation, at least this time, and rose and turned away to stroll about the chamber.

"Is this discussion not the way to do it, then?" Shandril asked.

"Well," Lanseril's voice floated back to her. "Let us say that few have sense enough to do it beforehand. Most rush into battle without thinking enough, and talk about it only to themselves."

"Do not think, though, that jaw-wagging is not good or necessary," Rathan said. "It is one of the most important things a priest does for lay worshippers who come to him."

"Aye, well said," Torm agreed. "Such talk is as necessary as the sword in an ordered life, and in the doings of kings and statesmen across the Realms. It was the sage Mroon who defined—almost a thousand winters ago, mind you—the famous 'circle of diplomacy': 'Why talk but to end the fighting? Why fight but to end the talking?' It is as true today as then. . . . Well, old mage? Did I remember, or did I not?"

"Ye did . . . perhaps the first thing I've told thee that ye have recalled, that I can tell," Elminster said severely. "But enough banter—it does not help these good people to make their decision, only hastens them to bed with weariness and lost time."

"Aye," Florin agreed. "Perhaps we should tell you of the Realms about so you can better decide your route. Would that help?"

"Indeed," Shandril and Narm answered together.

"Danger, you will find, lies on every hand. You want to wander freely, and hide yourselves, so places where few dwell that are near to us here are out, as are warlike and inhospitable lands. That bars you from anything north of the Moonsea, and from the Stonelands, Daggerdale, and Myth Drannor, all presently lawless places where much strife rages.

"Mulmaster, too, is an unfriendly place," Florin noted. "So, of course, are Zhentil Keep and the cities under its sway. Cormyr is friendly, but still too close to the cult's strength and spies for your comfort."

"Westgate is where Torm was reared—and look at him!" Torm grinned at Lanseril's comment. "It is a den of thieves and warring merchant houses, a city built on intrigue. Keep clear of it."

The druid paused to wet his throat from his flagon of spring water, and Merith spoke.

"You then have little choice as to what direction to travel. West you must go, overland to the Sword Coast cities. Silverymoon would be good, although you must be wary of the fell forces of Hellgate Keep and the orcs of the mountains. You must be alert for the long reach of the Zhentarim and of the cult—for if you do join the Harpers, and the cult hears of it, they will expect you to show up in Silverymoon sooner or later.

"The Moonshaes and Neverwinter are good, if you can remain unknown as the hurler of spellfire and her spellcasting companion. Everlund also, but Loudwater and Nesme and other places too favored by overland trade bring too great a risk of discovery. Loudwater lies between the Zhentarim, in Llorkh, and Hellgate Keep, and is isolated by wilderness and deep forest. Such places you must avoid, for they become traps all too easily. Have I left aught unsaid?"

"No," Illistyl said simply, and Jhessail laughed.

"If your heads are not spinning with that whirlwind tour of near Faerun," she added, "they should be!"

"Better they spin now than later, lost off the road somewhere in the wilderness of Faerun," Elminster said darkly. "We'll make thee a map on soft hide—Florin, ye and Lanseril can do it this night, if ye will. Remember the three Merith has told thee of, for I would avoid Everlund also. Seek ye Silverymoon, or Neverwinter, or the Moonshae Isles.

"Ye must, I think, leave the Inner Sea lands, at least for a while, and the South is no hiding place for thee. Go west, and find fortune."

Jhessail nodded. "Whatever you choose," she added, face serious, "do it quickly and quietly. Those who can slay you will be looking for you."

*   *   *   *   *

"Lord Marsh." The voice was cold. Its red-haired owner turned from a many-paned window inset with rubies. Fzoul Chembryl, high priest of Bane, master of The Black Altar and its priests and underpriests, laid cold eyes upon him and extended a hand that bore a black, burning banestone.

Lord Marsh Belwintle knelt and kissed it and rose with haste, carefully keeping his face impassive. The slave trade was too profitable to jeopardize it or his own standing with a quarrel. Marsh did not love the high priest, and one day there would a reckoning. Fzoul would then serve Bane far more directly than he did now, if Tymora smiled.

"I have called you here to discuss the matter of spellfire, in light of the continued absence of the Lord Manshoon. Sememmon, Ashemmi, Yarkul, and Sarhthor, as well as the priests Casildar and Zhessae, are here already."

"Almost everyone," Marsh said noncommittally, as he followed Fzoul down a short flight of stairs and along one of the drafty bridges that The Black Altar seemed to specialize in—railless spans of stone where one misstep would mean a killing fall to a stone floor twenty man-heights below. They climbed another stair, into a high chamber Marsh had not seen before. The assembled Zhentarim nodded coldly to him as he entered. He half-bowed to them all and took the sole empty seat.

The chairs of Sashen, Kadorr, and Ilthond had been removed; so had Fzoul's own, for he now sat in Manshoon's high, curving black seat. Marsh wondered what had happened to the others, but decided it would be safer not to inquire. He liked The Black Altar very little, with its priests and traps and guardian creatures, and liked this chamber, with its air of a prepared trap, even less. The last seat indeed!

"We are all here, now, save for our many-eyed friends and

the High Lord Manshoon, "said the red-haired high priest. "I will waste no time on pleasantries. Manshoon is yet absent from his tower and the city. Our best scrying spells cannot find him, nor can we contact him by other means. He can, of course, block or lead astray most magics, but we have no reason to believe he has done so. I fear, fellow lords, that Manshoon is dead.

"This may not be so, but too long we have waited for his return. We must act on one matter without further delay. If Manshoon likes our actions not upon his return, I shall bear the responsibility.

"The matter I refer to is that of spellfire, and the legendary and very rare power of wielding it. You all know, I think, what it is. Its precise limitations have never been determined, but you know what its presence means. I wish to know your minds on this matter." For a moment, no one spoke. Then Sememmon leaned forward.

"The last being who could wield spellfire that I know of previous to this Shandril was the incantatrix Dammasae, who dwelt in her youth in Thunderstone. Is it mere coincidence that two bearers of spellfire have been reared in the southern Dragonreach near the Thunder Peaks, or are they related by blood?"

Fzoul leaned forward in his seat in interest. "A most intriguing question! Does anyone have any knowledge on this matter?"

Sarhthor shrugged. "They could be mother and daughter. The years allow of it. But, with respect, what does it matter? Dammasae is long dead, as is her husband. This gives us no hilt with which to wield Shandril."

"Aye," Casildar agreed. "Her lover, Narm, is our means to move Shandril to our bidding. What I would know is the strength of his art. How easy a hilt to grasp is he?"

Sememmon shrugged. "He has been in Shadowdale, now, days enough for Elminster to teach him much. Whether that has occurred, I cannot say. I doubt that this art is terrifying whatever Elminster has done. Marimmar the Mage Most Magnificent was his tutor until recently."

There were dry chuckles from the mages at the table. The priest Zhessae frowned and asked, "Is ability or mastery of art a necessity to wield spellfire?"

There were shrugs. Fzoul spoke. "We do not know. I would tend to think not. This maid had no known skill or use of art before using spellfire openly against the dracolich Rauglothgor. Interestingly, the keep above the lair she destroyed was the Tower Tranquil—once the home of the sorcerer Garthond, husband of the incantatrix Dammasae."

"Does that mean," the mage Yarkul asked, excited, "spellfire may be contained in an item, or process, that was left in the tower by Dammasae? Which, in turn, argues that other wielders of spellfire could be created!"

"There have been several wielders of spellfire active at the same time before. It is not an ability the gods give to only one being at a time. An item or ritual is quite possible. Against that, one must place the strong likelihood that Dammasae never visited the Tower Tranquil," Fzoul said, and sat back again. The Zhentarim looked at one another around the table.

"That still," Casildar said carefully, "leaves open the question of what actions, if any, we should now take."

"We *must* gain control over the maid, or destroy her. Her spellfire threatens us all," Ashemmi said. The curly-bearded mage's dangling earring chimed as he turned his head sharply to look at Fzoul. "We cannot afford to sit idle. What if Mulmaster or Maalthiir of Hillsfar gains the power to wield spellfire? Even if those of Shadowdale use it only to aid their friends in Daggerdale, it will set our plans back. If someone sets out deliberately to destroy us with it, we could fare far worse."

"Aye, well said," Casildar agreed. "We must move. But how? Our armies?"

"I do not care to launch the armies of Zhentil Keep in Manshoon's absence," Fzoul said. "Shadowdale need merely spread the rumor that we have mastered spellfire, and Cormyr, Sembia, Hillsfar, and all will strike together to forestall the destruction they will expect at our hands. No, we must move more quietly than that, my lords. Yet as Casildar says, we must move. What say you?"

"What of our assassins?" Yarkul suggested.

"The replacements are young and poorly trained, yet,"

Zhessae said. "Even strengthened by our lesser brothers and the magelings, I fear they would anger Shadowdale more than harm it."

"Aye," Sarhthor agreed in his deep voice. "We have gone that way before. Always we must run, or die."

"Yes," Sememmon put in. "We have all seen what happens when we send the magelings. Everyone wants to be the hero, to make his name among us. Reckless and foolish, they overreach themselves and fall. Elminster is no foe to be mastered by a mageling."

"Are you suggesting that we go in force, ourselves?" Ashemmi asked. "Leaving aside our personal peril, does that not leave Zhentil Keep undefended? Surely the High Imperceptor of Bane has heard of Manshoon's absence by now. Will he not strike against you, Fzoul, and all of us?" His words fell into a deepening silence around the table.

"No doubt," Fzoul agreed coldly, "he will try. But The Black Altar, and Zhentil Keep about it, are not undefended, my friends." He waved a hand, and out from behind a curtain far down the large chamber floated Manxam.

The beholder was old and vast and terrible. Lichen grew upon its nether plates, and its eyestalks were scarred by old wounds and wrinkled with age. Its single great central eye turned slowly to survey them all as it drifted closer. In the depths of that dark-pupiled, bloodshot orb each man at the table saw his own death and worse. A deep, burbling hiss came from its closed, many-toothed maw; its ten smaller eyestalks moved restlessly as Manxam the Merciless came to the table.

The eye tyrant passed over them all to hang above the center of the table, and rolled slowly in awful majesty until its ten small eyes hung just above them, at least one looking at each man there. It said nothing, but merely hung in mid-air, watching.

"I feel we can all be persuaded," Fzoul said without a trace of a smile, "to come to some consensus now." The beholder did not blink.

Nervously Sememmon cleared his throat. "Aye, indeed . . . but what do you propose?"

"I believe," Fzoul said steadily, "that the most powerful

mages among us here now should go to Shadowdale immediately and do whatever is necessary to capture or destroy this Shandril, Elminster or no Elminster. As we are not sending incompetent or weak magelings, as you have so correctly advised us against, brother Sememmon, I have every confidence that you shall return with spellfire, if you return at all."

The mages Sememmon, Ashemmi, and Yarkul went white and silent. Only the wizard Sarhthor looked unsurprised. He merely nodded. Sememmon looked up to find that Manxam had silently rolled over so that its central eye, the one that foiled magic, gazed at them all.

Now the reason for seating the mages together around one end of the table was all too apparent. Manxam and Fzoul were just too far away for them both to be caught in a timestop spell, and no other magic would allow Sememmon to ready an item of art to strike at Fzoul or Manxam. Certainly he could not strike at both—nor was there a great chance of besting Fzoul here, in his temple. Against Manxam, the mage knew he stood almost no chance at all.

Sememmon doubted he could even escape alive from The Black Altar if he merely tried to flee. Perhaps if he, Ashemmi, Yarkul, and Sarhthor all worked together, with spells planned beforehand, they might have a chance to escape. If Casildar and Zhessae, as well as any number of loyal clerics hiding on all sides behind the tapestries, were ready to aid Fzoul in his trap, escape would be impossible. Sememmon kept his face expressionless with an effort, and turned to Fzoul directly.

"It certainly seems the right thing to do, brother Fzoul," he said, as if considering and approving. "However, I feel most uneasy in undertaking such a mission—or indeed, any major expedition outside the city—without even a single priest of Bane to pray for our success and aid us with the favor of the god's will. What say you, Lord Marsh, as one who neither serves Bane nor works art?"

Weaken them at least by one priest, Sememmon thought, and cut that one down as a warning to Fzoul. And if we win the spellfire, we'll come back and try it on one of the beholders. Had Fzoul done something to Manshoon? Sememmon wondered with a sudden chill. Perhaps Manshoon was behind this, to be rid of all his most powerful rivals in art in the brotherhood. If not, and he did return, would Fzoul tell him that all the mages had denounced him and gone off to act as they pleased?

Lord Marsh rubbed his jaw, frowning at the tabletop, thereby avoiding both the calm scrutiny of the beholder and the icy stares of Fzoul, Casildar, and Zhessae. He then looked up. "I must concur with you on this, brother Semem-mon. We have always won our greatest gains by careful use of all three of our strengths: the favor of great Bane; the versatile art of mages; and the might of the swords of our men-at-arms. It would go ill to deliberately neglect more than one of those strengths now.

"Our men-at-arms cannot reach the dale in time without use of art, or in numbers enough to be useful without alarming our foes. We must, therefore, forego our warriors. I believe that it would be foolish—as foolish as deliberately going into battle without shield and armor—to abandon also the strength of Bane in this matter. Moreover, I feel that the warriors under me, and probably many undercleries and magelings here and in Darkhold, would think the same—and seriously question our collective wisdom in doing so, whatever the outcome of the venture."

With that emphatic point, Marsh sat back and looked directly at Fzoul, fingers toying with a bauble at his throat which Sememmon, and no doubt most of the others at the table, knew to be an explosive globe from a magical necklace of missiles. Sememmon almost smiled. The hard-faced warrior was another who bore no love for the Master of The Black Altar.

The eye tyrant hung over them all this time, silent and terrible. Ignoring it, bearded Sarhthor rubbed his hands and said, "Well, I'm for such a strike, and the sooner the better. The spellfire must be ours."

Sememmon did not turn to look at his fellow mages, but nodded absently as he raged inwardly. Was the fool actually that simple and enthusiastic? Or was he working with Fzoul? Nay, listen to the way his words were spoken, the little soft twists at the end of the words that flashed like dagger blades turning over! Sarhthor was telling Fzoul, openly and cuttingly, that he knew Fzoul's game and thought very little of it.

"I'm so glad that we were able to come to an understanding so quickly," Fzoul said softly. His voice was like an assassin's bloody dagger being wiped clean on velvet.

The deep voice of the beholder rolled out from overhead, shocking them all with its sudden interjection. "Consider, and consider well, the nature of your understanding."

As Sememmon looked up to meet Manxam's many gazes for the first time, he took sudden satisfaction in the fact that Fzoul had to be more upset at the eye tyrant's comment than any of the rest of them. Its disapproval was directed at him. Sememmon nodded, deliberately, and saw all of the other mages nodding, too. Sememmon left that chamber feeling almost satisfied, despite the danger ahead.

*   *   *   *   *

The moon scudded through tattered gray clouds high overhead. The air was cold and still around the spires of the city. Fzoul stood on a high balcony of The Black Altar and smiled up at Selune in satisfaction. Strong magic protected his person from attack by art, and none but servants of Bane could enter the courtyard below.

The mages would have no choice. No doubt they would slaughter Casildar, but he was too ambitious anyway, and a small price to pay for the destruction of Manshoon's pet spellhurlers. The Zhentarim would serve Fzoul at last.

Even if Manshoon did return now, he would find himself isolated, with only upstart magelings—all too eager to betray him for their own advancement—to stand with him against the loyal of Bane, who served Fzoul. The beholders cared not which humans they dealt with, so long as their wants were met. The city would be his at last.

Until someone took it from him.

Fzoul never noticed the wizard eye floating above and behind him among the dark spires, keeping carefully out of sight. He could not see its invisible owner, regarding him from the dark window of a tower nearby.

He did hear the commotion in the courtyard below, as the

warrior-priests of the High Imperceptor crept over the wall, and were met by alert and waiting underpriests of the Altar. Fzoul leaned forward and indiscriminately cast a blade barrier down into the growing fray below, caring nothing for the fate of his own acolytes. Let them see Bane the sooner, all of them.

Sememmon heard the clash and clatter of many whirling blades and screams below, and suddenly saw the bloody slaughter as one of the attackers boiling over the temple wall cast magical light upon the scene. He leaned out swiftly before Fzoul could leave the balcony and attacked with his Ring of the Ram. He struck with all the force that the magical ring could muster, draining it of multiple charges to do the task quickly and surely. He did not aim directly at the Master of The Black Altar, for he knew Fzoul would be well protected, but struck instead at the balcony.

It shivered and cracked, as if struck by a battering ram, and then fell away, crumbling in midair, down into the shrieking and death below. It seemed to fall with awful slowness, but Sememmon watched Fzoul's fall closely. The cleric had no time to use an item or utter a word of recall—unless he managed to do so after the first blade had sliced crimson across his red mane of hair. A falling chunk of stone blocked Sememmon's view seconds before the balcony crashed to the ground.

Sememmon turned away in satisfaction, resolving that the attack on Shadowdale would begin and end with the destruction of Casildar, at least until the spellfire-maid was out from under the eye and thumb of Elminster.

He never noticed another wizard eye that floated just above the dark window.

The eye was gone, however, some six breaths later, when a great round shadow drifted out of The Black Altar's depths, its many eyestalks coiling and writhing like a nest of serpents. Then the slaughter really began.

* * * * *

The night was cold. Overhead, Selûne was scudding amid a few tattered gray clouds. Lower down there was little breeze, but Shandril had shut the windows against the chill.

She sat on the bed, facing Narm. "Well, my lord?" Shandril asked. Narm shrugged and spread his hands.

"What do *you* want, my lady?" he asked. Shandril looked at him, eyes dark and beautiful, and spread her own hands.

"To be happy. With you. Free of fear. Free to walk as we will, and neither cold nor hungry. More, I care little for, as long as we have friends."

"Simple enough," Narm agreed, and they both laughed. "All right, then," Narm continued, "we must travel west, as they all say. But, advice be damned, let us go by way of The Rising Moon and Thunder Gap, so you may see Gorstag once more. What say?"

"Yes! It if pleases you, it pleases me. But what of the Harpers?"

"Well . . ."

Outside in the night, Torm strained to hear, but slipped. He breathed a curse upon fickle Tymora as he slid slowly backward on the wet slates despite his splayed, iron-strong fingers. He soon ran out of roof and fell over the edge.

Desperately he swung himself inward as his fingers left the slates. Then he was falling, mind racing coolly. His fingers closed on a window ledge as he plummeted past it.

With a jerk that nearly wrenched his arms from their sockets he brought himself to a halt and hung grimly in mid-air. It was then that he noticed his left hand had come down hard upon a nesting evendove and crushed its frail body against the stone ledge.

"Ugghh," he said, suppressing an urge to snatch his hand away.

"How do you think I feel?" demanded the crumpled bird, opening one eye sourly.

At that Torm did fall. The bird sighed, became Elminster even as Torm fell helplessly away below him, and created a fan of sticky web-strands. These lanced down to the grounds far below, enveloping Torm on the way.

The thief came to a slow, rubbery halt only feet from the ground, and hung there helplessly. He began to struggle. "Serves you right," Elminster muttered darkly, and became a bird again.

Above the two eavesdroppers, Shandril and Narm had

decided to join the Harpers. "After all," as Narm put it, "if we don't like it, we can back out."

"Shall we tell them now?"

"No. Sleep on it, Elminster said." Outside, Elminster smiled quietly, though one couldn't see it for the beak.

"And so to bed again, you and I—and this time I would not hear your life story."

Outside, on the window ledge, the bird that was Elminster looked up at the stars glimmering above Selune. The Silent Sword had ascended above the trees. The night was half done. The bird's beak dwindled. It grew a human mouth, and sang, very softly, a snatch of a ballad that had been old when Myth Drannor fell:

> *. . . and in the wind and the water*
> *the storm-king's fire-eyed daughter*
> *came a-rolling home across the sea*
> *leaving none on the wreck alive but me . . .*

* * * * *

The sun rose hot that morning over Shadowdale, glinting on helms and spearpoints atop the Old Skull. Mist rose and rolled away down the Ashaba. Narm and Shandril rose early, and lingered not in the Twisted Tower, but set out for a brisk morning walk accompanied by six watchful guards that Thurbal insisted on sending with them. Their bright armor flashed and gleamed in the sunlight, and reminded the two lovers constantly of danger lurking near, and of spellfire.

They found themselves hungry again, despite a good breakfast of fried bread and goose eggs at the tower. They stopped in at The Old Skull Inn for bowls of hot stew. Jhaele Silvermane bid them fair morning as she served them, waved away their coins, and asked them when the wedding would be.

Shandril blushed, but Narm said proudly, "As soon as can be arranged, or even sooner." Their escort of guards developed sudden thirsts for ale that made Shandril shudder with the earliness of the hour, but all soon set forth again up the road toward Storm Silverhand's farm.

The dale was quiet despite the morning vigor of workers

in the fields. All Faerun seemed at peace. Birds sang and the sky was cloudless. Narm realized that he and his lady had only a vague idea of where Storm Silverhand's farm was. He turned to the nearest guard, a scarred, mustachioed veteran who bore a spear lightly in his hairy hands. "Good sir," Narm asked, "could you guide us to the dwelling of Storm Silverhand?"

"It lies before you, lord—from this cedar stump, here, on up to the line of bluewood yonder." Narm nodded and said his thanks, for Shandril had already hurried ahead. The guards trotted with him until they caught her again.

It lay behind a high, crown-hedged bank of grass-covered earth. Over the hedge could be seen the upper leaves of growing things. All was lush and green. On this bright morning, bees and wasps danced and darted among the curling blossoms of a creeper that coiled in gnarled loops. The men-at-arms walked watchfully and carried their blades ready, but Shandril could not believe that there could be anything lurking to offer ready danger, in such a place and on such a morning as this.

They turned where a broad track cut through the hedge, and followed it up a line of old, twisted oaks to a large, rambling house of fieldstone. Its thatched roof was thick with velvet-green moss and alive with birds. Vines on tripods and pole frames stretched away from them in rows, like choked hallways amid the green, rustling walls of a great castle. Far down one they saw Storm Silverhand at work, her long silver hair tied back with a ragged scrap of cloth.

The bard wore dusty and torn leather breeches and a halter, both shiny with age. Swinging a hoe with strength and care, Storm was covered with a glistening sheen of sweat, and stray leaves stuck to her here and there. She waved and, laying down the long hookhoe, hastened toward them, wiping her hands on her thighs. "Well met!" she called happily as she came.

"I'm going to hate leaving this place," Shandril said in a small, husky voice. Narm squeezed her hand and nodded.

"I am, too," he said, "but we can come back when we are stronger. We *will* come back."

Shandril turned to look at him, surprised at the iron in his tone. She was smiling in agreement as Storm reached them. The pleasant smell of the bard's sweat—like warm bread, sprinkled with spices—hung around her. Narm and Shandril both stared.

Storm smiled. "Am I purple, perhaps? Grotesque?"

Narm caught himself, and said, "My pardon, please, lady. We did not mean to stare."

"None needed, Narm. And no 'lady', please . . . we're friends. Come in and share sweetwater, then let us talk. Few enough come to see me."

On the way to the house, she said to Shandril, "So what is so strange about me?"

Shandril giggled. "Such muscles," she said admiringly, turning to point at the bard's flat, tanned midriff. Corded muscles rippled on her flanks and arms as she walked. Storm shook her head.

"It's just me," she said lightly, leading them through a stout wooden door that swung open before she touched it, into cool dimness within. "Sit here by the east window and tell me what brings you here on such a fine morning. Most seek Storm in fouler weather."

"Urrhh . . . as bad as Elminster," Narm said in response. She handed him a long, curving horn of blown and worked glass, in the shape of a bird. He held it gingerly, in awe. "It's real glass!"

"Aye . . . from Theymarsh in the south, where such things are common. It breaks easily," the bard said, filling another. Shandril held hers apprehensively, too. One of the guards backed away when offered one.

"Ah, no, lady," he said awkwardly. "Just a cup, if you have one. I'd feel dark the rest of my days if I broke such as that." Shandril murmured in agreement. The bard smiled at them all, hands on hips, and then turned and spoke softly to the guardsmen.

"We must be alone, these two and I, to talk. Bide you here, if you will. The beer is in that cask over there; it is not good to drink more sweetwater so soon. Bread, garlic butter, and sausage is at hand in the cold-pantry. Come with speed if you hear my horn." She took down a silver horn from where it hung on a beam near her head, and turned to Narm and

Shandril.

"Drink up," she urged simply. "There is much to talk about." She went to the back of her kitchen and swung open a little arched door there, into the sunlight. "Follow the path into the trees, and you shall find me." Then she was gone.

The visitors from the tower looked around at the low-ceilinged kitchen, the dark wooden beams, and hanging herbs. It was cozy and friendly, but ordinary, not the wild showplace of art and lore one might expect in the home of a bard. A small lap harp rested half-hidden in the shadows on a shelf near the pantry door. Narm almost dropped his glass when suddenly, and all alone, it began to play.

They stared at it as the strings plucked themselves. One of the men-at-arms half rose from his seat with an oath, clapping hand to blade, but a veteran turned on him. "Peace, Berost! It is art, aye, but no art to harm you, or any of us." The harp played an unfamiliar tune that rose and fell gently, and then climbed and died away to a last high, almost chiming cluster of notes.

"Sounds elven," Narm said quietly.

"Let us ask," Shandril said, standing her empty glass carefully upon the table. "I'm done." Narm drained his with a last tilting swallow and set it down with care beside hers.

They nodded to their guards, went out the little door, and found themselves on a path that twisted down a little ravine, around herbs and beneath overhanging trees. Down they followed it, to emerge at last by a little stream amid the trees that widened into a pool.

Storm stood beside it in a robe, hair wet. She was still damp from bathing, and as they came, she sat upon a rock and beckoned them to two other rocks at the pool's edge. Close by her head, the silver horn hung from a branch.

"Come and sit," she said, "and bathe, if you would . . . or just dabble your toes in the water. It is soothing." She turned serious eyes upon them, and said, "Now tell me, if you will, what it is that hangs upon your hearts."

"The harp that played by itself," Narm asked innocently, "was that an elven tune?"

"Aye, a tune of the Elven Court that Merith taught me. Is that all that troubles your mind?" she teased, shaking water from her silver hair.

"Lady," Shandril said hesitantly, "we think we would like to join the Harpers. We have heard only good of those who harp from all whom we respect. Yet we have heard only little. Before we set foot on a new road that we may follow most of our lives—and that may well lead us to life's end sooner than not— we would know more from you of what it is to be a Harper. If your offer still stands. Well, does it—?"

Storm held up her hand. "Hold, hold! No more queries until we've seen these clear between us. I shall try to be brief." She drew up her bare feet beneath her on the rock, and looked at the woods all around. Then she nodded, as if reaching a decision, and held out a hand to them.

"A Harper is one of a company of those with similar interests—men, and elves, and half-elves. Most bards and many rangers in the North are Harpers. More women than men are Harpers. We have no ranks, only varying degrees of personal influence. Our badge is a silver moon and a silver harp, upon a black or royal blue field. Many female mages, and most druids, are our allies, and we are generally accounted 'good.'

"A Harper is one who tolerates many faiths and deeds, but works against warfare, slavery, and wanton destruction of the plants and creatures of the land. We oppose those who would build empires by the sword or spilled blood, or work art heedless of the consequences.

"We see the arts and lore of fallen Myth Drannor as a high point in the history of all races, and work toward the careful preservation of history, crafts, and knowledge. We work toward that which made Myth Drannor great—the happy and willing sharing of life with all races.

"We work against, and must often fight, the Zhentarim; the Cult of the Dragon—who plunder the lore and art of the Realms to enrich their revered dracoliches; the slavers of Thay; those who plunder and willfully destroy tombs and libraries everywhere; and those who would overturn the peace and unleash fire and sword across the land to raise their own thrones.

"We guard folk against these, when we can. We also guard books and their lore, precious instruments and their music, and art and its good works. All these things serve hands and hearts yet unborn, those who will come after us.

"We seek to keep kingdoms small, and busy with trade and the problem of their people. Any ruler who grows too strong and seeks to take knowledge and power from others is a threat. More precious knowledge is risked when his empire falls, as fall it must.

"Only in tavern-tales are humans wholly evil or shiningly good. We do what we can for all, and stand in the way of all who threaten knowledge. Who are we to decide who shall know or not know lore?

"The gods have given us the freedom and the power to strive among ourselves. They have not laid down a strict order that compels each of us to do exactly thus and so. Who knows better than the gods what knowledge is good or bad, and who shall have it?"

Narm regarded her thoughtfully. "Does that mean, good lady, intending no disrespect," he asked quietly, "that there should be no secrets, and that wild six-year-olds should be tutored in the destroying spells, because knowledge should be denied to none?"

Shandril looked at him fearfully. Would Narm's tongue lead them into Storm's anger, losing any chance of aid—or welcome—from the Harpers?

Storm laughed merrily, dispelling the spellfire-maid's fear. "You have chosen well, Shandril," the bard said. "Unafraid, and yet polite. Inquiring, not hostile and opinionated. Well said, mage-to-be." She got up, drew on her soft, battered old boots, and rose to pace thoughtfully.

"The answer to your question is no. All in the Realms hold and guard knowledge as they see fit. That, too, we have no right to change, even if we had the art to alter every creature's mind. Much should be secret, and much revealed only to those who have the right or ability to handle it. If that sounds too simple, think on this: Harpers seek not to reveal the truth to all, but to preserve writings, art, and music for later years and beings. We work against things that threaten the survival of such culture, or erode its quality by influencing it with unchallenged falsehood.

"Harper bards always sing true tales of kings, as far as

truth is known. They do not, for any reward, sing falsely of the grand deeds of an usurper, or falsely portray as bad the nature and deeds of his vanquished predecessor. Even if such would make good tales and songs, a Harper cleaves to the truth. The truth—a thing slightly different for everyone—must be the rocks that the castle of knowledge and achievement is built upon.

"Strong words, eh? I feel strongly. If you come to do so, too, you will truly be Harpers. If one falls out of such belief, they should leave the struggle and our ranks. They will do themselves, us, and our cause ill.

"I hope only that whether you walk with us or no, or join and then leave us thereafter, that you walk always together, and take joy in each other's company. It is through such love —or longing, when in lack of it—that much learning and celebration comes about. It adds to the culture that we strive to save and nurture. More than that, whether you be Harpers or not, I would be your friend."

Shandril and Narm looked at each other, and then at the bard, and spoke together. "We would be Harpers."

"If you will have us," Shandril added awkwardly. Storm looked at them both with a smile and then stepped forward and gathered them into her arms.

" 'If you will have us,' " she repeated softly. "We would be proud and pleased to have you. You, Shandril and Narm, not your art and your spellfire. You need not stay here—indeed, I agree with Elminster, for we have spoken of this. You should not stay here. You should walk far and see much, and grow in your own counsel and powers. As you go, if you work against evil, you will be Harpers, whether you bear our badge or no. Fight not always with blade or spell. The slower ways are the surer—aid freely given, and friendships and trust built. These evil cannot abide. It shrinks away from what it cannot destroy with fire and blade."

"Where then should we go?" Narm asked, as they stood together there in the wood in each other's arms. They leaned together, and all three took comfort from the embrace. Storm spoke softly, words almost hidden among the sounds of the water.

"Go you by way of Thunder Gap. Watch for Dragon cult

agents. They are thick in Sembia, and there is one in Highmoon. His name is Korvan—" Shandril stiffened. "Go to Silverymoon itself. Seek out Alustriel, High Lady of that city, and say that you come from her sister Storm and would be Harpers.

"With Alustriel, too, is a good place to be if you intend to have a child by then." The bard looked meaningfully at Shandril, who blushed. "Well, you're not quite the first couple to make that mistake." She looked at Narm. "If your lady feels too sick to eat," she said, "feed her lots of stew. In the evenings, she'll feel more like dining."

Narm looked at her. "Pray, lady, let me get used to discovering I'm going to be a father, first," he said plaintively. Storm chuckled again.

"Think well, both of you, on the names your offspring must carry through life. I was born in a storm, and was named because I came out of it. It is an ear-catching name, I'm told, but I fought many larger and stronger lads and lasses when I was small because of it." She freed herself from them and undid her robe.

After a startled look, Narm politely turned his back. Unconcerned, the bard drew on her clothes. Shandril saw that her arms, back, and flanks were covered with faint white, twisting sword-scars. She looked up at Shandril's wondering eyes and winked. "I've walked many roads. Some roads leave little maps." She traced one scar with a long finger and tied her halter.

"You can turn about, Narm," Storm said dryly. "I'll soon grow tired of talking to your shoulders." Narm obediently turned about, grinning. "Now," Storm continued, "I'll tell you a few things about the journey ahead of you. First: trail marks. You'll see a few runes scratched or burned on rocks, trees, or in the dirt as you go." Storm picked up a stick and then shrugged. "Nay . . . I'll draw them for you in the house. It is Elminster's way to expect one to remember half a hundred things in a morning; I'll not do that. I will tell you the names of Harper agents along your way. Look to them for aid if you need it.

"These, too, I'll write for you, on a bandage. I'll need you to prick your finger and bleed on it afterwards. It must look

ED GREENWOOD

well-stained and disgusting if you don't want it to be looked
at too closely, if someone searches or robs you. But these I'll
tell you about, in case you get separated, or lose your list. If
you lose the list of runes, stay clear of all such that you see.

"First, in Cormyr . . ."

* * * * *

After a long time, Storm rose, belted her horn at her
waist, and led them back up the path to her back door.

"What if someone—by art, I mean—heard all this?" Narm
asked, looking at the trees all around. Storm shook her
head.

"I have art of my own to cloak this little, hidden place.
Manshoon himself could not hear us unless he sat with us."
She went in and set the men-at-arms to cutting cheese and
apples for all, while she prepared the bandages.

Storm vanished up a stair half-hidden in the shadows of
the old stone kitchen, taking Shandril's hand and drawing
her up, too. When they reappeared there was no sign of the
promised bandage. Shandril's eyes told Narm readily
enough that it was hidden upon her somewhere. The bard
now wore black fighting leathers and a sword.

"To the temple, then," Storm said briskly, "for we have
much to talk about with Rathan and Eressea."

* * * * *

West of the tower, over the bridge that spanned the river
Ashaba, rose the solid stone temple of Tymora without
ditch or palisade. Its open gates stood in tall green grass
without any wall, so that anyone could easily walk around.
Storm led them between the gate-pillars and along a wide
flagstone path to the temple. The path led to circular,
arched double doors of gleaming metal, fashioned to resem-
ble the disc symbol of Tymora. An acolyte stood guard
before them, manning a polished circular alarm-gong. He
was young and pimply and very earnest. "Why come you to
this house of honor to the Lady?" he inquired, in the words
of the ritual.

"To take our chances," Storm replied formally, "and to
speak with the Lady's servant, Eressea Ambergyles, and

🕭 286 🕭

with the faithful Rathan Thentraver if he is within."

"Yes, lady," said the acolyte with respect. "He is, and you are welcome. Enter, if you will." He opened the doors and stepped within to signal another to take his post as he escorted the visitors into the temple.

In a moment, he reappeared and beckoned wordlessly, leading them into a large circular chamber whose pillars held up a domed ceiling high overhead. He led them up a broad stair without haste, past a watchful priest who sat at the head of the stairs with plain brass rings gleaming upon his fingers and a bare mace laid across his knees. The mace glowed faintly.

Beyond the priest a gallery opened out to the right and left, running around the inside of the dome, past many closed doors. Their escort knocked upon a door straight ahead, and it swung open. Rathan and Eressea, both clad in plainspun robes, were seated at a small round table in a room with large windows. On the table between Rathan and the tiny, stern-faced Preceptress were six dice.

Storm nodded to them. "Well met, both of you. Games of chance?"

"What else in the service of Tymora?" Eressea replied. "It is sacrilege, mind you, to work upon odds, or cheat, or otherwise affect pure chance."

Storm nodded. "You know why we've come, Rathan?"

"Aye," he said, and rose. "Ye may go down to the doors, for we must now discuss holy things," he said simply to the men-at-arms. After a moment, they turned away with nods and murmurs and salutes. Rathan gestured to the acolyte to follow them, but left the door open. He turned to Narm and Shandril. "Ye wish to be wed before the bright face of Tymora," he said simply. "When?"

"As soon as possible, by your leave," Shandril said hesitantly.

"The day after tomorrow," Storm insisted. "I shall sponsor."

"Nay, lady," Rathan said with a grin. "The Lord Mourngrym hath already claimed that honor. All has been made ready, but for the asking of Her Grace, Eressea."

He turned to Eressea, who had risen. Her stern face was

alight. She smiled happily, and said, "I will give Tymora's blessing with pleasure. Is it to be here, or in the tower, or—?"

"Outdoors, Preceptress," Storm said softly, surprising them all. "Upon the site of my sister Sylune's hut, which is burned and gone now." There was a little silence. Shandril realized that Eressea was looking to her for her approval.

"Agreed," she said simply, unaware of what she should say. But Narm quietly echoed her, and made it somehow formal by doing so. Then Rathan spoke.

"Agreed," was all he said, and Eressea bowed.

"After dawnfry, then, the day after tomorrow," the Perceptress said. "Let the word go out." Rathan bowed, and went out and down the stairs before them.

* * * * *

"The young lord and lady to be wed? Gods' good wishes to them! I tell you, Baerth, I saw flames come from her very hand! 'Spellfire' they're calling it—but it was no spell like I ever saw cast! No dancing about or chanting, she just frowned a little, like Delmath does before he lifts a full barrel, and there it was! Aye, you wouldn't want to be marryin' that, now would you?"

Malark, in the shape of an owl on a branch overhead, grinned sourly to himself amid the coarse laughter, and thought on how to slay Shandril. All this skulking infuriated him. At every moment, the girl and her mageling were together, and at every moment, they were flanked by at least one accomplished in art, or one of the knights armed with powerful items of art—with others close at hand.

Malark would not soon forget the desolation of Rauglothgor's lair. A mistake in this matter could be his last. He turned tired eyes toward the Twisted Tower. She was guarded even now. Especially now.

The wedding ceremony would be one chance to get at Shandril-of-the-Spellfire, but not a good one. All of the most powerful protectors of Shadowdale would be gathered there. Perhaps later . . . these two had to leave the dale sometime. Malark had the uncomfortable feeling that others were waiting for just that to happen, and he might have to battle rival bids for spellfire, perhaps even Oumrath.

Malark growled to himself, and took flight restlessly, heading south across the road. Soon, Shandril of Highmoon, he thought. You'll feel my art soon. . . .

* * * * *

The day dawned cool and misty. Shandril and Narm had slept apart as custom demanded, Shandril in the Temple of Tymora with Eressea, and Narm in the Twisted Tower with Rathan. Both were up and awake before dawn to be bathed in holy water and blessed. Word had spread throughout the dale, and folk began to gather early by the banks of the Ashaba.

Rathan filled a glass from a crystal decanter and held it high. "To the Lady," he said, and emptied it into the bath. Then he turned his head to look down at Narm and grinned. "That's all the wine I'll touch this day."

Narm rose, dripping. "You mean you'll miss all the festive tippling, later?"

Rathan shrugged. "How else can I make this a special occasion? Eressea and I will go off together somewhere after it's all done and share a glass of holy water." He stared off into reverie for a moment and then blinked and said gruffly, "Come on, then. Out and dry yourself! If ye are so heedless as to get the chills, Shandril may wed a walking corpse!"

"Cheery, aren't you?" Narm observed, as Rathan unwrapped heated linens from hot rocks, grunting and licking his fingers, and held the linen out for Narm to take.

"If it's a clown ye want, I'll send for Torm straightaway," Rathan replied. "But don't blame me if he gets thee so drunk and distracted that ye forget to come to thy wedding—or if he locks thee in a chest somewhere so that he can have the pleasure of marrying your Shandril himself!"

"Torm?"

"Aye. And if he's busy misbehaving elsewhere, I may take his place in such adventures myself."

* * * * *

Eressea was kissing Shandril's forehead formally, and then hugging her fondly. "We must make haste now," she said. "Your lord-to-be awaits you. Shadowdale gathered awaits you, too. So let us 'scoot,' as Elminster says." Shandril rolled her eyes, and together they hurried down the stairs.

* * * * *

A lone horn rang out from where Sylune's Hut had been and echoed in the dale, to signal that Narm waited with Rathan. It was answered immediately from the battlements of the tower of Ashaba, as the bride-to-be and the Preceptress Eressea set forth on the long walk south.

Storm Silverhand walked behind them, blade drawn, as the guard of honor. Any hostile eyes watching and planning an attack on the maid who commanded spellfire could not help but notice the many bright glows of art that hung about the bard's person. She was armed with power and expecting trouble. There were not a few gasps and mutters among the dalefolk at the display.

Well ahead of them walked Mourngrym, Lord of Shadowdale, bareheaded but fully armored, the arms of the dale upon his breast, and a great sword at his side.

The trumpeters along the route bowed to him but did not sound their horns until Shandril reached them. One by one their calls rang out as the bride drew nearer.

Mourngrym saluted Narm and then stepped aside. A few bare stone flags among still-scorched grass marked the spot where Sylune's hut had stood. When she lived and was Lady of the Dale, no temples had stood in Shadowdale. All had come here to be wed before her. Now at least one more couple would be wed here.

Rathan stood square upon the stones, looking for Shandril. The disc of Tymora upon his breast began to glow as he cupped it in his hands.

Nearer they came, Shandril and Eressea, and the last trumpeter blew two high notes. A fanfare of all the trumpets joined him, loud and long and glorious. When the last, thrilling echoes had died away, Shandril stood before Rathan.

The priest smiled at her and cast the disc of Tymora, which he had taken off its chain, into the air. It hung a man's height above their heads, spinning gently, and its glow grew brighter.

"Beneath the bright face of Tymora, we are gathered here to join together Narm Tamaraith, this man, and Shandril Shessair, this woman, as companions in life. Let their ways run together, say I, a friend. What saith Tymora?"

Eressea stepped forward and spoke. "I speak for Tymora, and I say, let their ways run together." Rathan bowed his head at her words.

"We stand in Shadowdale," he said then. "What saith a good woman of the dale?"

Storm Silverhand took a step forward and spoke. "I say, let their ways run together."

"We stand in Shadowdale, and hear you. What saith a good man of the dale?"

The smith Bronn Selgard stood forth from the gathered Dalefolk then, his great grim face solemn, his mighty limbs clad in old, carefully patched finery. His deep voice rolled over them all. "I say, let their ways run together."

"We stand in Shadowdale, and hear you," Rathan said in response. "What saith the Lord of the Dale?"

Mourngrym stood forth. "I say, let their ways run together."

"We stand in Shadowdale, and hear you," came Rathan's voice, and it suddenly rose into a deep challenge. "What say the people of the dale? Shall the ways of these two, Narm and Shandril, run together?"

"Aye!" came the cry from a hundred throats.

"Aye, we have heard ye. We have heard all, save Narm and Shandril. What say ye two? Will ye bleed for each other?"

"Aye," said Shandril, first as was the custom. Suddenly she was dry-throated.

"Aye," Narm said, as quietly.

"Then let ye be so joined," Rathan said solemnly, and took their left hands in each of his. Mourngrym stepped forward with his dagger drawn.

In the throng nearby, Jhessail and Elminster tensed. Now their protection on Mourngrym might be tested by someone seeking to compel him to strike at the young couple. Rathan's face, too, was tense as he watched.

Gravely the Lord of Shadowdale reached out his dagger and carefully pricked the upturned backs of the two hands,

Shandril's first. Then he wiped the blade upon the turf before them, kissed it, and put it away. He stepped back in silence.

"Now, as we told thee," Rathan whispered to them, and stepped back.

Narm and Shandril brought their bloodied hands to each other's mouths, and then stepped into each other's arms and kissed, embracing fiercely. A cheer arose from those watching.

"Of one blood, joined, are Narm and Shandril," Rathan said. "Let no being tear asunder this holy union, or face the dark face of Tymora forevermore." Above their heads, the spinning disc flashed with sudden, intense light. There were cries of surprise and wonder.

"See the sign of the goddess!" Rathan shouted. "Her blessing is upon this union!"

The disc rose, shining brightly, as Narm and Shandril stepped back, hands clasped, to watch. From it sprang two shafts of white radiance, with a noise like high, jangling harping. They stretched down, one to touch Narm and the other Shandril.

Narm stood motionless, smiling, eyes wide in astonishment as he felt power rushing through him, cleansing and strengthening him. At the touch of the light, Shandril burst into flames, and as she moved to embrace Narm in wild joy, her spellfire rose above them both in a great teardrop of rising flame. Their clothes blazed and were gone, but their hair and bodies were unharmed.

Elminster clucked disapprovingly and began to move his hands in the gestures of a weaving of art, muttering spell phrases unheard by those around him. The Harpers stepped from trees all about, then, to play *The Ride of the Lion* on many harps that shone and glittered in the bright light of Tymora.

For a moment it seemed that another Lady stood with Elminster and the bridal couple on the fire-scarred flagstones, a smiling lady with silver hair. Only Jhessail saw the wraith-like figure before it faded silently away again. "Sylune!" Jhessail whispered, and tears came into her eyes.

Robes of illusion enclothed Narm and Shandril as the

flame died down. Rathan shouted, "It is done! Go forth in joy! A feast awaits you at the tower of Ashaba! Dance, all!"

Jhessail came forward amid the happy tumult then to where Elminster, Mourngrym, the clerics, and Storm stood guard about the happy couple, smiling.

"It is done," she said softly, and kissed them both. "It is time for me to give you what was given to Merith and I upon our wedding day. Foes are gathering even now in the woods to take you, and there will be battle. Mind you fly high, and take no part."

Elminster gravely began the casting of a spell of flight upon Shandril, and Jhessail did the same upon Narm. When they were done, Elminster said gruffly, "Remain aloft no more than ye must—this magic will not last forever. Go, now!" He guided them into another embrace, and patted Shandril's back awkwardly. "Rise!" he bid them, "before the fighting reaches us!"

Shandril thanked them all, and then, in Narm's embrace, rose slowly from the earth. Both were silent in awe as they rose up through a clearing sky together. The bright disc of Tymora silently rose with them and followed, leaving Rathan staring up into the sky. "I do hope Tymora sends me back her holy symbol," he said, watching the faint radiance moving eastward over the forest.

"And I hope," Storm said as gently, "that they have the sense to steer well clear of Myth Drannor."

"I'll see to that, sister," came a soft voice from above, as a black falcon swooped out of the mists and then climbed away from them, heading east.

Elminster growled. "Now I suppose I'll have to keep eyes alight for whatever *she* might do to get spellfire, too!" he said, and became an eagle, and was gone into the sky.

Those who still stood where Sylune's Hut had been looked at each other, and then at the dalefolk hastening back toward the tower as swords flashed and sang amid the trees. Harpers and guards of the dale were battling men in a motley of leathers—mercenaries, by their look.

Jhessail sighed. "Well, back to the battle again," she said.

"Aye," Storm agreed. "As always." They drew blades, a wand, and two maces, and charged into the fray. As always.

❧ 14 ❧

Talk Turneth
Not Danger Aside

Open the door, little fools: we wait outside.
                    The green dragon Naurglaur
                         Sayings Of A Wyrm
                    Year of the Spitting Cat

"We should go down," Shandril whispered into the wind. Narm's arms tightened about her, and he and Shandril flew for a time in silence. The great green expanse of the elven woods lay below them.

"Aye," he reluctantly agreed at last. "I shall not soon forget this."

"Nor shall I," she whispered. "As I should hope not!"

Narm chuckled at her mild indignation. Bending his will to turn northwest again over the seemingly endless trees of the Elven Court, they headed back to Shadowdale.

"I can't help but feel," he said, looking about them, "that we're being watched." It was an odd feeling to have while soaring naked high above the land.

"I'm sure we are, and we have been since we first rode with the knights," his lady replied. "How else could they protect us?"

"Well, yes . . . but now?"

"I'm sure they've seen such things before," she said. "Elminster's five hundred winters old, remember?"

"Aye." Narm sighed, looking all about them. They were gliding low over the trees, the sky clear but for a line of clouds to the north. They could see no other creatures in the air or below. Narm shrugged. "Would that none of this were necessary," he said, "and we could walk unafraid together."

Shandril fixed him with very serious eyes. "I agree with you," she replied softly. "But without spellfire, you and I would be bones by now." They passed over the bare top of Harpers' Hill and left it behind them again. "Besides, it is the will of the gods. Rage as we might, it is so, and shall be."

Narm nodded. "Aye. . . . Your spellfire can be handy enough, I'll admit. But does it harm you?"

Shandril shrugged. "I know not. I do not feel amiss or in pain, most times. But I couldn't stop it or give it up, even if I wanted to. It is part of me, now." She turned in his grasp to look back, and as she did so something circular and silver drifted out of the empty sky into her hands. Shandril caught it before thinking of danger. It was cold and solid, and the touch of its smooth weight sent her fingertips tingling.

"It is Rathan's holy symbol!" Narm said, astonished. "How came it here?"

"By the will of Tymora," Shandril said quietly. "To answer your doubts." Narm nodded slowly and almost sternly. The fine hairs upon his arms stood out stiff with fear. But he held her as gently and firmly as before.

"Where now?" he asked, as they saw The Old Skull Inn below. "The Twisted Tower?"

"No," Shandril said, pointing at chain mail flashing upon the backs of men below. "In all the alarm, the archers might well have us both down before they knew us."

"Or even," Narm muttered, "because they knew us."

Shandril slapped him lightly. "Think not such darkness!" she hissed. "Have any who are truly of the dale shown us anything but kindness and aid since we came here? We must be suspicious, aye, or perish—but ungrateful? But as I was about to say, I have little liking for the idea of greeting all the folk of the tower clad as we are."

Narm chuckled. "Ah, the real reason," he said, halting their flight over Elminster's tower. "My apologies, for such black thoughts. Still, it is better to look over one's shoulder than to die swiftly and surprised."

"Aye, but let not the looking make you sour," Shandril told him. "You would come down here?"

"Have we anyplace else?" Narm asked. "I doubt the art that protects Storm's home will be kind to us now, if we come calling when she is not there."

"True," Shandril agreed and took one last look around from their height, looking north over the Old Skull's stony bulk to the rolling wilderness beyond. The wind slid past them gently now. "Learn this spell yourself, as soon as you can," she urged as she clung to him. "It is so beautiful."

"Aye." Narm's voice was husky. "It is the least of the beauty I have known this day."

Shandril's arms tightened about him, and she and Narm sank gently to the earth in a fierce embrace in front of Elminster's tower.

Overhead, a falcon waggled its wings to an eagle and veered away to the south. The eagle bobbed in slow salute and wheeled about, sighed audibly, and dove earthward.

"Must ye stand about, naked, kissing and cuddling, and generally inflaming an old man's passions?" Elminster demanded loudly, inches behind Narm.

Narm and Shandril both jumped, startled, but barely had time to unclasp and turn about before the sage was pushing them roughly toward the door. "In! In, and try your hands at peeling potatoes. Lhaeo can't feed two extra guts on naught but air, ye know!" Shandril's fending hands encountered a deep and silky beard.

Elminster came to a dead halt and glared at her. "Pull my beard, will ye? Ridicule a man old enough to be thy great - great - great - great - great - great - and - probably - great-again-grandsire? Are ye mad? Or just tired of life? How would ye like to enjoy the rest of thy life from the mud, as a toad, or a slug, or creeping moss? Aye? Aye? AYE?"

He was pushing them both again, now, step by step to the door. Narm had begun to chuckle uncertainly. Shandril was still white and open-mouthed. The door opened behind them, and Elminster added in sudden calm, "Two guests again, Lhaeo. They'll be needing clothes first."

"Aye," came the dry reply from within. "It is cold in the corners, herein. How are they at peeling potatoes?"

Elminster's answering chuckle urged them in, and he closed the door with a brief, "I'll follow, anon . . . some tasks remain." They were inside in the flickering dimness with Lhaeo, already moving toward a certain closet.

"We've gone through more clothes since you've come to Shadowdale," he said. "You were a head shorter than I, were you not, Shandril?"

"Yes," Shandril agreed, and she began to laugh. After a moment, Narm joined her. Lhaeo shook his head as he handed clothes backward without looking. Truly they serve most who know when to laugh and when to listen.

* * * * *

The stew warm inside her, Shandril leaned back against the wall on her stool happily. She looked over at Narm, clad in the silk robes of a grand mage of Myth Drannor, and smiled at him, heart full. The hearth glowed, and Lhaeo moved softly back and forth in front of it, stirring and tasting and adding pinches of spice kept in a rack above his cutting board. Pheasant hung from the rafters above the scribe, and a plump gorscraw lay upon the table, waiting to be plucked and dressed. Narm sipped herbed tea and regarded Lhaeo's deft movements over his stewpots. "Is there anything we can do to help?" he asked.

Lhaeo looked up at him with a quick smile. "Aye, but it is not cooking. Talk, if you would. I have heard little enough speech that is not Elminster's. Tell me how it is with you."

"It is wonderful, Lhaeo," Narm said. "I am as happy now as I have ever been in my life. We are wed this day and henceforth. It is joyous indeed!"

"You, too?" the scribe asked Shandril. She nodded, eyes shining.

Lhaeo smiled. "Both of you," he said, "remember how you feel now, when times are darker, and turn not one upon the other, but stand together to face the world's teeth. But enough. I will not lecture you. You must hear enough of that from other lips, hereabouts."

They all laughed. Shandril stopped first and asked, "Those men—at the wedding? Who were they, do you know?"

"I was not at your wedding," Lhaeo said softly. "Forgive me. I abide here to guard—certain things. I did learn something from the Lord Florin of the men who drew swords and would have attacked you, if that's whom you mean."

Narm nodded. "Those men, yes."

The two men held each other's eyes for a moment, and then Lhaeo said, "There were over forty, we believe. Thirty-seven—perhaps more by now—lie dead. One talked before his life fled. They were all mercenaries hired, for ten pieces of gold each and meals, to grab you both—Shandril alone, if they could take but one of you.

"They were hired in Selgaunt only a few days back and flown up in a ship that sails the skies. Oh, yes, such things exist, though they be rare triumphs of art. They were hired in a tavern by a large, balding, fat man with a wispy beard, who gave his name as Karsagh. They were directed to take you to a hill north of here to be picked up by the skyship.

"They would then be paid in full. Each had received only two pieces of gold. Many died carrying it, still unspent. Who this Karsagh is and why he wants you, we know not. Have you any favorite thoughts as to who he might be?"

Narm and Shandril both shook their heads. "Half the world seems to be looking for us, with swords and spells," Shandril said bitterly. "Have they all nothing better to do?"

"Evidently not," Lhaeo replied. "It is not all bad, that. Look who found you, Shandril—this mageling called Narm, and the knights who brought you here."

"Aye," she said very quietly, "and it is here we must leave—friends and all—because of this accursed spellfire." Fire leaped and spat in tiny, crackling threads from one hand to another, as she stared down at her hands in anger.

"Not within these walls, if you please, good lady," Lhaeo said, eyeing it. "Things sleep herein that should not be so suddenly awakened." Shandril sighed, shame-faced, and let the fires subside.

"Sorry I am, Lhaeo," she said sadly. "I have no wish to burn down your house." The hearthfire let out a crack, then, that startled them all, as a tiny pocket of pitch in a branch blew apart. Narm stared from it to Shandril, a little fear on his face. At his look, Shandril nearly burst into tears.

"Nay, nay," said Lhaeo, turning to his cutting-board. "I know you do not, nor do I fear it coming to pass. You must not hate your gift, Shandril, for the gods gave it to you without such fury. And did not Tymora bless your union?" The scribe indicated the holy symbol that Shandril had carefully set upon a high table. As if in response to his words, it seemed to glow for a moment as they looked at it.

"Aye," Narm said, getting up. "So we are helpless in the hands of the gods?" He began to pace. Lhaeo looked up, sharp knife flashing as he cut up the tripes of a sheep.

"No," he answered, "for where then would be your luck, which is the very essence of holy Tymora? What 'luck' can there be, if the gods control your every breath? And how dull for them, too! Would you take any interest at all in the world beneath your powers, if you were a god and if the creatures in it had no freedom to do anything you had not determined beforehand?

"No, you can be sure that gods do not fate men to act thus-and-so often, if at all, despite the many tales—even those by the great bards—that would have it otherwise."

"So we walk freely, and do as we will, and live or die by that," Shandril agreed. "So where should we walk? You know maps, Lhaeo—I have seen your mark upon the charts here and in the tower yonder. Where upon the land of Faerun should we go?"

The scribe looked at her and spread his hands. "Where your hearts lead, is the easy answer," he said, "and the best. But you really ask me where you should run to now, this season, with half Faerun at your heels and with the Harpers your chosen allies. A good choice, know you by the road."

He paced alongside Narm for a few strides and then said, "I would go south, quick and quiet, and go by the Thunder Gap into Cormyr. There, keep to the smaller places and join with a caravan or with pilgrims of Tempus who seek the great fields of war that lie inland from the Sword Coast. Go where there are elves, for they know what it is to be hounded and will defend you with fierce anger."

He turned back to the cutting-board. "I daresay you would hear much the same advice from those who travel, if you could trust one to ask." Narm and Shandril traded glances in silence. Then Narm spoke.

"We have heard such directions before, yes," he agreed, "almost word for word. If the best way is so obvious as all that, will your enemies not be looking for us to take it, and be waiting?"

"Aye, most probably they will," Lhaeo agreed, with the ghost of a smile. "So you must take care not to get caught."

They both stared at him for a moment in frustration, and then Shandril laughed. "Well enough," she said. "We shall try to follow your advice, good Lhaeo. Know you any ways of avoiding those who search?"

"You both work with art and walk with those who are mighty in art, and you ask me?" Lhaeo replied, eyebrows raised. "If you would learn the ways of stealth and disguise without art, ask Torm. I have escaped thus far, true, but in my case I was cloaked in the Lady's Luck." He turned to Narm. "If you must pace about like a great cat in a cage," he added, "could you slice potatoes while doing it?"

* * * * *

Elsewhere, things were not so peaceful. In Zhentil Keep, two men faced each other across a table.

"Lord Marsh," said the mage Sememmon carefully, "does it seem to you that the priests of The Black Altar, through some unfortunate internal dispute or other, have fallen into confusion and disarray too great for us to leave the city with it unaddressed? I know my fellow mages feel that eye tyrants cannot be trusted and should not be given more authority than the minimum one is obliged to accord them to win their support. All reports indicate that the beholder Manxam presently holds sway in the temple, and the corpses of many hundred clergy, great and lesser, that lie there have begun to stink."

"I have heard those same reports," Lord Marsh Belwintle agreed smoothly. "I am forced to the same conclusions . . . as, I hold, any reasonable man would be. This matter of one girl who can create fire will simply have to wait, unless or until she shows up at your gates to do us harm. Whereupon I am fully confident that the power and skill of the gathered mages of the city would defeat her, so long as they have not all been destroyed or weakened in the interim by being sent off here and there on missions by one who had rather transparent reasons for wishing them out of the city."

"Exactly," Sememmon agreed. "I had thought to discuss with you the advisability of setting just one of your mages of power—Sarhthor, perhaps—to observing this maiden's doings, so that her seizure by any of your foes or other concerns could be noted or countered by us. Were she to reveal any power or method whereby she gained spellfire, we could benefit merely from such a watch, with no blood lost to us and no art or coin wasted. Prudence would seem to indicate some sort of vigilance on your part."

"An excellent plan, indeed," Lord Marsh agreed, reaching for a glass of blood-red wine before him. "The fighting arm of the Zhentarim would certainly concur with—and even expect—such a tactic. An eye must serve us where a claw might be cut off, if we are not to be taken unaware by some creeping enemy and ultimately overwhelmed. More wine?"

"Ah, thank you," replied Sememmon, "but no. It is excellent, indeed, but its taste lingers on the tongue and makes the sampling of potions when concocting them a chancy business, at best. Such onerous duties call, I fear."

"Quite so, quite so," Marsh agreed, rising. "Well then, we are agreed. I shall not keep you longer. We may have to speak with each other later, and speedily, should the beholders prove troublesome. But for now, oloré to you and your fellows-in-art."

"Oloré to you," Sememmon agreed. He walked away.

An eye that neither of them saw floating under the table watched Sememmon go and then winked out.

* * * * *

"The Wearers of the Purple are met. For the glory of the dead dragons!" Naergoth Bladelord said. The leader of the Cult of the Dragon was, as always, coldly calm.

"For their dominion," the ritual reply answered him, more or less in unison. Naergoth looked about the large, plain, underground chamber. All were present save the mage Malark. Well enough. To tongue-work, then, the faster to feast in some fine festhall of Ordulin, above, and then bed and then sleep. The ruling Council of the Cult waited expectantly.

"Brothers," he said, "we are gathered to hear of an affair that preoccupies your mages: this matter of spellfire and all that is drawn into it. Brother Zilvreen, what say you?"

"Brothers," Master Thief Zilvreen said with soft, sinister grace. "I have learned little from your loyal followers of the fates of the dracolich Rauglothgor and the mage Maruel. But it appears likely that Rauglothgor, its treasure, the she-mage, and even another sacred night dragon, the wyrm Aghazstamn, whom Maruel called on for aid and rode upon back to Rauglothgor's lair, have all been destroyed. Destroyed by the accursed archmage of Shadowdale, Elminster, a group of adventurers who call themselves the Knights of Myth Drannor, and by this young girl we have heard of, this Shandril Shessair, who can cast spellfire!"

"All?" rumbled Dargoth of the Perlar merchant fleet. "I can scarce believe they can all have been destroyed. What is so powerful, save an army of a size that we could see gathering for many days?"

"No such swords have been raised," Commarth, the bearded general of the Sembian border forces, added dryly.

"Men sent back by Malark have described the site of Rauglothgor's lair as a pit of freshly strewn rubble," Zilvreen answered. "Draw your own conclusions."

"So just what is this spellfire," Dargoth asked, "that it can destroy great mages and great wyrms alike?"

Naergoth shrugged. "A fire that burns and can be hurled as a mage casts bolts of lightning," he said, "and that affects magical items and spells as well as things not of art. More than that we do not know—which is why we sent Malark."

"What of him?" Commarth asked. "Has he spoken to you more recently than we know?"

Naergoth shook his head. "No, I have heard no more than I have told you. He is in or about Shadowdale now, as far as we know, seeking a time and a way to get at the girl."

"Shessair," one of the others mused. "Wasn't that the name of the mage that your brothers of art who preceded Malark slew at the Bridge of Fallen Men, in the battle that bought them their deaths?"

"Aye, it was," Naergoth said, "but no connection is yet apparent. We have at least three eyes in Sword Coast cities who have the last name of 'Suld' that I know of . . . and none are blood-related or even know of each other."

"What boots it?" Dargoth said. "Ancient history only

warms long tongues—it can have no bearing on what we decide to do in this matter."

"It certainly won't, if we do nothing," Commarth agreed in dry tones. "Have you any plans in mind, brothers?" Naergoth and Zilvreen shrugged.

"You first, brother," Zilvreen prompted.

Naergoth nodded and spoke. "The price of getting our hands on this spellfire seems far too high, and others—the Zhentarim, and the priests of Bane outside Zhentil Keep, for two—are known to seek it. Yet it is we who have already paid a price, and I am loath to turn away empty-handed. The price may seem too high to you . . . and yet we cannot afford not to gain spellfire for our own. No one can. I expect much bloodshed yet." He looked around the table. "How we go about getting it, I leave to you, brothers."

"Let the mages win it for us," said Zilvreen smoothly. "Waste no more swords—and especially no more of your bone dragons—on this."

"Well enough," Dargoth agreed. "But spellfire or no, we must not let this girl, or the knights, go unpunished for what they have done. We must never forget that we have lost much treasure, two dracoliches, and The Shadowsil over this. The girl must pay. Even if she becomes an ally, she must die after we have gained her secrets and her power. This must ride over all."

"Well said, brother," Naergoth agreed. There was a murmur of agreement around the table. "We are agreed, then—for now, we let your brother mages handle this affair?"

"Aye, it is his field," came one reply.

"Aye, it would be folly to do otherwise," said another.

"Aye—and if he comes not back, we can always raise other mages to the Purple."

"Aye to that, too!"

"Aye," the others all put in, in their turn. So it was agreed, and they all rose and left that place.

* * * * *

It was late in Shadowdale, and in the Twisted Tower the candles burned low. In an inner room of Lord Mourngrym's chambers off the great bedroom, there was much discussion over the remains of dinner—in low tones, as Lady Shaerl slept in her chair at one end of the table, and Rathan Thentraver dozed over one arm of his chair.

"We must leave," Shandril said, close to tears.

"Leave? Of course . . . how can you know yourselves and become strong if you are always in the midst of our hurly-burly?" Florin agreed. "But come back one day to see us, mind," he added softly.

"Have you a place in mind?" Jhessail asked, as she leaned drowsily upon Merith's shoulder. The elf's eyes gleamed in the candlelight. Tonight he had said little and listened much.

Narm shrugged. "We go to seek our fortune. The Harpers said to seek High Lady Alustriel in Silverymoon."

"Would you have some of us ride with you?" Lanseril asked. "There are greater evils in this world by far than those you have fought."

"With all respect, lord," Shandril answered him, "no. Too long you have watched over us and spilled much blood on our account. We must make our own way in the world and fight our own battles—or in the end, we will have done nothing."

" 'Nothing,' she says," Torm said to Illistyl. "Two dracoliches and a mountaintop and a good piece of Manshoon of Zhentil Keep, yet, and 'nothing,' she calls it! It's scary. What if she tries 'something' ?"

"Hush you," Illistyl said, stopping his mouth with a kiss. "You're a worse windbag than the old mage himself."

"Why, thank ye," said a familiar voice wryly from the far darkness of the room. Narm saw the battered old hat first, perched atop the staff that Elminster bore, as the sage's bearded old face came forward into the light and regarded them all. He looked last at Narm and Shandril.

"Ye might," he said dryly, "go to The Rising Moon for a night, at least. It would be a kindness to Gorstag. He has been worried about ye."

Shandril met his gaze in silence, and a breath had passed before Narm realized that she was crying. Silent tears rolled down her cheeks and dripped from her chin. He turned to her and took her in his arms, but her tears still fell.

"Don't cry, beloved," Narm soothed her. "You're among—"

"Shush her not," Merith said gently. "It is no shame to weep. Only one who cares not, cries not. I have seen what happens to those—Florin and Torm, at this table—who cry inside and try to hide it from others. It sears the soul."

Jhessail nodded. "Merith is right," she said. "Tears don't upset us, only the reasons for them."

"Cry here, lord," murmured Shaerl in her sleep, patting her own shoulder. "It is soft and listens to you." Mourngrym looked faintly embarrassed. Torm grinned.

"You see?" he said to Illistyl. "You could do that for me. . . . You have the shoulders for it." She slapped him fondly.

Shaerl stirred and frowned. "Oh, it is that game tonight, is it?" she murmured. "Well, my lord, you'll have to catch me first, I assure you." Chuckles arose from around the room. Mourngrym leaned forward and lifted his lady gently from the chair. Sleepily she clung to his neck and drew her legs up across his chest, settling herself with murmurs of contentment.

Mourngrym turned to them all with Shaerl cradled in his arms. "Good even, all," he said with a smile. "Shaerl should be in bed—and so should all of us."

* * * * *

"Now where were we?" Elminster asked, settling himself into a chair that looked as old, shabby, and well-worn as he did. "Oh, aye . . . your plans for the future, Narm and Shandril." Groans, silence, and faint snores answered him from elsewhere, as the newly healed knights lay sleeping upon couches and blankets. Jhessail looked at him and smiled ruefully, but she said nothing. Narm also kept silence, but the slow, disbelieving shake of his head was eloquent.

Shandril fixed the sage with her own tired eyes. "I suppose you'll tell us to steer clear of fights, or we'll be dead within a day, eh?"

"Nay." Very clear blue eyes looked deep into hers. "You two will be given no such choice. You must fight or die. But think: one mistake is enough when you're dealing with those who wield art. Remember that." His gaze shifted to Narm. "Ye too, Lion of Mystra."

Elminster cleared his throat, then continued. "If ye find

thyself facing a mage, stand not to trade spells with him. Throw rocks, and run right at him unless he's much too far away to reach. Then run away and find a place to hide where ye can grab rocks to throw. Simple, eh? Recall how thy lady first struck down Symgharyl Maruel before ye laugh."

"Five hundred-odd winters, eh?" was all Narm said.

*   *   *   *   *

The sun rose again over a very quiet tower of Ashaba. The Lord and Lady of Shadowdale, in the company of the sage Elminster, the young married lad and lass, and the knights all remained on an upper floor within a great, blinding sphere of shimmering colors, a prismatic sphere cast by Elminster. Rold warned everyone not to approach.

Several times the prismatic sphere melted away and was replaced by the art of the old mage. During one cessation of the sphere, a simpering Lhaeo was waiting. With the aid of several strong guards, he brought tea, a great cauldron of hot stew, bowls and a monstrous ladle, and two fat spellbooks for the old mage. The scribe then went away again and advised everyone else except the guards to do the same.

The envoys waited in their guestchambers, and the merchants went away from the forecourt again, for the lord and lady and all in the sphere rested that day and into the night. Once, in the dark hours, Elminster used a sending spell to deliver a message to a certain eye tyrant in a certain cold stone city, a message that left the tyrant black and seething with anger. But then, Elminster had five hundred years-worth of impudence saved up. He sat humming to himself in the tent he and Florin (who were both immune to the sphere's blinding effects) had erected to shield the eyes of their companions from the sphere's swirling colors.

"Elminster," Shandril asked hesitantly, "may I ask you something?"

"Aye," Elminster prompted her, waving a cooling hand over his bowl of stew. "Ask, then."

"Why is it that my spellfire was turned aside by a wall of force spell you created while testing me, and yet this prismatic sphere—a much more powerful spell, Jhessail tells me—can be destroyed by a mere wisp of spellfire?"

Elminster regarded her thoughtfully. "Like much else about thy spellfire, young lady, I know not. I could tell thee airy theories about the anti-spell nature of the wall and the many-layered and inherently less stable nature of the sphere, which focuses its energies more toward preventing attack from without than from within. Such words, however, would be just that—airy theories."

Elminster shifted uncomfortably. "The truth is, I know not, nor does any mage ye will ever face in Faerun, unless or until some new lore comes to light or ye are tested further. I do not care to test thee further myself, for such tests are dangerous to the one being tested. I have no desire to assure thy corpse—and Narm—that I have learned the precise limits of thy powers."

"My thanks for that," Narm said dryly.

"Many is the mage who would not scruple a moment, lad," Elminster told him gently. "The pursuit of an edge in art is all, for most. Some who care nothing for glory and battle-strength delight in learning what none have learned before. They'd not hesitate. Consider that, ye who hope to be a master of the art, and govern thyself accordingly.

"I do not want to hear news someday of how ye've turned thy bride into a weapon against rival mages, or burned her powers out in striving to further them or win them for thyself. Aye, aye . . . I know the very idea repels ye. But it is an easy road, step by innocent step, to such things, and dead is dead and wishing brings the past not back. Enough. Be not hurt or angry at my words, but sit and think upon them instead, and grow wise." Elminster grinned suddenly. "I'm in a mood to give away wisdom today . . . come all, and take some, until I have none left."

"I hear you," Mourngrym said wryly, from the great couch where he and Shaerl lay at ease in each other's arms. "I take it this is a mood that comes often upon you?" Elminster favored him with a look.

Jhessail chuckled. "Admit it, Master," she said. "Your wisdom is often in short supply."

"Aye," the old mage replied, looking around at them all

with a raised brow. "Its like is rare indeed in this company."

Torm had lost his sight for a time because of an incautious look at the whirling, shimmering sphere. "Why do we cower here like—like—"

"Like blind men?" Rathan put in helpfully. Torm gave him a sour look. There were chuckles. Elminster rolled his eyes and picked up one of his spellbooks without replying. Jhessail gave Torm a pitying look.

"Listen, little snake-brains," she said lovingly. "How well could you have fought Manshoon, say, without the light of your eyes to guide you?"

"Aye, but I'm better now," the thief told her. "Why must we sit caged up like this? Time slips away! Armies march, and mages weave! The gods sleep never, and orcs—"

"Will do as they always do, aye, and spill the blood of others and beget more orcs between bloodlettings—we know the sayings. If there is such a thing as patience in your mind, in some dark and seldom-visited corner, seek it out, and hunt it down, and once you have hold of it, let it not go from your grasp." Jhessail fixed him with dark eyes. "Use your knot, man. Or I'll teach you to."

"That might be fun," Torm said to the tent above him.

"I wouldn't, Torm," Merith said calmly from where he lay. "I just wouldn't. It is unwise."

"Threats, dire warnings, and sinister words he heeded not," Torm sang lightly, "but rushed in and took the crown for his own."

"If it's crowning ye're looking for," Rathan grunted, hefting his mace and leaning forward, "I could see my way clear to obliging ye."

"Why, darling," Torm said, mocking the tones of a high court Cormyrean lady (Shaerl frowned, and then couldn't hold it; her severe expression slipped into laughter). "I knew not the depths of your caring. My champion!" (Squeal of excitement, breathy delight.) "My brave warrior! My—"

"—bringer of slumber," Rathan grumbled, flinging Torm's half-cloak over the thief's head and holding it down firmly to muffle his cries. "Silence, now," he added as the thief struggled, "or I'll just bounce my mace off this nasty lump here"—he patted Torm's enshrouded head—"until it goes down."

"Sleep now, all of ye," Elminster told them. "Narm and Shandril begin a long journey in the morning." He darkened the glowing globe that hung by his shoulder. A few half-hearted jests were tossed back and forth by the weary knights, but sleep came swiftly.

* * * * *

Shandril awoke much later in a cold sweat, pursued through the crumbling tunnels of a ruined city by a black-winged devil who cornered her at last and reached for her, with Symgharyl Maruel's cruel, smiling face. She caught a shuddering breath and started up. Florin sat nearby with Elminster, talking in low tones through the blue haze of the sage's pipe. He leaned over with concern on his ruggedly handsome face and laid a soothing hand on her arm. She smiled gratefully at him and held to his arm as she sank back down beside Narm, who slept peacefully. Florin gently wiped the sweat from her forehead and jaw, and she smiled and must have drifted off to sleep again, for when next she knew her surroundings, morning had come.

Jhessail was laughing with Merith over hot minted tea. Sunlight shone warmly all about, for the tent and the sphere were both gone, and the knights, variously clad, were sitting up on their couches or bedrolls, or walking quietly about.

The clear tones of a horn floated up to them from some-where below, where an unseen player was blowing his delight in a fine morning. Shandril looked around at the old stone walls of the chamber and said aloud to herself, "I'm going to miss this."

"Yes," Narm agreed, suddenly beside her. Shandril turned to him in pleased surprise. He grinned. "You seemed ready to sleep forever," he said, hugging her.

Shandril hugged him back. "You're mine, now!"

"A-aye," Narm managed from within her arms.

"Not for much longer, if you break him like a clay cup," Torm said dryly. "They're more useful, you know, when they're whole . . . back and arms able to carry, and all. . . ."

Shandril burst out laughing. "You're utterly ridiculous!"

"It is how I get through each day," Torm told her earnestly. It was much later when she realized he'd spoken the sober truth.

* * * * *

"Well," said Florin at last. "Here we part." He nodded at the weathered stone pillar just ahead. "Yonder is the Standing Stone." The pillar rose, watchful and defiant, out of the brush, overlooking the fields back to Mistledale and south toward Battledale. Florin pointed. "Down that road lies Essembra. Take rooms at the Green Door. It once had a talking door, but we took a fancy to it, so that door is back at the tower. Somehow," he grinned, "we forgot to show it to you in all the excitement."

The white horse under Shandril snorted and tossed its head. "Easy, Shield," Florin said to her. "You've barely begun, yet."

There was a sudden lump in Shandril's throat at his words. She turned in her saddle to look back. Past the pack mules on their reins, past the watchful crossbowmen who rode behind with quarrels at the ready, back to where the knights rode with an ever-grumbling Elminster. She'd miss them all. She felt Narm's hand clasp hers hard. She held back sudden tears.

"None of that," Rathan ordered her gruffly. "All this sobbing robs an occasion of its grandeur."

"Aye," Lanseril agreed. "You'll be too busy staying out of trouble to cry, soon. So get in the habit now, and let's have dry eyes. Remember that Mourngrym serves his best wine at Greengrass. We'll be looking for you, some year."

Narm nodded. Shandril was too busy wiping away tears that would not stop. Her shoulders shook in silence.

"Go now," Torm said gruffly, over his shoulder. "Or we'll be all day a-weeping and a-saying farewells."

Rathan nodded and urged his large bay forward to take a hand of both Narm and Shandril. "Tymora go with ye and watch over ye," he said fervently. "Think of us when ye are downcast or cold—such thoughts can warm and hearten."

Torm stared at his friend. "Such bardic soft and high glory," he said in amazement. "You've not been drinking, have you?"

"Get on with ye, snaketongue, to the nearest mud, and fall from thy saddle into it," Rathan said kindly, "and mind ye get lots of muddy water in thy mouth."

"Peace, both of you," Jhessail chided them. "Narm and Shandril should be well away before highsun, if they are to make Essembra even two nights hence." She turned to the young couple. "Mind you stay on the road. The Elven Court is not the safest place in Faerun these days."

"Let not fear or pity stay your hand, either," Florin said gravely. "If you are menaced on the road, let fly with spellfire before hands are laid upon you. A swinging sword often can't be stopped in time by spellfire or art."

"Oh, aye . . . one last thing," Elminster said. "I know something of illusions. This will make ye both look rather older, and a trifle different in appearance—save to each other's eyes. It will wear off in a day or so, or ye can end it at any time, each of ye affecting only thyself, by uttering the word *gultho*—nay, do not repeat it now, or ye will ruin the magic. Let me see . . ." He drew back his sleeves and sat upon his placid donkey and worked magic upon Narm and Shandril while the knights drew their mounts around in a respectful circle.

When it was done, the knights moved their mounts in closer for careful, critical looks. Narm and Shandril looked to each other and could not see the slightest difference in each other's appearance, as Elminster had said, but it was clear that they looked different to the eyes of others.

"Go now," Elminster said gently, "or ye'll be seen. We shall ride north toward Hillsfar with illusions of ye for a time to confuse any who seek ye, but those who pursue ye are not weak-minded. Go now, and go swiftly. Our love and regard go with ye." His clear blue eyes met theirs fondly and steadily as they slowly turned their mounts about, and then, with a vast wave, spurred away.

Looking back as they thundered south along the road with tears stinging their eyes, Shandril and Narm saw the knights sitting their saddles watching. Florin raised something that flashed silver to his lips as they rode on over the first rise, and as the descending slope of the road hid the knights from their view, the clear notes of the knights' battle-leader's war-horn rang out in a farewell. He was playing the *Salute to Victorious Warriors*. Shandril had heard it played by bards at the inn, but she had never dreamed it would someday be played for her!

"Will we ever see them again?" Narm asked softly, as they slowed.

"Yes," said Shandril, with eyes and voice of steel, "whatever stands in the way." She brushed her hair out of her eyes. "It is time we learned to look after ourselves. If I must slay with this spellfire every jack and lass seems so eager to take, then so be it. I'm afraid I can't laugh at devils and dracoliches and mages and men with swords the way Torm does. They just make me angry and afraid. So I'll strike back at them. I hope you won't be hurt . . . I fear much battle lies ahead of us."

"I hope *you* won't be hurt, my lady," Narm answered her, as they rode on. "You're the one they'll be after."

"I know," Shandril said softly, and steel shone in her eyes again. "But it is I who'll have spellfire ready when they find me."

They slowed their horses to a steady trot. The road was lightly traveled that day. They saw no one traveling south, and only a few merchants heading north. All rode ready-armed, but nodded without incident or ill looks.

Great old trees of the Elven Court rose on both sides of the road. Between them and the road itself stumps rose out of the ditch like the gray fingers of buried giants, all that remained of saplings cut by travelers as staves and litter-poles and firewood. Narm watched these narrowly as they rode, half-expecting brigands to rise up out of them at every bend and dip of the way.

They rode in silence for the most part, until the sun glimmered low, and the trees laid dark shadows across the road.

"We should find a place to sleep, love," Narm said as shadows lengthened and their horses slowed.

Shandril looked at him and nodded soberly. "Aye, and soon," she said. "We are almost upon the vale. A cursed place. Let us stop here—at that height, ahead—and hope none find us."

They reined to a halt, and Narm swung down. "Ohhh," he groaned. "Stiff . . . ohhh. Tymora watch over us." He patted his mount's head and listened. "Water, down there," he said after a moment, pointing.

Shandril swung down into his arms. "Good, then," she said lightly, inches from his nose. "You fetch some while I tie the horses, oh mighty conjurer."

Narm growled and kissed her, and then unhooked the nosebags from the mules and went down to get water. Somewhere nearby a wolf howled. Overhead, as the last light faded and the moonlight began, a black falcon came silently to a branch above Shandril, and clung, watching.

* * * * *

They awoke in each other's arms on a hard bed of canvas tent laid flat upon mossy ground. Birds called in the brightening morning. It was damp and misty among the trees. They were in a beautiful place, but somehow it was not welcoming. They were intruders, and could feel it.

Once Narm thought he saw elven eyes far off in the gloom, regarding him steadily, but he blinked and they were gone. The Elven Court itself may have gone from these woods, but the hand of man had not tamed them—yet. Narm felt more comfortable with his hand resting on the hilt of his drawn dagger, beneath the cloak that covered their shoulders and throats. He turned to Shandril, who smiled through tousled hair, looking sleepy and vulnerable. "Good morn, my lady," Narm greeted her softly, rolling over to draw her close.

"And to you, my love," Shandril replied softly. "It is nice to be alone for once, without mages attacking us and guards watching over us always, and Elminster fussing about. . . . I love you, Narm."

"I love you, too," Narm said quietly. "How lucky I've been to see you in the inn and then be parted, only to find you deep in ruined Myth Drannor again. I would have come back to The Rising Moon someday when I was free of Marimmar, only to find you long gone."

"Aye," Shandril whispered against his chest. "Long gone and probably dead. Oh, Narm . . ." They lay in each other's arms, warm and safe and unwilling to rise and end this feeling of peace.

Then they heard the dull thudding of hooves from the road nearby, and the creak of harness leather. Shandril sighed and rolled free of Narm. "I suppose we must get up," she said, long, blond hair hanging about her shoulders as she rose to her knees, pulling the cloak about her against the chill. "If we stop in Essembra only to buy feed and to eat and then hasten on, we could camp on the southern edge of the woods this night. I would be out and away, west of the Thunder Peaks, before the Cult of the Dragon and Zhentil Keep and whoever else is after me know we have parted from the knights. Come, now. You can kiss me more later."

Narm nodded a bit mournfully. "Aye, I know." He sat up and looked all about at the drifting mist in the trees, and the horses chewing on leaves patiently. He sighed too, then, and scrambled up to draw on his clothes. His thighs were raw from yesterday's riding. He drew on his belt, then stopped abruptly, listening. He could have sworn he had heard a chuckle, but there was no one to be seen. All was quiet from the road, too. After a long time he shrugged and continued on, glancing back often at his lady. He never saw the black falcon winging low over the treetops to the east on the long flight home.

In falcon shape, The Simbul shook her head and chuckled again. They were good folk, she thought, and then rose on powerful wings to look around at the trees below. Children, still, but they'd not be for much longer. She had other concerns, too long neglected, to see to now. Perhaps they'd be killed—but then again, it was entirely possible that they'd do the killing if any in Faerun quarreled with them. Farewell, you two. Fare-you-very-well. The lonely queen of Aglarond flicked raven-black wings and rose higher.

* * * * *

They made good time across the strangely still place known as the Vale of Lost Voices. Sacred to the elves, it was, and men whispered that something unseen and terrible guarded it. Something that destroyed axe-wielding men and great mages alike, and left no trace behind. In the vale the elves of the Elven Court buried the bodies of their fallen, but those who dared to dig for treasure there vanished in the mists and were not seen again.

Narm and Shandril, and those who passed them there, said not a word all the time they rode across that tree-choked valley. The largest trees they had seen yet grew in the vale, some as big around as Elminster's tower back in Shadowdale. The light was eerily blue under the trees where mists coiled slowly far off, and faint glowing lights drifted and danced. No one stepped off the road while they traversed the vale.

They left it at last, Shandril shivering in sudden relief as they came up over the crest of the steep hill that marked its southern edge.

"The Lost Dale, they call it in Cormyr," Narm said, low-voiced. "Forever lost to men, because of the elves."

Shandril looked at him. "They say in the dales that every elf in the Elven Court would have to be dead before one tree of the vale could be safely cut."

"But all the elves are gone now," Narm said. Shandril shook her head.

"No. I saw one in the woods at Storm Silverhand's. She waved to Storm and went away as we came down to the pool." Shandril turned to peer all around into the trees.

"But that's far from here," Narm protested.

"Think you so?" asked Shandril very softly. "Look there, then." Narm followed her gaze and saw a motionless figure in mottled green-gray standing upon the mighty branch of a shadowtop that towered high above the road ahead. The figure was an elf, and he leaned easily upon a bow that must have been a head taller than Narm. He looked at them with steady blue, gold-flecked eyes. Shandril bowed her head, spread empty hands, and smiled. Narm did the same. A slow nod was their only answer. The horses carried them past at a steady pace, and Shandril said, "A moon elf, like Merith."

"A possible enemy, unlike Merith," Narm replied grimly. "We must watch our every step." He peered ahead. "The trees thin," he said. "We must be nearing Essembra. I can see fields."

A caravan rumbled toward them, then, a dozen wagons

pulled by oxen. The wagons were surrounded by hard-eyed outriders who rode with crossbows at their saddles and short spears in their hands. The wagons bore no merchant banner, but passed without incident.

Well behind the caravan rode a family on heavily laden draft horses, leading strings of pack mules. They were led by a single excited youth with a halberd that dipped and swung alarmingly as he rode forward to challenge them. "Way, there! Way, if you be not foes! Declare yourselves!"

Narm stared at him in silence. The halberd lowered upon them.

"Declare yourselves, or defend yourselves!"

"Ride on in peace," Narm replied, "or I'll turn your halberd into a viper and turn it back upon you!"

The boy recoiled, his horse dancing uncertainly as its rider waved about trying to draw his blade wrong-handed while keeping the halberd menacingly upon Narm. "If you be a mage," he said shrilly, backing away as Narm and Shandril rode steadily on, "give your name, or face swift death!" Beyond him Narm saw small crossbows raised ready upon saddles, and calm, wary eyes above them. He could not hesitate longer. Beside him, Shandril rode serenely silent.

Narm drew himself up in his saddle. "I am Marimmar the Magnificent, Mage Most Mighty. I and my apprentice would pass you in peace. But offer us death, and it shall be yours!"

Beside him, Shandril burst into muffled giggles. Narm kept his composure with an effort, as the boy cast him a frightened look and hastened by. Narm nodded pleasantly and then stared straight ahead as he rode past the other men and the mules behind, managing to hide a smile that kept creeping onto one side of his face.

* * * * *

"Sarhthor?" Sememmon asked aloud, peering into the depths of the crystal ball before him. Its magical telepathy was always difficult to focus at first. In its depths he could see flickering lamps and an expressionless, elegantly bearded face. Sarhthor looked back at him and sent his thoughts without speaking. Sememmon tried to hide his own irritation at the other mage's precise ease of art and apparent fearlessness.

"Well met, Sememmon. I have searched the dale. Elminster and the knights have just returned, using the road south from Voonlar. The girl with spellfire and her consort mageling are not here, as far as I can determine."

"Not in Shadowdale?"

"Not. They may be here in hiding, but I doubt it. None of the knights—or those Harpers I can observe in safety—have gone anywhere out of the ordinary or met with anyone. The folk of the tower know they left two nights ago."

"Two nights?" Sememmon almost screamed. "Why, they could be almost anywhere!"

Precisely why I'm returning to you, as soon as possible, Sarhthor thought flatly, then said aloud, "By the way, who is that with you?"

"With me?" Sememmon asked, angry and startled. "I am alone!"

"You are indeed—now. A moment ago there was an eye floating above your left shoulder—the ocular construction of a wizard eye spell. A spy, then. Guard yourself, Sememmon."

Sememmon had already turned angrily away from the ball, to stare wildly about his chamber. "Show yourself!" he thundered, casting a detect magic spell. Dweomer—the auras of familiar objects imbued with art—glowed all around him. The faint traceries of spells, too, shone in the field of revealed magic created by his spell, but they were all spells he knew about, preservative and defensive, all art that should be there. There was no sign of any intruder.

At last Sememmon turned angrily back to the crystal ball, but it was dark. No one waited at the matching globe at the other end any longer. Sememmon cursed the shadows about him, but they did not answer.

*　*　*　*　*

The sun was low again. Shandril and Narm passed a skin of hot spiced tea between them as they rode, their bellies full of warm roast phledge, the plump ground-partridge of the woods, smoky-tasting and delightful in a thick pea gravy. No one had acted suspicious of them at the inn Florin had recommended.

"How do you feel, my lady?" Narm asked suddenly, not meeting her eyes. "About the spellfire, I mean. Does it . . . change one?"

A little startled at the suddenness of the question, Shandril looked at him with something close to pity in her eyes. "Yes, no doubt. But not in the larger sense, I think. I am still the Shandril you rescued from Rauglothgor." She hesitated, then added in a much softer voice, "I am still the Shandril you love."

Narm looked at her, and there was a little silence as they regarded each other. And then the attack came.

Shandril felt something was wrong an instant before the boulder struck Narm's shoulder, and his head flew back. The jarring made her bite her lip. Narm was whirled about, his arm striking her head solidly as he spun, and he toppled and fell.

Stunned, Shandril stared at the huge, mossy boulder as it settled past her to hang above Narm's head. He lay crumpled, unmoving. The boulder sank slowly, and over the grassy bank beyond where Narm lay, Shandril saw a man in robes.

He grinned at her without humor. His eyes glittered black and deadly. She drew breath to scream, as wild fear rose and choked her from within.

❦ 15 ❦

The Crushing
of the Soul

*I have known the crushing of the soul that
defeat brings, and the burning, sickening pain
of deep wounds—and would not have it otherwise. Such dark things make the bright spots
burn the brighter.*

Korin of Neverwinter
Tales Told By The Warm Fireside
Year of the Blazing Brand

"No . . . make no sound," the man in robes warned. "Speak
not. Cast no spells. Use no spellfire, Shandril Shessair—or I
will let fall the rock on the head of your husband." His eyes
bore into hers. "Do not think to trick me or take me
unaware," the man added calmly, "for I am not such a fool—
and yonder stone can hardly miss its mark."

Shandril sat still in her saddle, cold fear trickling slowly—
slowly and chillingly—down her spine. She stared at the
mage and wondered for an instant who this one was. How
to win free? her mind screamed then. How to win free?

"I am Malark," the man said with cold pride, "of the Cult of
the Dragon. I come for revenge, and I will have it." His eyes
flickered. "Get down off your horse slowly, and stay just
where you land, or your husband will die."

Shandril did as he commanded, never taking her eyes off
his. He watched her with the cold patience of a snake.

"Lie down. Slowly. To your knees, and then upon your
belly, arms outstretched toward me. Do not touch any
weapon." Shandril did so, heart sinking as she pressed her
face into the rocky ground. "Good," said the voice coldly.

"Spread your arms and legs apart. Do not try to rise."

He was nearer. Shandril obeyed, wondering how much she'd have the courage to endure. She gathered spellfire within her, silently. Malark walked around her, staying at a safe distance. Angry warmth filled her chest and throat. She glared at the grass before her eyes, and it began to smoulder. She hooded her fire, hastily, and held herself ready. Tymora aid me!

"You have cost us much indeed, Shandril Shessair. The Shadowsil, the dracolich Rauglothgor, his lair, and the forti-fied tower above it, with all his treasure, the dracolich Aghazstamn, many devout worshippers—the worth of all these, you owe us. The price is your spellfire—that, and your service and that of your husband. You may serve us, or die. Lie still." The cold voice began the mutterings of spellcasting.

Gods aid me, Shandril thought. What will become of us? There are no knights here to rescue us, now.

Malark's cold chanting ended in a sudden squealing, gur-gling sound. Shandril, waiting to absorb his spell, froze and then rolled over in breathless haste. If that rock fell on Narm . . .

But Narm was safely to one side, in the grip of a grinning Rathan. Malark stood staring at her, black eyes very dark and very large, and over his shoulder Torm was grinning.

In the thief's hands were the ends of the waxed cord that had choked off Malark's spell in mid-word. Malark was hanging from the cord now, face terrible, frantic fingers clawing at the cord about his throat growing feeble. Malark's eyes rolled up into his skull, and he began to sag. Torm held the cord tight as he lowered the mage slowly to the ground.

"Well met," the thief said cheerfully as he rolled the body over, drawing his dagger in one fluid motion, and beckoned Rathan over with a jerk of his head. "His purse, quickly, before he is fully dead . . . these damned mages all have spells set to trigger all manner of mischief at their deaths."

Rathan bent to work obediently. "Ho, Shandril—thy lad's all right," he said quickly. Shandril stared at the boulder, now sunk into the grass nearby, and shuddered. "Nothing but a bit of rag and a handful of coppers," Rathan told Torm.

"His boots," Torm directed, still holding the cord tight. Malark's face looked so dark and terrible that Shandril turned away.

"Is—is he dead?" she asked weakly.

"Nearly. I'll cut his throat in a moment. . . . Then, lady, it would be best to burn the body completely, or some bright-minded bastard of the cult will raise him to lurk on your trail." Torm turned professional eyes upon the boots. "Try that heel."

"Hah!" Rathan said in satisfaction a moment later, holding up six platinum pieces. "Hollow, indeed!"

"Hmmph," Torm said, wrinkling his nose. "No magic? Scarce worth all this trouble. Have off his robe, Rathan, and we'll cut his throat and be done with it."

"His robe?"

"Aye, his robe. Where he conceals the components for his spells, a few extra coins, and the gods know what else . . . which we'll soon learn. Come on—my arms grow weary!"

"They do? Pretend they're around a wench, and ye'll have no trouble at all," Rathan told him gruffly, tugging off the mage's robe. He stepped back, looked at the body as Torm laid it down with both ends of the cord in one fist and a dagger gleaming long and wickedly in the other, and then grinned at Shandril.

"Not unimportant, are you?" he said. "Malark, one of the rulers of the Cult of the Dragon. An archmage in his own right. You watch out, now. There are lots of other rats like this one in Sembia, mind, and there's one in Deepingdale, too. . . ."

"Yes," Shandril said. "Korvan."

Rathan nodded. "Aye, that's the name! You've been warned, then? Good. Well, you're doing fine thus far!"

"Fine," said Shandril bitterly, looking at Malark as Torm freed his cord at last and slashed with cruel speed. Her gaze fell next on Narm, who still lay silent in the grass. "Oh, yes. Fine indeed." She burst into tears.

Rathan sighed and went to her. "Look, little one," he said awkwardly, "Faerun can be a cruel place. Men like this have to be slain—or they will kill thee. Nor is there any shame in defeat at his hands—this one could have slain any of us knights, in an open fight. He was an archmage." He enfolded her in a bear hug. "Ye wouldn't be thirsty, perhaps?"

Shandril's shoulders shook helplessly then, as tears were overwhelmed by laughter. She laughed for a long time, and a little wildly, but Rathan held her tight, and when at last she was done, she raised bright eyes and said, "Are you finished, Torm? I think I'd like to wield a little spellfire."

Torm nodded and stepped back, and Shandril raised a hand and lashed the body with flames, pouring out her anger. Oily smoke arose almost immediately, and the horses snorted and hurried off in all directions.

Torm and Rathan let out brief despairing cries and ran after the horses, just as Narm rolled over and groaned, and then asked faintly, "Shandril? Wha—why did you do that? Am I not to kiss you?"

*　*　*　*　*

"They could be dead by now!" Sharantyr said angrily. "I ride patrol for a few days and return to find you've put your toes to the behinds of two of the nicest young people I've met! One struggles with half-trained art, and the other bears spellfire that every mage in the Realms would slay her to gain or destroy, and both are mad enough to seek adventure. And but days married, too! Where is your kindness, Knights of Myth Drannor? Where is your good sense?"

"Easy, Shar," Florin said gently. "They joined the Harpers and wanted to walk their own road. Would you want to be caged?"

"Caged? Does a mother turn her infant out of the house because it's reached twenty nights of age? Alone, you sent them!" She turned upon Elminster. "What say you, old one? Can they best even a handful of brigands on the road? Brigands who attack by surprise in the night? Speak truth!"

"I have never done aught else," Elminster answered her. "As to the fight ye speak of, I think ye'd be surprised." He drew out his pipe. "Besides," he added, "they're not alone. Not by now. Torm and Rathan rode after them."

Sharantyr snorted. "Sent the brightest lances, didn't you?" She paced, sword bouncing on her hip, and then sighed.

"Well enough. They are not unprotected." She folded her arms and leaned back upon the wall by the hearth. "Gods spit upon my luck," she said more softly. "I wanted to say farewell, not just ride away and never see them again."

"They'll be all right, Shar," Storm said, "and they'll be back again."

"Sharantyr raises a good point, though," Lanseril said from his chair. "The wisdom of sending them alone, with only a rescue squad hurrying along behind, can well be questioned." He raised thoughtful eyes to Mourngrym and Elminster. "I take it you considered their slipping away while we rode a distraction to Hillsfar a good risk?"

Elminster nodded. "It had to be. Think on that, Sharantyr, and be not so angry, lass."

"They passed the vale without loss or upset," Merith put in. "I heard from one of the people who was watching the road there."

Sharantyr nodded. "Since then?" she prompted. Merith shrugged.

"I scryed Torm and Rathan yestereve," Illistyl spoke up. "They were cutting across country, southeast of Mistledale, and had met with no one then. I'll try them again tonight."

"Soon?"

"Aye . . . you can watch, if you like. You too, Jhess, if you have no greater game afoot"—she looked meaningfully at Merith, who grinned—"at such an early hour of the evening. We might need your spells if there is danger or alarm."

Jhessail chuckled. "It is a good thing none but the gods look over your shoulders to see all we—and Narm and Shandril, gods smile upon them—get up to. It would make a long, confusing ballad."

Elminster scowled. "Life is seldom as clear-cut, smooth, and as easily ended as a ballad," he said and put his pipe in his mouth with an air of finality. The fire crackled and flared up in the hearth. The sage stared at it thoughtfully. "She's so young to wield spellfire," he murmured.

* * * * *

"He lies within," the acolyte said fearfully, hastening away from the door.

Sememmon thanked him curtly and said, "Open it."

The acolyte stood a moment in silence. Then he glided forward and swung the heavy oak and bronze door wide. Sememmon motioned him to pass through. The acolyte nodded and stepped forward, face impassive. The mage followed, through very thick stone walls, into a vast chamber that glowed a faint and eerie blue.

This was the center of The Black Altar, the Inner Chamber of Solitude, where one was said to be closest to the god. The forces of the High Imperceptor had not penetrated this far, although Sememmon felt much hidden satisfaction at the extensive damage he'd already seen. The priesthood would be a while recovering its strength, indeed. Perhaps, Sememmon thought, never, if certain misfortunes befall them now, while they are weak and disorganized.

Sememmon came fully into the chamber, and such thoughts ceased. Vast and dark above him hung a beholder, its great central eye gazing down upon him maliciously. The acolyte had darted back behind Sememmon. He heard the door clang and the crash of a heavy bar falling into place. He was imprisoned. The eye tyrant was not Manxam. Sememmon cursed inwardly even as he strode forward, his cloak about him concealing nervous fingers that had gone straight to the hilt of a useless dagger.

The floor of the chamber was of highly polished marble. In the center of that vast, cold expanse rose a black throne—a throne that the High Imperceptor had not sat at the foot of for many a long year. It was gigantic, a seat for a giant, the seat of a god. It was occupied.

Red silk stood out against the black stone. Fzoul Chembryl lay asleep upon a bed across the seat of the god's throne, recovering after the frantic healing efforts of the priests who served Bane under him. Sememmon gazed at him as he approached, uncomfortably aware without daring to look up that the beholder was moving with him, floating directly overhead with its great unblinking eye staring down.

The mage was no more than a dozen steps from the base of the throne, able to see clearly the rope ladder the priests were wont to ascend by, when a deep, rumbling voice from overhead said, "You have come to find death, Sememmon the Proud, but you have found not Fzoul's death, but your own." As Sememmon looked up and broke into a run, he saw the dark body of the beholder sinking lower and lower. The beholders were making their own bid for leadership of the Zhentarim.

Within a breath the beholder would be close enough to use the eye that dealt death or that turned one to stone. Or it might simply charm him into obedience or pursue him about the chamber like a trapped rat and wound him from afar. In the end, he knew, it would use the eye that destroyed one utterly, and there would not even be dust left of Sememmon.

So Sememmon ran as he had never run before, diving frantically around the edge of the throne where the vast central eye, the one that foiled all magic, could not see. He hastily began the casting of an incendiary cloud. He did not have the right spells for a fight this grave. . . . Buy time and cover, then use a dimension door to teleport directly above the beholder, he told himself. Use paralyzation—or, no, use magic missiles now! Or . . . ah, gods spit upon it all! Raging, Sememmon applied himself to spellcasting.

He finished, and sprinted along the back of the throne, nearly tripping over a ringbolt on the floor that obviously was a trap-door—if one were very strong or had four or five acolytes to lift it. Sememmon reached the corner, gasping for breath, and steadied himself. To cast a magic missile spell, he must see the target—and if he could see the behold-er, its eyes would also be able to see him. He tensed himself to take a rapid peek, and—

There was a flash and a roar, and the very floor heaved up, knocking Sememmon to his knees. Up, get up, he urged himself frantically. But there was a reddish haze of dancing spots before his eyes. He could not seem to grasp which way 'up' was.

"Well met, Sememmon," said a dry, coldly familiar voice. Sememmon looked up into the calm gazes of Sarhthor and Manshoon. The High Lord of Zhentil Keep was robed in his usual black and dark blue, and he looked amused. "You can get up now," he added. "It's gone." He flexed his open hand.

Sememmon found his voice. "You've returned! Lord, we

have missed you, indeed—"

"Aye. No doubt. I've watched you and seen the, ah, troubles with Fzoul. Come, now, and slay him not. He is needed." They hurried across the marble floor toward the door Sememmon had come in by. It was blasted and twisted into shards of metal beneath their feet. "Sarhthor," Manshoon explained briefly.

The three mages went out through strangely deserted halls and sought the starlit night outside. Wordlessly they walked out of The Black Altar, past dim piles that had already begun to stink; the bodies of those who had fallen in the battle between Fzoul's forces and those of The High Imperceptor. They walked straight to Sememmon's abode, and the two mages left Sememmon there.

"Cheer up," said Manshoon in parting. "You'll have your chance to fight with the others for all this"—he shrugged his shoulders and looked around at the dark spires that rose all about them—"someday. I can't live forever, you know." With that he turned on his heel and was gone down the cobbled street into the night, Sarhthor at his heels.

Sememmon stared after them in the faint light and tasted fear. When would Manshoon feel that Sememmon had lived long enough? He entered hastily, the little eyeball that Manshoon had sent to spy floating in, unseen, with him, too.

* * * * *

"We just happened to be riding this way," Rathan said gruffly. "It's an open road, is it not?"

"No," Shandril said with a crooked smile. "You came after us to protect us. Did you not trust Tymora to look after us!"

The burly cleric grinned. "Of course Tymora watches over ye. . . . Am I not an instrument of Tymora's will?"

"Is that why you moved a sleeping man and left all the fighting and dirty work to me?" Torm said. "Not a copper's worth of value in the pockets of his robe, too."

"Dirty work, is it? Who took off his boots, I'd like to know!" Rathan teased him.

"I thank you both," Narm said, "despite your feeble attempts at humor. Again my lady and I owe you our lives. And our horses', too, it seems. Your spell even took away the pain in my head."

Rathan grinned. "If ye want it back, I can lend thee Torm for a few breaths." Torm favored him with a sour look.

Shandril giggled. "I don't think that will be quite necessary, Rathan. I have a man to drive me beyond endurance, now." Narm gave her a hurt look, to which she replied with a wink, but Torm looked delighted.

"Oh, you can leave him with Rathan, to learn how to ride and fight and worship and all," he said, "and I'll ride with you. I'm witty, agile, clean, quick, and experienced. I know lots of jokes, and I'm an excellent cook, so long as you're partial to meat, tomatoes, cheese, and noodles all cooked together. I'm fully conversant with the laws of six kingdoms and many smaller, independent cities, and I'm an excellent gambler." He batted his eyelashes at her. "What do you say? Hmmm?"

Shandril gave him a look that would have melted glass. "Is there nothing you can do about him?" she asked Rathan.

"Oh, aye," Rathan agreed. "Ye can give him first watch, so we can all get some sleep. Narm and I'll sleep on either side, close against ye, and ye won't have to worry about him getting cold and wanting to snuggle up."

"Ah, hah," Shandril agreed dubiously. She rolled her eyes and flopped down into the bed of folded tent without replying. Rathan grunted and lowered himself slowly to a lying position, rolling his cloak up as a pillow. He lay on the grass fully clad, without bedding or blanket, grasping his mace. He nodded then, as if satisfied, and within a few breaths he was snoring. His booted feet twitched now and then.

Torm winked at Narm and reached out to pinch one of them. His fingers were still inches away from their goal when Rathan rolled open one eye and said, "Ye can forget pinching, stroking, and tickling honest folk—or even us—who're asleep in the arms of the gods. Just see that the fire stays high."

Narm fell asleep chuckling.

* * * * *

The soft morning sun breaking over the rolling hills and fields of Battledale and northern Sembia lit up the sky to the east, and found Rathan Thentraver thoughtfully warming water for tea over the dying fire.

He looked around at his sleeping companions, got to his feet with a slow grunt of effort, and clambered up the bank to look at the land about. It was bare of all but grass, rolling and very empty. He nodded in satisfaction, tucked his mace under his arm, and sat down again and cleared his thoughts of all but Tymora, as he tried to do every morning.

He opened his heart to her and prayed that the two young folk beside him—aye, and Torm, too, hang him—would see only her bright face until they had at least reached Silverymoon and befriended Alustriel. Everyone needs at least one safe journey—and these two, more than most, because of the spellfire, he told himself.

Rathan looked across the twisted blankets to Shandril's sleeping face and thought about her weeping spellfire and lashing out angrily with spellfire and tearing open her tunic to pour spellfire out the faster upon a foe. He would not want to carry such power for all the gold in the Realms. . . .

He sighed. If they'd ridden a bit slower, that snake of a mage might have had her yestereve. So close, he'd been. A matter of breaths. Yet one couldn't nursemaid one who could blast apart mountaintops!

They'd be running into trouble soon enough, these two, and they'd need someone. Rathan sighed. Ah, well, some things ye must leave to Tymora. He got up and began to make tea. Soon they'd be wanting morningfeast, too.

He looked at all the sleepers, and a smile touched his lips. Why wake them? The younglings needed a good, long sleep when they were guarded and could relax. Let 'em sleep, then. He peered south to see if he could glimpse the River Ashaba, but it was too far away yet. Ah, well. We'll ride with them until they're up at dawn tomorrow, and then turn back. If Elminster is half the archmage he pretends to be, surely he can hold Shadowdale together that long.

Scratching under his armor, Rathan opened his food supply pack. Ah, well . . . another day, another dragon slain.

* * * * *

"Will ye never be done all that scratching and scribbling?"

Elminster demanded. "You're not writing an epic, ye know!"

Lhaeo turned calm eyes upon him. "Stir the stew, will you?" Elminster snorted, shifted his unlit pipe from hand to mouth, and began to stir.

"You miss those two, don't you?" the scribe asked him softly without turning.

The old mage stared at Lhaeo's back angrily for a long breath and then muttered, "Aye," around his pipe, set the ladle back in its place, and sat down upon the squat cross-section of a large tree that served as a seat next to the tiny kitchen table. " 'Tis not every day one sees spellfire destroy one's own prismatic sphere without delay or a lot of effort. Or see the high-and-mighty Manshoon put to flight by a young girl who's never cast a spell in her life."

"A thief, she said she was—or at least, she joined the Company of the Bright Spear as a thief."

Elminster snorted again. "Thief? She's as much a thief as you are. If we had a few more thieves like that girl, the Realms would be so safe we'd not need locks! Swords, aye, but no more locks. Which reminds me . . . locks, and locked-away books, that is—Candlekeep—Alaundo. What did old Alaundo say about spellfire? We must be getting fairly close to that prophecy now, too, so it's no doubt Shandril he's talking about."

Lhaeo smiled. "As it happens, I looked up the words and sayings of Alaundo the last night they spent here. To your left, under the jam jar, on the uppermost scrap of paper, I've copied the relevant saying. If a certain 'war among wizards' has already begun in Faerun, it is next to be fulfilled."

Elminster halted his flailing about in the vicinity of the jam-jar to fix Lhaeo with a hard glance, but the scribe went on with his writing.

"What're you doing?" Elminster demanded. "There you sit, scribbling, while the stew thickens and burns. What is it?"

Lhaeo smiled again. "Stir the stew, will you?" he asked innocently. Then, before the old mage's fury could erupt beyond a rising growl, he said, "I'm noting down the limits of Shandril's power, as observed by you and the knights. The information may prove useful some day," he added very quietly, "if she must ever be stopped."

Elminster stared at him a moment and then nodded, looking very old. "Aye, aye, you have the right of it, as usual." He sighed. "But not that little girl. Not Shandril. Why, she's but a little wisp of a thing, all laughter and kindness and bright eyes—"

"Aye. Like Lansharra," Lhaeo answered simply. Elminster nodded, very slowly, and said nothing. There was silence for a long time. Lhaeo finished his work, blew upon the page, and got up. The sage sat like a statue, his eyes on the fire. Lhaeo reached over him, slid a scrap of paper from under the jam-jar, and laid it before Elminster. He turned away to see to food, without a word. Perhaps four breaths later, he heard the old mage's voice behind him, and he smiled to himself. Put a recipe for fried sand snake in front of Elminster and he'd be reading it in a trice.

" 'Spellfire will rise, and a sword of power, to cleave shadow and evil and master art.' " Elminster read it as though it was a curious bard's rhyme or a bad attempt at a joke. Lhaeo waited. Elminster spoke again. " 'Master art'? What did Alaundo mean by that? She's to become a mage? She has not the slightest aptitude for it—and I'm not completely new to teaching art, ye know!"

"I have found that Alaundo's sayings make perfect sense after they have happened, for the most part," Lhaeo said, "but they help precious little beforehand."

"Ahhh . . . stir the stew!" Elminster grunted. "I'm going out for a pipe." The door banged behind him. Lhaeo grinned.

The stairs creaked as Storm came down them barefoot, silver hair shining in the firelight.

"Leave the stew," she said softly to Lhaeo. "It's probably been thrashed into soup by now, between the both of you."

Lhaeo smiled and put strong arms around her. "Let us go back upstairs," he said gently, "before he returns for a flame to light his pipe. Haste, now!"

The bed creaked as they sat upon it, a scant instant before the door, below, banged open again. Outside, Elminster chuckled and then hummed his favorite of the tunes Storm had devised. One didn't get to be five hundred winters old without noticing a thing or two.

* * * * *

They rode steadily south all that day on a road busy with wagons rumbling north out of Sembia. Hawk-eyed outriders and shrewd, watchful merchants looked them over often, and the scrutiny always made Narm and Shandril uncomfortable.

Torm had acquired a moustache from somewhere about his person, as well as some brown powder of the sort used as cosmetics in the Inner Sea lands. Skillfully he rubbed it about his eyes and jaw and cheekbones, until his face seemed subtly different. He rode in silence for the most part—a mercy upon his companions—and affected a soft, growling voice when he did speak. He remained to the rear as they rode.

Looking back, Narm could see the glistening whites of his eyes darting this way and that in the shadowy gloom of a cap that hid his face. The conjurer gathered that Torm was a little too well known in Sembia or nearby to ride openly on the high road this far south without his fellow knights around him.

Rathan, however, paid such cautions no mind. He rode easily before Shandril, speaking loudly of the kindnesses and spectacular cruelties of the Great Lady Tymora, and occasionally pointing out a far-off landmark or the approaching colors of a merchant house or company of the Inner Sea lands. But he seemed to be addressing her as Lady Nelchave, and occasionally comparing things to 'your hold, Roaringcrest.' Shandril answered him with vague murmurs, trying to sound bored. In fact, she was enjoying riding in the comfortable security of Rathan and Torm's presence, with a guided tour of the countryside.

Torm and Rathan preferred to lunch in the saddle without halting. Shandril found it fascinating to watch them fill nosebags with skins of water and lean forward to hang them carefully about the necks of their mounts and mules, after first letting each animal taste and smell the contents of such a bag. They deftly passed bread, cheese, and small chased metal flasks of wine about. Torm even produced four large, iced sugar rolls (probably pilfered from some passing cart or other) from somewhere about his person. Shandril began to wonder if he had endless pockets, like those of Longfingers the Magician in the bards' tales.

A light rain squall came out of the west in the afternoon and lashed them briefly as it passed overhead. Torm nearly lost his moustache, but he regained his high, sly spirits. He danced about on his dripping horse, firing jests, rolling his eyes, and mimicking the absent knights.

The day passed and the road fell away steadily behind them, until in high eventide they came to Blackfeather Bridge, where the road between the Standing Stone and Sembia crosses the River Ashaba. There Sembia maintained a small guardpost of bored-looking, hardened men armed with ready crossbows and long pikes bearing the Raven and Silver banner of Sembia.

The guards looked long and coldly at the four travelers. Narm noticed a cleric of Tempus and a silent man in robes standing off to one side with two veteran warriors, watching them steadily. His throat went dry, but he tried to keep his face unconcerned and impassive. Dragon Cult and Zhentarim agents could be anywhere—and everywhere. Narm was certain Rathan was recognized, but nothing was said and no one barred their way.

Two hills later, as the sun sank lower, Narm looked back, but he could not see any pursuit. An uneasy feeling persisted, however, and he was not surprised when at sunset Rathan led them wordlessly westward, well off the road, until it grew too dim to ride safely on.

"This seems as good a place as any," Rathan said gruffly, waiting for Torm's soft-spoken assent. "Ready watch tonight," the cleric added. "If you must go off to relieve yourself, Shandril," he added, "go not alone."

The knights seemed to share Narm's feeling of trouble ahead. Narm and Torm had barely drifted off to sleep, long after an exhausted Shandril, when there was a thudding noise, as someone tripped amid the webwork of black silk cords Torm had strung in an arc behind where Rathan sat watch. Rathan lifted the mace from his knees as he whirled and let out a warning bellow.

The attacker was already coming to his feet, cursing softly, sword drawn—and there were others behind. Narm rolled upright with frightened speed. Torm was up and away into the night like a vengeful shadow before he could even draw breath.

"Defend thy lady, lad!" Rathan bellowed back over one shoulder, as his mace struck aside attacking steel with a shrill clatter. Two faced him, with a third rushing up.

Narm saw a man fall as he looked all around for danger on his way to stand over Shandril, who was rolling over drowsily. More men with blades were coming out of the night. Narm saw another fall, and this time he saw the glint of steel as Torm leaped onward to deal death again. Then a man rushed right at Narm, steel gleaming in the firelight.

Coolly, Narm cast a magic missile spell. Then he drew his dagger and braced himself. The glowing pulses of his art swooped and struck. The man, who wore dark leathers and wielded a hooked sabre, staggered and fell. Narm set his teeth and leaned over to finish the job. Blood wet his fingers, and he felt sick as he looked up and around again for new dangers approaching.

There were none. Torm dispatched another from behind—Narm saw the man stiffen and groan—and Rathan was chatting jovially to those he slew.

"Do you not realize what moral pain—nay, spiritual agony—striking thee down causes me? Hast no consideration for my feelings?" The heavy mace fell again, crushing. "More than this, aye, ye—uhh!—grrh!—wound me. Instead, of challenging me in—ahhhh—the bright light of day, before men of worth to bear witness, with a stated—hahhh!—grievance, ye seek to do the dishonor upon my poor holy bones in the dark of the night! At a time when all good and—ahhh!—lucky men are abed, with better—unghh!—things to be doing than cracking skulls asunder! Don't ye agree—ahh!—now?" Rathan's last opponent fell, twitching, jaw shattered and bloody.

Torm looked up. "The horses don't like this. We'd best move them, and us, in case there are others lurking. Narm, is your lady awake?"

Shandril answered him herself. "Yes." She shuddered involuntarily at the sight of his bloody dagger. "Must you enjoy it so much?"

Torm looked at her in silence for a time. "I do not enjoy it at all," he said quietly. "But I prefer it to getting a knife in the ribs myself." He bent down and wiped his blade on something that Shandril mercifully couldn't see in the darkness, but he did not sheathe it. "Shall we ride?"

"Walk, pigeon-brain," Rathan rumbled, "and lead the horses. Who knows what we'll stumble over or down into if we try to ride in this? See to these, will ye? I want none alive to tell thy names and route, and this mace is not as sure as a blade."

"At once, Exalted One," Torm said with sarcastic sweetness. "Mind you don't forget any of your baggage. I'll see if our late friends were carrying anything of value with them."

Rathan nodded in the light of the dying fire. "Mind more don't come upon thee while ye're slavering and giggling over the gold. See to the campfire, will ye?"

In quiet haste, they gathered their gear and led their mounts and mules into the night. Westward Narm and Shandril followed Rathan, pace by careful pace, over rolling ground.

Torm caught them up before long. "The fire's scattered and out. I can find no one else following, but listen sharp everyone."

"It seems I'll be doing that the rest of my life," Shandril said in a bitter whisper.

Torm put his head close to hers. The faint light of Selune caught his teeth as he grinned. "You might even get used to it. Who knows?"

"Who indeed," she replied, pulling a reluctant Shield up an uneven slope in the dark.

"Not much farther now," Rathan said soothingly from up ahead. Loose stones clacked underfoot, and then Rathan said in quiet satisfaction, "Here. This place will do."

Shandril fell into sleep as if it were a great black pit, and she never stopped falling. She awoke with the smell of frying boar in her nostrils. Narm had just kissed her. Shandril murmured contentment and embraced him sleepily as she stretched. He smelled good.

Close at hand, a merry voice said, "Works like a charm, it

does. Can I try it? Shandril, will you go back to sleep for a moment?"

Shandril sighed. "Torm, do you never stop?"

"Not until I'm dead, good lady. Irritating I may be, but I'm never dull."

"Aye," Rathan rumbled. "Thou art many things, but never dull."

"Fair morning to you both," Shandril laughed.

"Well met, lady," Rathan answered her. "Thy dawnfry awaits thee . . . simple fare, I fear, but enough to ride on. We were not bothered again in the night, but ye had best watch sharp today. It will not be long before those bodies are found."

Narm looked around at the grassy hills. "Where exactly are we?"

"West of the road, in the hills west of Featherdale," Rathan supplied. "Turn about. Do ye see that gray shadow—like smoke—on the horizon? That is Arch Wood. Between here and there lies an old, broad valley with no river to speak of anymore. That's Tasseldale. I would not go down into the valley. Though it's a pleasant place, indeed, with many fine shops and friendly folk, it is also full of people ye want to avoid. Nay, keep to the heights along the valley's northern edge.

"There, ye'll meet with no more than a shepherd or two and perhaps a Mairshar patrol. Tell them—they police the dale and always ride twelve strong—that ye're from Highmoon, going home, Shandril, with this mage ye met in Hillsfar. Call thyself 'Gothal,' or something, Narm. Stick to the truth about Gorstag and the inn, lady, and ye'll fare the better. Give no information to any others until ye meet with the elves of Deepingdale."

"Elves?" Shandril asked, astonished.

"Aye, elves. Don't ye know anything of Deepingdale, where ye grew up?" Rathan's voice was incredulous.

"No," Shandril told him. "Only the inn. I saw half-elven, under arms, when I left with the company, but no elves."

"I see. Know ye that the present Lord of Highmoon is the half-elven hero of battles Theremen Ulath, just so ye don't say the wrong thing." The burly cleric rose and pulled on his helm. "Now eat. The day grows old."

They ate, and soon the time came when all was ready, and Rathan sighed and said heavily, "Well, the time has come. We must leave ye."

He turned on his heel to look southwest. "One day's ride should take ye to the west end of Tasseldale, in the Dun Hills. That's one camp. Keep a watch—sleeping together's for indoors. Peace, Torm, no jests now. Another day's careful riding west—just keep Arch Wood to the left of ye, whatever else ye come upon—will bring thee to Deepingdale. Ye can press on after dark once ye've found the road, and make The Rising Moon before morning. All right?"

They nodded, hearts full.

"Good then," Rathan went on in gruff haste, "and none of that weeping, now." He held out a wineskin to Narm. "For thy saddle." He fumbled at the large pouch at his hip and brought out a disc of shining silver upon a fine chain and hung it about Shandril's neck, kissing her on the forehead. "Tymora's good luck go with thee," he said.

Torm stepped forward next. "Take this," he said, "and bear it most carefully. It is dangerous." He held out a cheap, gaudy medallion of brass, set askew with glued-in cut glass stones on a brass chain of mottled hue that did not match the medallion. He put it about Narm's neck.

"What is it?" Narm asked.

"Look at it now," Torm said. "Take care how you touch it." Narm looked. About his neck was no cheap medallion, but a finely detailed, twist-linked chain of heavy work. Upon it hung two small, golden globes, with a larger one between them. "This is magical," Torm said, "and keep it clear of spellfire or any fiery art, or it may slay you. We call it a necklace of missiles. You, and only you, can twist off one of these globes and hurl it. When it strikes, it bursts as a mage's fireball does; mind you are not too close. The larger globe is of greater power than the other two. It needs no ritual or words of command to work. Keep it safe; you'll need it, some day . . . probably sooner than you think." He patted Narm's elbow awkwardly. "Fare you both well," he said.

The knights mounted, saluted them with bared blades, tossed two small flasks of water, wheeled their mounts, and galloped away. Hooves thudded briefly upon the earth and then died away and were gone.

Narm and Shandril looked at each other, eyes bright and cheeks wet, and slowly embraced. "We really are alone now, my love," Narm said softly. "We have only each other."

"Yes," said Shandril softly. "And that will do." She kissed him long and deeply before she spun away, leaped into her saddle, and said briskly, "Come on! The sun waits not, and we must ride!"

Narm grinned at her and ran to his own saddle. "Spitfire!" he called as he swung himself up.

Shandril raised her eyebrows and spat fire, obediently, in a long rolling plume that winked out just in front of him. The horses snorted in alarm, and she grinned. "Ah yes," she agreed, "but thy lady." She looked west then and tossed her hair from her eyes. "Now," she commanded, lifting her chin, "let us away!"

Away they sped from that place, leaving only trampled grass and silent, unseen spectral warriors.

* * * * *

The stars were clear and cold outside, but Elminster saw them not. He gazed into a twinkling sphere of crystal on the table before him in the upper room of his tower. Within the crystal he saw a rich, red-carpeted chamber with tapestries of red and silver and gold, a fine, roaring fire, and a lady in a black, tattered gown sitting at a table, gazing back at him.

"Well met, sage, and welcome," she said with the faintest of smiles.

"Well met, lady queen and mage. Thank ye for allowing this intrusion."

"Few enough call upon me, old mage, and fewer still do so without some plan to harm or hamper me. I thank you."

Elminster inclined his head politely. "I have further thanks for thee this night, lady. Thank ye for protecting Narm and Shandril on several occasions—possibly more—these past few days. I am most grateful."

The Simbul gave him a rare smile. "My pleasure, again." There was the briefest of silences, and then the old mage asked a careful question.

"Why did ye aid them so, when the maid is such a threat to thy magic, and with it, the survival of Aglarond—and of thee?"

The Simbul smiled. "I know the prophecy of Alaundo and what it may mean. I like Shandril." She looked away for a moment, and then back at the old mage. "I have a question for you, Elminster. Answer not if you would not. Is Shandril the child of Garthond Shessair and the incantratrix Dammasae?"

Elminster nodded. "I am not certain, lady, but it is very likely."

An eyebrow lifted. "Not certain? Did you not hide the girl and shelter her as she grew?"

Elminster shook his head very slowly. "Nay. Not I."

"Who, then?"

"Again, I am not sure. I believe it was the warrior Gorstag, of Highmoon."

The Simbul nodded. "So I have come to suspect these last few days. I thank you for trusting me so, to answer me openly. I promise you, old mage, that I shall not betray your trust. The girl Shandril is safe from my power—unless the passing years change her as they did Lansharra and she becomes too dangerous to leave unopposed."

"That is my present burden," Elminster said heavily. "Such a fall must not happen again."

"What, if I may ask you without offense, will you do differently this time?" The Simbul was watching him closely, her eyes very dark.

"Leave her be," Elminster replied. "She will choose her own path in the end. Her choice may be the clearer and happier for her—if not easier in the making—if I do not sit upon her every act and speak upon her every thought." Elminster met The Simbul's gaze thoughtfully. "The Harpers can protect her nearly as well as I could, without locking her in my tower and thus keeping her under my eye . . . and I could not do that without ruining her choice, even had I the cruel heart to do it."

The Simbul nodded. "That is the right road for you to ride, I think. It is good, indeed, that I needn't force you to take that route."

Elminster smiled, a little sadly. "A good thing, indeed," he said very softly, "for such an attempt would likely have destroyed ye."

The Simbul regarded him soberly. "I know." She nodded slowly and then almost whispered, "I have never doubted or belittled your power, Elminster. You take the quiet way and play the befuddled old fool, even as I take beast-shape and hide often. But I have seen what your art has wrought. If ever I should have to stand against it, I expect to fall."

"I did not disturb ye this night to threaten ye."

"I know," The Simbul said, rising slowly. "Will you allow me to teleport to you now?"

"Of course, lady," Elminster said. "But why?"

The Simbul's eyes were very dark as she let fall her tattered gown. Beneath it, she wore a garment of thin, black silk strands that reached from her throat to cuffs at her wrists and a broad cummerbund belt. The outfit covered little. Set with many small, twinkling gems that winked out when she did, her garment shone the more brilliantly when The Simbul reappeared beside Elminster. Unsmiling, she stood almost timidly amid the dark room's clutter of papers and books. Elminster gaped at her and then deliberately composed himself and smiled.

"But, lady, I have seen some five hundred winters," Elminster said gently. "Am I not too old for this?"

She stopped his lips with slim white fingers. "All those years will give us something to talk about, you and I," she said, "instead of art." She was slim and very light as she sat in his lap, and her skin as she leaned forward to embrace him was smooth and soft. "I would tell you something," she whispered, as Elminster's arms went gently around her. "My name, my truename, is—"

"Hush, lady," Elminster said, eyes moist. "Keep it safe. We shall trade them, soon. But not now."

The tears came. "Ah, old mage," The Simbul said, sobbing into his chest, "I have been so lonely. . . ."

Lhaeo, who had come up the dark stairs with tea, the pot wrapped in a thick scarf to keep it warm, stopped outside the door and heard them. He set the tray down carefully on a table nearby and went softly downstairs again for a second cup. What is the weight of secrets? he wondered to himself. How many may a man carry? How many more, a woman, or an elf?

*　*　*　*　*

It was dark outside, but in the little cottage near the woods candles flickered and the hearthfire blazed merrily. A woman straightened up from the cauldron as they came in. She was no longer young, and the clothes she wore were simple and much patched. She gasped. "My lords! Welcome! But I have nothing ready to feed you. My man's not to be back from the hunt until morning."

"Nay, Lhaera," Rathan said kindly, embracing her. "We cannot stay, but must hasten back to Shadowdale. We have an errand for thy daughter that is urgent, and I would renew Tymora's bright blessing upon this house."

Lhaera looked at them in wonderment. "With Imraea? But she's scarce six—"

Torm nodded. "Old enough that her feet are firmly on the ground." He was interrupted then by the precipitous arrival of a small, dark-haired whirlwind who fetched up against his legs, laughing. As he reached down to embrace her, she danced back out of his reach and announced solemnly, "Well met, Torm and Rathan, Knights of Myth Drannor. I am pleased to see you."

Both knights bowed, and Rathan answered solemnly, "We are pleased to see thee, lady. We have come to discharge our duty to ye. Are ye in good health and of high spirits?"

"Aye, of course. But look how beautiful my mother is since you healed her! She grows taller, I think!"

Torm and Rathan regarded the astonished and smiling Lhaera carefully. "Aye, I think you are right. She does grow taller," Torm said solemnly. "Be sure to send word to us when she grows too tall for the roof, for you will need some help rebuilding then."

Imraea nodded. "I will do that." She eyed Torm. "You are making me wait, Sir Knight. Is my patience not well held? Am I not solemn enough?" Then she fairly danced. "Did you bring it?"

"It is not an 'it.' It is a 'he,' as you are a she," said Torm

severely, drawing open his cloak and letting something soft
and furry into her arms. Its fur was silver and black, and it
had great, dark, glistening eyes. It let out a small and inquiring meow. Imraea held it in wonder as it stretched its nose
out to hers.

"Has it—he—a name?"

Rathan regarded her severely. "Aye, it has a truename,
which it keeps hidden, and a kitten name. But you must give
it a proper name, the name you can call it. Take care you
choose wisely. The kitten will have to live with your choice."

"Aye," Imraea agreed seriously. "Tell me, please, its kitten
name that I may call it so while I think on such an important
choice." Lhaera smiled broadly.

"Its name," said Torm with dignity, "is Snuggleguts." Torm
dropped nine pieces of gold into her hand.

"What is this?" Imraea asked in wonder.

"Its life," Rathan said. "The kitten will need milk, and meat,
and fish, as it grows, and it will need much care, and to be
kept warm. You, or your parents, must buy those things.
You must take the mice and rats it will kill, thank your pet
without any disgust or sharp words, and bury them. It is
your duty. Know you, Imraea, that the gods gather back to
themselves cats and dogs and horses even as they do you
and me. There is no telling when Snuggleguts may die. So
treat it well and enjoy its company, but let your kitten roam
free and do as it will. Each time you see your pet may be the
last."

"I will. I thank you both. You are kind, you two knights."

"We but do the right thing," Torm replied softly.

"Aye, that you do," Lhaera said to them. "And there's few
enough, these days, who take the trouble to do that."

❧ 16 ❧

Sunset at
The Rising Moon

*By night dark dreams bring me much pain —but
always comes, after, bright morning again.*
　　　　　　　　　Mintiper Moonsilver, bard
　　　　　　　　　Nine Stars Around A Silver Moon
　　　　　　　　　Year of the Highmantle

"The Wearers of the Purple are met," Naergoth Bladelord
said. "For the glory of the dead dragons!"

"For their dominion," came the ritual response from sullen throats. Naergoth looked around the chamber.

Malark had not shown his face again. Naergoth was beginning to worry that something ill—and probably final—had
befallen him. By the looks others were giving his empty
seat, he was not the only one thinking along such lines. Long
faces aplenty looked back at him.

"Well enough," Dargoth said. "What say you, Zannastar?
You stand for our mages in the absence of Malark, and the
doubt grows in my mind that we shall ever see him alive
here again."

"It is not my place to speak as one of you," said Zannastar, a
balding, bearded man of middle years. "I do not wear the
purple."

His hard face turned to look down the table. "But I do
think that the more one listens, the more one learns. Something, whether it's spellfire or not, is striking down brother
after brother, and many of your sacred ones, too—
Rauglothgor and Aghazstamn were both of great power.
Can the dracolich Shargrailar be any the safer? Its lair is on
the other side of the Peaks, true, but still near."

"Yes," Zilvreen agreed, "and yet the Sacred Ones can look after themselves far better than we can defend them, if we know not where the blow may fall. Better we go after this Shandril ourselves and destroy her. If we cower in lairs awaiting her attack, we have already conceded the victory."

"Yes, yes, we have heard this line before and agreed to it," Naergoth said. "Our absent mage may have died following it."

"Let this Shandril and the fledgling mage Narm go, then," Dargoth said. "The cost is too high."

"Too high already," agreed the cleric Salvarad in a soft voice that warned of sharp things beneath its purr. The triple lightning bolts of Talos, worked in silver, gleamed upon his breast. "Yet, brothers, consider the cost if it becomes widely known that a young girl—a young girl who commands an unusual and powerful ability of art—has defied us and destroyed so many of us! Can we afford to let her go—at any price—now? What think you?"

"Oh, aye, for the cost of a loss of reputation, let her go," Zilvreen said. "What loss is that? A few butcherings and maimings and menaces and that sort of loss is mended, at least among those folk with whom it works at all. But can we afford to pass up our chance of wielding spellfire, when our enemies could end up using it against us? There is the real price, brothers."

"Yes, we cannot afford to face this spellfire—that we have seen clearly. But we cannot let our foes gain it!" one of the warriors said. The man beside him turned to look in surprise.

"You think your enemies can stand against it? Hah! I've heard it whispered that Manshoon of Zhentil Keep was put to flight by this girl! I say we keep our ranks safe and war no more upon this Shandril—unless time and Tymora weaken her so that our chances are improved. Let others go after her and be the weaker for it! We shall reap the reward of their folly as the vulture dines upon the fields of fallen.

"Swords have got us where we are today. Aye, not without art and divine favor, I'll grant, but swords have kept rulers and bandits at bay. We do not need this spellfire. Waste not our best blood on it!"

"Well said, Guindeen. Yet," Salvarad responded, "can we afford to let our foes win spellfire to wield against us? We should all then be destroyed."

"You bring us to the hard choice, indeed," Naergoth Bladelord said quietly, "and that brings us to the choice behind it: Who wants to go up against this young maid?" He looked around the table, but the silence that followed grew heavy.

No one moved or spoke. After a very long time, Naergoth said softly, "So be it. We are agreed. We put spellfire behind us and go on to work for the greater glory of the dead dragons in other ways."

There were reluctant nods, but no one said anything. It is difficult to laugh at fear when one regularly dealt it often to others.

*　*　*　*　*

They rode west, steadily. Narm peered warily all about as they traveled, expecting another attack. But Shandril found this forest somehow friendlier than the Elven Court. Amid the thick tangle of trunks and gnarled limbs, one could see into the deep, hidden places. Vines hung in spidery tangles from high branches to trunks. Ferns grew thick upon the ground, broken only in places where limbs had fallen.

Shandril looked here and there, at moss upon rocks and trunks, and at great thick trees as large about as some cottages. But Narm saw only danger, possible ambushes, and concealing shadows. But as the day grew older and no attack came, he too began to enjoy the road to Deepingdale.

"It is beautiful," he said, as they came to the crest of a gentle rise in the road and saw sunlight streaming down through the trees in a small clearing.

"Aye," Shandril said in a small voice. "I've never seen these woods before, even though I lived just a day's ride from here." She peered about. "Sometimes I wish I'd never known this spellfire, and I could just come home now with you, instead of fleeing a hundred or more half-mad mages."

"Why not stay?" Narm replied. "You have the power to slay a hundred half-mad mages."

Shandril sighed. "Aye, maybe. But I'd lose the dale and my friends and even you, I don't doubt, in the process. Powerful mages always seem to destroy things about them. They work worse devastation than forest fires and brigands. Sometimes I think life would be much simpler without art."

"I said that to Elminster," Narm replied, "and he said not so. If I could see the strange worlds he's walked, he said, I'd understand."

"No, thank you," Shandril replied. "I've troubles enough, it seems, in this world." The road rose again through a leafy tunnel of old oaks, then gave way to an open area.

Narm and Shandril rode close and quiet, side by side, looking all about them for danger. Tiny, whiplike branches that had fallen from the trees above lay amid the dead leaves and tangled grass and ferns like thin, dark faerie fingers, waiting to clutch or snap underfoot. They rode on, and still no attack came, nor did they meet travelers upon the road.

"This is eerie," Shandril said. "Where is everyone?"

"Elsewhere, for once," Narm said. "Be thankful, and ride while we have the chance! I would be free of the dales, where everyone knows us. Your spellfire cannot last—triumph—forever."

"I have thought about that," Shandril said in a small voice. "Thus far, we have been very lucky. More than that, we've fought many who did not know what they faced, even as I do not. Before long, mages will come against us with spells and devices of art prepared specifically to disable me or foil spellfire. And then how shall we fare?"

"Ah, Shan, you moan a lot," Narm replied, exasperated. "I'm worried about you. You at least can strike back. Did you expect a life like in the ballads, all cheering and triumph and happy endings? No. Adventure, you wanted, adventure you have. Did you hear Lanseril's definition of adventure, at that first feast in Shadowdale?"

Shandril wrinkled her brow. "I did overhear it, yes. Something about being cursedly uncomfortable and hurt or afraid, and then telling everyone later that it was nothing."

"Aye, that was it." They rode over another rise with still no sign of other travelers on the road. "It is a long way to Silverymoon," Narm added thoughtfully. "Do you remember all the Harpers Storm named for us, along the way?"

"Yes. Do you?" his lady replied impishly, and Narm shook

his head.

"I've forgotten half of them, I'm sure. I was not suited to be a world traveler," Narm replied ruefully. "Nor was the tutelage of Marimmar very useful in that respect."

Shandril laughed. "I'll bet." She looked at the woods about them. "If the Realms hold places as beautiful as this, mind you, I won't mind the trip ahead."

"Even with a hundred or so evil priests and mages after our blood?"

Shandril wrinkled her nose. "Just don't call me 'Magekiller,' or anything of the sort. Remember—they come after me. I have no quarrel with them."

"I'll remind the next dozen or so corpses of that," Narm replied dryly. "If you leave enough for me to speak to, that is."

Shandril looked away from him, then, and said very softly, "Please do not speak so of all the killing. I hate it. Never, never do I want to become so used to it that I grow careless of my power. Who knows when this spellfire might leave me? Then, Narm, I will have only your art to protect me. Think on that."

They rode down into a dell where moss grew in knobs and clumps of lush green amid the dead leaves. Small pools of water glistened under dark and rugged old trees. Narm looked around warily, as always, and said soberly, "Aye. I think of it often."

* * * * *

"It seems the fate of this Shandril to grow old unhindered—by us, at any rate," Naergoth said dryly to Salvarad, when they were alone at the long table. "Is there any other business?"

"Aye, indeed. The matter of your mage. Malark was destroyed in Shadowdale—how, I know not—but Malark perished at the hands of Shandril."

"You are sure?"

"I watch closely, and others watch for me—and, all told, we miss little."

Naergoth looked at him expressionlessly. "What then have you seen in the way of mages to take the Purple in the place of Malark?"

"Zannastar, certainly. You could even give him the Purple now. We have seven warriors and one mage."

"Well enough. Why Zannastar?"

"He is competent at art, but even more, he is biddable, something Malark was not."

"Aye, then. Who else?"

"The young one, Thiszult. A wild one—quiet but very reckless. He could be dangerous to us, or brilliant. Why not, alone and in secret, send him after the spellfire with four or six men-at-arms? He'll either bring it back or kill himself—or learn caution. We cannot do ill by this."

"Oh? What if he comes back with spellfire and uses it against us?"

"I know his truename," Salvarad replied smugly, "though he doesn't know that any have learned it."

Naergoth nodded. "Send your wolf, then. Who knows? Perhaps he'll succeed where all the others have failed—ours and those of Bane and Zhentil Keep. This gauntlet we've made the girl Shandril run will have its effect on her in the end, even if we've paid the price for it in blood thus far."

Salvarad nodded. "Yes. She's only one maid, and not a warlike one at that. We'll have her in the end, spellfire or no spellfire. I mean to have the spellfire, too . . . but if we take her alive, she's mine, Naergoth."

Naergoth raised an eyebrow. "You can have women much easier than that, Salvarad."

"Nay, you mistake me, Bladelord," Salvarad replied coldly. "The power she has handled . . . does things to people. I must learn certain things from her."

Naergoth said, "Then why not go after her yourself?"

Salvarad smiled thinly. "I am intrigued, Bladelord. I am not suicidal."

"Others have said that, you know."

"I know that well, Naergoth. Some of them even meant it."

*   *   *   *   *

Night came upon them while they were still in the woods. The night grew cold, and the couple drew their cloaks about them as they rode on. Mist rose among the trees.

Narm watched it drift and roll and said in a low voice, "I don't like this. An ambush would be all too easy in this mist."

"Yes," Shandril replied, "but all the wishing in the world won't make any difference. We're not far, now—we can't be, for travelers who left the inn mid-morning fully expected to make Tasseldale by nightfall. And there is no other road. We cannot have missed our way." She looked into the soft silence of the trees. Tangled branches hung still and dark in the mist. Nothing stirred, and no attack came.

Shandril sighed. "Come on," she said, spurring her horse into a trot. "Let's get safely to The Rising Moon. I would see Gorstag again."

* * * * *

The fire burned low in the hearth, and it fell quiet in the taproom of The Rising Moon as the last of the few guests went up to bed.

Lureene quietly swept up fallen scraps of bread as Gorstag made the rounds of the doors. She heard his measured tread upon the boards in the kitchen and smiled.

So she was smiling in the dim glow of the dying fire when Gorstag, who carried no candle when he walked alone by night, preferring the dark, came into the room.

"My love," he said softly. "I would ask something of you this night."

"It is yours, lord," Lureene said affectionately. "You know that." She reached for the lacings of her bodice.

Gorstag coughed. "Ah . . . nay, lass, I be serious . . . ah, I mean, oh, gods look down!" He drew a deep breath as he walked slowly up to her in the dimness and asked very quietly and formally, "Lureene, I am Gorstag of Highmoon, a worshipper of Tymora and Tempus in my time, and a man of some moderate means. Will you marry me?"

Lureene looked at him, mouth open, for a very long time. Then she was suddenly in his arms, looking up at him with very large, dark eyes. "My lord, you need not . . . marry me. It was not my intention to—ah, trap you into such a union."

"Do you not want to be my wife?" Gorstag asked slowly, roughly. "Please tell me true. . . ."

"I would like nothing more than to be your wife, Gorstag,"

Lureene said firmly. His smile then was like a sudden flash of the sun in the darkness, as his arms tightened about her.

"I accept," Lureene added, gasping for breath. "Kiss me, now, don't hug the life from me!" Their lips met, and Lureene let out a little moan of happiness. Gorstag held her as if she were a very fragile and beautiful thing that he feared to break. They stood together so, among the tables, as the front door of the inn creaked gently open, and a cool breeze drifted in about their ankles.

Gorstag turned, hand going to his belt. "Aye?" he demanded, before his night-keen eyes showed him who had come.

Lureene turned in his arms and let out a happy cry. "Shandril!"

"Yes," said a small voice. "Gorstag? Can you forgive me?"

"Forgive you, little one?" Gorstag rumbled, striding forward to embrace her. "What's to forgive? Are you well? Where have you been? How—"

Outside, there was a snort and a creak of leather, and in mid-sentence, Gorstag said, "But you have horses to see to! Sit down, sit down with Lureene, who has a surprise to tell you, and I'll learn all when I'm done."

"I'm married, Gorstag," Shandril said quickly. "He's— Narm's with the horses."

Gorstag threw her a surprised look, but he never slowed his step. By the light of the fire, Shandril saw tears wet upon his cheeks, and then he was gone.

Lureene threw her arms about Shandril. "Lady Luck be praised, Shan! You're back and safe! Gorstag has been so worried about you, ah, but now . . . but now—" She burst into tears and held Shandril tightly.

Shandril felt tears of her own stinging her eyes, and she gulped quickly to forestall a happy flood. "Lureene . . . Lureene . . ." she managed, voice breaking. "We cannot stay. Half the mages in Faerun are after us, and we're a menace to you even by being here."

Fearfully, she stared at the barmaid. She was touched that Lureene had missed her so—she'd always thought the older girl must find her tiresome. Now she feared to lose what she had so fleetingly seen, swept away by fear. Lureene met her gaze and smiled, shaking her head slightly.

"Ah, little kitten, you have been hurt indeed, to fear these doors shut to you," Lureene said sadly. "If to see you again, we must entertain a few thousand angry mages, entertain them we shall, Gorstag and I, and think it a small price to pay.

"Ah, Shan, thank you! Thank you! You've made Gorstag so happy, he's like a youngling again—did you not see him stride and spring to the door? You've made him happy again, the way he has not been since you left."

"But we must leave again, on the morrow," Shandril said, teetering on the edge of tears. "How—?"

"He will understand, Shan. He knows you are not ours any more—I don't doubt that he's taking the measure of your man right now! It's just that he didn't know what had befallen you. Could you not have left a note or some word?"

Shandril cried uncontrollably, emptying out all the fear and regrets and homesickness of the days since she'd fled the inn, seeking adventure. Lureene held her tightly and rocked her wordlessly, until at last Shandril's sobbing had died away to shuddering breaths.

Then she kissed Shandril's bent head and said softly, "Do not be so full of sorrows, little kitten. I am most grateful to you." The body in her arms made a sort of bleating, questioning sound. Lureene hugged it still more tightly and said, "Gorstag was so upset over you, one night, that he could not sleep. I came to comfort him. He'd never have permitted me to do as I did, if he'd not been so in need of comfort. And he would not have asked me to be his wife."

Shandril looked up, hair all across her reddened eyes in disarray. "He did? Gorstag? Oh, Lureene!" Her tears were happy this time, and she hugged Lureene with bruising force. Ye gods, Lureene thought, stepping back to hold her balance, if this is what adventure does for a woman . . .

A woman? Shandril? But—aye! She is a woman, now, Lureene thought, holding her by the shoulders and meeting her delighted laughter with a fond smile. This was not the girl who'd slipped away from the kitchen.

This was a lady with a lord of her own—and something else. Something beyond the weapons worn so easily at hip and boottops . . . a quiet sort of confidence, of power hidden. Yet none of the loud arrogance of the adventurers who came to the inn for a night of revelry and often left, made wiser by Gorstag's hands and tongue, shamefacedly.

"Shandril, what has happened to you?" she asked quietly.

Shandril gave her a strange, almost haunted look. "Oh," she said in a whisper. "You can see it so clearly then, can you?"

Lureene nodded. "Aye. But I know not what it is." She raised a hand to Shandril's lips. "No . . . tell me not, if you would not. I do not need to know."

"But you should know," Shandril said simply. "It is not something easily believed, though. I hope Gorstag will be able to tell me more about why I have it."

Lureene grinned at her suddenly. "Then it can wait until after you've sat down and soaked your feet and eaten. I'll wake Korvan."

"No!" Shandril said sharply. Lureene turned to look a question at her. "No, please," Shandril pleaded. "Wake him not. I cannot trust his cooking—no offense to you—for my own good reasons. I'll cook, if you will have me."

Lureene nodded, looking troubled. "Did Korvan . . . bother you?" she asked with a little frown.

"It is not that," Shandril said. "Please trust me, and wake him not. I'll tell you, but it is better not to rouse him."

"Then I'll not leave your side unless your man or Gorstag is at hand to protect you while you are here," Lureene said firmly. "You can tell me what you like after you've rested." She reached out her hand. "Come here by the fire."

Shandril let herself be led and sat in a warm chair with a high back. Lureene poked the fire up into new flames and set fresh, dry wood on it, and went for a bowl. When she returned, Shandril's head had fallen onto her shoulders, and she was asleep.

* * * * *

Narm held the bridles of both horses, tense—ready to flee hurriedly if need be. He looked about him in the moonlit mist of the road, but he heard no creature moving in the rolling silence. Wait, Shandril had said. Come after me only when you have stood so long that you grow cold—and if you wait that long, mind you come most careful, ready for war. Narm shifted nervously. Was he cold enough, yet? There was noise within.

Then the door that Shandril had entered was flung wide. A burly, craggy-faced man with gray-white hair and level gray eyes wet with tears strode out. He stretched out a strong arm to Narm and said, "Well met, and welcome to the inn! I am Gorstag. You are Shandril's Narm?"

Narm met his gaze squarely and swallowed. "Yes. I was here almost two months back with the mage Marimmar. Shandril has told me of you, sir. I am at your service."

Gorstag chuckled. "Well, you can be of service," he said gruffly, "by leading one mount around to the stables with me." He set off with a horse and three mules in tow.

Narm followed him into a place where a sleepy boy on night watch unhooded a lantern for them and fetched water, brushes, and feed. In companionable silence, they set to work.

"You know the art?" Gorstag asked softly, as they both bent to the same bucket. Narm nodded.

"I was trained in Shadowdale as a conjurer. Shandril and I have come straight from there, where we were wed under Tymora." Narm felt suddenly shy under this old man's stern, clear eyes. He said no more, then, as he turned back to Warrior, who rumbled appreciatively. He turned from the horse's flank a few breaths later to find his gaze collected by Gorstag's. Unconsciously, Narm took a step back, but he said nothing. At last, Gorstag nodded and turned back to the first of the three mules.

"Tell me, if you will, how you met Shandril Shessair," he said softly. The mule pricked its ears at him, but it was clear that he expected no answer from it. Narm studied the innkeeper's broad shoulders for a moment.

"I saw her first here and . . . liked what I saw, though we did not speak. In the morning, I left with my master, and we made our way to Myth Drannor."

Gorstag's arms stopped their rhythmic brushings for a moment, and then resumed. "We met with devils, and Marimmar, my master, was slain. I was rescued from the same fate, by the Knights of Myth Drannor, who patrol there.

"Later I returned to Myth Drannor and saw Shandril from afar. She was the captive of a cruel mage, The Shadowsil, and I tried to free her. I called on the knights for aid, and we ended up in caverns where a dracolich laired. Shandril and I were trapped together when the cavern collapsed during a mighty battle of art. We thought we'd never get out, so . . ." Narm paused, studying the mule before him, and then sighed and turned to face Gorstag. "We came to care for each other. I love her. So I asked her to marry me."

To Narm's surprise, Gorstag nodded and chuckled. "Aye. It is the same for me." He made a clucking noise, and the stableboy reappeared immediately. Gorstag nodded. "See to them all . . . the very best, mind, as if a fine lord and lady rode them." He waved to Narm to follow him out, and then turned back to the boy and added, "Because they do."

As they went back around the side of the inn in the moonlit, misty night, Gorstag said, "My house is open to you both, but you seem in much haste. How long can you stay?"

Narm hesitated. "We must leave on the morrow, sir," he said quietly. "Many have tried to slay us—slay Shandril, actually—these past days, and they will no doubt try again. We dare not tarry. Elminster told us to be sure to call on you, and Shandril insisted too, but there is danger to us here, waiting, and we would not bring it upon you."

"Can you say more?" Gorstag asked. "I will not stay you, and Elminster is a name I set great store by, but I would rest easier, Narm—and call me Gorstag, mark you!—to know where and why the little girl I raised these years passing is riding, and who would do her ill, and why."

"I have not the right to answer you, Gorstag," Narm replied. "Only my lady should speak on this. I can say that those who pursue us are of different causes, but all, it seems, are powerful in art. Therein lies your peril and Shandril's secret."

They went inside the inn, only to find Lureene regarding them with a finger to her lips, as she knelt beside a chair before the fire. Narm raced forward at the sight. Behind him, Gorstag smiled.

"She sleeps," Lureene said softly as Narm bent anxiously near. Shandril moved her head and murmured something.

They all came close to listen.

"Narm," she said. "Narm, we're here. We're home. Wait here . . . wake Gorstag . . . come carefully, ready for war . . ."

Narm kissed her cheek, and in her sleep she raised a hand slowly to pat at his head, smiling. Then, suddenly, she was upset. "She went for you," Shandril cried faintly. "She went for you, and there was not time! I had to burn her!"

"Shan! Shan!" Narm said urgently, shaking her awake. "It's all right . . . we're safe."

"Yes, safe," Shandril said, awake now, looking up at him. "Safe at last." She kissed his hand on her shoulder.

Then her eyes moved to Gorstag, who stood looking gravely down at her. "I am sorry," she said slowly. "I did not wish to be such a trial to you. I should have told you where I'd gone. I was a fool."

"We all play at fools," Gorstag said with a smile. "You are back safely, and nothing else matters now."

Shandril thanked him with her eyes and said, "We cannot stay, I fear. We are fleeing from far too many to vanquish or avoid if we stand and stay. We must ride on in the morning."

"So Narm said," Gorstag replied. "And he said it was for you to tell us why. Will you, lass?" Shandril nodded.

"Have you ever heard of spellfire?" she asked.

Gorstag nodded, sadly. "Your mother had it," he said softly. "Oh, lass. Oh, Shandril. Beware the cult."

"Beware the cult, indeed," Narm said ruefully. "We have fought them half a dozen times or more already, if you mean the Cult of the Dragon."

"Aye," Gorstag said, "I do." But he said no more, for Shandril was gaping at him, flame flickering in her eyes.

She calmed herself and asked quietly, "Please, Gorstag, who were my parents?"

"The sage did not tell you?" Gorstag asked, gaping at her in his turn. "Why, your mother was a companion-at-arms of mine. We were adventurers together, long ago: Dammasae the Incantatrix. If she had a last name, I never knew it. She was born in the Sword Coast lands. She would not talk of herself."

"Are you—my father?" Shandril asked softly. Gorstag chuckled.

"No, lass. No, though we were good friends, Damm and I, and often held each other by the campfire. Your father was Garthond. A sorcerer he was, by the time he died, Garthond Shessair. I never knew where he was born either, but in his youth, he became apprentice to the mage Jhavanter of Highmoon."

"A moment, if you will," Lureene said gently. "This grows confusing. Let me go to the kitchen. Gorstag, pour ale, and tell your story as a story. If you ask question upon question, Shan, it grows as tangled as a ball of wool."

Shandril nodded. "You have told me the two things I wanted most to know. Unfold the rest as you see best, and I'll try not to break in. By the gods, master, why did you not tell me all of this before? Years I've wondered and worried and dreamed. Why didn't you tell me?"

"Easy, lass. And I am not your 'master.' You are your own master, now." Gorstag was solemn. "There were good reasons. Folk were looking for you, even then, and asking me where you came from. I never wanted to tell you a lie, girl, not since I first brought you here. Oh, you had wise eyes from the first. I could not say false to you. I knew that these same prying folk asked you and the other girls questions when I was not about. If you knew the truth, they'd have tricked or drawn it out of you.

"So I said nothing of it to you, and let the rumors of my fathering you pass unchallenged, and waited for you to be old enough to tell. You are that, now, and past time. I'm sorry you had to run away to find your adventure. The fault was mine, not to have seen your need sooner, and made you happier."

"No, Gorstag," Shandril said. "I've had nothing but good from you, as the gods witness all, and I blame you not. But tell me the tale of my parents, please. I've waited many a year for such news."

"Aye. Well, then. Enough of dates, and all. We can puzzle that out later. Here's the backbone of the tale. Garthond, your father, was an apprentice of the mage Jhavanter.

"Jhavanter, and Garthond with him, fought several times against the Cult of the Dragon in Sembia hereabouts. Jhavanter held an old tower on the eastern flanks of the

Thunder Peaks, which he called the Tower Tranquil. Garthond dwelt there with Jhavanter until mages of the cult destroyed Jhavanter in a fight. After that, Garthond continued his studies—and his feud with the cult.

"At every turn he would work against them, destroy their lesser mages, and terrorize any among them not protected by art. He grew in power, Garthond did, and survived many attempts on his life by the cult. Eventually he rescued the incantatrix Dammasae from cult captivity—they had her drugged, bound, and gagged, in a caravan heading to one of their strongholds.

"Dammasae had adventured with me and others before this. She had become known for a natural power she had—a power she wanted to develop, by practice and experiment. She could absorb spells and use their force of art as raw energy, held within her. She could use her power to heal, or to harm in the form of fiery blasts. The cult took her to learn the secrets of spellfire for their own use, or at least control her use of it to further their own schemes. No doubt, if they seek you now, it is for the same reasons."

"That," Shandril agreed softly, "or my destruction. But please, Gorstag, say on!" To know her life at last! Her eyes were moist as Narm put his arms around her shoulders comfortingly.

Gorstag took down his axe from behind the bar and lowered himself into a chair facing hers, laying the axe near at hand on a table beside him. He turned his chair so as to better see the front door. Outside, moon-dappled mist drifted past the windows.

"Well," the innkeeper continued, "Garthond rescued Dammasae and protected her and worked magic with her . . . and they came to love each other. They traveled much, seeking adventure as many of we fools do, and pledged their troth before the altar of Mystra in Baldur's Gate.

"Here I must leave what I know occurred and relate to you some guesswork—of my own, of the sage Elminster, and of some others. We believe that a cult mage, one Erimmator—none know where his bones lie now to question him—cursed Garthond in an earlier battle of art. The curse bound a strange creature called a balhiir from another plane of existence"—Shandril gasped, and Narm nodded grimly—"in symbiosis with Garthond. Perhaps it was a cult experiment to find the possible powers of any off-spring of a spellfire wielding incantatrix's union with a mage 'ridden' by a balhiir."

"I fear so," Narm replied. "But your tale, Gorstag . . . what happened after they were wed?"

"Why, the usual thing betwixt man and maid," Gorstag said gruffly. "In Elturel they dwelt, then, in quiet. In due time a babe—a girl, one Shandril Shessair—was born. They did not return to the Tower Tranquil and the dales, where the cult waited in strength and the danger to their babe was greater, until she was old enough to travel. Eight months, that wait was."

Gorstag shifted in his chair, eyes distant, seeing things long ago. "They rode with me. East, overland, we went, and the cult was waiting for us, indeed." The innkeeper sighed. "Somehow—by art, likely—they knew, and saw through our disguises. They attacked us at the Bridge of Fallen Men on the road west of Cormyr.

"Garthond was thrown down and utterly destroyed, but he won victory for his wife and daughter, and for me. That day he took nine mages of the cult with him, and another three swordsmen. He did not die cheaply.

"He was something splendid to see that day, Shan. I've not seen a mage work art so well and so long, from that day to this, nor ever expect to. He shone before he fell." The old warrior's eyes were wet again, as he stared into dim night and saw memories the others could not.

"Dammasae and I were wounded—I the worse, but she could bear hurt less well. She carried less meat to lose and twice the grief and worry, for she feared most, Shan, for you. The cultists were all slain or fled from that place, and we rode as fast as we could to High Horn for healing. We made it there, and Dammasae had some doctoring. She needed the hands and wisdom of Sylune, though, and we could not reach Shadowdale in time.

"Your mother is buried west of the dale, on a little knoll on the north side of the road, the first one close to the road west of Toad Knoll. A place holy to Mystra, for she appeared there to a magister once, long ago."

Gorstag looked down at the flagstones before his chair. "I could not save her," he added simply, old anguish raw in his voice. Shandril leaned toward him, but she said nothing.

"But I could save you," the warrior added with iron determination. "I did that." He caught up his axe and hefted it.

"I took you on my back and went by way of the woods from Shadowdale south to Deepingdale. It was in my mind to leave you with elves I knew and try to get into the Tower Tranquil to get something of Garthond's art and writings for you, but I was still on my way south when elves I met brought word that the cult had broken into the tower and plundered it, blasting their way into its cellars. Then they used the great caverns they'd created as a lair for a dracolich—Rauglothgor the Proud— whose hoard had outgrown his own lair.

"So I counted on my obscurity in the eyes of the cult—that few who had seen me riding with Dammasae and Garthond yet lived to tell the tale—and came openly to Deepingdale, where I used some gems I'd amassed on my travels to buy a run-down inn and retire.

"I was getting too old for rough nights spent on cold ground, anyway. Few of my former companions-at-arms were alive and hale, and an old warrior who must join or gather a new band of younger blades is but asking for a dagger in the ribs at first argument.

"I brought you up as a servant here, Shan, for I dared not attract attention to you. Folk talk if an old retired warrior lives alone with a beautiful girl-child, you know. I had to hide your lineage—and, as long as I could, your last name— for I knew the cult would be after you if they guessed.

"That fight at the bridge, you see—they could have slain us all by art from afar without exposing themselves to our blades and spells for anything near so high a cost, if all they'd wanted was us dead. No, they wanted you, girl, you or your mother. I let them have neither! It was the greatest feat I ever managed, down all those years of acting and watching my tongue and yet trying to see you brought up proper.

"For they've kept nosing, all these years, the cult and others. I suspected your Marimmar, Narm, of being yet another spying mage—who knows, now? Some, I think, were fairly sure, but they did not want to fight rivals for you unless you were the prize, so they watched closely to see if you'd show some of your mother's powers. I dreaded the day you would. If it were too public a show, I might not have time to get you to the elves or the Harpers or Elminster.

"I was more wary of the old mage, for it is great mages who fear and want spellfire the most and will do the greatest ill to get it. Even if I had the time to run, then, I might not have the time to get Lureene and the others safe away. The cult might well burn this house to the ground and slay all within, if they came to take and found me gone."

He shook his head, remembering. "Some days, I was like a skulking miser, looking for those coming to plunder under every stone in the yard and behind every tree of the woods and in the face of every guest."

Chuckling, he shook his head. "Now you are wed, and I am to be wed, and you went to find yourself because I would not tell you who you were. And you've come back, with all my enemies and more besides upon your trail, and you wield spellfire. And I am too old to defend you."

"Gorstag," said Narm quietly. "You have defended her. All the time she needed it, you kept her safe. Now all the Knights of Myth Drannor must scramble to defend her! She drove off Manshoon of Zhentil Keep and wounded him perhaps unto death! My Shandril needs friends, food, and a warm bed, and a guard while she sleeps. But if others give her those, it is not she who needs defending now when she goes to war!"

Shandril chuckled ruefully. "There you hear love talking," she said, wearily pushing her hair out of her eyes. "I need you more than ever, now. Did you not see how lonely The Simbul was, Narm? I would not be as she is, alone with her terrible power, unable to trust anyone enough to truly relax among friends and let down her defenses."

"The Simbul?" Lureene gasped. "The Witch-Queen of Aglarond?" Gorstag, too, looked awed.

"Aye," Shandril said simply. "She gave me her blessing. I wish I could have known her better. She is so lonely, it hurts me to see her. She has only her pride and her great art to carry her on."

* * * * *

In a far place, in a small stone tower beneath the Old Skull, The Simbul sat up in the bed where Elminster lay snoring, and tears came into her eyes. "How true, young Shandril. How right you were. But no more!" she said softly.

Elminster was awake, instantly, and his hand went out to touch her bare back. "Lady?" he asked anxiously.

"Worry not, old mage," she said gently, turning to him with eyes full. "I am but listening to Shandril speak of me."

"Shandril? Are you linked to her?"

"Nay, I would not pry so. I have a magic that I worked long ago, that lets me hear when someone speaks my name—and what they say after, for three breaths, each time—if they are near enough. Shandril is speaking of me, and my loneliness, and how she wished to know me better as a friend. A sweet girl. I wish her well."

"I wish her well, too. She is at ease, then, and unhurt, would you judge?"

"Aye, as much as one can judge." The Simbul regarded him impishly. "But you, lord! You are at ease and unhurt. Shall we see to changing your sloth into something more— interesting?"

"Aaargh," Elminster replied eloquently, as she began to tickle him, and he tried feebly to defend himself. "Have you no dignity, woman?"

"Nay—only my pride, and my great art, I'm told," The Simbul said, skin gleaming silver in the moonlight.

"I'll show you great art!" Elminster said gruffly, just before he fell out of the bed in a wild tangle of covers and discarded garments.

Downstairs, Lhaeo chuckled at the ensuing laughter, and began to warm another kettle. Either they'd forgotten him, or thought he'd grown quite deaf—or, at long last, his master had ceased to care for the proprieties. About time, too.

He began to sing softly, "Oh, For the Love of a Mage," because he was fairly confident that Storm was busy, far down the dale, and would not hear how badly he sang.

These are the sacrifices we make for love, he thought. Upstairs, there was laughter again.

* * * * *

"It grows early, not late," Gorstag said, as he saw Shandril's head nodding into her soup. "You should to bed, forthwith—and then it is in my mind, Narm, that you both stay and sleep as long as your bodies need, before you set off on a journey that is long indeed, with no safe havens anywhere."

"We have not told you all yet, Gorstag," Narm said quietly. "We have joined the Harpers—for now, at least—and we go to Silverymoon, to the High Lady Alustriel, for refuge and training."

"To Silverymoon!" Gorstag gasped. "That's a fair journey, indeed, for two so young, without adventurers to aid you! Ah, if I was but twenty winters younger! Still, it'd be a perilous thing, even then. Mind you stay with caravans for protection. Two alone can't survive the wilderness west of Cormyr for long, no matter how much art they command!"

"We'll have to," Shandril said in a grim, determined voice. "But we will try to take your advice and stay with the caravans. And if you don't mind, we will sleep over tomorrow. Foes or no foes, I can't stay awake much longer."

"Come," Lureene said, "to bed, lass. In your old place, in the attic. Gorstag and I'll sleep by the head of the stair, the other side of the curtain. I'm not leaving you alone while you're here."

"Aye," Shandril murmured, rising slowly by pushing upon the table. In the darkness of the passage that led out to the kitchen and the attic stair, cold eyes regarded them for a last instant and then turned with their owner and fled silently into the dark. So the wench had returned, had she? Certain ears would give much, indeed, to hear speedily of this. . . .

* * * * *

"Gorstag?" Lureene asked sleepily. "Happy, love? Put that axe down at hand here, and come to bed now."

"Aye," Gorstag replied. "There's something I must find first, love." He ducked into the darkest corner of the attic, at the end beyond the stairs, and dragged aside a chest bigger than he was. He did something to one of the roof beams, down low behind it in the dust, and part of the beam came away in his hands. He took something from a small, heavy coffer, and then replaced everything as before.

Bearing whatever he had unpacked with him in his hand, he came back across the broad boards of the attic floor to the curtain and called softly, "Narm? Shandril?"

"Aye, we are both awake. Come in," Narm said in reply, from where they lay together.

Gorstag came in quietly, and lowered something by its chain from his hand to Narm. "Does your very touch drain items of art, Shan, or only when you will it so?"

"Only when I call up spellfire, I think," Shandril told him. She gazed at the pendant Narm held. "What is it?"

"It is an amulet that hampers detection and location of you, by means of art and the mind, such as some foul creatures use. Keep it, and wear it when you sleep. Only try to take it off when you must use spellfire, or you'll drain its art. Wear it tonight, and you may win a day of uninterrupted rest tomorrow. I only wish I had one for each of you—but the dark necromancer whose neck I cut it from, long ago, only found the need to wear one."

Narm chuckled. "You should have gone looking for his brother."

"Someone else had slain him already," Gorstag replied with a grin. "It seems he liked to torment everyone around with summoned or conjured nasty creatures. Someone finally grew tired of it, walked to his tower with a club, threw stones at the windows until he appeared, and then bashed his brains out. The someone was eight years old."

"A good start on life," Narm agreed with a yawn, and put the amulet about Shandril's neck. "This has no ill effects, does it?"

"Nay, it is not one of those. Good night to you both, now. You've found the chamber pot? Aye, it is the one you remember, Shandril. Peace under the eyes of the gods, all." The innkeeper ducked back through the curtain. Lureene grinned up at him, indicating the empty bed beside her, and the great axe lying on the floor beside it.

"Now close the bedroom door, love, so the gooblies can't

come in and get us," she said gently. Gorstag looked at the trapdoor at the head of the stairs.

"Oh, aye," he said, and closed it down, dragging a linen chest over it. "There. Now to sleep, at last, or it will be dawn before I've even lain down!" Clothes flew in all directions with astonishing speed. Lureene was rolled into a bear hug, and kissed with sudden delicacy. She chuckled sleepily and patted his arm.

"Good night to you, my lord," she said softly, and rolled over. She had barely settled herself before she heard him breathe the deep, slow, and steady draws of slumber. Once an adventurer, always . . . she fell asleep before she finished the maxim.

* * * * *

It was highsun when Narm awoke. The sun was streaming in the small round windows at either end of the attic, and the curtain had been drawn back. Lureene sat upon a cushion beside them, mending a pile of torn linens. She looked over at Narm and smiled. "Fair morning," she said. "Hungry?"

"Eh? No, but I suppose I could be." Narm sat up and looked at Shandril. She lay peacefully asleep with the amulet gleaming upon her breast, Narm's discarded robe clutched in her hands. Narm chuckled and tugged at it. A small frown appeared on Shandril's face. She held hard to it and raised a hand in an imperious, hurling gesture. Narm flinched back, but no spellfire came.

"Shandril," he said quickly, bending close to her. "It is all right, love. Relax. Sleep."

Her hands fell back, and her face smoothed. Then, still deep asleep, she muttered something, turned her head, and then turned it back and murmured quite distinctly, "Don't tell me to relax, you . . ." and she trailed away into purrings and mutterings again. Lureene suppressed a giggle into a sputter. Narm did likewise.

"Aye, we'll let her sleep some more. If you want to eat, there's a pot of stew in the taproom, untouched by Korvan's hands, on the hook over the hearth. I've bread and wine here. Go on . . . I'll watch her."

"Well, I—my thanks, Lureene. I'll . . ." He looked about him.

Lureene chuckled suddenly, and turned about on the cushion until her back was to him. "Sorry. Your clothes are over there on the chest, if you can live without that robe Shan's so fond of."

"Urrr . . . thanks." Narm scrambled out of the bed and found his clothes. Shandril slept peacefully on. Lureene gave him a friendly pat as he climbed down the stairs past her. He was still smiling as he went down the hall from the stairs, past the kitchen, and came face to face with Korvan.

The cook and the conjurer came to a sudden stop, perhaps a foot apart, and stared at each other. Korvan had a cleaver in one hand and a joint of meat in the other. Narm was barehanded and weaponless.

Silence stretched between them. Korvan lifted his lip in a sneer, but Narm only stared straight into his eyes and said nothing. Korvan raised the cleaver suddenly, threateningly. Narm never moved, and never took his gaze away from Korvan's own. Silence.

Then, giving a curse, Korvan backed away and ducked into the kitchen again, and the hallway was free. Narm strode forward without hesitation into the taproom, and greeted Gorstag as though nothing had happened. Elminster had been right. This Korvan wasn't worth the effort. A nasty, mean-tempered, blustering man—all bluff, all bravado. Another Marimmar, in fact. Narm chuckled at that, and was still chuckling as he went back past the kitchen door. There was an abrupt crash of crockery from within, followed by a clatter, as if something small and metal had been violently hurled against a wall.

* * * * *

Thiszult cursed as he looked up at the sun. "Too late, by half! They'll be out of the dale and into the wilderness before nightfall! How, by Mystra, Talos, and Sammaster, am I to find two children in miles of tangled wilderness?"

"They'll stay on the road, Lord," one of the hitherto grimly silent cult warriors told him. Thiszult turned on him.

"So you think!" he snarled. "So Salvarad of the Purple thinks, too, but I cannot believe two who have destroyed

The Shadowsil, an archmage of the Purple, and two sacred dracoliches can be quite so stupid! No, why would they run? Who in Faerun, after all, has the power to match them? No, I think they'll turn aside and creep quietly about the wilderness slaying those of their enemies they come upon, while the rest of us search futilely elsewhere, until we are all slain or overmastered! I must reach them before dark, before they leave the road!"

"We cannot," the warrior said simply. "The distance is too great. No power in the Realms could—"

"No power?" Thiszult fairly screamed. "No power? Why think you I follow these two, who felled such great ones! Hah! That which I bear is power enough, I tell you!" He reined in sharply and cast his eyes over the warriors in leather who rode behind him. "Ride after us, all of you—to Deepingdale, and the Thunder Peaks beyond! If you see my sigil—thus—upon a rock or tree, know that we have turned off the road there, and follow likewise."

"We?" the warrior who had spoken before asked him.

"Aye—you and I, since you doubt my power so much. Trust in it, now, for it is all that stands between you and spellfire!" He gestured at all of them. "Halt!" Turning to the warrior, "You, dismount . . . No, leave your armor behind!" He touched the warrior, and spoke a word.

They both vanished, warrior and mage, in an instant. The other men-at-arms stared. One of the now riderless horses reared and neighed in terror; the other snorted. Quick hands caught bridles. "Stupid beast," one warrior muttered. "There's no danger, now. Why'd it take fright?"

"Because the smell of the man that was on its back a breath ago is gone," another, older fighter told him sourly. "Gone—not moved away, but suddenly and utterly gone. It would scare you, if you had any wits. A stupid beast, you call it? It goes where you bid it, and knows not what waits, but you ride to do battle with two children who have destroyed much of the power of the cult hereabouts in but a few days, and know they await you, and still ride into danger . . . So who, of man and mount, is the stupid one?"

"Clever words," was the reply, but it was made amid chuckles. The reins of the two mounts were lengthened so that they could be led, and the warriors hastened on.

"Is it in your mind, then," one asked the older warrior, "that we ride on a hopeless task?"

The older warrior nodded. "Not hopeless, mind you—but I've seen too many young and over-clever mages who follow our way—like that one, who just left us—come to a crashing fall, to think that this last one has any more wisdom or real power than the others."

"What if I tell Naergoth of the Purple of your doubting words when we return? What then?" asked the one he had rebuked earlier. The old warrior shrugged and grinned.

"Say the word, if you will. It is my guess you'll be adding them to a report of Thiszult's death, unless he flees. I've served the cult awhile, you know. I know something of what I say, when I speak." His tone was mild, but his eyes were very, very cold, and the other warrior looked away first. They rode on.

* * * * *

A wild-eyed Shandril was buckling and lacing and kicking on her boots for all she was worth, at the head of the stairs. "We must away," she panted to Narm, as Lureene fussed about her. "Others come . . . I dreamed it . . . Manshoon, again, I tell you—and others! Hurry and get dressed!"

"But . . .but . . ." Narm decided not to argue and began to eat stew like a madman, wincing and groaning as he burned his lips on hot chunks of meat. Lureene took one look at him, as he danced about Shandril on bare feet, and fell back onto the beds hooting in helpless laughter.

"Forgive me," she gasped when she could speak again. By then Shandril had straightened her belt and started down the stairs, and Narm had halted her with a firm arm to the chest. He handed her the bowl of stew.

"—You two," Lureene continued, "but I doubt I shall ever see a mage of power so discomfited! Whhooo! Ah, but you looked funny, gobbling like that!"

"You should see me casting spells," Narm said dryly. Then he asked, "When did she awake like this?"

"Scarce had you gone down when she sat upright, straight awake, and called for you. Then she scrambled up, grabbing for clothes and the like, all in haste. She dreamed that enemies follow fast upon your trail."

"She's probably right," Narm said ruefully, and began scrambling for clothes himself.

* * * * *

"Did your art have the desired effect?" Sharantyr asked softly.

"Yes,' Jhessail said heavily. "This dream-weaving's wearisome work. No wonder Elminster was so reluctant to teach it to me. Yet, I think I scared Shandril enough to get her moving before the cult tries again." She lay back in her chair wearily, rubbing her eyes. "Ahhh, me," she said. "I'm ready for bed."

Sharantyr arose. "I'll get Merith," she said, but Jhessail shook her head.

"Nay, nay . . . it is sleep I need, not cuddling and companionship . . . you have no idea, Shar—it is like a black pit of oblivion before me, I am so tired . . ."

With that the lady mage of the knights drifted forward into the pit, and was gone. Sharantyr found a pillow for her head, drew off her boots, wrapped her in a blanket, and left her to sleep.

Then she drew her sword and sat down nearby where she could watch Jhessail, laying it across her knees. After all, it had been overlong since Manshoon had worked his last mischief in Shadowdale.

* * * * *

They kissed Lureene good-bye in excited haste, thrust the empty bowl into her hands, and were downstairs and out through the taproom, and into the sunshine, before they drew breath again.

There in the innyard Gorstag stood with their mounts and mules ready-harnessed. The latter two mules of each train bulged suspiciously here and there where they had not bulged before.

"Bread. Sausages. Cheeses. Two casks of wine. Pickled greens—this jar, sealed with clay. A crate of grapes and figs. A coffer of salt. Some torches," Gorstag said briefly. "And the gods watch over you." He enveloped Shandril in a crushing hug, and swung her up into her saddle. "Carry this," he said, and pressed a bottle into her hands. "Goat's milk . . . drink it before highsun tomorrow, or it may well go bad."

He turned to Narm without waiting an instant, like a swordsman turning from a kill in battle, shook the conjurer's hand in a bruising grip, took him by both elbows and lifted him bodily into the saddle. He then thrust a small, curved and polished miniature disc of silver into his hands.

"A shield of Tymora, blessed by the priests in Waterdeep long ago. May it bring you safe to Silverymoon."

He stood looking up at them. "You are in haste," he said gruffly, "and I was never one for long good-byes. So fare you well in life—I hope to see you again before I die, and you both as happy and as hale as you are now. I wish you well, both of you." He stretched up to kiss them both. "You have both chosen well, in each other." He patted the rumps of their horses to start them on their way, and raised his fist in a warrior's salute to an honored champion as they called their good-byes.

As they turned out of The Rising Moon's yard, Shandril burst into tears. When Narm looked from comforting her to wave, Gorstag still stood like a statue with his arm raised in salute. He stood so until they were out of sight.

When Lureene came down to him, standing there, she heard him muttering prayers to Tymora and Mystra and Helm for the two who had gone. When she put her arms around him from behind, and leaned against the old might of his many-muscled back, she could feel the trembling as he left off praying and began to cry.

* * * * *

It was dark in the meeting chamber of the Cult of the Dragon. Only a single oil-lamp flickered on the table between the two men who were there.

"Do you really think this boy-mage can defeat Shandril, after she has destroyed your best and most powerful?" Dargoth of the Purple said angrily.

"No," Naergoth Bladelord replied simply. "Another of our dragons pursues her right now."

"Another dracolich?" Dargoth said in angry astonishment. "We haven't many more sacred ones to lose!"

"True," Naergoth said, turning cold eyes upon him. "This one went of its own will. I did not compel it or ask it to go to war—but I did not forbid it, either. One does not forbid Shargrailar anything."

Dargoth looked at him. "For the love of lost Sammaster! Shargrailar the Dark flies? Gods preserve us!" He sat back, shocked, shaking his head.

"They will hardly start doing that after all this time," Naergoth said to him dryly, reaching to extinguish the lamp. Darkness descended.

*   *   *   *   *

Suddenly they were in a place of fragrant vapors, pots, and knives. The warrior looked around and snorted. "A kitchen!" At his words, the cook, who stood with his back to them over a bloody cutting board, gave a start and whirled around, cleaver rising.

Thiszult smiled coldly at him. "So pleased to see us, Korvan?"

The sour-faced cook struggled to regain his composure; hatred, envy, fear, and exultation chased rapidly across his mean face. "Why, Thisz—"

"Hush. No names! How long ago did the wench leave?" Thiszult strode forward. "Which is the way out of here?"

"Outside, the back, that way. Or, in front: that way, right into the taproom, then left across it to the front door," Korvan said. "She and the boy-mage left but ten breaths back, if that. You may well be able to catch them if you—"

"Have horses. Where are the stables?"

"Around the side; that way. There's a good strong black, and a stouter but slower bay, down the end, and—"

"The cult thanks you, Korvan. You will receive an appropriate reward in time." Thiszult strode coldly out into the hallway with a snap of his dark cloak, the warrior at his heels. As the man went out, he drew his broad, stained sword and held it ready in his hand.

"Korvan," Lureene whispered as she came out of the open pantry, eyes dark with anger, "do you know those—those folk?"

The cook stared at her, white-faced, for a moment—and then he raised his cleaver again and went for her, determined. Lureene cast the tin of flour she held at his face and fled out the door, into the hall and then the taproom beyond. It was empty.

She ran across it, dodging between tables, and burst out the front door in time to see the dark-cloaked mage spur out of the innyard like a vengeful whirlwind.

Before her, in the mud, Gorstag stood with his hands locked about the forearms of the warrior who had come with the mage. They stood straining against each other, the warrior's sword shaking in his grasp as he tried to force it between them. Lureene ran as hard as she could toward them, sobbing for breath.

Behind her, the front door of The Rising Moon banged open again. Korvan. Her death. Lureene ran on, slipping and sliding desperately, knowing she had to warn Gorstag before Korvan's cleaver could reach him.

The two men were only ten paces away, now . . . now six, now three . . . Suddenly Gorstag slipped to one side and pulled hard on the man's wrist instead of pushing against it, and the blade lunged forward—harmlessly past Gorstag's shoulder. He crashed into the man's chest and drove his fist as hard as he could into the man's throat.

Throat, neck, and man crumpled without a sound, and Gorstag turned in time to catch Lureene about the shoulders and spin her to a halt. "Love?" he asked, and Lureene pointed past him.

"Korvan!" she gasped. "He serves the cult! Look out!" As she spoke, the cook put on a last burst of speed and chopped at them as he came. Gorstag pushed Lureene hard to one side so that she staggered and nearly fell, and leaped away in the other. The cleaver found only empty air.

Korvan looked about, wildly, at both of them—too late, as fingers of iron took him by the neck from behind. The cook staggered and lashed out blindly to that side with the cleaver—only to have that wrist deftly captured and twisted. Korvan let out a little cry and dropped his weapon from suddenly numb fingers. Gorstag wrenched him around bodily until they were face to face.

"So," the innkeeper said, "so . . . first you molest my little one . . . and now you would slay my bride-to-be! You threaten me with steel here in the yard, and you serve the Cult of the Dragon—in my own kitchen." His voice was low and soft, but Korvan twisted in his grasp like a frantic, hooked fish, face white to the very lips.

"This has been coming for a long time," said Gorstag slowly. "But at least I've learned something about cooking." The hand that held Korvan's wrist let go and darted to his throat, whip-fast, and the two old hands twisted mercilessly. There was a dull crack, and Korvan of the cult was no more.

Gorstag let the body fall into the mud grimly and turned to Lureene. "Are you all right, my lady?" he asked. "Is there fire or ruin behind you in The Moon?"

Lureene shook her head, wide-eyed. "No, Lord," she said, close to tears. "I am fine . . . thanks to you. We are safe."

"Aye, then," Gorstag said, and he looked down the road. "But will Narm and Shandril be? Find me the fastest horse, while I get my axe."

Lureene stared at him in horror. "No!" she said. "You'll be slain!"

"Leave my friends to die because I did nothing?" Gorstag's face was like iron. "Find me the fastest horse!"

Lureene rushed toward the stables, tears blurring her sight as she ran. "No," she whispered. "Oh, gods, no." But the gods did not hear before she reached the stables.

There was a slow thudding of hooves, then, as Gorstag came back out of the inn with axe in hand. Frightened faces were gathering about the yard.

A dwarf on a mud-spattered mule rode heavily in at the gate, and came to a sliding halt before Gorstag. The dwarf heaved himself sideways and rolled down out of the saddle with practiced ease, using the axe he bore naked on his shoulder like a walking-stick. Crippled, he leaned heavily on his axe as he limped over to Gorstag. The innkeeper was looking grimly toward the stables, where a worried Lureene was leading out a horse.

"Well met," the dwarf said to Gorstag. "You are Gorstag?" The innkeeper, who was intent upon Lureene and the approaching mount, looked down in surprise.

"Aye, I am."

"Have you seen a companion of mine, the adventuress Shandril? She waited on tables here, once," the dwarf rumbled. "I hear she rides with a young mage, now, and hurls spellfire."

"Aye. I have," Gorstag said, axe coming up. "Who then are you, and what is your business with Shandril Shessair?"

"I am come from Shadowdale," the dwarf said gruffly, looking up at him with a gaze as harshly steady as his own. "From Sharantyr and Rathan and Torm of the knights I have heard where Shandril headed and followed on. I am sent by Storm Silverhand of the Harpers and Elminster the sage, and bear a note to ye, to tell you to trust me in this. Here; read it. Now tell me where Shandril is, for time draws on and my bones grow no younger."

Gorstag grinned at that as he unrolled the parchment. "Not so sour, Sir Dwarf. Life is less a trial to the patient."

"Aye," the dwarf replied, "most of them lie dead. Tell me where Shandril is!"

"A moment." Gorstag read the parchment. Lureene brought the horse to his shoulder, and he moved so that she could read what was written, too:

> To Gorstag, of Highmoon, By these words, well met! The bearer of this note is the dwarf Delg, once a swordmate of Shandril in the Company of the Bright Spear, just after she left your house. He serves no evil master and bears Shandril no ill will; trust us in this—he has submitted to all our tests of art in this regard, and it is true. The Cult of the Dragon destroyed the company, and it was thought only Shandril survived. This Delg, left for dead in Oversember Vale, made his way to the shores of the Sember, where he was found by elves and taken to priests of Tempus. While they were healing his wounds and praying to the god for guidance as to what task they should set him in return, a messenger of Tempus appeared and said that Delg's task was to defend the girl who wielded spellfire against

seeking swords; and so he has come to you for
word. Your part in defending Shandril is done,
valiant Gorstag; we tend Dammasae's place of
rest and remember. Aid this one as best you
can, and you will be honored greatly. You shall
have then in your debt,
                    Elminster of Shadowdale and
                    Storm Silverhand of Shadowdale

Gorstag read it, frowning a little, and then looked up at
Delg. "You've missed them," he said simply. "They rode west
from here some short time ago, now. A mage hostile to them
follows them, close indeed."

"I've missed them? Then there's no time left to wait
about!" the dwarf said, and hobbled back to his mule. "Up!"
he commanded it, "and ride like the wind . . . or she'll be in
trouble again, and in need of old Delg, before we get there!"

"Will you not take a faster mount?" Gorstag asked, waving
at the horse Lureene held. Delg shook his head.

"My thanks, but how fast would I travel if I fell off it at the
first bend in the road? Nay, I'll stick to what I know, and
make haste in my own way. Fare thee well, Gorstag. Stay by
your lady. It is the greatest adventure you can have." And he
grinned then, and rode away, raising his arm in a warrior's
salute. Gorstag returned it, watching him go, and Lureene
stroked his arm thoughtfully and said nothing.

After a time Gorstag looked away from the road and said
gruffly, "Well, you can put the animal away. We shan't be
needing it."

Lureene nodded. "Of course," she said, turning, "and
there's a little matter of corpses lying about, too . . ."

Gorstag growled and went to put away his axe and find a
shovel. He carried the letter very carefully in his hand, and
looked at it again as he went.

* * * * *

Shargrailar the Dark circled high above the Thunder Gap,
cold winds whistling through the spread, bony fingers that
were all that was left of its wings. Shargrailar was the
mightiest dracolich in Faerun known to the cult, perhaps

the most powerful bone dragon there had ever been. Its eyes were two white lamps in the empty sockets of a long, cruel skull. It looked down with the cold patience of a being who has passed beyond the tomb and yet can fly, and it flew lower, watching and waiting.

So a human female dared to destroy dracoliches? Death must find her. Lucky she must have been, and her victims young fools, but still, she must die. She was headed toward Shargrailar's lair. Armed with spellfire, they said. Interesting. Shargrailar glided among the clouds like a silent shadow, peering at the tiny road men called the East Way, far below. It had been a very long time since Shargrailar had been interested in anything.

There below, on the road. Two human riders, with mules . . . one was female. Silently Shargrailar descended, skeletal head peering. Yes . . . yes . . . this must be her. If not, what matter? What pair of humans could hurt Shargrailar? The great dracolich dove down out of the sky like a gigantic arrow of death, for that is the way of dracoliches. As it descended, Shargrailar could see that the she-human was beautiful . . . it opened bony jaws to give her death, silently, patiently . . .

* * * * *

Thiszult rode hard, hauling upon the reins savagely. He had to pass the maid and mage and get ahead of them, to have to time to call up his special magic—or find a height or their camp, to have some time with them in view to do it. It would not do to miss them now—or to get too close and warn them, without his swordsmen to chase them and bring them to a stand.

He thought furiously as he rode. He wore no insignia, and rode alone. There was nothing to say that he was a mage, nor that he wished anyone ill. Yet, he was riding in brutal haste—dangerous, as the road climbed toward the Peaks, and a warning to anyone that all was not right—especially to a couple no doubt wary indeed, by now, of attacks. He slowed his mount, cudgeling his brains for a plan. In darkness they could too easily evade him. Yet, one had to sleep, and they would halt, to camp. Perhaps then would be the best time to attack, but only if he had their close trail by then and remained unseen. There was no other way.

With a sigh, he brought the horse to a shuddering halt, leaped clear and then tied its reins to a sapling before the winded horse could move away. He checked what he carried with him. It was all secure. Well and good. A quick glance up and down the road—empty, as far as he could see from here—and he quickly cast spells of invisibility and flight upon himself, and leaped into the sky.

He was gone before Delg found the exhausted horse and wasted several breaths in puzzlement, as he looked about for traces of anyone leaving the road nearby or continuing on foot, but found nothing. The dwarf shook his head and rode on, thinking of Burlane and Ferostil and Rymel, all dead now, all never to laugh with him again . . . well, perhaps he'd join them soon, if there were hostile mages about. He kicked his mule into reluctant hurry, and watched the road ahead narrowly, his axe ready in his hand.

* * * * *

"Someone follows us," Narm said, peering back over his shoulder as they rode.

"Some *one*?" Shandril asked him. "One? Alone?"

"Yes . . . a child, or one of the short races, on a mule," Narm said doubtfully. "Seems an odd traveler, to ride alone through the wilderness."

"Well, it is an open road," Shandril replied. "It cannot be untraveled, by any means." She turned in her saddle. Behind them, the land fell away in gentle hills to the dark woods and Deepingdale, and she thought she could see The Rising Moon, or where it must be. Tears touched her eyes for a moment, again—and then she saw bony death gliding coldly down out of the sky behind them.

"Narm!" she screamed, as she kicked heels to her mount and climbed forward onto its neck in sudden, wild urgency. "Get down!"

Narm looked, and saw. In frantic haste, he tore Torm's gift from his neck and threw it away. Shandril had one glimpse of his white face before the world exploded around them.

* * * * *

What in the name of the Soul Forger was that? Delg stood in his stirrups, open-mouthed, as the great skeletal bulk arrowed down out of the sky ahead of him. It was like a dragon, but it was a skeleton! It was . . . oh, by the lode-luck of the dwarves, it must be one of those dracoliches Elminster had told him about! Delg swallowed and sat down in his saddle again. He was getting too old for this sort of thing. . . .

No dwarf stood a chance against that! Nor, he thought grimly, did little Shandril, even if she had married a boy who could cast a handful of spells and gained some fire magic of her own. The mule beneath him had slowed to a walk as he had sat thinking.

Delg booted it mercilessly in the ribs then, waving his axe so that it flashed in the sunlight. "Get you going!" he snarled into the mule's ears. "I'm late for a battle, and they'll be needing me, never fear!"

* * * * *

Thiszult flew low over the trees to one side of the road, the wind of his flight whipping past his ears in his haste. He had to find them, and get ahead of them. Soon, now . . .

There was a flash and roar of flame ahead. Startled, Thiszult veered off to one side, rising in the air for a better look. Were they in a fight? This might prove even easier than he had thought!

A vast, dark skeleton wheeled in the air, and Thiszult gasped in astonishment. A Sacred One! But how did it come to be here? And—who was it? He had never seen one so large and terrible before! As he stared at the dracolich, its cold orbs met his gaze, and it rose toward him. Its skeletal jaws looking somehow amused.

But I'm invisible! Thiszult thought in amazement. How can it see me? Or is that a power of the Sacred Ones?

From the great dracolich's maw, a blue-white bolt of lightning leaped and crackled. Thiszult did not have time to protest that he was a friend before it struck him. All his limbs convulsed at once, and he was dead, mouth open to speak, even before Shargrailar's bony claws struck his body and tore it apart. Thiszult's secret, powerful magic fell to earth. It was lost in the trees below.

Far away, Salvarad of the cult sighed and turned from his scrying font. Thiszult would never take the Purple now.

* * * * *

Shandril got up, grimly. The stink of cooked horseflesh was strong in her nostrils. Faithful Shield had lived up to her name all too well. The dracolich's flames had poured strength into Shandril, not harmed her. She only hoped Narm had survived.

Lightning cracked overhead as Shandril ran across the smoking road. She did not look up; she had eyes only for her man. A heart-twisting, blackened tangle of horse's legs met her gaze. Where once she would have turned away, sick, she now ran forward without hesitation, peering anxiously into the smoking slaughter. Narm! Oh, Narm!

He had no protection against dragonfire. He could well be dead. Their child would never know its father . . . Shandril snarled at herself. None of that! Find him, first!

There he was, moving weakly, half-buried under scorched baggage. He was alive! Oh, gods be praised!

Tears ran down Shandril's face as she knelt beside him, tearing aside smoldering straps and canvas with frantic haste. Narm moaned. His hair smoked; the left side of his face was black and blistered.

"Oh, Narm! Beloved!" Shandril wept. Cracked lips moved; lids that no longer had lashes flickered open. Watery eyes met hers, lovingly—and then looked beyond, and widened.

"Look out, love!" he hissed, painfully. "The dracolich comes!" Shandril followed his gaze.

The great Shargrailar wheeled directly above them, vast and dark and terrible. For all that it was only empty, hollow bones, the undead creature was awesome. Shandril shivered as she gazed up at its fell might. It turned and dove silently down the sky at them again.

"Run, Shan!" Narm croaked from beneath her. "Get you hence! I love you! Shandril, go!"

"No," Shandril said, in tears. "No, lord, I will not!" As the great bony jaws opened, she carefully climbed forward until she lay gently atop Narm's blackened body, shielding him as much as she could. Narm groaned in pain. She braced herself to lift her weight off him, and said softly, "I love you."

As the roar of the dracolich's approaching flame grew in the air about them, Shandril put her lips to Narm's and gathered her will. Then blasting flame swallowed them again.

* * * * *

"Clanggedin aid me!" Delg muttered, as the mule bucked beneath him. The road before him was one great smoking ruin. A roaring cone of fire had just raked it again. In a moment the swooping dracolich would be above him. The mule bucked again. "Oh, blast!" Delg burst out, as he found himself somersaulting forward in the air. His frantic grab for the saddle-horn missed. Well, at least he still had hold of his axe. He tucked it close against him so that it would not be chipped in the hard landing to come.

So the mule's saddle was empty when the raking claws of Shargrailar swept the poor beast skyward, rending and tearing. The dracolich let out the first sound it had uttered in many long years as it rose into the air—a long, loud hiss of anger and frustration. It shredded the mule as if it were a rotten rag, and wheeled again. Destroying an enemy had never taken this long before.

* * * * *

Shandril desperately drew in all the flame that struck her, and strained to reach the dragonfire that ravaged Narm's helpless body and draw it into her, too. Through their joined lips she felt the fierce energy flowing; sluggishly at first, then faster and faster. Gods, the pain! Her lips were seared as if by hot metal; tears blinded her. Her body shuddered at the pain, but she held fast to her Narm as the last of the flames swept over them and were gone.

Still energy flowed into her. She realized with a start that Narm's own energy was stealing into her now; she was killing him, draining him to death! Hastily she broke their kiss and stared anxiously down at the slack, silent face. Oh, Narm! She had no art to heal him! What had she done?

Bitterly, Shandril felt the swelling energy burning within her. Her veins were afire; she was bloated with more than she could hold for long. The pain . . .

Into her mind then came Gorstag's voice, telling of her mother: ". . . to heal or harm . . . !" Heal! Could she heal as well as burn? She gathered her shaking limbs to lie tenderly upon Narm again, and set her lips to his. Closing her eyes, Shandril willed energy to flow out of her gently, slowly, like a cooling flow of water, through her lips. It did.

Through their kiss she could feel her released energies flowing into Narm. She willed it so, fiercely, and felt his feeble heart grow stronger, and his body began to rally. He moved beneath her, struggling to speak.

Shandril shed fresh tears as she poured still more energy into her beloved, until he was whole and strong and—

Bony claws raked shrieking agony across her back. Shandril was torn free of Narm and flung to the road beyond by Shargrailar's angry strike. Pain almost overwhelmed her; she shrieked aloud, flame gouting from her mouth in her agony. Ohhh, Tymora, the pain!

She had ignored the strike of another bolt of lightning and the numbing impacts of a shower of magic missiles while healing Narm, but the great dracolich could slay her this way, destroying her as surely as if she had no spellfire. Shandril twisted and writhed in the dust of the road in her agony. She could feel her blood flowing out of her. Blood, blood . . . she had seen more spilled these last tendays than in all her life before this, and she was heartily sick of it!

Well, now she could do something about it. Shandril opened her eyes and looked for the dracolich. A fierce anger was upon her. Exultation rose within her to join it; she could heal! She could use spellfire to aid as well as to do battle! On hands and knees, Shandril turned and saw Shargrailar sweeping down again, its cold eyes glimmering at her from its cruel skull, its claws outstretched to rend and tear. The onetime thief from Deepingdale met the dracolich's chilling gaze and laughed.

From her eyes flames shot forth, in two fiery beams that struck the undead dragon's own eyes. Smoke rose, and Shargrailar screamed.

Bony wings sheared away to one side in agony; Shandril was still laughing in triumph as she spat a white inferno of flames into the blinded dracolich. It reeled backward in the air, blazing, and crashed to earth.

She ignored its snappings and thrashings and turned back to heal Narm. Shandril felt a tingling in her own torn back. She bent her will to cleanse and heal herself as she crawled back to join her husband where he lay among all the dead horses. She sighed at the soothing relief from pain that spread across her back. Ahhhhh . . .

Her energy was much lessened, now, and Shandril became alarmed as she gave more of it to Narm. She shouldn't have healed herself . . . she had too little left, and the dracolich was still dangerous. It was not wasting spells on her any longer; she could not gain any more spellfire from it. Oh, Tymora! Was her luck always to be bad?

No, a small voice said within her, it could be fatal, just once—now, perhaps—and all her worries would be over. Shandril got up, hastily, looking for the dracolich. If it clawed her now . . .

She could hear a strange smashing and hollow splintering sound from where Shargrailar had landed. Peering cautiously over the unfortunate horses, she saw an axe rise and fall amid the dracolich's weakly crawling rib cage. Bone chips flew. The dracolich had already lost its wings and two claws. It was trying feebly to turn its head to blast its attacker with flame, but the bones of its neck were smashed in two places, and smoke still rose from its blackened skull where Shandril had burned it.

A hearty kick sent more pieces of bone flying. The descending boot was planted firmly on one of Shargrailar's claws, and its owner chopped brutally downward.

"Delg!" cried Shandril in happy astonishment, and then she was laughing and crying at the same time as she hurried toward the small, burly figure whose gleaming axe still chopped and smashed methodically up and down the splintered bulk of the helpless dracolich.

The dwarf grinned up at her. "Well met, Shandril! Long days pass, and you've gotten into trouble, as always . . . only this time you're in luck: Delg's here to lay low your dracolich from behind!"

Then he was swept up into a happy embrace, clear off his feet, before Shandril let out a whoof of effort and staggered forward to set him down again.

"Delg! Delg—I thought everyone of the company was dead!" Shandril cried. The dwarf nodded soberly for a moment before his fierce grin came again.

"Aye. So did I," he said, beard bristling. "But I've found you at last."

"Found me? Do you know what's happened to me? This bone dragon you're destroying is but the latest. Scarce a day passes without someone trying to slay us because of the spellfire I wield."

"Spellfire, aye, so they've all been telling me."

"All?"

"Aye, Elminster and Storm and the knights and Harpers and all. I rode the legs of my mule a good two fingerwidths shorter following you. You've become important indeed, lass, in less time than I've seen most heroes and legends rise, in my years." The dwarf waved his axe. "So let's see this spellfire again, before we move Narm somewhere safer."

"Well enough," Shandril said, and turned to where the dracolich lay. "Do you know this one?"

"Never seen it before I buried this axe in it," Delg replied, raising an eyebrow. "Does it matter?"

"No, I suppose not," Shandril replied, and let fly with roaring spellfire that blasted Shargrailar's helplessly flopping skull to bone shards. As the smoke died away, Shandril looked at Delg and shrugged, expressionless.

"Beware, Delg, I'm not safe to be near, these days," she said with a sigh. "So much killing, since first I left The Rising Moon. . . . Is butchery what all the legends are built on?"

"Aye," the dwarf said gruffly. "Didn't you know?" He turned to Narm. "Let's drag your lord a goodly distance from all this carnage, and see what we can salvage before sunset."

" 'We? You'll come with us?"

"Aye, if you'll have me. On your bridal journey, and all."

The dwarf looked embarrassed, and then squinted at her defiantly, hands twisting nervously on his axe as he spoke. "I am a friend to you, Shandril, and will stand true by you and your lord. Few enough such you'll find, mark you, and you need but little more in life than good food and good friends. The company's gone now, all save for you . . . so old Delg'll ride with you.

"If you make it to Silverymoon all well, and are sick of me by then, I'll leave you. I hope you won't be . . . it is a trial indeed, when you be my age, befriending pretty girls anew to ride with . . . folks get all the wrong ideas, y'see."

The old dwarf handed her his axe. "Hold this, while I carry your mage here—easy, lad, you'll feel better soon enough; I know, I've lived through battles enough to tell, by now—down the road apiece. The sun waits not for all my talking." Nor did it, but it was a happy camp that sunset.

* * * * *

In the morning, the dwarf walked with the young couple as they headed west up into the mountains. It was a clear day, and the green Dalelands spread out behind them as they went up the rolling hills toward the Thunder Gap. All was peaceful. A lone black falcon soared high above in the clear blue air, and the day passed on with no attack or hurling of spellfire. Delg told Narm fierce tales of Shandril's daring with the company, and Narm, recovering, told Delg of the struggle in Myth Drannor and Rauglothgor's lair, and how she blasted apart the mountaintop. The dwarf looked at Shandril with new respect, and chuckled, and said, "I won't ask you to hold my axe, next time!"

Near sunset, on the heights of Thunder Gap, they turned at last and looked back over the marching trees, and the road dwindling down, down, down from where they stood to Highmoon, hazy in the distance.

"Who could know, looking at it, that this beautiful land could be so dangerous?" Narm asked quietly. Delg looked, and smiled, and said nothing.

"Never mind," Shandril replied, putting a hand on his arm. "We found each other, and that is worth it all."

They walked off into the evening together, and thought on many mornings ahead as the soft stars came out above them, and were very happy.

Elminster:
The Making of a Mage

Ed Greenwood

From the creator of the FORGOTTEN REALMS® world comes the epic story of the Realms' greatest wizard!

Elminster. No other wizard wields such power. No other wizard has lived as long. No other book tells you the story of his origins. Born into humble circumstances, Elminster begins his life of magic in an odd way – by fleeing from it. When his village and his family are destroyed by a being of sorcerous might, young Elminster eschews the arcane arts. Instead, he becomes a journeyman warrior and embarks on a mission of revenge . . . until his destiny turns in on itself and he embraces the magic he once despised.

The PRISM PENTAD

Troy Denning

Searing drama in an unforgiving world . . .

The Obsidian Oracle
Book Four
Power-hungry Tithian emerges as the new ruler of Tyr. When he pursues his dream of becoming a sorcerer-king, only the nobleman Agis stands between Tithian and his desire: possession of an ancient oracle that will lead to either the salvation of Athas – or its destruction.

ISBN 1-56076-603-4

The Cerulean Storm
Book Five
Rajaat: The First Sorcerer – the only one who can return Athas to its former splendor – is imprisoned beyond space and time. When Tithian enlists the aid of his former slaves, Rikus, Neeva, and Sadira, to free the sorcerer, does he want to restore the world – or claim it as his own?

ISBN 1-56076-642-5

The Verdant Passage
Book One
ISBN 1-56076-121-0

The Amber Enchantress
Book Three
ISBN 1-56076-236-5

The Crimson Legion
Book Two
ISBN 1-56076-260-8

On Sale Now!